Smarter Than Elvis

Matt Davis

Part One: The Courtship

Chapter 1

April 1, 1967

It was a hazy early spring night in Coverdale, Alabama and there was no traffic, save for the nearly unidentifiable rusted-out late-50's model sedan struggling down the two-lane highway with a slight hitch in the giddy-up. Inside the sedan, local townie Derlin Spurlock and his young girlfriend Mavis Clapp were on their third date, coming from what Derlin had considered to be a very romantic fish fry at his Uncle Vern's pond-adjacent trailer. As Derlin drove Mavis home, the car had begun to shake, sputter and smoke even worse than it usually did, but Derlin had been planning for that to happen. He'd peanut-buttered his own gas tank, sneaking away at the fish fry during one of Uncle Vern's famous stories.

Mavis was under the impression that Derlin was eighteen like herself, however he was actually seven years her senior. He had begun attempting to woo Mavis a few weeks prior when Cupid's arrow had brought them together by pure storybook happenstance. Wandering under the bleachers of Coverdale High School one day in an attempt to get out of the midday sun, Derlin had begun absentmindedly looking for change. He soon became distracted, crouching in the dirt in an attempt to pry up what he'd hoped was a quarter but ended up being a Nehi soda bottle cap. Muttering a profanity and flicking the cap away from him, he rose from his concentration to discover that during his quest, the bleachers had filled above him and a large pep rally had begun. Not wanting to be caught by some school-children (again) while rummaging for dropped change, Derlin loitered under the bleachers for the duration of the pep rally, fighting the urge for a cigarette. At one point, digging out a handful of pennies from the dirt, he happened to glance upward, seeing up Mavis's skirt in the process. His heart leapt in his chest and he imagined he was experiencing love for the first time. Spitting into his dirty hands and using the saliva to brush back his unwashed mullet, Derlin sought Mavis out as the rally ended, identifying himself as "the new boy from across town" and casually asking her if she'd like to go out for a milkshake.

Mavis had bashfully declined the offer at first, but she was taken by Derlin's forwardness, long hair and stubbly mustache. Though he was skinny as a rail and smelled vaguely of turpentine, he was taller than most of the other boys at her school and he'd alluded to the fact that he had his own car. Her thoughts racing as she gave Derlin a quick up-down and glanced over her shoulder, she'd changed her mind before Derlin had even had the chance to get out the entirety of his "Aw man, really?"

Since that day, Derlin had spent the better part of the past two weeks trying to coax some action out of Mavis, being spurned multiple times during their brief courtship. However, hc was sure that this was to be his evening. If the ambiance of the fish fry in itself wasn't enough to set the mood, his concocted plan was pure gold. He pulled into the parking lot of Lumpy's Feed & Seed and the car slowly ground to a stop next to the gas pumps. Here began to unfold what Derlin had considered to be the ace up his sleeve.

"Wait here for just a minute baby, I'll figure out what's wrong with her," Derlin said sweetly, hopping out of the car to go "check under the hood."

His plan from there was simple enough: Pretend to tinker with the car for a little while, banging around under the hood. Once enough time had elapsed, Derlin would return to the car, shrugging, claiming to not be able to fix it right away. Next, he'd go pick some flowers from somewhere behind Lumpy's, hop back in the car, see what he could talk Mavis into while they waited on a hypothetical tow-truck. Afterwards, he'd go grab a stick to dislodge the peanut butter from the gas tank, the engine would magically roar to life and he'd drive her home. Flawless, absolutely flawless.

However, in what would become a recurring theme in his life, while Derlin was out there tinkering under the hood he got to thinking. If after their romantic tryst in the Feed n' Seed parking lot, he hopped back out of the car and "fixed it" in a few seconds, she might become suspicious; but if he went ahead and took care of the peanut butter beforehand, he could just crank the car up after their hanky-panky, feign surprise and mutter something about gaskets and shc'd presumably be none the wiser.

"Derlin, you old dog!" he chuckled to himself. Casanova himself would havc been proud. He picked a few disheveled daisies sprouting from a clump of dirt next to the gas pump and began to search the parking lot for sticks.

Scampering back to the car moments later with a fine stick, Derlin snuck around the back to the gas tank to complete the final preliminary step in his plan. Indeed, upon unscrewing his gas cap, the top of the tank was crammed with thick, scalding hot peanut butter. Making haste, Derlin immediately took to stabbing at the peanut butter with his prized stick, oblivious to the pressure clearly building beneath it.

"Come on you bastard son of a bitch," he whispered, jabbing feverishly. In hindsight, he regretted using crunchy peanut butter.

"Let's go you sticky-ass mother-" the words were still coming out of his mouth when the pressure blew. He was immediately covered in a spewed blend of hot crunchy peanut butter and low-grade, leaded gasoline. He did his best to muffle a painful yelp.

"Are you alright Derlin?" Mavis shouted from the front seat, clearly worried. "What happened out there?"

Derlin was stunned, but didn't want to blow his chance at finally rounding second base with Mavis because of some fluke concussion or gas burns. He was covered neck to belt in a sludgy, viscous deep brown liquid and reeked like some bastard hybrid of an offshore oil rig and a child's sandwich, but all he saw was the opportunity to return to the car a conquering hero. A man to be trusted. A fixer of sedans. A man who clearly solved any problems that got in his way.

His only hurdle, as such, was being covered in the aforementioned gasoline and peanut butter.

"Yeah baby, don't you worry I'm fine," Derlin shouted. His eyes darted around the parking lot and he thought deeply about what to do next. Suddenly, a light went on in his mind as he remembered a conversation with his Grandpa Hoyt on the topic of dating from when he was eleven or so. As hard as he tried to remember some specific point of grandfatherly advice or wisdom, the only piece of the conversation that had stuck with Derlin over the years was his Grandpa Hoyt's steadfast and repeated assertion that using low-grade leaded gasoline as a cologne was a surefire way to gain the amorous attention of a lady no matter the circumstance.

"If I had enough gas and a big enough neck, I could woo the Queen of England herself," he'd say. Derlin could vaguely recall Grandpa Hoyt mentioning the gas as a masking agent for horse manure and, looking down at his dripping brown shirt, only imagined that the same could be true about the muck gradually drying on his face and chest. Gasoline was strong, after all.

"It's like catnip to a dame, but none of that hoity-toity ethanol shit they got now," Grandpa Hoyt said, if he recalled correctly. "Gotta have enough lead in it to make your neck tingle."

"Just a dabble behind your ears, Tommy" he'd say. Derlin never understood why he said "dabble." Or why he called him Tommy. At any rate, he was out of other ideas and ready to trust his grandpa's bizarre wisdom. Spraying a small bit of fresh gasoline into his hand from the unlocked pump, Derlin sloshed what he could only hope was an appropriate "dabble" behind his ears and across his neck.

Mavis herself sat in the car patiently, a little curious at all the crashing and yelping coming from outside, but as Derlin had claimed to be alright she was content to sit and tap her foot to the radio, faintly playing Glen Campbell's new hit song "Wichita Lineman." She liked Derlin a great deal and was struggling more and more to heed her mother's advice about "young ladies who go around giving out milk for free." Quite frankly, after restraining herself romantically for their past few dates, Mavis hoped Derlin was unable to get his old rust bucket running again just so she could drag him into the back seat once he got done banging around the parking lot.

"I'll be back in a second," Derlin continued, "Just fixin' the engine was a little messy is all and I'm putting some of my fancy new France Europe cologne on." He removed his shirt and began to use it to sop up as much of the grease on his face and chest as he could manage. He tried to toss it away into some tall grass nearby, missing badly. It made a dull thwack when it hit the ground next to the pumps.

"Oooh! I can't wait," Mavis hollered, grinning to herself.

Derlin took a deep breath and stepped back into the car. As he exhaled and began to explain the mess, Mavis cut him off, commenting immediately on the sensuality of his new cologne and offering to go to the back seat to help him find a way to relieve the stress of dealing with his busted ride.

Much to Derlin's surprise, Grandpa Hoyt's advice had a few seeds of truth in it after all. Initially only armed with peanut butter and a dream, Derlin had indeed succeeded in his master plan, his dual role as sexual conqueror and vanquisher of engine problems complete. To a fly on the wall (there were a lot of flies), he was the happiest guy in the world in that moment, though it may have been the gas fumes.

Little did they know at the time, but it was a fateful night for the both of them aside from just the banging. In a graphically detailed scene of conception, which Derlin would vividly recreate in a one-man play with a variety of props and sound effects in the living room at family gatherings for decades to come, that night he and Mavis started their journey toward parenthood. He'd knocked her right on up.

Chapter 2

April 18, 1967

The first few weeks of their young relationship passed with relative ease and tranquility compared to the times that would soon follow. Derlin and Mavis continued dating as any young couple would, going to movies and hamburger restaurants and sneaking away into the back of the old sedan whenever possible. Derlin popped into high school events just often enough that Mavis would think he actually attended her school and he'd scrounged up an old science textbook which he kept in his floorboard as a testament to his learning. Young love blossoming, their relationship was progressing rapidly and Derlin was quite pleased with the situation he'd stumbled into. His father Clovis had spent most of Derlin's actual high-school days mocking his inability to get a girlfriend and Derlin was very proud to prove to him that "he could too get a pretty high-school girl to like him" even if it had taken an extra seven or eight years for the stars to align. Derlin smiled whenever he thought of mentioning his good fortune to his father, as not only had he and Mavis fallen for each other quickly and genuinely, but she was still quite busy in school five days a week, allowing him to plenty of time to maintain his own rigorous schedule of drinking beer, doing burnouts in the sedan and throwing eggs at passing trains with his father and uncle.

Mavis wasn't the type of girl to skip school despite Derlin's periodic amorous pleading, but she and Derlin were still finding ways to see each other every day of the week. The more that he came around, swerving up into their yard and honking, the more her parents began to get the sense that he may have been a bad apple. In addition, the more he hung around, the more her parents had trouble believing that Derlin was eighteen as he said. They'd found him to be shady from the outset without being able to quite put their finger on it. This had fueled their initial suspicion of him, especially Mavis' father Clebert, who recognized Derlin's face from what he was certain were years of loitering in front of a variety of local businesses.

While Mavis was never going to be on a Hollywood marquee or cure polio, she was a pleasant girl who got good grades and it pained the Clapps to see their only daughter so enamored with someone who Clebert considered a do-nothing roustabout. Clebert had lived in Coverdale long enough to know how far the "Spurlock" name tended to get folks. He was at least passingly aware of most living members of the family in town, considering them to be clinging to the fringes of society at best. He had attended school a few years ahead of Derlin's father Clovis, before Clovis had dropped out to pursue a career in unemployment. The two had never interacted personally, but it's easy to remember the kid that gets suspended for driving his go-kart onto the football field during the homecoming game and a name like "Clovis" tends to stick in a person's mind.

It was fair to say that thus far in their acquaintanceship, Derlin had done nothing to distinguish himself from what Clebert knew of the Spurlock clan and it caused him to wince a little bit every time he saw how big Mavis smiled when she looked up at Derlin's stubbly and inevitably slack-jawed face.

Sighing from behind his newspaper as he saw the headlights flash through his living room window and heard the accompanying screech of brakes, Clebert was quickly getting tired of Derlin showing up as a surprise guest every evening right before dinner was ready. After Derlin's regular routine of giving one-word answers to questions and playing footsie with a giggling Mavis under the table culminated with Derlin taking the last chicken leg, Clebert had decided that he couldn't hold his tongue any longer. "Derlin, let's you and me have a little talk on the porch while the girls start cleaning up," Clebert said abruptly as Derlin was still devouring the cartilage on the end of his drumstick.

Derlin looked up, wide-eyed, nodding as he finished chewing. Wiping his hands on his jeans and winking at Mavis, Derlin stood. Clebert grabbed his Lucky Strikes and matches off of the counter, motioning Derlin out the front door.

Derlin stretched and patted his stomach as he joined Clebert on the porch, accepting a Lucky Strike and puffing on it mightily. The weather, seemingly, had warmed every day since Derlin and Mavis had consummated their relationship in the Lumpy's parking lot and Derlin felt a pang of heat as he looked at Clebert's glare. A bead of sweat began on his forehead.

"Nice weather, ain't it?" Derlin said nervously. He looked around Clebert at the closed front door, seeing the light in the kitchen from the windows as Mavis and her mother Eudora cleaned. He fidgeted, unsure of what Clebert was after.

"Yeah," Clebert replied dryly. "Yeah, I suppose it is."

"Thanks for letting me crash your supper," Derlin offered, attempting to break the tension he suddenly felt on the porch. "My mama ain't exactly made for the kitchen."

"Don't mention it," Clebert said, clearing his throat. "Eudora is a fine cook."

"Yeah she sure is," Derlin said, "I reckon I must've put down six or eight of them drumsticks."

"Oh yes," Clebert said flatly. "You had two at a time going there for a little while. One in each hand. You've got quite the appetite. Must be that teen metabolism."

"Yeah, that's probably it," Derlin said, nodding quickly despite being unsure quite what a metabolism was. "I am still growing I reckon."

"Sprouting up like a weed," Clebert said, chuckling ominously and without humor. "You know, you seem like a pretty smart young fella."

"I would reckon to suppose that I am," Derlin replied, trying to hide the surprise in his voice.

"I know you and my daughter have gotten rather cozy over the last few weeks," Clebert began.

"Yes sir, I sure do like her," Derlin smiled. "I just wish we'd met sooner instead of way at the end of senior year."

He coughed lightly.

"Here's the thing," Clebert said. "I don't think you go to her high school."

The blood drained from Derlin's face and his eyes went blanker than usual. Clebert took a step toward Derlin. He was several inches shorter than Derlin and just as skinny, but it was Derlin felt himself shrink back as Clebert's gaunt, reddening face stared up at him.

"I know your face, son," Clebert said sternly. "I know I've seen you smoking cigarettes in front of the gas station and hunting nickels in the storm drain in front of the pool hall since my Mavis was in middle school."

It was Derlin's turn to wince.

"Yeah," Derlin said, shrugging and taking another heroic puff of his Lucky Strike. "Yeah, I reckon you might have."

"Well, how old are you?" Clebert asked.

"I'm twenty two sir," Derlin lied, coughing lightly.

"Try again," Clebert said firmly.

"Twenty five," Derlin moaned. "I'm twenty five years old."

"Does my daughter know this?" Clebert asked.

"Yeah, I told her," Derlin lied.

Clebert sighed.

"And what do you do for a living?" Clebert asked.

"Well, you see," Derlin started, rubbing his neck sheepishly. "I'm kinda in between jobs right now. I did some wood working for a while, some glass working."

Both jobs he was referring to were one-time tasks that took him no more than two hours to complete, but the way he felt this conversation going, he decided he might need to pad his resume beyond the actual "experience" he had. He made the mental note to avoid using his usual fall-back career when asked what he did for a living, "pool hustler," since Clebert had apparently seen him fishing for nickels in front of the pool hall and he felt that as such, his cover was likely blown.

"Son, by the time I was your age, I was years into my career already," Clebert said, still not breaking his stare. "I had a vision of success, and I worked hard and followed it, and it's enabled me to move up the ladder over the years and build a skill set. Do you have any kind of skill set?"

Derlin thought back to earlier in the afternoon, when he'd chugged a Panther Cat pint can in under five seconds and successfully karate kicked it onto the hood of his car.

"No sir," he said. "I don't reckon I do in the traditional sense of the word."

"Well, what are your intentions when it comes to my daughter?" Clebert asked. Derlin thought of the day of the pep rally and smiled.

"Well," Derlin said. He paused. "Well, I know I love her and she loves me, but as she's still finishing up her schooling, I don't reckon we've got much in the way of intentions as it goes."

Clebert sighed.

"I'll tell you what, Derlin," Clebert said. "You not having a job and all, I bet that that makes money pretty tight, with rent to pay and all."

"Oh, I've been staying at my Grandma and Grandpa's," Derlin said. "They've got me a cot set up on their porch. I ain't gotta pay them rent as long as I don't tear up the driveway coming in and out."

Clebert sighed again.

"Still, I bet you don't have much 'walking around' money," Clebert said. "Being out of work and all."

Derlin produced a half dollar from his wallet and fished around in his pockets, producing another eight cents.

"Hell, I got most of a dollar," Derlin offered. The fifty cent piece belonged to his Grandma Vondene, who'd tasked him with going by the store for milk. He'd failed to run the errand, but was pleased in that he had more than the eight cents from the storm drain to show Clebert when he asked about "walking around money."

"Look son, I'm gonna come right out and say it," he said. "I've got a check for $500 with your name on it if you get into that car and drive off into the sunset and never bother Mavis again. You can even do a burnout when you go if you like."

A look of hurt crept over Derlin's face.

"What?" Derlin stammered. His eyes stung and watered as though Clebert had just popped him in the nose.

"I don't want you around my daughter. I think you're bad news. I think she can do better and I'm offering to pay you handsomely to go away." Clebert said, raising his voice but keeping it low enough not to alert Mavis or Eudora.

"You can't buy no Spurlock man," Derlin said forcefully, doing his best not to raise his voice. "We love each other and can't nobody change that."

Derlin stomped around Clebert and, much to his chagrin, back into the house.

Though Clebert wasn't happy, he admired Derlin's resolve. He'd wholeheartedly expected him to take the money and run. In the fact that an unemployed man with 58 cents in his pocket was turning down $500 to hit the bricks, Derlin had passed some small test in Clebert's eyes. He still didn't think much of anything of him, but maybe if Derlin was actually in it for "love" like he claimed, Clebert was content to sit back and keep an eye on him for a while. He'd always trusted his daughter's judgement of character up to this point, but Derlin was a stretch to say the least. Clebert sighed as he headed back in the front door behind Derlin, shaking his head slowly as he decided that he could probably wait it out a little while if it made his daughter happy.

May 10, 1967

As April quickly turned into May and graduation neared for Mavis, Derlin began floating the idea of eloping to Mexico. Mavis laughed and deferred any time Derlin brought it up, but the idea of a life of adventure on the open road in a foreign land was beginning to sound exotic to her, even if Mexico was just a few hundred miles to the south. She was actually weighing the pros and cons of his idea one morning as she was looking in the mirror getting ready for school when she first noticed her baby bump beginning to form.

Mavis spent most of the school day worried and unable to concentrate, fully expecting Derlin to flee for the hills (or Mexico) when she told him the news of his impending fatherhood. He was waiting for her in the parking lot after school as per usual, having just finished a brown-bagged Panther Cat beer a few moments prior. He sensed something was amiss as Mavis approached and soon began to worry that Clebert had offered her a similar bribe or, even worse, let slip how old he actually was.

"Derlin, honey, we gotta talk," Mavis said quickly.

"'Bout what, baby?" Derlin asked curiously as they climbed into his car, doing his best to hide that he'd turned white as a sheet.

"Well, I don't know how to say this," Mavis sighed. "So I reckon I'll just come right out and say it."

Derlin winced, expecting the worst. He'd been kicked to the proverbial curb a time or two in his day and knew how these "talks" had ended up in the past.

"Well," Mavis continued, beginning to form her words slowly. "Derlin, I don't know quite how else to say it." She paused to bite her lip and for Derlin, time briefly stopped.

Finally she spoke. "I'm pregnant with a baby and you're gonna be a daddy."

Derlin's eyes widened and he gasped in excitement. He let out a yip and began to cackle and honk the horn happily, revving the engine and drawing stares from around the parking lot. People covered their ears at the noise of the horn but Derlin kept at it for a good thirty seconds.

"Does this mean you're excited?" Mavis asked hopefully.

Derlin leaned in, wiping some of the sweat from his upper lip and kissing Mavis half on the cheek, half on the mouth.

Suffice it to say that the Clapps were less than thrilled to learn of their only daughter's deflowering and subsequent impregnation when Mavis finally broke the news to them a few days after Derlin. Clebert had retained a mild admiration of Derlin's resolve in refusing the $500 check, but had retained hope that his "Derlin problem" would eventually solve itself, even if it took time. Even as that admiration slipped into the ether, Clebert was a deeply religious man and certainly wasn't going to take the chance of letting his first grandchild be born out of wedlock. Regardless of how little he thought of Derlin, it seemed Clebert would be stuck with him for the long haul and it pained him greatly as he demanded that Derlin marry his daughter. Derlin maintained a fervent insistence that he was going to happily marry Mavis as soon as possible and was overjoyed at Clebert's sudden acceptance, but Clebert had still insisted that he was bringing his shotgun to the small ceremony just in case.

May 17, 1967

The wedding was held as soon as Clebert was able to secure a preacher of discretion and was held at the Clapp's behest on a small hillside on the outskirts of town and far away from the local church, with only the Clapps and Derlin's Uncle Vern in attendance. The Clapps hadn't informed their other relatives of the wedding due to both the nature and the necessity, but most of Derlin's family missed it too despite Derlin's invitations. They skipped it not in protest of the out-of-wedlock intercourse necessitating it, but because of a major dirt track car race happening in the next county over. Derlin didn't blame them, as if it wasn't for his own wedding he'd have been there right along with them, Vern included.

Though not quite the dream wedding she'd always pictured, Mavis was still ecstatic to marry Derlin and a single tear ran down her cheek as she replied "I do" to the preacher's matrimonial inquiries.

"I do, too!" Derlin pledged loudly, not waiting for his recitation of vows to continue. He leaned in to kiss Mavis but was spurned by the preacher.

"Son, I haven't pronounced you man and wife yet," the preacher smiled.

"I know, but we both said we was gonna," Derlin said happily. "I didn't get where I am today waitin' on folk to finish saying everything written on their fancy piece of paper."

The preacher was clearly taken aback by such abrupt words, no matter Derlin's good intentions and leaned in to rebuke him.

"Perhaps your inability to wait is exactly what got you where you are today son," he whispered sharply, alluding to Mavis's small but growing belly.

"Come on man, that ain't nice," Derlin returned. "I wouldn't come to your wedding and say something like that. That's dirty pool, I-"

Mavis's father cleared his throat and cocked his shotgun firmly.

"What I mean to say is please continue, sir," Derlin said quietly, head hung down. "Accept my apology for shit talking at you on this holy day."

Perturbed, the preacher ran through Derlin's side of the vows with the quickness of a radio advertisement, reminding Derlin of recent ads he'd heard for the dirt track race he was currently missing.

"I said I do," Derlin smiled, winking at Mavis as the preacher finished the vows.

"Then by the power vested in me by the State of Alabama, I now pronounce you man and wife. You may kiss the bride."

Mavis embraced Derlin and he leaned in for what could fairly be described as a long and sloppy kiss. The Clapps, Uncle Vern and the preacher had all averted their eyes by the time it concluded and once Derlin finally pulled away, lipstick stained the stubble of his poorly-trimmed mustache in a pasty magenta. Like Mavis, it was the happiest day of his life, but unlike Mavis, Derlin was able to celebrate with a drink.

Uncle Vern had lugged a case of Panther Cat, Derlin's personal favorite malt liquor, to the top of the hill with him as a "wedding gift" and within 45 minutes of the nuptials the two of them had nearly drained it. While Mr. Clapp had half of a can before discarding the rest behind a tree, Derlin and Vern took care of the remaining twenty three cans and were soon quite drunk. Mavis looked on lovingly as the two of them wrestled on the hillside.

The Clapps whispered to themselves, aghast at what their young daughter had gotten herself into. Derlin did indeed seem to mean well, but that didn't mean that they viewed him as anything more than a do-nothing townie. They'd once maintained hope that he'd grow past it "once he's older than 18," but this idea was abandoned once Clebert had pried Derlin's actual age out of him. He'd always intended to speak to Mavis about the matter, assuming she knew the truth and was keeping it from him by simply avoiding bringing it up. She would learn his actual age in time, but was presently unaware that since dropping out of Coverdale High at 16, the young, go-getting Derlin had basically just spent nine years drinking beer and leaning against things, only taking periodic odd jobs around town when he needed tires for his sedan.

May 18, 1967

Derlin cherished his spotty history of aforementioned odd jobs, but until he'd become a married man he'd never had the reason or inclination to seek full-time employment. "Conventional working," as his Grandpa Hoyt called it, was foreign to him, but seeing as he'd promised both his new wife and his new father-in-law that he'd find a job, he decided he might should give this "conventional working" a try. The morning after the wedding, Derlin woke up with the sun, shaking the cobwebs of a slight hangover and rolling over to kiss Mavis on the forehead.

"Good day and good morning, wife of mine," Derlin smiled.

Mavis returned his smile and sighed happily. "Good morning, Derlin."

"I'mma get a job today, baby!" he said enthusiastically. "I'mma get a real good job, then we can get our own place and then next thing you know that baby in there will be signing up for football teams and boy scout camps!" He tapped lightly at her belly and grinned.

Mavis smiled from her bed, wishing him encouragement as he pulled on his nice jeans from the wedding, now stained with grass, and stomped out the door in search of employment. Derlin passed the Clapps in the kitchen, making a pot of coffee. He wished them a good morning as he headed out the door, getting no response aside from a small nod from Mr. Clapp.

His trusty sedan had been even more sluggish than usual since the peanut butter fiasco and Derlin was tinkering with the idea that he'd lost part of his stick down in the gas tank. As such, Derlin opted to leave the sedan where it was, parked diagonally across the driveway, deciding to enjoy a walk toward town.

Derlin was not particularly sure how to go about finding conventional employment somewhere beyond the realm of unloading bales of hay from a truck or removing rocks from a field, but he was confident as he began his search. Walking toward town from the Clapp's small neighborhood, Derlin thought about what his first stop may be. It seemed daunting to just waltz into a business and ask for a job.

Luckily, as Derlin loped down the roadside in the early morning light he saw a familiar sight: Lumpy's Feed & Seed, the very gas station Derlin had parked at on the night that he and Mavis had copulated. Derlin was not a religious man, but took the appearance of Lumpy's as a bit of a sign from above. He'd done a few odd jobs for Lumpy over the years, which he'd referenced to Clebert when describing his work history. These jobs, the "woodwork" and "glasswork", included moving a stack of 2x4s from one side of the building to the other and the removal of several hundred old glass soda bottles, which Derlin had simply taken into a nearby cornfield and smashed instead of taking them to the dump. Figuring with that strong a track record, he might already have a foot in the door, Derlin headed up to Lumpy's to give it a shot.

Derlin was again surprised at his own good luck when he walked out of the Feed & Seed a few moments later, having obtained a modest position as a part time gas station attendant. He'd spoken with Lumpy himself and started the job right there on the spot.

Derlin had known Lumpy since he was just beginning to hone his loitering skills as a boy and didn't feel that the old man had changed in appearance much over the years. Now in his mid-sixties and easily 300 pounds, clad in overalls with a dirty rag crammed in the back pocket, Derlin could barely understand what Lumpy was saying from beneath his ragged "Feed & Seed" hat. Missing a handful of teeth, Lumpy's thick Alabama drawl was impenetrable to all but the most soil-smeared local folks around the town and Derlin felt proud to catch more than a word here or there. Supposedly, Lumpy had been struck by lightning on two different occasions in his life and most discernible anecdotes he told ended with him bleeding from the face. He'd ran the Feed n' Seed for most of his adult life since taking over for his father Greasy and, though he knew he probably wasn't going to get much hard work out of Derlin based on his track record, he was happy to have someone to take care of some of the more "shit-wipin'" tasks in his daily workload.

Lumpy's aforementioned rag in hand, Derlin's first task was to give the pumps a good wiping, after which he would dispose of the crusted remains of his own peanut butter and gasoline soaked shirt, which had now been baking in the Alabama sun for over a month and had been long-confused by Lumpy for a discarded diaper.

He scrubbed at the pumps for a good twenty minutes, quickly turning his rag to an even grimier off-brown than it was to begin with. He could see his discarded shirt out of the corner of his eye and though he'd intended to save it for last, he was growing tired of looking at it and was downwind from the smell to boot. Tossing his rag to the ground at the pump, Derlin stomped over to where his shirt lay and began swatting away the horseflies. He reached down quickly, grabbing the sopping, sour mass between his thumb and forefinger. He turned and threw the shirt into the nearby woods, wincing as a few warm flecks of liquid spattered against his face. He stared after it for a moment before shifting his attention to putting the finishing touches on the fuel pumps and returning to the counter for his next task.

By noon, he'd not only sifted the dead worms out of the nightcrawlers bin and cleaned the nickels out from the weeds under the pay phone, but he'd raked nearly the entire gravel parking lot. Lumpy was ecstatic with Derlin's hard work, especially knowing the younger Derlin's penchant for lethargy from his days of moving lumber. Over the course of the early afternoon, after busting his hump to the best of his ability, Derlin worked up the courage to ask Lumpy for a $50 advance in his pay so that he and Mavis could put a deposit down for their own place and, once learning of Derlin's marriage and Mavis' status as an expecting mother, Lumpy was happy to oblige. Derlin neglected to tell Lumpy that his future son or daughter was conceived in the very parking lot he'd spent the past ninety minutes raking as Lumpy counted out five ten dollar bills from the register, simply telling him that they'd met each other in high school. This was technically true, as they did meet in a high school, just maybe not in the conventional way that one would associate with the phrase. Derlin smiled widely as he said it, thinking back fondly once again on that fateful day looking for change under the bleachers.

Lumpy cut Derlin loose for the day at a little after two o'clock so that Derlin could contact a small apartment complex called "Applebottom Acres," where Lumpy's brother Greasy Junior was the maintenance man. Though the apartment complex was a bit on the squalid side, both under power lines and railroad track adjacent, it was the only place in town that fell under Derlin's $50 deposit threshold and he'd soon signed his name to a six month lease. The unit was available immediately and, though Derlin had yet to see the inside, he grabbed the keys and bolted as soon as they were handed to him. Not wanting to waste any daylight, Derlin headed for the Clapp house excitedly, running up into the yard some twenty minutes later, sweaty and yelling.

"Mavis, baby!" Derlin hollered. "Mavis I got a job and got us a place to live!"

Mavis came running out of the house as Clebert yelled after her to tell Derlin to cut out all the racket.

"Derlin, I knew you could," Mavis began, elated. "Where are you working?"

"They hired me up at the Feed & Seed," Derlin said proudly. "Lumpy says I work real good and I'll be getting 20 hours of work a week!"

Clebert scoffed and rolled his eyes and Mavis shushed him. He shook his head and turned his attention back to his mashed potatoes, continuing to half-listen as he ate.

"That's wonderful Derlin!" she encouraged. "That's certainly a good start."

"Twenty hours is a damn lot," Derlin said. "I reckon I'll get pretty tired. But that's how I had enough money to get our dream castle!" Derlin shrugged nonchalantly, as though his day of mild conquering was no big deal.

"You bought us a house?" Mavis gasped.

"No… well, no, not exactly!" Derlin began.

"Here it comes," Clebert chided from the porch.

"Well, I rented us an apartment," Derlin continued.

"That's great sweetheart!" Mavis said, still as happy as she could be. "Where at?"

"Applebottom Acres!" Derlin beamed. "We've got a unit right on the first floor so you don't have to walk up no stairs or anything."

"Applebottom Acres?" Clebert hollered. "You're taking my daughter to Applebottom Acres? That's the worst apartment complex in town. They sell drugs down there, you know. My hunting buddy Merle said one time he saw a Mexican selling dope cigarettes to some teenagers!"

"It didn't look bad to me, Pop," Derlin said. "I didn't see no drugs or Mexican fellas. Besides I'm real strong and I ain't gonna let anything bad happen to your daughter or our baby."

"Don't call me that!" Clebert hollered.

"Sorry, Pop!" Derlin smiled, winking much to Clebert's dismay. "It's all I got the money for right now but I'll get Miss Mavis her real dream castle someday."

Mavis hastily threw together some of her clothes in an overnight bag, kissed her parents on the cheek and joined Derlin, now leaning against the front of his already-running car. She shouted a promise over her shoulder that she would soon be back for the rest of her things. Derlin waved and climbed in the car, slamming the door and revving the engine in his customary manner. The two of them sped off before the Clapps could get out much more of a reaction. Clebert stared after Derlin's car, hands on his hips and mouth agape, as it disappeared down the road.

Derlin sped through town, humming to himself and soon slammed to a stop in his "official parking space" in front of their new apartment.

"You can tell it's mine cause it says 'Apartment 3' on it," Derlin mused.

Jiggling the lock as instructed, Derlin opened the door to their new palace with a flourish. It smelled slightly of mothballs and a water stain decorated the rear wall, but Derlin and Mavis both fell in love with it instantly. Derlin had been lucky enough to acquire a unit that was basically furnished, as neither of them owned a stitch of furniture. Derlin had briefly considered asking his family for some assistance in setting up the apartment, before remembering an earlier attempt to borrow a chair from his parents to attend a friend's poker match. The conversation escalated quickly and had ended with the chair being smashed and thrown in the fireplace so "no one could use it." As such, Derlin was reticent to ask after anything else.

Derlin grabbed a beer for himself from the fridge as he and Mavis settled in, getting her a glass of water from the sink. He turned on the TV as he walked into their tiny living room, hoping to find a wrestling program but settling for an episode of Andy Griffith. Patting the side of the TV with satisfaction, Derlin plopped down beside Mavis on the couch and put his arm around her. Dream castle or not, they were home.

Chapter 3

June 3, 1967

    The high school graduation ceremony was held, like most events of great importance in Coverdale, on the same football field the pep rally was held the day that Derlin and Mavis first met. As Derlin climbed the steps of the bleachers with Clebert and Eudora as they trudged behind Uncle Vern, whom he'd insisted on bringing, he stared through the cracks in the wood to the dirt below. Proudly, he thought of the changes in his life in the two months between crouching beneath the very same bleachers looking for change and climbing up them as a husband and soon-to-be father. He marvelled at life's ability to come full circle.

    Derlin had assumed The Clapps as a "polite applause family" when it came to ceremonies such as this and was determined to make sure Mavis had the loudest ovation, even though some of her classmates had a seemingly endless parade of distant aunts, cousins and well-wishers joining their families in attendance. Once again, Derlin had an ace up his sleeve designed to impress his beloved Mavis. Moreover, he had an ace crammed into the back of his jeans, taking the form of two air horns he'd recently gotten Vern to acquire during his bi-weekly trip to loiter at the marina of a nearby lake.

    Correctly postulating to the Clapps that they were "probably gonna do peoples names in the order of the alphabet," Derlin was pleased as first the "A" names quickly turned to the "B" names and began to nod enthusiastically as the names progressed. Having never graduated himself, nor having a family member do so, Derlin had never attended such a ceremony and was wholly enjoying the pomp and circumstance of the occasion.

    "Myrtle Cordelius Brown," the principal called from the podium to a smattering of applause as an elated young potato of a girl came galloping across the stage in her robe. Derlin clapped absentmindedly as he watched Mavis slowly approach the stairs to the stage.

    "Hershel Jerome Calloway," the principal continued. Calloway, a beaming, yellow-haired brick wall of a boy, was a star on the high school football, basketball and baseball team and generated a large round of whoops and cheers in an extended ovation that also included a whistling Clebert Clapp. Derlin remained seated and silent, his hands in his lap. The "sport boy" had gotten quite the ovation and Derlin's mind raced to figure out how he was going to make a larger racket.

    "Jackie-Sue Chubb," the principal continued. Derlin simmered.

    Uncle Vern jabbed Derlin with his elbow. He leaned in, whispering. "Man, that Jackie Sue Chubb sure is a looker, ain't she?" He grinned and nodded.

Derlin squinted, holding the program over his eyes to shield the sun.

    "Well, I like the view from the nosebleeds," Derlin chuckled, but I sure wouldn't wanna be ringside."

    Vern began a wet, smoky cackle that was soon interrupted by a familiar name. Derlin shushed him violently.

"Mavis Adeline Clapp," the principal said, almost immediately gasping in fright as Derlin set off both air horns at the same time and began chanting his wife's name at the top of his lungs. Taking the "chanting" clue from his time spent under the bleachers during the pep rally, Derlin had expected to quickly get the entire crowd raucously chanting "Mavis! Mavis! Mavis!" at the top of their lungs but few, if any, of the people in attendance joined him. He'd made his way, blasting the horns, yelling and dancing, all the way down the bleachers to the front of the stage before looking up to notice some 500 people staring at him in silence. He stared at them for a moment, eyeing the crowd up and down for familiar faces. He tossed the air horns aside and turned to face Mavis, who stood at the edge of the stage staring at him with her mouth open.

"I love you, baby!" Derlin shouted, cupping his hands around the sides of his mouth even though she was only ten or so feet away.

"I love you too, Derlin!" Mavis shouted.

"Congratu-lations on getting graduated baby!" Derlin shouted, giving her an enthusiastic thumbs up.

"Thank you, Derlin" Mavis yelled, smiling, waving and blowing him a kiss. Derlin turned back to face the crowd, realizing that he had unintentionally ground the ceremony to a halt.

"Sorry y'all," he said sheepishly, waving at the bleachers. "My fault."
As he began to slowly trudge back up the bleacher stairs, Derlin felt the daggers of several hundred eyes on him as the principal resumed the ceremony. He felt confident that even if he hadn't quite made as much noise as the "sport boy" got during his ovation, that he'd at least caused a bigger scene and in the end that was a victory in itself.

July 4, 1967

As the summer progressed, Mavis grew ever-larger. Applebottom Acres was far from the "dream castle" Derlin consistently referred to, but he and Mavis spent those first months as though their small one-bedroom apartment was a boundless paradise. Derlin slaved away, five hours a day, four days a week down at Lumpy's, keeping Mavis as comfortable and happy as he could as a soon-to-be mother. Mavis, for her part, was overjoyed to be an expectant mother. It didn't seem as though it was going to happen quite the way that she'd always dreamed of it as a little girl, with Derlin being a dumpy, mulleted gas station attendant instead of the burly, horse-riding, tanned Clark Gable-type she'd imagined over the years. He certainly had the mustache, but regardless of his lacking further attributes of her daydreamed Prince Charming, she'd grown to love Derlin quickly over their months together. He wasn't particularly handsome, with his perpetually furrowed brow, his slack jaw and untrimmed neck hair, but in him Mavis saw something special which she'd grown to cherish. His efforts to make things right for the arrival of the baby only fostered her love more.

At Derlin's insistence, she spent most of her days at home, relaxing, keeping from "getting her blood angried up" so that the baby would be born calm. She spent most of her days listening to records, watching television and jotting down little stories on a yellow legal pad which she kept hidden in her bedside table. Always an avid reader in school, she'd come across her two favorite authors in her recent Senior English class, learning to love Flannery O'Connor from her teacher and Isaac Asimov from the boys passing magazines at the back of the class. She found her own work somehow influenced by both as she began to fill her legal pad, though she felt her prose was plodding and not nearly as good. Regardless, it helped to fill her lonely days while Derlin was at Lumpy's and she thought to herself that maybe, if she ever wrote something she thought was decent enough, she might send it into the local newspaper.

It was nearing dusk that evening as Derlin finally arrived home from Lumpy's. It was the fourth of July, but it was a weeknight and as such aside from watching some fireworks on TV Mavis didn't particularly expect to have any plans.

"Hey baby," Derlin smiled, waving as he waltzed through the front door. "Get your shoes on, I got a surprise for ya."

"Are we going out to dinner?" Mavis asked excitedly.

"Oh, I've got dinner taken care of," Derlin said slyly. "Don't you worry about nothin' baby, just get in the car!"

He'd left the sedan running in his parking space and hustled Mavis out the door as soon as she'd gotten her shoes.

Mavis tried to question Derlin as to where they were going as he drove, but he rebuffed her inquiries, only saying that he had a "surprise" and that she'd find out soon enough. He flicked on the radio to break the silence, nodding as the guitar-riff jingle for a local fair filled the silence.

Derlin slowed as he pulled off the road into a large construction area where it appeared land was being cleared for a car dealership. Weaving through it, past iron beams and tractors and "no trespassing, property of Dodge Motors" signs, Derlin had soon crept the sedan to the crest of a small hill overlooking what remained of the pasture the lot was atop of. Derlin reached into the back seat, producing a picnic blanket, a bucket of chicken and a pack of bottle rockets.

"I figured since we didn't have no big New York City fireworks show in town, I'd give you one out here," Derlin said, unfurling the blanket on the hood of the car and offering to help Mavis climb atop it. "You can sit here and eat chicken and I'll shoot bottle rockets off the hill and we'll have ourselves a time!"

"Aw, Derlin, that's the most romantic thing anyone's ever done for me," Mavis said as Derlin hunted the back piece out of the bucket of chicken and began to gnaw at it hungrily.

The sun was just finishing its descent behind the horizon of the Alabama countryside as Derlin lit his first bottle rocket, hooting as it zipped from his hand and popped in the sky a few seconds later. He cranked the car radio and rolled the windows down, smiling each time he heard Mavis "ooh" and "ahh" over the bottle rockets until he'd exhausted the entirety of his supply. Gazing out at the evening sky as the last bottle rocket burst above him, Derlin turned to walk back to his beaming bride. Noticing the radio blaring Ray Charles' version of "Georgia on My Mind," Derlin wondered why no one had ever written a song about Alabama.

Six Months Later: January, 1968

Mavis had been attending regular checkups with her mother, mostly letting Derlin avoid the "doctor speak and lady parts" he felt would fill the visits. Had he chosen to attend the visits, he would have learned that Mavis was experiencing a perfectly normal, healthy pregnancy, just as she'd tell him upon returning home from the doctor's. However, he'd have also learned something that Mavis had decided to keep from him for the time being; that she was having twins.

As her due date crept closer, the burden of this secret began to wear on Mavis. Derlin had gotten a holiday raise based on his performance at Lumpy's and was now pulling in an even two dollars per hour, but $40 a week was hardly a salary to raise twins on and Mavis confided in her mother how worried she was that they would be able to make ends meet. The Clapps took to having Mavis and Derlin over for dinner as often as possible to ease their burden on groceries and though Eudora had softened her stance on him, Clebert mostly just stared at Derlin in silence.

By the doctor's calculations, Mavis's due date should have been January eighth, but that day came and went without babies or even a pang of labor pain. After the next two days passed with radio silence, Mavis scheduled an appointment and for the first time during her pregnancy Derlin attended with her.

"Say, Doc Leslie," Derlin started, as soon as the doctor entered the exam room. "Is this baby gonna live in my wife forever or what?"

"Oh, I imagine they'll both be along shortly," Dr. Leslie said absentmindedly. Sometimes babies do take a *little* longer, but-"

"What do you mean 'they'll both be along?'" Derlin asked, tilting his head. Mavis grimaced.

"Honey, I may have found out we're having twins a couple months ago and may have forgotten to tell you," Mavis said tensely.

"You mean there's gonna be two of them?" Derlin asked loudly.

"Well, that's generally what 'twins' means, Mr. Spurlock," Dr. Leslie said.

"I ain't no scientist, doc, I'm just making sure," Derlin said, pausing to put his hands on his hips and think for a moment. "Man, doc, that means my goose juice is awful strong if two of my boys made it upstream like that, huh?"

He smiled and nodded affirmatively at his own crotch.

"I guess it is a good indication of virility, sir," Dr. Leslie said.

"Do what now?" Derlin asked.

"You mean you're not mad?" Mavis asked, a look of relief creeping across her face. "I've been worried sick that you'd be furious."

"Why come would I be mad?" Derlin asked.

"Well, money is tight as it is," Mavis said. "It's gonna be hard with two extra mouths to feed."

"Aw hell, we'll make it work," Derlin said confidently, dismissing Mavis' worry with a wave. "I'll ask Lumpy if I can get more work down by the Feed n' Seed and I'll pick up enough to keep us along. Plus, babies don't eat that much besides."

Part Two: The Run

Chapter 4

February 2, 1968

For three weeks, each day passed with the expectation that Mavis would make the fateful phone call to Lumpy's or holler into the living room that it was time for Derlin to take her to the hospital. For three weeks, Derlin maintained a cat-like state of readiness for when the time came. He had a suitcase with all the necessary items for her hospital stay waiting by the front door and had been limiting himself to two Panther Cats a day, whether he had worked that day or not. Each day, Mavis grew larger and larger until finally, exactly nine months and 23 days after that infamous encounter in the Feed n' Seed parking lot, the night came where she roused Derlin from his slumber and told him that it was time to go.

Derlin awoke with a start, smacking himself in the face and shaking his head to wake him from his slumber. Quickly throwing on jeans and an old white t-shirt. He helped Mavis from the bed

Derlin hastily grabbed her prepared bag and helped her out the door and into the passenger seat of his beloved rusty sedan. Once she was securely in place, with seatbelts fashioned "and a pillow for squeezing," Derlin attempted to slide across the hood in an effort to save time, catching a hole in the outer thigh of his jeans on his bent, disheveled hood ornament, both wrenching it from its tentative hold on the car hood and twisting Derlin to the ground. He regained his footing quickly enough, grabbing the mangled hood ornament from the ground and throwing it through an open window into the back seat to replace later. He stomped on the gas as the car sped across their parking lot, leaving muddy ruts through the front yard of the small apartment complex. The old sedan gained traction once it hit pavement and Derlin sped in the direction of the hospital. At the cost of a small metal trash can and three clusters of azaleas, Derlin managed to get "the front space" at the hospital as they arrived, parking among the shrubbery next to the front entrance.

A pair of nurses led Mavis safely to a delivery room with Derlin close at their heels, and as the doctor arrived without a moment to spare, out came baby Randy. Derlin cheered, and was facing away in the midst of a slow-motion 360 dance a few seconds later as Randy's twin brother Ollie was born. He was still facing away when he heard the doctor utter a low "holy hell" as he cradled Ollie in the light.

"Oh Lord, not this again," Dr. Leslie muttered to himself. He'd been delivering babies in Coverdale the last time he'd encountered the problem that lay before him, but had blocked out most of the details over the twenty five years that had elapsed since.

Derlin, Mavis and a pair of nurses all let out a hushed gasp at about the same time the third attending nurse fled from the room in a frenzied panic.

"What's that on the top of their heads?" Derlin asked loudly, clearly rattled. "Is that a big fuckin' '666'?"

"I think it is!" whispered one of the remaining nurses, beginning to cry.

"No, no!" Dr. Leslie insisted, doing his best to remain calm. He knew from experience that this was a situation that could get out of hand quickly. "Look closer! It's not a '666'. I've seen this before. It's just three lowercase b's. These baby boys ain't the devil anymore than you or I. It's nothing to be afraid of. Just simple, harmless b's. Coincidentally three in a row."

Derlin and Mavis sighed in relief as the doctor pored over their twin boys, checking that they'd arrived in good order. He counted their fingers and toes, something Derlin noted to double-check later.

"Thanks Doc Leslie," Derlin said. "I was really worried there for a second that we had ourselves a case of devil babies. You're right though, if you look close it really is just lowercase b's after all. Clear as day."

"Well, oddly enough it's a problem that comes up every so often," Dr. Leslie. "You see, it seems there comes a time every so often in this town, mostly with you Spur--"

A large rock came hurtling through the window of the hospital room, sending shards of glass flying, smashing into a machine against the wall.
Dr. Leslie sighed deeply, inching closer to the broken window and peering out.
He gasped, backing away from the window in shock.

Derlin noticed the glow emanating from outside and had to shield his eyes as he took his turn looking out the window and soon, his turn to gasp.

"Oh, shit!" Derlin whispered, ducking below the window and scampering back to his wife's side.

Gathered in the grassy pavilion along the side of the hospital were fifty or so Coverdale townsfolk. Some held pitchforks while others were hard at work building and lighting torches. More people were arriving by the dozens, looking angry and determined.

The crowd began to swell quickly.

Dr. Leslie, regaining his wits, flung open the window and accosted the mob, hoping he'd be able to diffuse the situation.

"What do you people want?" he yelled. "You're making too much noise, this is a hospital for goodness sake!"

"We want those demon babies!" a man yelled from near the entrance.

"Yeah!" the crowd shouted in unison.
As it turned out, the attending nurse who had fled from the hospital moments after the birth had taken to the streets. She'd begun by banging on doors, shouting about a "demon birth" and through word of mouth had soon roused half the town.

"Them boys got the mark of the beast." the nurse hollered from the front of the crowd. "We're here to send 'em back to Hell."

"You people have it all wrong," Dr. Leslie assured them. "These precious young babies aren't demons at all. They're perfectly normal little boys."

"The nurse lady said they have the devil's mark on 'em," shouted a farmer, brandishing his pitchfork at the second story window from the grass below.

"No such thing!" Dr. Leslie replied, waving his hands and trying to calm the increasingly unruly mob with medical science. "These boys simply have three lowercase b's as a birthmark. Not a '666' or any sort of demon sign at all. It's a totally harmless birthmark. They're just normal babies."

"Well, what do three lowercase b's mean, then?" the farmer asked, clearly puzzled. He rested his arms on his pitchfork for a moment as he stared up expectantly awaiting his answer, tilting his wide-brimmed hat to the back of his head and slowly chewing a piece of hay.

"It means they're not the spawn of the devil," Dr. Leslie offered, hoping that this would be the end of it. "It means this whole business is nonsense and that you can all go home because nothing's the matter. At all."

The crowd went quiet for a moment. The good doctor could feel all of 300 faces staring up at him, and he could see the wheels of thought slowly turning behind most of them. It would seem, particularly to his highly-educated mind, that upon such a revelation about the normalcy of the birthmarks, the fervor surrounding the boys would quickly die down, the crowd would disperse without a riot and the evening would return to normal.

However, it was soon clear that the mob was choosing to unanimously disregard the information that the doctor had given them. They continued to uneasily mill about outside the hospital, muttering amongst themselves as more and more people arrived from the furthest reaches of the county. Torches stayed lit, pitchforks remained in brandishment formation, and some of the neighborhood toughs began to form a posse with the intent of storming the hospital doors.

"How do you know that three b's don't mean the devil?" the farmer shouted up again at Dr. Leslie as he stood firm in the window above.

"Well, I guess I don't," the doctor began. "But I---"

"That's all I needed to hear!" the nurse shouted.

"Let's burn them devil babies up!" the farmer cried.

Derlin and Mavis began to panic, looking at the ravenous group of people that stood beneath them. As the mob continued to swell, another rock was thrown, this time breaking a window in the room next to theirs. The window crashed and before the rock clattered to a stop, Dr. Leslie had turned and fled. Moments later, his black station wagon peeled out of a back street behind the hospital, speeding away into the night. Though Dr. Leslie had practiced medicine in the town for 40 years, that night he would leave it for good, never to be seen nor heard from in Coverale again.

Derlin and Mavis stood silently for a moment, looking down at the babies laying wide awake in their crib.

"If I help you, can you run to the car?" Derlin asked.

"I think so," Mavis said quietly, her eyes filled with worry.

After a few quick seconds of jostling, Derlin grabbed Randy, Mavis grabbed Ollie and Derlin grabbed Mavis with his free hand. He looked back at the suitcase he'd prepared for Mavis and her hospital stay but didn't have the hands to grab it. They hustled out the door and as quickly as they could manage down the hallway, limping and weaving toward an exit. Derlin knew that they couldn't very well just waltz out the front door to where he'd left the sedan and did his best to follow signs and lead them downstairs to the basement.

Finally locating an exit sign, Derlin led his family through a service entrance shrouded in bushes and made it along the side of the hospital just in time to see members of the torch and pitchfork-brandishing mob storming past Derlin's poorly-parked car and heading inside. Using the mob's new focus of attention to their advantage, Mavis and Derlin waited till the last of the crowd rushed inside. Remarkably, Derlin's car was unscathed in the rush and they were able to make it unseen to the trusty old sedan, still parked diagonally across the curb at the entrance. Derlin got Mavis and the babies situated in the backseat as comfortably as he could manage before flinging himself into the front seat and grabbing for his keys, which he always kept hidden safely in the floorboard just in case he needed to grab them quickly. The engine whirred to life with a rumble and Derlin quickly burned out of the parking lot, middle finger out the window. With one hand on the steering wheel, he was unable to compensate for the rush of horsepower from his gas pedal stomp, misjudging the exit and careening into a bench which wedged itself under the front end. Using his continuing momentum, Derlin kept at it and kept the gas pedal pressed firmly to the floor, sideswiping a mailbox and gunning it down the road away from town. The racket of the encounter attracted the attention of the mob, gathering in the torch light along the second story windows as they discovered that Mavis and Derlin's room lay empty. They rushed back toward the lawn, pouring out of the front entrance of the hospital and quickly began to chase after Derlin's badly damaged sedan, following the high streams of sparks shooting from underneath his car into the predawn sky.

The sedan shook as a small part of the park bench broke off and clattered past the back wheels. He was able to pick up a little bit of speed to separate them from the pursuing mob, but with half of a park bench still wedged under his front axle, Derlin knew the family wasn't going to get much farther down the road before the mob started gaining ground on them. He could hear the bench grinding into the pavement as he drove and listened intently to the whine of the engine as it struggled to overcome the burden. Soon, smoke started to billow from under the hood.

Derlin could soon see no better option, so he pulled his shuddering sedan over to the side of the road, finding a small gully where he could at least get it a few feet off the road to try and hide it, should the mob pass by. As the babies lay blanket-swaddled in a patch of leaves, Derlin and Mavis frantically concealed the sedan as best they could under some tree branches and brush. After a few moments of covering, Mavis and Derlin stopped for a moment and silently locked eyes again. They could hear the faint approaching murmur of a large group of people and could vaguely make out the warm orange glow of torches growing brighter in the distance. Instantly, each grabbed a baby in their arms and took off running into the woods, Derlin helping Mavis keep pace as he scoured the distance for any kind of landmark. Somehow, after only a few minutes of running, they managed to make it through the trees and brush and reached a small clearing. They could no longer see torches in the distance from where they stood, nor could they hear the shouts of townsfolk or barks of hounds and for a moment they began to feel safe. Derlin estimated that they'd gotten roughly half a mile from the main road. Between the distance covered and the hiding of his car, Derlin hoped that they'd done enough to be in the clear, at least for the night. For the first time since they fled the hospital, Mavis was able to catch her breath.

"What do we do now?" Mavis cried, leaning against a tree, wiping a mixture of sweat and tears from her face.

"As long as that mob of folks is still after us, I reckon we don't have much of a choice but to keep going," Derlin shrugged. He did his best to hide the worry he felt but knew that this was among the most important moments of his life.

"The doctor himself said they weren't sixes," Mavis cried, looking down at her newborn sons and their shining "bbb" birthmarks. She was weak from childbirth and had exhausted her last drops of energy during their harrowing escape. "Why are these people still chasing us? These boys didn't do nothing to nobody."

"I know, baby," Derlin sighed. "We just got to keep going and get to a safe place where y'all can rest. We can figure all this out in the morning."

A branch crashed in the distance behind them and Mavis stood with a start.

"Baby, we gotta go," Derlin said, grabbing Randy and Ollie as gently as he could.

"I know," Mavis whispered. With that, they left the clearing and set off deeper into the forest, not knowing what lay ahead of them. Derlin wondered to himself if any other new fathers in history had gotten their first "baby-holding" practice while sprinting through the forest.

Nearly two hours passed, full of wandering. Long past the clearing, Derlin thought he had begun to recognize the lay of the land and soon began to lead his young family down what he dearly hoped was a path. After a few hundred yards, he was elated to realize his suspicions had been correct.

"Baby, I know where we are," Derlin whispered excitedly. "I used to come out here all the time when I was a young'n. I know a place we can go."

Mavis nodded silently, her eyes again wide as she followed Derlin further down the path. Just as the sun was beginning to creep over the horizon, their wood-lined path came into another clearing of trees, one Derlin had expected to find.

"There," he said plainly, pointing across the little meadow through the pre-morning fog.

Mavis hadn't really known what to expect when Derlin had told her he knew of a "place they could stay" that night. Thinking back, she supposed she'd expected a cousin's dilapidated hunting shack, an old indian cave, or perhaps even an old hollow log, but she certainly wasn't expecting what awaited their arrival. Jutting up into the early morning sunshine, alone in this meadow in the middle of the forest, was an ancient stone windmill.

Derlin had remembered playing in the long-abandoned windmill from his days roaming the Coverdale forest as a child, when it was frequently used as a fort during games of "Cowboys & Indians" or "Northern Aggression." He knew the winding, gnarled forest path to the windmill like the back of his hand and it felt like a natural choice for sanctuary when leading his family to safety as they fled from town. As he saw it, fate and circumstance could not have landed them in a better place to collect their bearings and rest. They were a good four miles from the outskirts of town and Derlin speculated that no one would come looking for them down a dusty old forgotten road in a dustier, older, even more forgotten windmill.

It had been built in the early eighteenth century as a friendly outpost by a mostly-forgotten band of enterprising Dutch settlers, in an area of Coverdale they referred to as "Schijtendal," loosely translating as "Shitty Valley." Using a mixture of stone, mud, clay and some of the finest lumber in the forests of the King of Spain's New World territories, the windmill was ranked among the largest and sturdiest in the pre-Louisiana Purchase United States. The sizable stone fireplace warmed many a weary traveler throughout the eighteenth and early nineteenth centuries. It had even served as a drummer boy practice hall by various local militias and even a small handful of deep-south Confederates during the Civil War. It may have been a bit past its prime as a dwelling, but there was no surprise that it still stood, hulking above the trees in a dark, forgotten corner of the Alabama countryside.

The windmill was nearly pitch-black inside as they pried open the door and made their way inside. Derlin took to securing the perimeter while Mavis used the small bits of daylight creeping through the front door to search the musty room for candles or matches. While Derlin stalked purposefully around the outside of the windmill, eyeing the treeline for trouble, he found a discarded rake which he began carrying for defense. He carried it as a military man would a rifle, stepping proudly and periodically pausing to untangle it from a low-hanging tree branch. Once he was confident that they had indeed lost the angry mob for good he concluded his march, doing one more lap around the perimeter for good measure. Still seeing no torches lighting up the horizon in the growing daylight, he headed inside to check on Mavis and the boys.

Mavis was surprisingly successful in her quest to light the windmill, but not quite perhaps in the manner she'd hoped or expected. In a shabby and dated supply closet, she'd discovered three oil lanterns atop some 20 canisters of Dutch whale oil which the label indicated dated to the 1830's. Mavis couldn't read Dutch however and was happy to find an illustration of a lantern on the dusty lead canister. The whale oil left a distinct musk hanging in the already stale air, but it burned slowly and would keep the babies happy and warm however long they'd need to stay there. The canisters were certainly not the end of their problems, and seemed a better find than the four 50 pound sacks of ancient salt sharing the closet.

"Aside from the windmill not being a boat and us not being in the ocean," Derlin remarked, taking a deep breath of the musky, whale-tinged air. "I bet this must be what it's like to be a sea captain like in the movies."

They slept in the windmill that morning, the four of them atop an ancient pile of hay with the babies swaddled in blankets in between. Derlin stroked her hair as Mavis slowly fell asleep and the two promised to formulate a plan later in the day when they awoke.

"Why don't we just live in the windmill?" Derlin shouted excitedly just after noon, waking Mavis and the twins with a start. Both babies began a round of what would become their own specific brand of crying, a tearless holler which basically sounded like someone with a gravelly voice half-heartedly yelling as they unenthusiastically rode a ride at the fair.

"Why don't we what?" Mavis asked, bewildered, briefly forgetting where she was as she rubbed the sleep from her eyes. Randy continued yell-crying. Ollie was already back asleep.

"Why don't we just live here?" Derlin asked again, pointing downward at the hay covered windmill floor, smiling.

"Aaaaahhhhhhhhh," Randy continued, still agitated.

Mavis shook her head.

"Look," he continued, trying to talk over his son's strange crying, which began to sound a bit like a disjointed meow. "Those people in town wanna kill all of us because they think all those B's on our boys heads are sixes. That's nobody's fault. That ain't on us, that ain't on them babies. Nothin' we can do about that."

"Right," Mavis replied. "But we can't just up and live in a windmill."

"Now, baby, hear me out on that," Derlin said assuredly. "This windmill don't have no rent. I won't have to have no job. We can just live out here till the kids grow enough hair to cover their heads up and till then I'll just find food in the woods!"

Mavis stared at him silently, slowly placing her hands on her hips.

"Now, listen," Derlin said, beginning to frame an idea in the air with his hands.

"What'll Lumpy do if you just disappear on him?" Mavis asked sternly.

"Oh, he'll manage," Derlin said dismissively. "Always does."

"There's plenty of hay for the babies," he began again. "I know you could spruce this windmill up into a cozy little homestead in no time. By the time the babies is three or so we can go back to town and nobody there will even remember or wanna kill us anymore. We can start back fresh just like before and I'll get a new job and everything will turn out just fine!"

Mavis was resistant to the idea as most sensible folks would be, but as Derlin looked at her biting his tongue, eyebrows raised, nodding, with a double thumbs up, she realized that she really didn't have a better option to present. She conceded to the plan to stay, at least for the time being and Derlin let out an excited yip, leaping to his feet and pumping his fist in the air.

As Derlin bounced happily outside to grab his rake for a day of "securing the perimeter," he hollered something Mavis half-caught about the windmill being her castle and he being her "Prince Sherming."

She sighed deeply shook her head, vowing to herself to do her best to turn the windmill into a suitable home for her family until Randy and Ollie grew enough hair to cover their birthmarks. As a new mother with a violent mob still presumably after her children's lives, she didn't see many other options. It wouldn't be forever after all. Besides, as Derlin had continued to reiterate, "Spurlock men do tend to hair early."

Chapter 5

February 3, 1968

The morning progressed slowly as Mavis attempted to get used to her surroundings. She was still clearly in shock after the whole affair, not expecting to experience her first morning of motherhood in a drafty abandoned windmill after fleeing for her life from the town she'd grown up in. Mavis nursed the boys and did her feeble best to search the now day-lit windmill top to bottom for anything else that could be of use in making the 250-year-old tower more "homey," as Derlin had put it, for her little family. As Mavis searched, the boys' progressively flatter yell-cries echoed constantly off of the high stone walls and ceilings and she wondered how long it had been since the windmill had heard a baby's cry.

Derlin had been gone since the decision to stay was made, purposefully scouring the forest for lunch and dinner alike, hoping that his foraging without any weapon beyond his trusty rake could indeed keep his family fed as he had so recently boasted. He planned on stalking, ambushing and bludgeoning a rabbit or possibly a deer, but had nothing schemed out beyond this. Gradually, he shed his confidence from earlier in the morning. While his Grandpa Hoyt was a beloved hunting legend in the region, the skills hadn't been passed down to Derlin.

Deciding he best hide if he planned on ambushing anything, Derlin crouched under a large bush near what he incorrectly assumed to be the well worn path of a local rabbit or squirrel. The path was actually the result of a recent heavy rain draining to the lowest levels of the underbrush, which Derlin had failed to notice while stomping through the resulting nearby mud.

Derlin kept his rake cocked behind him like a baseball player ready to swing for the first 15 minutes or so of his "hiding" before abandoning his Harmon Killebrew stance and leaning casually on the rake for support, waiting for supper to hop by. It was not the first or the last time that Derlin had propped himself upon a rake and he was quite in his element when doing so. It was a trait he would pass down to his sons, just as his father Clovis had done for him and just as Grandpa Hoyt had done for Clovis. It was a skill that Spurlock men had honed since Derlin's Great-Great-Great-Great-Great-Great-Great Grandfather Bonaventure Spurlock had first arrived in America, clinging to the side of a whaling vessel destined for the gulf.

Nearly an hour and a half had passed before Derlin finally shook himself from his prop, realizing that dinner was not just going to come wandering up to him and his rake, doe-eyed like a Disney cartoon. If he wanted Bambi, he was going to have to stalk him and kill him. He thought about this reality for a few moments; his poor skill as a hunter, his arsenal of weaponry including only his rake, his fists and the well-worn size six cowboy boots on his feet.

Right then and there, he had an idea that might provide some salvation from the fact that he'd wasted an entire afternoon. The sun had already begun to fall from the sky in his first day of providing for his family and he hadn't found so much as an acorn, but

Derlin remained undeterred. As the sun faded from view, Derlin felt a new light shining down on his family's fortunes. It was time again to be a man of action. In yet another instance that was neither a first or final, Derlin tore the sleeves from his T-shirt. What followed next, however, was a first. He tore a small hole in one sleeve before pulling it down over his nose and mouth. Tearing two holes in the second sleeve, he pulled it down over his eyes and forehead. Suddenly brimming with a newfound confidence, Derlin decided that Mavis would surely understand if he was a little later than planned getting back to the windmill. He'd only been gone for seven hours at this point. He took a deep breath, picked up his trusty rake and prepared to get his family dinner.

Derlin knew the vague direction of town from the windmill even at night from the time he'd spent there as a child and once he'd passed through the thickest of the woods he was able to see faint lights of civilization. He walked purposefully toward town, lurking in the darkness as best he could and keeping a lookout for passing cars. Once the streets of Coverdale became a little brighter, Derlin crept through the shadows and, when necessary, the back-alleys on the way to his destination. He noticed several broadsides pasted to telephone poles reading "Wanted: Devil Babies" with a crude illustration of his children and a tip hotline at the bottom.

After miles of scampering through what he now considered hostile and treacherous territory, Derlin finally reached his destination, illuminated against the black backdrop of the evening. The A&P grocery store sat nearly empty as it neared its 8pm closing time and Derlin could not have arrived at a more perfect time if he'd tried. He paused on the curb in front of the store as he adjusted his poorly constructed sleeve mask.

The eyes were off-center and the mouth hole was much too small, but he had to concentrate. His plan was about to come to fruition.

Derlin took a deep breath as he stepped into the parking lot, crouching in a manner that stretched his hamstrings and calves. He spent another minute on these preparations clearly visible in the parking lot, just a run of the mill masked man with a rake lucidly doing rudimentary P.E. warm up exercises in the dark. Concluding his stretching and filling his lungs with air once more, he sprinted into the A&P, rake in hand, and began immediately yelling at the top of his lungs.

"Everybody get down on the ground, I'mma steal me some food," he shouted. It came out with the intended intensity but garbled and strange to everyone else inside due to the poor construction of his mouth hole.

"Git down! Don't nobody wanna get hit with this rake! Rake scratch!" he yelled, both terrifying and bewildering the few remaining customers as he mimed scratching them with his rake.

He began brandishing the rake wildly, hollering about meats and cigarettes and all the things he was going to steal while he was there. Again, it came out in a frightening jumble. One wild swing of the rake unintentionally ripped the A&P phone from its cord, knocking it down an aisle. Both cashiers and the three remaining customers all hit the deck quickly as this happened, screaming in unison and hoping that this strange man with the rake would leave them alone if he was left to his quest for the aforementioned "Bacon, baby milk & Lucky Strikes."

Derlin grabbed a shopping cart and continued to brandish his rake with his free hand. He didn't want to say anything else disturbing to the customers, as he sensed that they couldn't quite understand the words he was trying to say. However, he did want to maintain his edge and confident demeanor while in front of them so he began to hiss menacingly. No one in the store moved as he stuffed his cart to the brim with canned fruits and vegetables, piles of meat and beer, a few dirty magazines and of course, a few cartons of Lucky Strikes.

He usually smoked "Old Indian" cigarettes, a local Coverdale brand he'd been loyal to since pre-adolescence. They were by far the cheapest cigarettes around and were rumored to be blended with lead shavings, but Derlin loved the tang they had and had smoked them religiously since he was eleven. He just figured if he was going to be stealing smokes, he might as well grab good ones. He even had the foresight to throw a large armful of candles to light the windmill into the cart, noticing them on a nearby shelf as he browsed for rake polish.

Derlin headed toward the exit, quietly at first. He scanned the store slowly from the checkout area, pausing to see if there was anything particularly nourishing or expensive that he'd missed in his haste. As he browsed the impulse items, something caught his eye.

"Candy for the babies!" Derlin shouted incoherently, grabbing a fistful of Charleston Chews from a checkout aisle display and hurtling out the door and into the darkness. He kicked a dent in the Coca-Cola machine on his way out for added emphasis, sprinting through the parking lot as quickly as he could manage with the cart and retreating quickly back into the shadows of the night.

It would be among the more difficult tasks in his life to that point for Derlin to wheel the 250 pound malt-liquor and bean can-laden goliath through the rutted paths and leafy underbrush that made up his woodland trek back to the windmill, but he had managed to fill the cart with some $300 worth of sundries and was quite proud of himself. Had there been a police pursuit, they would have found him easily as it took him 90 minutes of strained jogging, pushing the cart down the side of the two-lane highway away from town, before he reached the edge of the woods. For the first time, he was thankful that he'd knocked the phone from the wall as he had. A&P was the last local business to close for the evening and it was half an hour before a cashier had made it to a phone to report the robbery.

Letting out a victorious yelp as he reached the edge of the woodline, Derlin removed his sweat soaked shirt sleeve masks, tucking them carefully into his back jeans pocket. He wiped the sweat from his brow, looking down fondly at his rake and nodding to himself. Mavis was going to be proud. Ducking into the woods with the cart as sirens finally blared in the distance, Derlin wasn't worried in the least. Maybe this was going to work out alright after all.

Chapter 6

February 4, 1968

It was nearly dawn by the time that Derlin reached the bottom of the small hill that lead to the clearing where the windmill stood. He'd sweat out nearly all of the beer he'd drank as he slowly dragged the cart through the forest and though a combination of adrenaline and self-preservation had kept him going this far, his flame was waning. The hill involved maybe seven feet of total incline, but the six-hour, three-mile cart dragging jaunt through the woods had taken its toll. Derlin paused to rest for a moment, opening a still-cool can of his prized Panther Cat Lager and consuming it as Popeye would spinach. He wiped his dripping brow and mouth in one fell swoop and took a deep breath. Gaining undeterminable strength as the malt liquor pulsed through his veins, Derlin gazed down at the small fistful of Charleston Chews he'd pilfered on his way out of the A&P as a treat for his infant children.

"Candy for the babies!" he said loudly to himself as motivation, feeling a swell of fatherly pride before exhaling mightily and beginning the final cart-shove back to the windmill.

When he burst through the door, Mavis let out a startled scream that caused Randy and Ollie to both burst into a fresh bout of their yell-crying.

"Honey, I'm home," Derlin hollered happily. He drug the cart in from the doorway, checking the treeline once more for the possibility of anyone following him. He closed the door and blockaded it with a large log he'd found a few days prior that he'd since been using as makeshift home security. "Lookit all this stuff I got!"
Mavis gasped and began to rummage through the cart excitedly. Discarding the two copies of the February, 1968 issue of "Plumpers" Magazine, she was ecstatic to see what an incredible bounty Derlin had brought back into their home. She grabbed a jug of water and began guzzling it with the ferocity that Derlin had been downing Panther Cats since his return.

"Derlin, I can't believe it," Mavis began. "How in the world did you afford all of this? We don't have any money. What happened to the sleeves on your shirt?"

"Woah, woah, woah, baby. One question at a time," Derlin started, slurring his words slightly. "Don't you worry about none of that. I caught my shirt sleeves on some briars and they came off cause I was runnin' real fast because of… of a panther cat I seen in the woods and I didn't wanna get bit."

Mavis narrowed her eyes but nodded silently.

"And the groceries," Derlin continued. "I got them… from those nice people at the A&P. They just had me do some rake work for them first. Cleaning up leaves and making their mulch and gravel smooth, stuff like that."

Mavis smiled. She'd worried immensely during Derlin's absence and was surprised and relieved to find that he'd apparently been away working.

"That's great news Derlin," she said. "I'm so proud of you."

"I'm prideful of it too baby," he beamed. "I got all this meat and cheese and cigarettes and baby food for once the boys get done titty-feeding on you. Plus, that candy there, them Charleston Chews," he pointed.

"Yeah?" Mavis asked.

"Them's for the babies, too." he said, as though it was particularly important.

"Okay, Derlin," Mavis nodded.

Mavis put the candy into a makeshift cabinet she'd fashioned out of a few large pieces of board in the corner of the room. She began to put away things as best she could as Derlin grabbed a bottle of lighter fluid and began to douse kindling in the windmill's stone hearth for what he referred to as "a meat cooking fire."

Mavis sat happily next to the fireplace nursing Randy and Ollie as Derlin slowly and meticulously cooked and ate two pounds of bacon, one strip at a time. From time to time he'd turn and offer Mavis a small piece from the end of his fork, but she'd refuse each time. He'd had a hard, if vaguely mysterious last 24 hours and, as she assumed, probably needed all the bacon he could get. She did make herself a sandwich after Derlin finally fell asleep, her grimy hero snoring away in a pile of hay next to two empty packets of bacon and five empty cans of Panther Cat Lager. The firelight danced and played as it reflected from the grease on Derlin's stubbly chin and Mavis watched it flicker with fascination as she slowly ate her sandwich, ruminating over the less-than subtle changes she'd experienced in her life since first becoming a Spurlock.

February 5, 1968

Derlin awoke the next morning feeling greasier than he'd expected. Though never a particularly avid bather, he felt an intense need to take a shower. Reeking of bacon and smoke, he gurgled as he rolled over in the hay, doing his best not to disturb Mavis or the babies. He staggered out into the early dawn hours of the day with the intention of finding a small creek he'd stumbled across during an earlier "woods patrol." He planned on lowering himself into it for a bath. He didn't expect to be lucky, but he hoped to find a pool deep enough that he could at least submerge himself. Derlin planned to lead Mavis and the babies back later in the day, hoping the pool could become sort of a family bathtub as Mavis recovered from childbirth. Even a rube such as Derlin knew that a creek in the woods wasn't the ideal place for Mavis to tend to her birthing injuries, but as he thought back on "settler times" when "people pretty much just lived outside," he decided finding the big pool in the creek was probably the best they were going to do in their current predicament. He'd forgotten to grab any for himself as he left the windmill, but he'd had the foresight to steal "lady soap" from the A&P, along with a "whole shit ton of different medicines and salves" to aid Mavis in her recovery.

Derlin thought of Mavis as he walked listening for the sound of the water. To paraphrase Dr. Leslie, the doctor had "patched Mavis up real good," before the mobs came, and he was expecting a fairly smooth convalescence. Though the twins had spent nearly an extra month in the womb, they took after their father's scrawny physique at birth and all things considered came out uneventfully. Still, the idea that Mavis had been able to flee with Derlin, first to the car and then through the woods, only hours after giving birth to Randy and Ollie was something that Derlin would always marvel at. He'd always considered himself "probably one of the strongest people in town" but learned that night that Mavis had a certain strength that he could never hope to match. He thought of his young wife, trying to find a word for that strength. He'd never quite find it, reaching a mental dead end at the phrase "like 'spry' but way more bigger," giving up once he heard the unmistakable trickle of water.

Derlin followed the noise, bounding through the underbrush and soon finding himself creekside. He wandered down the bank, following the creek in hopes that it would get wider. After a few hundred yards, he had a stroke of luck as the creek wound down a hill, forming a foot deep pool among a cluster of smooth rocks at the bottom. Sliding down the hill, nearly losing his footing in his boots, Derlin began gathering rocks to dam up the area around the pool. Soon, he'd managed to get the pool's depth up to over two feet and, satisfied that he'd made a worthy makeshift bathtub, Derlin began to remove his tiny boots.

Soaking naked in his proudly constructed pool, Derlin splashed himself across the stomach and dunked his head under the cold water, scrubbing the bacon grease from his stubbly face. He wallowed there for a good while as the morning light got brighter. As he finally pried himself from the silty bath, Derlin stood next to the creek air-drying himself and surveying the woods around him. Something caught his eye at the base of a tree about 50 feet further down the creek and, as soon as he'd dried himself sufficiently to put on his jeans and boots, Derlin sauntered down to investigate. Discarded at the base of the tree sat a five-gallon plastic bucket, on its side, partially buried under dirt and moss. Derlin wrested it from the ground, holding it aloft as though he'd just found treasure. Returning to the creek, Derlin scrubbed the moss and dirt away as best he could, slowly filling the bucket with creek water to take back to the windmill.

"Mavis!" he hollered as the windmill got within sight. He walked awkwardly, carrying the bucket by the handle at his side, sloshing it everywhere. "Mavis!"

Mavis opened the windmill door slowly and waved. She came outside, a look of worry on her face as she encountered her damp, panting husband bounding up from the forest with a bucket.

"What's that?" Mavis asked.

"Oh, it's creek water," Derlin said nonchalantly.

"Creek water?" Mavis asked.

"Yeah," Derlin nodded. "I spent all morning makin' you a big old rock bathtub in a pool down at the creek so you can soak your lady parts and heal up proper and even relax a spell. It's real nice, and I bet we can probably wash the babies in it. I got baby soap from the grocery folk too."

"Really?" Mavis smiled. "That's amazing, honey. You're the best husband in the world. I'm sure we could all use a bath."

"I don't know about 'best in the world' but I'll take 'best in the woods.' Derlin laughed. "I took me a soak this morning, I feel like a forty dollar bill! I do reckon I got a little more silt on me than when I started but that's fine."

Derlin scratched at his back over his shoulder.

"So, where'd you get the bucket?" Mavis asked.

"Oh, some asshole just left it sitting right there by the creek, and I seen it," Derlin started. "I figured I could fill it up with creek water and we could at least wash our hands up here or give the boys a quick dunk."

"That's a great idea, honey" Mavis smiled.

"I might even take a Tennessee car wash if I don't feel like going all the way down to the creek," Derlin said.

"What's that?" Mavis asked, her look of confusion returning.

"A Tennessee car wash?" Derlin replied. "That's a bath where you don't get your hair wet."

"Oh," Mavis said plainly.

"Yeah, baby," Derlin said. "Sometimes a man just ain't got the time."

February 6, 1968

Over the next few days, Mavis slowly and diligently prepared and cured the 40-some pounds of meat that Derlin had stolen, preventing it from spoiling on the windmill floor where Derlin had left it in a heap. Refrigeration was not something that had crossed his mind as he ransacked the butcher's stash at the A&P, but Mavis wasn't about to let Derlin suffer the indignity of such lack of foresight. Using the knowledge gained as a child helping her grandmother prepare batch after batch of horse jerky, the massive sacks of closet salt had come in handy after all.

Derlin, meanwhile, recuperated by spending those next few days laying in the hay, reading "Plumpers" and thinking about what lay ahead. There were enough canned goods and Panther Cat to last for two or three weeks. Enough smokes for a month and enough meat and rake polish to last for two. He didn't know how "titty-milk" worked, but assumed he already had enough formula and baby food stashed for the boys' first month or so away from their mother's breast.

Thinking he had at least a little bit of time to let ideas simmer, Derlin took a few days off from plotting his next move. With each crack of a Panther Cat, he began to understand that his A&P bounty was likely going to dry up more quickly than he anticipated and soon, he'd unpropped his feet from the hearth and began to think seriously about his next move as a strange abstract form of an armed robber. He had natural reservations about going back to the A&P for another attempted heist so soon, but luckily for him it was not the only grocery store in Coverdale. Far on the other side of town, a two-hour twilight scamper at minimum, was a much larger and nicer Piggly Wiggly. Successfully knocking it over would take a great deal of his less-than-ample cunning, but he knew the time would come when he'd have to make that run if he wanted to continue to be able to provide for his family in the unconventional manner which he'd chosen.

February 16, 1968

The present grocery stash and subsequent bucket discovery had been a boon to the success of life in the windmill and the next week and a half passed with relative ease as Derlin and Mavis began to fall into a routine for the first time since fleeing the hospital. Each morning, the family would rise early. Mavis would nurse the boys then cook breakfast in the hearth for her and Derlin as the babies "played" laying next to each other in the hay, occasionally lightly pawing at each other's faces and staring at each other blankly. One would inevitably injure the other with a finger jab to the eye or a slow claw at the face and yell-crying would ensue on both sides. Nap time for the twins would soon follow and this was when Derlin, now full of dry cereal and breakfast meat, would head out the door with rake in hand on his daily "woods patrol."

He would wander through the forest and the meadow immediately surrounding the windmill, looking for clues of foot-traffic or animal activity, never actually noticing any of either. There was no "foot-traffic" nearby but his own, and spotting his own from an earlier "woods patrol" would only have inevitably startled him. He missed numerous clues to animal activity, but it's pretty unlikely at this point that he would have been able to capture something anyhow unless a rabbit leapt at him and died in midair.

Upon securing the area on his morning rounds, Derlin would return to the windmill for lunch. He'd pat the babies on their heads, running his thumb along their birthmarks, which like the rest of them were growing larger by the day. He'd kiss Mavis, eat a sandwich and stretch loudly for a few minutes, explaining to the babies how important it was for him to "stay limber" if he was going to protect them. After his lunch and vigorous stretching routine, Derlin would go on a "scouting mission" for more supplies, constantly referencing his bucket as a reason to keep searching. This would inevitably turn into four or five cans of Panther Cat and a nap atop a pile of brush somewhere deep in the woods. It was in the time immediately preceding these beer naps, when alone and drinking under the shade of some ancient oak tree, that he began to formulate his next move.

The Piggly Wiggly was indeed going to be his "huckleberry," but he knew after the jaunt to the much closer A&P that he didn't have it in him physically or mentally to do the Piggly Wiggly run totally on foot. He thought about the condition of his trusty old sedan, hoping that it was still there, next to the highway tucked safely into the underbrush. Yes, there was a parking bench wedged under the front bumper, but if Derlin's father Clovis had taught him anything at all, that was nothing that a bunch of revving the engine in reverse couldn't fix.

He was certain that after his years of running it hard, nothing could kill the old sedan and that, come hell or high water it was going to play a major role in the evening. He was unsure if the A&P heist had gotten enough news coverage to draw attention to his rake, but Derlin knew that he needed a bigger and better plan this time than just running into the store and yelling. He needed a plan with flair and bombast. A plan that popped like the Fourth of July fireworks he'd shot off for Mavis in the construction lot so many months ago.

It hit him one afternoon, as he lay sprawled on some particularly leafy underbrush beneath a shadowy tree sipping his third Panther Cat of the early afternoon. His trusty old sedan wasn't just going to get him to and from the Piggly Wiggly when the night finally came. It was going to take him right through the front door.

Chapter 7

February 27, 1968

Randy and Ollie pawed lazily at an empty can of beans on the floor as Derlin watched them from his propped position against the windmill wall. Mavis was asleep, napping in the hay, so Derlin cracked his last Panther Cat as quietly as he could, wincing at the sound it made as he did so. His gaze moved from his twin boys to his can of Panther Cat, the final in a long and proud line of beers consumed in or around the windmill since they'd arrived there two weeks prior.

"We've had a pretty good run, boys," Derlin whispered to Randy and Ollie, crouching down beside them as they stared back at him, blank-faced and slack-jawed, a look that had been identifying Spurlock men for centuries.

As Derlin stood, he inadvertently kicked the can of beans laying between them, sending it clattering across the floor and causing them to break into a fresh and vibrant round of yell-crying.

Thinking quickly and doing his best not to wake Mavis, Derlin sprinted to the other side of the room, retrieving a Charleston Chew from the makeshift cabinet.

"Here you go boys, heads up!" Derlin whispered. He tore the wrapper and tossed the candy bar underhanded to the floor between them, apparently expecting one of them to catch it. It bounced once between them and landed in the hay as they eyed it blankly. Lacking the necessary motor skills to do so, neither boy moved to retrieve it.

"Oh yeah, you're babies," Derlin said, shaking his head and laughing as he sat down on the floor with his sons, retrieving the candy and brushing it free of dirt. Neither of the boys yet had any semblance of teeth to speak of, but they both seemed to enjoy gnawing and gumming at the candy and had stopped yell-crying almost as soon as Derlin had given it to them.

"Charleston Chews is like nature's pacifier," Derlin said to himself.

It was then that Derlin had his first truly proud moment of parenthood. Not only had he ceased their crying, but he felt he'd bonded with them in the process. However informal and unsuccessful, they had technically just shared their first game of "catch" and Derlin was briefly lost in a daydream of the boys roaming the outfield for his beloved Atlanta Braves, their baby heads atop large, muscular bodies, yell-crying as they tracked down dramatic fly balls. Derlin smiled as he looked down at the boys gumming at the increasingly dusty Charleston Chew. Windmill upbringing or not, he could still be an excellent father. A solver of problems. A fixer of things. A provider of candy for the babies.

His children satiated, Derlin returned to his casual lean against the wall and the remaining few swigs of his Panther Cat. As he moved his stare around the room, he noticed how bare the cupboard was becoming. To Derlin's surprise, the boys still showed no interest in the baby food he'd acquired, failing to react as he held up the jars and tried explaining the flavors as best he could. Derlin's closet of salt pork that Mavis had stashed away was still ample, but the remaining canned fruits and vegetables were only going to get them so much farther down the line before he would have to act on his aspirations and head to the Piggly Wiggly.

Derlin held the last sip of his Panther Cat in his mouth for a moment before swallowing and crumpling the can in his hand. The sound of crushing aluminum provided him just the focus he needed and it was a moment of clarity unlike any he'd felt since he'd first decided to rob the A&P at rake point that fateful day standing in the forest. After weeks of careful planning and deliberation, Derlin chose this moment as his time of action. The time had come for him to finally knock over the Piggly Wiggly. He sighed softly, for the first time feeling a twinge of regret in the manner that he'd come upon to be a providing father. He certainly had jitters, wary of the difficulty of the task that lay ahead of him, but he was determined to succeed. He left the babies tucked away safely in a small, protective corner "fort" made mostly of hay and empty Panther Cat cans, and quickly scrawled Mavis a note explaining everything clearly on the side of a grocery bag. "*Dear Baby,*

Gone to do some big time rake work for some people in town. Be home win I can. Tell the babies I say hey. Will bring smokes and lady sope. I love you.
Roll Tide,
Derlin"

It was still early in the afternoon when Derlin began his trek down the familiar rutted path toward town. It was a little earlier than he'd originally planned on starting out, but as he walked he remembered that he was going to need all the daylight he could get in locating his trusty old sedan by the highway. Besides, digging the car from the underbrush and successfully removing the hunk of park bench from underneath it alone was a task that Derlin expected was going to take him well into nightfall.

He stomped through the woods, imagining himself moving along stealthily like a deer, or perhaps an Indian. In actuality he was making a great deal of racket, and were it not for the tiny cowboy boot prints he left in the mud and dirt, a hunter likely would have mistaken him by noise alone for an injured bear. He smashed his way through the woods, karate chopping branches and swatting down spiderwebs with his rake and soon, he'd located the old two-lane highway and set to looking for his car.

Derlin couldn't remember the exact spot where they'd hidden the car, but knew it wasn't very far past the billboard for his favorite local restaurant, The Screaming Captain Seafood Emporium. The billboard leered over the desolate stretch of highway, depicting a massive, elderly sea-captain, mouth agape, with squarish Teddy Roosevelt teeth and black eyes, forcefully cramming a whale, octopus and mermaid into a deep fryer. In vivid technicolor, it was colorful and easy to spot even in the approaching darkness. It had been there by the side of the highway since the mid-1930's but had somehow lost none of its luster or vibrancy. The restaurant itself was a staple of Coverdale cuisine, still being run solely by the giant, mysterious "Captain" even as he approached his 110th birthday. Staring longingly at the billboard, Derlin's mouth began to water and pangs of hunger crept into his stomach. His breakfast of salt pork had worn off hours before and he briefly thought of stopping by The Screaming Captain on his way home, but while he was able to dismiss something like robbing grocery stores at rake point for beer and baby food, he couldn't quite lower himself to the level of behaving in that manner at a fried seafood buffet. He stood, wavering slightly in the breeze but otherwise unmoving beneath the billboard for a good five minutes. Thinking about seafood, thinking about his rake.

Thinking about seafood, thinking about his rake. Finally, he shook himself from his stupor.

"You ain't gonna steal fish from that restaurant, Derlin," he told himself quietly, mouth still watering. "That ain't something Spurlocks do." He wandered past the billboard, toward a leafy mass that he hoped was his sedan. Looking back over his shoulder, he paused again.

"I'mma have me some fish, though!" he said sternly. "The day I get us out of that damn windmill and into a real home again, I'mma have me some fish."
He nodded to himself in confident affirmation of his goal and began walking again. While most men would dream of items of sport or luxury upon returning to civilization, the top of Derlin's mountain did indeed seem to be respectable access to the fried fish buffet. He laughed loudly.

"I'll be seeing you, Captain!" he hollered as he turned to dig through the underbrush. He let out a small howl as he began his work.

The leafy mass he'd spotted was indeed the sedan, which sat undisturbed by the road where they'd left it fleeing the mob. They'd done a better job of covering it up than Derlin had remembered and it took him a good twenty minutes just to get the car fully clear of woodland debris. Still wary of the possibility of police interference or the continuing town-wide hunt for the "devil babies," Derlin had to dive behind the sedan into the underbrush to avoid being spotted by passing cars a handful of times. He'd remained undetected despite badly skinning up his forearms and elbows on the jagged branches piled around him. Soon, with the car finally free of leaves and branches, Derlin turned his attention to the park bench wedged beneath the front axle.
First, as any good Spurlock man would, Derlin attempted to pry the park bench loose with the handle of his rake. When that was unsuccessful, he attempted several kicks with his cowboy boots with little success. It was then that his father Clovis' voice popped into his head, clear as day.

"Just rev the engine a bunch in reverse, boy," Clovis whispered from Derlin's conscience. "Just rev it a bunch in reverse."

Derlin hopped into the driver's seat, scouring the floorboard for his keys. He began to panic upon not seeing them and upon looking up was elated to find that they were still in the ignition. It took three tries before the engine turned over and the sedan finally sputtered to life. When it did Derlin revved the engine with gusto, letting out a triumphant holler.

As daylight was nearly gone, Derlin wasted no time in his attempt to free the bench from beneath his getaway car. Flooring the gas pedal while in reverse the first time sent smoke flying up from the tires as the car lurched back a few feet. Just as Clovis had taught him, the park bench was indeed loosened by the foretold revving in reverse. A second attempt sent just as much smoke flying up from the tires but eventually shook the bench out from underneath the car entirely. The bench had been acting as somewhat of an anchor and as it sprung loose, Derlin and the sedan shot quickly backwards, running over a series of saplings before crashing into a support post on the Screaming Captain billboard.

"Oh shit man," Derlin yelled. "Oh hell fuckin' shit man!" He shifted the car into drive and floored it once again, coming loose of the billboard post and careening back out into the early evening darkness of the two-lane highway. As he rode away, the post crumbled and the entire billboard toppled to the ground in a majestic technicolor heap. "Captain," Derlin yelled out the window as he drove. "Oh, shit Captain I'm so goddamn sorry!"

In his panic, Derlin had gone three miles before he realized that he was heading in the wrong direction. He whipped the sedan around in an attempted 180, sending it into a sideways spin that eventually knocked out two mailboxes and landed him partly in a ditch by the side of the road. Pausing, Derlin took a deep breath and gathered himself for a moment, trying to regain his composure after the unexpected destruction of the billboard of his beloved seafood parlor. He did his best to put the accident out of his mind and focus on the major task that lay ahead of him. The Piggly Wiggly now lay seven miles away instead of four, but as Derlin gazed first at his quarter-full gas tank and then over at his rake buckled into the passenger seat, his confidence rose. Once again stomping on the gas pedal, he spun the tires until the sedan was free of the ditch and jolted haphazardly back onto the darkened highway toward Coverdale.

Derlin only passed a handful of cars on his way into and through town and most importantly no policemen. He wasn't sure if the torch-brandishing mob was still searching for them and by extension was also unsure if the police would be looking for his car. He did notice several "Wanted: Devil Baby Twins" broadsides still stapled to telephone poles and placed in storefront windows, just as they'd been two weeks prior, though he was happy that he still did not see any posters identifying he or Mavis as the offending parents. Either way, he'd donned his haphazard shirt sleeve mask as soon as he'd arrived inside the town limits just to be on the safe side.

He crept through the nearly empty downtown Coverdale at 15 miles per hour, doing his best not to attract any attention. It was only as he approached the Piggly Wiggly that he began to gain speed. As he rolled down the final few hundred yards of street and through the parking lot, he hit the gas pedal and got the old sedan up to nearly thirty. Veering through the parking lot, yelling at the top of his lungs, Derlin lightly clipped two parked cars before smashing through the double doors, sending glass flying through the store and grinding to a stop against the row of cash registers. He unbuckled his rake from the safety of the passenger seat and clambered out of the car.

"Alright now everybody get on the fuckin' ground right now," Derlin yelled. "I got me some shoppin' to do here at the Piggly Wiggly! Where y'all folks keep the Panther Cat at? I hope it's icy cold!"

The store was more crowded this time and Derlin could tell by the shared fear and bewilderment of the dozen or so customers that he had neglected to improve the shoddy mouth hole in his mask.

"I. Said. Get. Down. On the ground," Derlin hollered as slowly and plainly as he could, pointing the rake at the customers while using his free hand to point emphatically at the ground.

The message was received slowly as the customers and cashiers gingerly lowered themselves to the ground, eyeing Derlin peculiarly. Sure, half the town had heard of the evening Derlin had robbed the A&P. The cashiers all certainly knew of it. But the newspapers had dismissed the event as so strange and borderline psychopathic that they attributed the attack to a drug-addled hobo passing through town on a bender. Everyone from the newspapers to the police to the grocery store owners themselves basically assumed that the perpetrator was a few hundred miles down the rail by the time Derlin crashed through the storefront. They were as shocked as anyone to see this poorly-masked, rake-brandishing man in the flesh, having driven some rusted monolith of a sedan through the doors of their own Piggly Wiggly.

As it had worked so well the first time at the A&P, Derlin began to swing his rake wildly, hissing menacingly at his petrified onlookers. On purpose this time, he used the rake to knock the phone from the wall. This time it hit a startled old man in the foot as it skidded to a stop. Derlin nodded, pleased with his handiwork.

Derlin began to fill the first of his several carts and planned to take full advantage of having the entire sedan as his takeaway vehicle this time as opposed to the single buggy of goods he'd managed to wrestle from the A&P. He first filled up an entire cart of baby food, mostly from a display for a new "Salisbury steak" flavor, dumping it into the backseat. Next, naturally, was an entire cart of Panther Cat, which he loaded carefully into the trunk. He proceeded to stuff every square inch of the sedan with potted meats, bread, cigarettes and canned goods while the shoppers and cashiers watched in bewildered silence. Finally, with a large ham under his arm, Derlin tossed his rake atop the pile of groceries in the back, gave a pleasant salute to the crowd and climbed back into the sedan. Slamming the gears into reverse, just as his father Clovis had taught him so well, he quickly cleared the debris of the damaged storefront while the onlookers watched in a mix of horror and confusion from the floor of the store. Waving goodbye once more and honking as he swung the car around, he was soon speeding back toward the windmill with enough supplies to last the family for months.

Chapter 8

Derlin sped through the Coverdale night with his headlights off at around 50 miles per hour, relying solely on the glare from street lamps and business signs until he'd reached the outskirts of town. Doing so meant that he ran up onto a curb or two and "possibly" drove through a bus stop rain shelter, but in his mind he was going to be more difficult to hypothetically track in the darkness by the local police force despite all of the racket he was making without his lights on.

Derlin had often thought of the old sedan as indestructible over the years, and after making it nearly undamaged through a billboard post, a few mailboxes, the bus shelter and the storefront of one Piggly Wiggly, Derlin was certainly testing the boundaries of this theory. During the later part of the escape, the sedan did lose a hubcap, clattering off into a rain gutter during one of Derlin's wild, curb-hopping turns. He was briefly worried that the hubcap could act as evidence were he apprehended, before recalling that it was the final hubcap to go in a vehicular life filled with such wild, curb-hopping turns and that it almost certainly couldn't be traced back to him, as a result.

Getting the car itself to the windmill was going to be a little more difficult than simply wheeling a grocery cart through the woods along old deer paths, but Derlin was certain that he knew a way to make it happen. When he had frequented the windmill as a child, passing his days idly with his Uncle Vern and long-lost cousin Gooch, they would often stomp down the same woodland path that Derlin used to first lead his family there on the fateful night running from the hospital. Occasionally, however, they would cross the clearing, pass through a few feet of brush and reach the edge of a large cornfield which allegedly belonged to the mayor's brother. From there they'd weave their way through the rows of corn until they'd reach a dirt road, which came out directly behind Lumpy's Feed & Seed, the very same gas station where Derlin & Mavis would conceive Randy and Ollie years later.

Derlin thought nostalgically about Lumpy's for a moment as he drove, both as the site of these fond childhood memories and of first depantsing his beloved Mavis. He had been too distracted to notice if the old road was still there the evening he was courting Mavis, though he was disappointed in himself for not at least taking a look when he was hunting the parking lot for sticks.

Derlin had no doubt that the old sedan, despite its hallowed sturdiness, would simply not be able to handle careening through the forest, busted shocks and all, with several hundred pounds of beer and groceries in tow. Not many would. He'd end up with it wedged between two trees and certainly wasn't keen to carry his bounty to the windmill one armload at a time. He was going to have to take a chance that at least some ruddy remnants of the old dirt road remained accessible because, as the night crept closer to daylight, he was losing the only cover he had for his incredibly suspicious vehicle and its quarter-ton of stolen cargo.

Barreling down the road toward Lumpy's, the parking lot came up on him so quickly as he crested the hill that he nearly drove right past it. He slammed on the brakes, swerving into the loose gravel lot and skidding to a stop some thirty feet later. As Derlin sat there for a moment, blinking firmly in an attempt to regain his bearings, he saw a glorious sight in his driver's side mirror. There, with only a disheveled rope and a badly misspelled "Privat Proppety" sign blocking his access, was the old dirt road. Weeds had grown up a bit around the entrance, obscuring it from view, but it remained there just the same. Derlin was ecstatic.

Not wanting to waste the time necessary for removing the sign or loosening the rope to pass through cleanly, Derlin simply mashed his foot to the gas as hard as possible as he had so many times before in his life. What was left of his tires spun in place, kicking up gravel wildly for a few seconds before gaining traction and sending him hurtling through the parking lot. The two dilapidated wooden posts holding the rope snapped instantly as Derlin flew by, the "Privat Proppety" sign sticking to his windshield as he passed. What was left of his windshield wipers did nothing to dislodge it, and 100 yards down the path, Derlin had given up on its removal and was already planning on placing it somewhere near the windmill as added security.

The old road itself had seen better days. It appeared as though it had been mostly untraveled by anything but wildlife since Derlin was a child. Grass sprouted randomly, large puddles formed and rocks jutted out of the dirt. The road itself, like Lumpy's, was out of the way enough that not a whole lot of people ever really noticed it anyway and Derlin speculated that few people other than himself, Lumpy, Uncle Vern, Clovis and maybe Grandpa Hoyt even remembered that it existed at all.

After speeding down the first stretch of the path to further distance himself from the town, Derlin slowed down to a crawl as the path become more dilapidated. Every so often a rock would hit the undercarriage of the sedan, sounding like an iceberg ripping through the hull of a ship, but it never really seemed to do any damage. Lurching forward, grinding against stumps and rocks and spinning his tires in the mud, nearly twenty minutes passed before Derlin saw a familiar landmark. Illuminated briefly by his headlights, Derlin yipped as he saw the large flat rock just off the path where, as eight and ten year olds Clovis and Vern had painted a very large, graphic and anatomically confused mosaic of several beavers "having sex" in a pile. Derlin smiled proudly as he passed it, awash in the late evening moonlight. He was nearly home.

If his memory served him correctly, Derlin knew that he couldn't be anymore than a mile or so from the windmill and very close to the old cornfield. As soon as the thought crossed his mind, cornrows began to appear on his right. In his childhood days of wandering with his uncle, he and Vern had always just walked randomly through the corn rows to the windmill, making their own way and never leaving the path at any specific point. As such, Derlin didn't particularly have aim when he suddenly gunned the engine and swerved off the road across and through the field, leaving a wake of destruction in the corn behind him. Ducking as the sharp, dry, season-old corn stalks whipped into his open window as he drove, Derlin's head and left arm took quite the beating as he fishtailed across the field, struggling to gain traction, wiping out hundreds of stalks in the process.

At the far end of the field, just as he'd remembered, lay the small row of brush that separated the cornfields from the meadow and the windmill. He veered the sedan in the proper direction as though he were steering an old wooden ship toward shore. Soon, he'd crashed through the row of brush and into the meadow, skidding slowly toward the windmill and coming to a stop by gently bumping against it.

The sun was just creeping above the treeline as Derlin emerged from the sedan.

He stretched mightily, surveying his surroundings in the early morning light.

Birds were just beginning to chirp and, more importantly, no sirens could be heard in the distance. He quietly popped the truck, un-wedging a can of Panther Cat from his massive stash. He cracked it and sipped it slowly.

"This is the life," he stated proudly to no one in particular. He paused for a moment to reflect on his surroundings, staring back at the field as the morning dew glistened on each side of his path of destruction. He sighed in satisfaction and quickly powered down the remainder of his beer, tossing the can into a pile of brush near the base of the windmill. He jogged to the front door, anxious to see his family and show off his fabulous haul of booze and sundries.

The bump of the sedan against the windmill, though not structurally damaging, had already jostled Randy and Ollie from their early morning slumber and their flattened yell-cries were the first sound to greet Derlin as he arrived inside.

"Mornin' boys!" he hollered, waving to them in their hay nest on the floor. "How you doin?" Randy and Ollie paused from their yell-crying long enough to stare up blankly at their father, slack-jawed and blinking.

"That's my boys!" Derlin shouted, shooting "finger guns" at them complete with his own devastatingly inaccurate bullet noises. Randy began to yell-cry once again while Ollie continued his magnificent blank stare unabated.

Mavis was waiting for him next to the fireplace, smiling.

"You're so good with the babies, Derlin," she said sweetly.

"I know I am," Derlin began proudly. "I sure do like 'em. They're both real nice."

"You sure are back late, they must have had a lot of rake work for you to do at the Piggly Wiggly," Mavis continued.

Derlin didn't reply, distracted by patting his sons on their heads.

"Did they give you a place to sleep at least?"

Derlin stared at her for a moment, slack-jawed and blinking not unlike his young sons bellowing flatly in the hay. He'd drawn a blank for a brief moment, completely forgetting his janitorial ruse. As he'd laid things out to Mavis after the A&P robbery, he had been acquiring these piles of groceries as payment for performing rake-related maintenance around local businesses. He certainly had no plans to tell her that he was robbing these places, let alone robbing them with the very same rake that he was supposedly using to ply his newfound trade as a "legitimate maintenance man." He'd been staring at her for a few seconds by this point and decided that he should probably say something.

"Yeah," he replied. "Yeah, they sure did, I guess. Plus I took longer cause I went and got the car and drove it up here through the cornfield."

"I did wonder why you were gone so long, honey." Mavis said. "I was getting worried about you."

He muttered something about a "leaf truck" overturning in the parking lot enabling him to get more rake work than expected and how the Piggly Wiggly folks were proud of him because there "wasn't a single leaf left in that whole goddamn parking lot" by the time he was done.

"That's wonderful news Derlin," Mavis exclaimed happily. "Maybe folks around town will start calling you 'The Rake Man!'"

"Yeah," Derlin agreed quietly, averting his eyes and quickly looking at the floor. "Yeah, I reckon they might."

Chapter 9

Due to what Derlin had personally attributed to the "practice" gained in his first rake-point grocery store robbery, the haul from the Piggly Wiggly was at least thrice as big as the haul from the A&P. He had taken the careful time necessary to ensure that not only did he get each and every one of his desired items from the store during his hold-up, but that in his parlance, he acquired a "goddamn shit ton" of each of them. When he burst dramatically into the meadow and skidded to a stop against the windmill, he had done so with 16 cases of Panther Cat in tow (minus a couple of "roadies"), enough baby food and "regular sized people food" for at least four months, five cartons of Lucky Strikes plus five cartons of Old Indians for when he was feeling nostalgic. He also made certain to point out that he'd acquired "enough lady soap to bubble up the whole damn stream."

He'd learned a lesson on refrigeration with his first attempt at feeding his family as it was only due to Mavis's resourcefulness that Derlin's massive pile of A&P meats hadn't gone to waste. As a result of his wife's quick thinking and to Derlin's utter delight, the windmill was now crammed with a few years worth of dried and salted meats. The experience had taught him not to waste valuable car space on something so "keen to spoil" and aside from a few irresistably succulent choices he hoped to throw in the salt pile, Derlin had certainly gone easier on the butcher's section on this particular trip. However, he remained a man of celebration and while browsing for things to throw in the salt, he'd grabbed four of the finest T-bone steaks he could find for grilling over the fireplace upon his return.

"One for each of us!" Derlin said excitedly as he handed them to Mavis while they were unloading the car that morning. "We're gonna be eatin' good tonight!" he continued, smiling and looking to Randy and Ollie for some sort of affirmation.

"Derlin, the babies can't have steak," Mavis started, carrying a load of lady soap to the corner next to Derlin's bucket.

"Well why the hell not, baby?" Derlin said. "It's a special occasion!"

"Honey, they're infants," she continued. "They don't have any teeth yet."

"Oh yeah," said Derlin, defeated. He shuffled his feet quietly and stared down at Randy and Ollie, laying in the hay at his feet. He looked at their perpetually bald, shining heads and the twin "bbb" birthmarks that had necessitated their shoddy and unorthodox windmill upbringing. Slowly, the wheels began to turn in his head.

"Does that mean I can have three steaks?" he asked.

"Sure Derlin," Mavis smiled. "You can have three steaks."

"Ow!" Derlin howled in celebration, pumping his fist and heading to a nearby pile of unsorted groceries to dig for the ketchup.

Three steaks, eight Panther Cats and half of a bottle of ketchup later, Derlin was asleep in the hay next to the fireplace, his beloved Mavis and the boys curled up at his side. He'd sleep long and hard that night, dreaming vividly of the future and of what life might be like once the babies had hair and everyone got to live in a house. The family home in this dream was basically the house from the television show "My Three Sons" and Derlin found himself smoking a pipe, wearing a Fred MacMurray-style sweater as he and the boys tossed a football around the kitchen while Mavis baked tray after tray of cookies.

He dreamed too of his beloved rake, brandishing it on horseback as he charged into some long-ago medieval battle. He was clad in armor and had long, flowing blond locks of hair and a crest with three lowercase b's emblazoned across his chest. He galloped across a misty field toward an unknown foe, scattering away from him as he shouted and waved his rake about. Later in the dream, riding through a muddy village square, gaggles of peasants marveled at Derlin's rake, bowing to him, kissing his hands and wishing him blessings. In this dream, the family still lived in a windmill, albeit a much larger one, and Derlin would spend most of the following morning wondering if any Spurlocks had ever been Lords or Knights in the "old country." They hadn't.

February 29, 1968

When Derlin awoke that day, he decided to do a little calculating. The initial bounty from the robbery of the A&P had given them enough supplies to get them through nearly a month in the windmill. The Piggly Wiggly haul would get them four to five more, if Derlin's "figurings" were correct. That would put the babies at six months old. He knew that, despite what he'd told Mavis about Spurlock men "tending to hair early," in a genetic quirk as far back as the family could trace, Spurlock men actually stayed totally bald until they were nearly three years old. Derlin imagined correctly that he'd have never gotten to convince Mavis to stay in the windmill to begin with if he'd started off with a three-year timetable, but now that he'd established his method for the acquisition of goods, he couldn't see her disagreeing too heartily anyway.

The potential for complication remained, however, as Derlin knew he'd have to sweep farther and farther away from Coverdale to keep finding fresh grocery stores to knock over whenever the cupboard needed refilling. It would be particularly difficult to just cycle back and forth between the A&P and the Piggly Wiggly time and time again and, coupled with his unconventional methods, this just seemed like a sure path to apprehension and incarceration. Derlin had spent very little of his life outside of Chubb County at this point, but was certain that he could locate enough other stores in the area to keep his family's lifestyle afloat. By his calculations, if he could just successfully rob six or seven more grocery stores, one every four months or so, then Randy and Ollie would finally be able to grow enough hair on their toddler heads to each cover up their unfortunate birthmarks. At this point, Derlin could move the family back to town without being tarred and feathered. They could move into a proper home somewhere with electricity and water, he could manage to get a regular job again and they could just raise the boys "like normals."

It all made perfect sense to him in his head, "where I do my thinkin,'" as he'd put it to Mavis. As he explained it all to her in detail, replacing any notion of "robbery" with rake-work and light sweeping, she balked slightly at the idea of spending an additional 32 months in the windmill. She begged him to try to come up with another better plan, but the only idea the ensuing six hours of thinking in the woods netted him was that "maybe the babies could wear hats" and that didn't strike either of them as a particularly feasible long term solution.

Warily, Mavis consented to Derlin's plan, realizing that at least for the time being, they didn't have any other viable options on the table. He'd hesitated at first to tell her of the broadside posters mentioning the hunt for "devil babies" he'd seen on his way through town, but once he did Mavis was quick to change her mind about leaving. She agreed to stay in the windmill at least until Derlin's periodic bounties dried up and they were forced to consider other options. She felt continually isolated in the windmill, only occasionally leaving to visit the creek, but she knew that her babies had been safe during their time there and that remained the top of her list in importance. She assumed that, despite her husband's seeming prowess in the art of raking, that there was almost certainly a "rake season" that at some point had to end, leaving Derlin with little to no work in the off-season once the leaves or grass had been properly maintained.

"Rake season ain't got no end," Derlin stated plainly, quashing the notion as soon as Mavis brought it up.

"See baby," he continued, "it ain't just leaves and shit that people need raked. Sometimes it'll be big tall grass. Sometimes it's mulch. Hell, this bad-boy can even handle raking gravel if I don't go at it too hard."

"I understand that, Derlin," she began. "But-"

"And dirt." He interjected.

"I know, honey," she continued, "But-"

"And mud, you know, if the dirt's wet," Derlin said.

"Right honey," she continued, a little more sternly. "But what I'm trying to ask-"

"Dirt don't just get wet in one season," Derlin said.

"Derlin!" Mavis shouted, raising her voice at her husband for the first time in their strange but happy young marriage.

"Yes, baby?" Derlin asked calmly, not seeming to notice that Mavis raised her voice at all.

"I just have one question," she began.

"Okay, shoot," he replied, leaning back on a wide plank of wood he'd laid on some hay to simulate a recliner. He placed his hands behind his head and spent a few seconds clearing his throat.

"Since you're so good at it, what if you started raking more often for more people and maybe getting paid money we could save for going to live in a house?"

"Well, baby," he began slowly, searching his head wildly for a plausible reason. "See, we gotta wait till the babies get hair before we can get a house is all. And that's gonna be a really long time. So, since we're gonna be living out here anyway, maybe I'll keep raking for groceries for now and maybe I'll start raking for money when they get a little older."

"Well, what if you started doing it for money some now and we just saved the money somewhere?" Mavis asked.

"Baby, we ain't got no bank we can go to. There's nowhere safe to hide it here but under the hay and even there the babies are probably gonna get their pees and poops on it," he concluded.

"But what if we hid it somewhere in the woods," Mavis asked. Like a hollow tree or something?"

"Just out in the woods where anybody can come grab at it?" Derlin snapped. "I ain't gonna do that. Been down that road before."

Derlin was referring to the fact that each of the past three generations of Spurlock males, being his father Clovis, Grandpa Hoyt and Great Grandpa Shakey had all at some point attempted to stash their life savings in honey jars in the woods (two in hollow trees, one atop a particularly tall rock) only to have them stolen within a week by enterprising local bears. None of the Spurlock men actually knew that bears and not "robbers and bandits" had absconded with their life savings, nor the role the honey played in attracting them. All Derlin knew was that he wasn't going to be the fourth Spurlock to fall victim to such turmoil and thus was never going to be keeping any of his hypothetical rake money in the woods.

Mavis seemed to accept this logic, as she'd learned quickly to just pick her battles in regard to Derlin's quirks and if he seemed to think that it was better to rake for cans of beans than money for the time being, so be it. It wasn't like she had any shopping to do. She turned to play with Randy and Ollie on the floor. As she did so, Derlin opened a Panther Cat and began to think. Mavis had indeed struck a chord. Sure, all the grocery stores had cash registers too, right there on the counter, but that logical next step had never crossed his mind. Mavis had caused a light-bulb to go off for him, however, and as the wheels slowly turned in Derlin's head, his mind began to drift from scouting grocery stores and he began to plan his first bank robbery.

March 5, 1968

Derlin crept out into the night and climbed into the sedan. He did his best not to wake Mavis and the babies but, as per usual with the hard life it had lived, the sedan required a bit of engine revving to get its juices flowing and Derlin had had far too many beers to be able to back it quietly through the hole he'd torn earlier in the small row of brush that separated the windmill's clearing from the cornfields.

Derlin had been thinking hard for the past four days about what Mavis had said about "maybe raking for money" and he'd had about fourteen Panther Cats over the course of the afternoon and evening. As he weaved slowly in and out of his earlier path through the corn stalks, inadvertently widening it as he went, he reviewed the outline of the plan he'd come up with earlier in the afternoon while he'd consumed his first three beers of the day.

Part one of the plan was something he already had well-started by this review and that was simply to get the car to the highway and head west from Coverdale. Thus heading in the proper direction, he was going to drive three towns over and across the state line into Chicken Wipe, Mississippi which at seventeen miles away would be the farthest he'd been from Coverdale to that point in his life.

He'd planned to arrive in town before dawn and lurk in the shadows of the First Regional Bank of Chicken Wipe, waiting for the first "manager type" or bank president to show up to open the doors for the morning. Derlin expected to be able to recognize him by the wearing of some kind of sash. At the point of their arrival, an ambush would ensue and Derlin would accost the poor man with the rake, forcing him to empty the contents of the bank into a large burlap sack which Derlin had scrawled a large dollar sign on with some black tar paint he'd found in the windmill. If all went according to plan, Derlin would be well on his way back to Coverdale before any police or bank employees arrived. He could make it smoothly back across the state line into Alabama and he'd return to the windmill in time for lunch with a large sack of cash. He thought back to one of his pre-marriage dates with Mavis in which they saw "Bonnie & Clyde" at a local drive-in theater. At the time, he'd paused their vigorous making out during the "gun scenes" just to see the robberies and shoot-em-up's and was now quite glad that he had, as he planned to appropriate the knowledge gained there into his own heist if the bank manager planned on trying any "funny business."

Derlin arrived in Chicken Wipe in the predawn hours just as he had planned, stashing the sedan behind a large row of bushes on a street adjacent to the bank. He had his rake and his mask at the ready but he had a bit of time to kill before any bank management arrived and decided to fill the void with yet another Panther Cat from the back seat. One quickly turned into three, and upon cracking the fourth (and eighteenth of the journey) Derlin lost balance in his crouch and fell backwards into the bushes. Out of context, it would have been remarkably impressive that Derlin was able to remain in a still crouch for what were his fifteenth, sixteenth and seventeenth beers of the morning, but his subsequent toppling over and passing out in someone's shrubbery ended the showing with a marked failure on his part considering the importance of the task that lay ahead. In his later days, consulting his own personal history, he'd readily admit that he should have stuck with the family creed ("Stop at 15.") and that if he had, everything probably would have gone just fine.

"Never should'a passed out in those fuckin' bushes kids," he once told Randy's Kindergarten class.

It would be the warmth of the sun that finally woke him some time later and as Derlin lurched to his feet and grabbed his rake, he couldn't help but let out a "Shit!" loud enough for the entire neighborhood to hear.

He lumbered down the street in the direction of the bank in a slurred jog, frantically trying to put on his mask without losing grasp of the rake, swearing all the while. When he finally found the bank, it was clearly already open, with customers quite busily coming and going in the early morning business hours.

"Goddamnit!" he shouted, kicking at the pavement clumsily. A few of the customers eyed him strangely on their ways to and from the bank but no one paid him more than a moment's attention.

Derlin, still quite lit and reeking of alcohol, decided that he had come too far to abandon what he considered to still be a feasible plan. He'd crossed the state line into Mississippi for the first time in his life, by God, and wasn't going to let something as trifling as a major miscalculation of timing stand in his way. As he hyped himself up to continue the haphazard course of his plan, he adjusted the top and bottom of his mask and began stomping toward the bank with a blurry confidence.

Derlin elbowed his way in through the bank doors brusquely, bumping shoulders with a few customers who weren't quick enough to slide out of his way. He left a wake of jostled hats and purses behind him as he shuffled through the crowd. Doing his best, he was slowly able to stumble up to the nearest teller. As per what he considered a burgeoning personal trademark, he hissed menacingly and began to scratch the rake slowly down the glass separating him and the clearly perplexed teller.

"Sir, you need to wait in line," she said impatiently.

"Heh?" Derlin shouted, wobbling slightly as he leaned closer to the glass.

"Sir, you need to wait in line like everybody else," she continued, agitated. "Everybody else here has waited in line."

Derlin swung around wildly to cast his obstructed gaze in the direction of the dozen or so confused people waiting in various lines behind him. He waved his non-raking arm dismissively at them and turned back toward the teller.

"Hissssss…" he began again, once again lightly scratching the teller window with the tip of his rake. He hiccupped, but the hiccup soon turned to much, much more than that. Derlin's vomit came out with a force, but the woefully inept cutting of his mouth hole caused most of the vomit to stay trapped inside his mask, running slowly down his neck and onto his shirt. The teller screamed, jumping back from the window and grabbing the phone to call 911. Derlin fell woozily to the ground, cracking his head on a small metal trash can as he went. His rake clattered to the floor next to him and both lay motionless on the floor as a crowd of onlookers slowly began to inch forward and form a circle around him.

The next thing Derlin knew, he was being helped to his feet by two very large men. As his gaze steadied, Derlin noticed that these men were Mississippi police officers. It was a few blurry seconds later that he noticed the handcuffs. Derlin was under arrest.

He'd also pissed himself.

Chapter 10

Derlin tripped as he was being led to the police car, cracking his forehead once again on the lower door frame and hitting the ground with a groan and a thud.

"Oh shit," one of the officers snickered before he and his smirking partner piled Derlin into the back of the car.

The knock of the door frame marked the second concussion Derlin had received in the last half hour along with the bank trash can and he quickly passed out in the back seat, periodically belching. The next thing he knew, he awoke in a very small and brightly lit holding cell. His face, stubble and chest hair was still caked with vomit and his shirt and mask appeared to have been taken from him while he was being processed. He immediately recognized the inside of a jail cell, but his mind was still quite cloudy from the dual concussions and near-case of beer and he decided to remain quiet as he cleared his thoughts and surveyed his surroundings.

He could remember very little of the preceding several hours. He remembered stumbling into the bank and vaguely remembered being led to the police car before his second fall, but not much else between or beyond that. He knew he'd driven to Chicken Wipe with the intention of robbing the bank and that he was most definitely in jail now, he just wasn't sure where he was or how far along he'd gotten on his plan before he'd been arrested.

As Derlin sat silently in his cell, he thought of Mavis, alone with the babies in the windmill and expecting his return. He fully expected that he'd been arrested for attempted bank robbery and with his rake as hard evidence, he wondered how long that it would be before they traced him back to the grocery store hold-ups in Coverdale. As near as Derlin could figure, the dominoes were about to begin to fall. He was up shit creek without a paddle and he'd be going to jail for a long time. His mind raced, trying to think of what Mavis and the boys would do without him as their supplies dwindled. Derlin grew frantic the more he thought. He couldn't be a provider and a protector to his family while in handcuffs and he couldn't be their rake-wielding Robin Hood of the Alabama forest if he was sitting in jail.

After a few minutes of being alone with his panicked thoughts, a deputy sauntered by in front of Derlin's cell, not even glancing his way. He was quite fat and pale, and a shock of bright red hair was visible even beneath his policeman's cap.

"Hey man!" Derlin shouted hoarsely. "Where am I?"

"You're in jail, asshole." The deputy replied bluntly, giggling to himself as he finished.

"I know that, dipshit," Derlin countered, raising his voice at the officer's rudeness, "I meant what town."

"Chicken Wipe," the deputy shouted, his sweaty face reddening. "Don't you know nothin'?

"What y'all got me in for?" Derlin asked. He tried to ask confidently, but was bracing for the worst. He winced as the deputy stepped toward his cell to reply.

"For being a big ol' puss!" the deputy laughed. He eyed Derlin keenly, awaiting any type of "resistance" on Derlin's part, happy to look for an excuse to rough him up a bit beyond his already battered state.

"Naw man, come on," Derlin pleaded. "I hit my head a bunch and I was drunk and I still kinda am and I just don't know. Just tell me, man, I didn't do nothing to you."

The deputy sighed, unimpressed, placing his doughy hands impatiently on his vast hips and shaking his head slowly.

"Please, man," Derlin continued, reaching deep for some Disney-style cartoon innocence in his voice. "I'd tell you what you did if I arrested you when you were drunk."

"Fine, if it'll shut you up," the deputy began. "You went into the bank yesterday mornin' drunk as shit, cut in line and acted like an asshole. You hissed at the lady workin' teller and almost hit some old man with your goddamn rake before you puked all over yourself and passed out. We got you for drunk and disorderly."

"Is that all?" Derlin asked, elated.

"Is that all?" the deputy snapped. "Yeah, that's all! Ain't it enough? You scared old Miss Wilkins at the bank so bad she had to go home early and the bank still smells like your stank-ass beer vomit. What were you drinkin', Panther Cat?"

"Yeah," Derlin said proudly. A huge weight had been lifted from his shoulders and as such, his confidence with the deputy rose sharply.

"That shit's nasty," the deputy replied, raising his voice to a nasally whine as he continued his walk down the hall. "We're gonna keep you in here the rest of the weekend and then you can take your grimy ass back to Coverdale and stay there. You want your phone call or what?"

Derlin thought deeply for a second, feeling a brief moment of shame for not knowing the phone number to the windmill before remembering that it lacked both phone lines and power.

"No," Derlin replied. "No, I don't reckon that I need one. It would be nice to have a shower though."

"I'll bring in the hose," the deputy called back from down the hall.

"That's fine," Derlin hollered. A free bath was a free bath.

After being sprayed down, Derlin spent most of his next day and a half of incarceration taking the opportunity to sleep on a bed. After being denied a request for a magazine, he spent most of his time in his imagination, reviewing old pickup ads and "tittie pictures" from magazines he'd read in the past. He knew that at some point he'd have to come up with a story to tell Mavis, but after over a month in the windmill, his small jail cell seemed like a penthouse and he was going to "live it up" on his mattress until the law sent him on his way the following afternoon. He could think of a story and decide what to tell her on his way home.

The next morning, Derlin was led from his cell to be processed and dismissed from the jail. After his paperwork went through, he was led to the room near the exit where prisoner belongings were held and was thankfully reunited with his rake. Much to his chagrin, he was also reunited with his vomit stained T-shirt and mask, which apparently had not been discarded as he thought and was simply being left in a damp pile to await his later collection. Derlin winced as he took the sopping mass. It weighed at least a pound and a half and dripped onto the floor.

"What about my goddamn car?" Derlin shouted, looking down into his empty box again to double check for keys.

"You didn't have a car, asshole." The clerk replied plainly.

"Fine!" Derlin shouted, sauntering off toward the exit. He smiled as he walked, for that was exactly what he wanted to hear, aside from being called an asshole.

His chariot awaited, just where he'd left it.

Chapter 11

As Derlin exited the jailhouse and shuffled happily, if sorely, down the steps to the street, he began to strut. At least as much as anyone who'd just suffered two concussions and was more or less covered in bruises and scrapes could strut. He was proud, free and damn lucky to boot. Derlin had assumed, justifiably, that the police would have noticed that he was attempting to rob the bank in his drunken stupor instead of just harassing a cashier and being strange. Luckily for Derlin, Chicken Wipe wasn't near the top of the heap in of the world of criminal investigation and aside from absorbing some verbal abuse, Derlin was set free without a clue known about his plans of grander exploits.

He paused at the bottom of the stairs, gazing down at his vomit soaked rag of a t-shirt and mask. Wadding them slowly and determinedly into a ball, Derlin heaved them onto the roof of the police station where he heard them land with a satisfying "thwack." He wiped his hands in the grass before patting them dry on his jeans and continuing on his merry way.

The sunlight hurt his eyes and he struggled to walk in a straight line, but Derlin gradually made it through downtown Chicken Wipe to where he'd left his trusty old sedan a few days prior. He gained steam as he grew closer to the car, yearning to be home at the windmill with Mavis and the babies, breaking into a slow, limping jog. He even tried to attempt another "Dukes of Hazzard" style slide across the hood in celebration once he reached the car, as he had done the night he and Mavis had conceived. Assuming he'd be danger free with the hood ornament safely mangled in the back seat, Derlin lunged at the car, only to catch his bare back on the hood, sticking and rolling off into a crumpled heap under his bumper.

Derlin gasped for air as he lay on the pavement, which was already quite hot in the late morning sun. He used the grill of the sedan to pull himself back to his feet, using the hood and side mirror as support before ripping open the driver's side door and collapsing into his seat. Despite the sun beating down from the sky, the bushes Derlin had parked beside in an effort to conceal his car were actually keeping his interior rather cool and he soon passed out, partially reclined in the driver's seat.

It would be nearly nightfall once again before Derlin awoke to a vigorous tapping on his window. He awoke with a start, meeting the glare of a small old woman holding a poodle on a short, pink leash.

"What?" Derlin asked angrily, rubbing his eyes as they adjusted to the early evening light and sighing as he slowly rolled down his window.

"No bums!" the woman shouted, immediately setting down the poodle and walking it briskly down the street.

Derlin cranked the car and as it sputtered to life he leaned out the window.

"Hey, suck one you old bitty, I didn't do nothin' to you," he hollered as she continued her evening stroll. "I ain't no bum! I got a car!"

The woman stopped in her tracks, glaring angrily at Derlin. She snatched up the poodle again and began to march back toward the sedan.

"Oh shit," Derlin said to himself, snickering as he slammed the car into reverse and hit the gas. He slammed on the brakes and cut the wheel a few yards down the road, whipping the sedan around approximately 100 of his intended 180 degrees. Not having the time for a five point turn, Derlin simply curb-hopped the sedan and took out a row of metal trash cans as he peeled off back down the street.

It may have been three days later than he'd initially planned on, but he was finally heading home to his family.

As Derlin drove, he racked his brain trying to come up with an idea to tell his beloved Mavis about where he'd been and why he'd been missing for 72 hours. Obviously, he wasn't going to tell her that he'd gone to jail, even if it was only for "drunk & disorderly." She'd known Derlin was often both of those things when they'd begun courting, but under the circumstances as Derlin saw it she didn't necessarily need to know about some harmless weekend in a drunk tank three towns over in a whole different state if she didn't have to.

He knew that, no matter her thoughts on his limitless skill, she wouldn't believe he'd been at a raking job for four days. He was returning to the windmill with no food, no money and without a shirt. After nearly five and a half miles' driving worth of thought, Derlin finally decided on what he figured to be the most plausible, reasonable idea he'd come up with: that he'd been kidnapped. Between the various bruises sustained in his many accidental falls over the weekend and a general lack of hydration, Derlin certainly looked the part of a disheveled kidnapping victim.

Derlin drove slowly once he reached the outskirts of Coverdale, now in full darkness, to maximize the time he had to formulate the details of his supposed kidnapping. One by one, details in his mind seemed to be falling into place to make his story believable and Derlin greeted each new detail with a nod and an affirmative "uh-huh!" as he crept down the path past Lumpy's Feed & Seed with his headlights off. By the time he'd begun to weave through what was left of the ransacked cornfields, he was certain that Mavis would never doubt him for a second.

Derlin parked the sedan as quietly as he could, wincing as it ground to a stop, not wanting to compromise the dramatic entrance that he'd planned on making. He steadied himself as he walked up to the windmill door. He took a deep breath and burst through it, collapsing to the ground and panting.

Mavis screamed and rushed to his side in a shock.

"Oh my God, Derlin! Are you okay?" she asked, terrified.

"I got kidnapped," Derlin sputtered, gasping for air. "I escaped!"

"Oh my Jesus, Derlin!" Mavis continued, "Who kidnapped you?"

"The bad man!" Derlin shouted, "The bad man and his friend!"

Derlin wove quite the tale to avoid telling of his brief incarceration, one he would retell to the family on a whim for decades, never missing the tiniest detail of his brave and harrowing escape. As the story went, Derlin had been minding his own business, innocently raking the gravel in front of Lumpy's in exchange for some gasoline. This was a mistruth on multiple fronts as, not only had Derlin never done any "rake work" for Lumpy's, even during his brief employ there, but he'd been stealing gas from an unlocked pump there since before he and Mavis had ever even met.

Anyhow, supposedly as Derlin had put the finishing touches on yet another fine session of raking, a van pulled up with the word "BEER" scrawled on the side. A large man in a trench coat and a black hat rolled down the window slowly, leaning out and commenting on how Derlin looked mighty thirsty because of all the rake work that he'd been doing. Derlin obliged that he was indeed thirsty, as he'd been in the sun for "hours and hours," but that doing that much rake work really wasn't that big a deal to him as he did larger raking jobs "all the time."

The man in the trench coat offered Derlin a tall, cool Panther Cat, fresh from the refrigerated keg in the back of the van and Derlin excitedly accepted. However, upon opening the rear of the van and preparing to hop in, Derlin discovered that there wasn't any beer to be had and was soon overpowered and thrown into the back. He tried with all his might to fight back but the "big motherfucker" in the trench coat had caught him off guard and gotten the better of him. It was at this point, Derlin acknowledged, that he'd first struck his head.

He pointed to one of the many bruised lumps visible atop his head and turned to Randy and Ollie's blank faces, staring up at him wide-eyed from the hay.

"How 'bout that one boys?" he asked, smiling.

After a few seconds of silence, he continued his vivid tale.

Derlin had ridden in the back of the van for what seemed like hours before it finally came to a stop. He heard the "big motherfucker" start talking to some other guy about how they were going to have to be careful extracting Derlin from the back of the van on account of how he was really strong. It was here that Derlin overheard names exchanged, learning that the "big motherfucker" was named Friday and his partner was named Gannon.

Mavis narrowed her eyes at this and began to speak, but Derlin kept talking so quickly she was unable to interject.

After a few moments of tense waiting, the van doors swung open and the two men grabbed Derlin and wrestled him into a small nondescript building, down a short hallway and into some sort of dirt-floored holding cell, where they'd left him without food, water or additional contact for two full days.

"What do y'all want with me?" Derlin asked from the ground of his cell once they'd finally approached some 48 hours later.

"You know exactly what we want, Spurlock," Friday shouted sternly. "Did you really think you could just keep getting away with it and we'd never catch on to what you were doing?"

Derlin shook his head violently.

"I don't know what you guys are talking about," he pleaded.

"We saw you had a pretty nice rake out there in front of Lumpy's," Gannon spoke up from a shadowed corner of the room."

"Yeah," Derlin said flatly, his eyebrows raising slightly.

"Looks like it could handle lots besides gravel," Gannon continued as he slowly lit a cigarette. He offered one to Derlin. They were Old Indians. He accepted.

"Yeah, I reckon it can," Derlin replied. Gannon leaned forward and lit Derlin's smoke. He took a giant puff and blew it directly into the man's face.

"Looks like it could handle mulch, big tall grass," Friday interjected. "Dirt, maybe even mud, you know"

"If the dirt is wet," Derlin interrupted, finishing Friday's sentence confidently and taking another puff of his Old Indian.

"If the dirt is wet," Friday continued, removing his black hat and locking eyes with Derlin.

Derlin laughed.

"Don't you know who we are?" Gannon shouted angrily, grabbing the bars of Derlin's holding cell and shaking them with force.

"No sir," Derlin began, "No I don't reckon that I do."

"Well, Spurlock," Gannon continued. "I've got some sour news for you. We're the Rake Mafia."

"The what?" Derlin asked incredulously.

"The Rake Mafia!" Friday shouted. "We control the raking in this town. You wanna rake in Coverdale, you've gotta go through us!"

Derlin laughed again.

"That don't make a whole lotta damn sense man," Derlin snickered.

"How's that?" Gannon asked.

"Because," Derlin began, confidence rising. "The last time I checked, this was the United States of America. And in the United States of America, and here in the great state of Alabama, if a man wants to rake he don't have to answer to no man but the man what's paying him to rake."

"That's quite a dangerous attitude to have," the Friday said menacingly, opening the cell door and cracking his knuckles.

Derlin quickly surveyed his surroundings and did his best to do an inventory of his cell and the small, poorly lit outer room as a whole. He saw his raked propped against the corner of the room some thirty feet away, but aside from that, if he could get to it, it looked like it was just going to be Derlin and his bare hands.

Friday swung wildly with a haymaker from the right, which Derlin ducked before "karate kicking" the man in the kidney with the point of his cowboy boot, sending him tumbling to the floor in agony.

Gannon immediately jumped to action, grabbing Derlin's rake from the corner and twirling it with a skill reminiscent of a Hollywood Kung Fu master. Derlin landed the first punch in their combat, but was quickly knocked to the floor with a blow to the head from his own prized rake.

"And that's where I got this one boys!" Derlin pointed proudly to another purple lump on the side of his head near the temple which he assumed was his trash can wound. "What do 'y'all think about that?"

Randy let out a solitary yawn of a yell-cry and Ollie began to gnaw on a piece of hay he'd procured from the ground beneath him. Other than that, as per their usual, they exhibited no reaction to their father's anecdotes or inquiries. As Mavis would often remind him, they were babies, and Spurlock ones at that.

Returning to Derlin's harrowing adventure, at this point in the story,\ Derlin would have the presence of mind to sweep the legs out from under Gannon. He would retrieve his rake in a heated scuffle, badly scratching his opponent's face with a backhanded rake swing and leaving him in a crumpled pile, screaming on the floor clutching at the remains of his eyes. In his subsequent many years of retelling the tale at family gatherings Derlin would over time waste nearly sixty dollars in ketchup while providing this scene's special effects.

He'd run through the doorway on the far side of the room and into some sort of warehouse/compound, where he'd snuck through the shadows in secrecy, occasionally felling a security guard via rake scratch or rake-strangulation. The compound had fences topped with barbed-wire remarkably similar to those surrounding the Chicken Wipe, Mississippi jail and Derlin had to scout the perimeter for several minutes until he reached a low point in the fence. At this point, he scaled the small compound building which had housed him via a conveniently placed dumpster, after which he was able to leap over the lower fence from a very windy point on a roof corner. Once he'd tumbled to safety in the brush below the fence he'd continued with rake in hand through the woods until he'd reached Lumpy's, where he'd hopped in the sedan and hauled ass back to the windmill as quickly as he could.

Mavis and the babies each stared at him with a similar confused, blank look. "And that's what really happened," Derlin concluded, limping over to the corner of the windmill and grabbing a warm can of Panther Cat.

"I gotta get hydrated!" he proclaimed, draining the can of half of its contents during his initial swig.

"Aren't you worried about that Rake Mafia coming after us here?" Mavis finally asked, her face tense with fear.

"Naw, baby." Derlin said confidently, "I'm pretty sure it was just the two of them, and they got roughed up pretty damn good, on account of I'm real strong and tough and I don't think we'll have to worry about them bothering us no more."

"Okay Derlin, if you say so," Mavis sighed.

"Your man done won him a rake war, baby," Derlin shouted proudly. "That ain't something to sneeze at."

He eased himself down into the hay, picking up a copy of "Plumpers" magazine from his stash and soon falling asleep.

Chapter 12

March 10, 1968

The next few days around the windmill were quiet, as Derlin nursed his various "kidnapping wounds" and Mavis tended to the babies. Mavis had grown increasingly apprehensive since Derlin's vivid descriptions of the apparent rake war he'd become entangled in, and she reacted to each creak of the windmill as though the dreaded rake mafia was about to bust down the door. Derlin noticed this behavior, but dismissively assumed it would pass. In his haze of Panther Cats, he sat blissfully unaware of how life in the windmill was beginning to change Mavis, well beyond her growing fear that her beloved husband was in trouble with the mob.

She loved Derlin and didn't particularly plan on stopping, but living in seclusion in a damp, drafty 18th century windmill, minding the babies alone while her unemployed husband drunkenly roamed the forest wasn't exactly the life that she'd signed up for. She didn't expect mansions and jet-setting, but necessities like electricity, heat and running water were things that she had more or less assumed would be part of the package of married life. Sure, she and Derlin had gotten married awfully quick, but she still didn't regret the move. She'd loved him from the start and even if her own father hadn't insisted upon a shotgun wedding, she'd have felt compelled to adhere to the Spurlock family's longstanding "no bastards" rule, happily agreeing to marry Derlin on her own when she'd found out that he had indeed knocked her up.

Mavis didn't have any big city aspirations. She didn't particularly feel the need to learn a trade or start a career. She was perfectly content with being a homemaker and a stay at home mother, as motherhood and a family of her own was all she'd ever wanted growing up. She'd just always thought, when dreaming of her future Prince Charming, that some sort of actual house would be involved and she was becoming increasingly unsure of her want or her ability to stay living crammed into the windmill for the duration of the time it would take Randy and Ollie to grow a full head of hair. She missed her yellow legal pads to aid in the passage of time if nothing else, and thought of asking Derlin to get her some the next time he did a raking job. They'd certainly provide a necessary distraction on long days alone in the windmill.

Derlin stretched mightily from his hay pile next to the fireplace, rolling over onto his stomach and reaching for a can of Panther Cat that lay just beyond his grasp. He inched himself forward on his stomach, grunting softly, reaching again and knocking the can over, sending it rolling a few feet further away.

This got Mavis' attention and she eyed Derlin warily. He smiled, pointed to the most prominent lump on his head and shrugged before continuing his stomach crawl across the floor until he reached the beer. Sitting up, he cracked it with satisfaction and offered a "cheers" salute at Mavis as foam spilled all over his bare stomach and the windmill floor. Derlin took a warm, foamy sip and sighed happily.

"Derlin, I think maybe you should quit raking," Mavis said.

She caught Derlin off guard with the statement and it took a few moments for him to stammer a response.

"Wh-what are you talking about baby?" he asked, furrowing his brow and killing the last swallow of his Panther Cat.

"I think it's gotten too dangerous," Mavis continued. "With the rake mafia and them kidnapping you. They could have killed you Derlin! What would me and the boys have done then? These boys need their daddy! I need you too! You just can't be getting into wars with the mob over who gets to rake the gravel in some parking lot, Derlin. You just can't. It's not worth the risk!"

For the first time, Derlin felt a little bad about the story he'd concocted. He was seeing first hand what it was doing to Mavis and, while she'd have probably been angry at him for a while if he'd told her about spending the weekend in the Chicken Wipe drunk tank and vomiting all over his good shirt, that anger would have passed and almost certainly wouldn't be causing her the psychological trauma that his wild tale of karate and dehydration so obviously had.

He briefly thought about coming clean but ultimately decided against it. Aside from Mavis' breakdown, he'd really enjoyed the "man of action" persona that he felt the story was helping cultivate in his family. He wanted more than anything to be a hero to Randy and Ollie and despite their basic developmental inability to follow the details of his fanciful tale of escape, he felt that the story had helped cement his status of conquering hero in their eyes. After all, they had a father who'd won a rake war single handed and not a lot of boys could say that.

It was in continuing to cultivate such an image that Derlin decided against telling Mavis the truth of his incarceration. She'd be worried about the rake mafia for a little while, sure, but he was certain that soon everything would be back to normal with her and he could focus on better, more streamlined plotting in regards to robbing the bank.

"Baby, everything is gonna be fine," he assured. "There ain't gonna be no rake mafia coming for us and we ain't got nothin' to worry about with me rakin' except how much rakin' I'm gonna do."

He'd go on to tell her how no "black hatted mafia goon" was going to stop him from raking every parking lot in the entire town if he wanted to. He was quite proud of how the words were spilling out of his mouth but Mavis didn't seem to share his enthusiasm.

"Derlin, if you up and disappear I'm gonna have to go back to momma and daddy's. I can't keep the boys in a windmill forever if you go off getting yourself beat up or killed because you're messing with the mafia."

"I ain't gonna get killed!" Derlin hollered. "Besides, you can't take the boys to your momma and daddy's because they live too close to town and folks'll see the boys birthmarks and shit'll just hit the fan all over again!"

Mavis knew deep down that Derlin was correct. If they ended up back in town before the babies had proper hair coverage, the townsfolk would inevitably see their birthmarks once again, those cursed three lower case "b's." In all likelihood, she imagined, they'd resume their frenzy as a pitchfork-wielding, torch-brandishing mob without missing much of a beat.

"Just be careful is all," she replied quietly. "I love you, Derlin."

"I love you too, baby!" Derlin said. "Besides, I won't even have to do much raking for a while. We've got this windmill full of stuff to eat and drink for us and the babies. All the heat'll have cooled off by the time I gotta go back to work."

"I guess you're right, Derlin," Mavis said, resigned for the time to her fate as the wife of a rake man.

"Yeah, baby, you know I am," Derlin continued. "I'd tell you I'll try not to be a hero but you know I'm gonna. It's the Spurlock way." He sniffed mightily to clear his nostrils, grabbed his rake and began to twirl it the way the "karate man" had during his disappearance. Randy and Ollie stared from their hay-bed on the floor, for the first time entranced by their father's vigorous movements and finely-honed combat skills. This loud, strange man seemed to be a hero.

Chapter 13

It was barely a week before sedentary life in the windmill began to get under Derlin's skin. He'd begun to tire of his "woods patrol" and had begun using the time allotted to them to secretly drink behind the base of the windmill. He could hear Mavis and the boys inside going about their days, but couldn't bring himself to just lay around inside the windmill with them.

He'd begun to get claustrophobic in the windmill, side-eyeing the mound of baby food jars he'd acquired and the amount of space they took up. Though Mavis told him clearly on multiple occasions that the boys were too young to start eating food from the jars, Derlin reckoned that they "had to be getting sick of just milk, breakfast, lunch & dinner" and vowed to expand the boys' dietary horizons whenever Mavis slept. Beginning simply enough by dipping his fingers into a jar of sweet potato baby food and rubbing them onto his sons' gums, Derlin was soon secretly weaning his children onto a variety of flavors. He'd attempted early on to give the boys a healthy balance of vegetable flavors while he fed them, but after a few days he only had the 60-something cans of Salisbury steak remaining.

Randy and Ollie had each taken to the vegetables fairly well, developing a balanced diet, but once Derlin began offering the babies the Salisbury steak flavor, they began refusing their mother's milk altogether. When Derlin noticed this as Mavis attempted to feed the boys one evening, he nonchalantly offered to try and see if the boys liked any of the baby food he'd gotten. He tossed Mavis a jar of Salisbury steak, which they gobbled up ferociously to Mavis' astonishment. Derlin giggled to himself. His boys were going to be eating steak after all.

This sense of accomplishment buoyed his mood, but he was beginning to see Mavis' side of things a little more clearly when it came to their living situation. He didn't want to spend another two and a half years living in a windmill anymore than Mavis did, and he really didn't want to keep having to find new grocery stores to rob every couple of months for those two and a half years. Derlin knew that his family deserved something better than the old windmill, as well as it had treated them in their times of need, but he also knew that it would most certainly take money to get it.

When Mavis had asked him to start raking for money instead of food, his mind had raced through a scenario where holding up the First Bank of Chicken Wipe was just as easy as stealing that first cart of meat and beer from the Piggly Wiggly and that simply was not the case. Aside from being blackout drunk, Derlin had gone into his prospective bank heist woefully unprepared. He'd learned from his mistakes, at least the ones which he remembered, and vowed to himself to do better on a second attempt as soon as he was fully healed and able.

In this second attempt, aside from being (relatively) sober, Derlin planned on a focused, more pointed scheme of attack. Instead of meandering up to a teller and hissing, Derlin would begin violently swinging his rake and screaming for money from the outset.

He would kick over the trash cans both to assert his dominance and to avoid any possible head trauma should his vomiting and collapsing incident somehow repeat. Confident in his ability to karate kick through a teller window, Derlin simply planned on grabbing a cash box and sprinting from the building as quickly as he could, where he would most likely spend a few hours hiding in some underbrush, or perhaps underneath an overturned above-ground pool.

Three very quiet days and nights passed as Derlin fine tuned the hypothetical chain of events for his latest attempted heist. He would emerge from his concentration long enough to eat meals, pound a few Panther Cats and maybe grab Mavis by the backside, but aside from that he remained totally invested in the construction of his plan. At the end of the third night, Derlin was confident that his plan was as concrete and effective as it was ever going to get. He waited until an hour before dawn and crept from the windmill to his sedan, driving it with the headlights off through the cornfields and toward the road to town.

March 21, 1968

The sun was beginning to creep over the horizon as Derlin rode slowly down the highway toward Chicken Wipe. He took a deep breath as he headed once more into town. He circled the bank a time or two, cruising the side streets and looking for a place to stash the sedan. He finally found what he thought was a perfect spot, at the end of a street facing away from the bank and towards home, but in his haste he neglected to pull far enough forward to clear a fire hydrant, which he left blocked by his back wheels and bumper. He hopped from the car deep in concentration, scanning his surroundings, taking off for the opposite side of the street and entirely missing the hydrant as he walked away.

In an unusual moment of clarity, Derlin arrived at the bank rake in hand, just as it was opening. He was one of the first few people in the door and immediately began swinging the rake with fury, yelling "karate noises" at the top of his lungs. He spun around in a circle as he swung, gradually working his way closer to the nearest teller booth. As he worked through his second 360, he detected movement out of the corner of his eye. By the time he realized what was happening, Derlin was being tackled to the ground by the very same pasty, red-headed deputy with whom he'd crossed paths during his last jail stay. His rake was thrown from his hands and he was pinned to the floor by the deputy's girth.

The deputy mashed Derlin's face into the ground and forced him into handcuffs as Derlin hollered in pain.

"Just what in the hell is wrong with you?" the deputy screamed in his high-pitched whine as he held Derlin down with a knee to the small of the back.

"I'm not drunk this time!" Derlin hollered, repeating the claim four more times as he attempted to slide out from under the deputy's weight.

"Son, you're under arrest!" the deputy shouted.

"Aw, shit…" Derlin began, wincing again in anticipation of an arrest for attempted bank robbery. "Man, I didn't mean to-"

"For attempted assault!" the deputy interjected. "You're damn lucky your stupid rake swings didn't hit anybody or you'd be looking at three to five."

Derlin breathed yet another a sigh of relief. His unconventional choice of weaponry had once again led to local police failing to detect that he was attempting to rob the bank in question, simply thinking he was high on some kind of drugs or just plain off his rocker.

"You're still going away though," the deputy continued, forcefully applying handcuffs and wrenching Derlin's arms as he tightened them. "Attempted assault, you're gonna be going down for six months, at least."

"Attempted assault?" Derlin hollered. "But I didn't even hit nobody!"
"That doesn't matter, you tried to," the deputy replied.

"I tried to, yeah, but I didn't," Derlin continued, clearly agitated.

"That's what attempted assault means," the deputy barked, growing increasingly exasperated with Derlin's lack of understanding of the law. "It means you tried to do it, but you failed."

"If you're gonna charge me for it at least let me get back up and get my rake and actually hit somebody!" Derlin pleaded.

"That would be assault!" the deputy boomed.

"Well, what's the damn difference?" Derlin hollered.

The deputy yelled in frustration, coming down with a vicious right fist to the back of Derlin's head, rendering him unconscious. For the second time in less than a week, Derlin was piled unceremoniously into the back of a police car. Though he would later remark to the family how proud he was to be sober during this particular arrest, he still managed to piss himself.

Chapter 14

Derlin knew he was in a pretty good bit of trouble by the time he'd awoken in the back of the police car a few minutes later. Even if it didn't make sense to him, the deputy seemed pretty serious about the whole "attempted assault" racket before he'd knocked him out. Derlin still didn't believe it was an actual crime that existed, assuming the deputy was out to get him from their first encounter a few weeks prior and that he'd be summarily released once the rest of the police force invariably confirmed that it was not a real crime. He lay silent in contemplation, face still mashed against the seat and door, for the duration of his ride to the police station.

As his mind fluttered back to consciousness, his thoughts quickly turned from his troubles to the ramifications his trouble would have on Mavis and the boys. He had no way of contacting her if he became stuck in jail for any duration and was worried that because of his previous tale of action-crime drama that she'd assume him to be captured or dead, leaving the windmill for her parents' home near town. He thought of Randy and Ollie and the inevitable turmoil if their birthmarks were again discovered.

"Sit up, Spurlock, we're here!" the deputy barked from the driver's seat. "Let's get your ass inside."

"I can't sit up, I need help," Derlin shouted into the door and seat cushion.

The deputy exited the car, opening the rear door quickly as Derlin tumbled out, shoulder and face first onto the ground with a dull thud.

"There you go, son!" the deputy shouted, grabbing Derlin by his arms and helping him to his feet. He patted Derlin on the back firmly before leading him up the stairs and into the police station.

Derlin had spent a good portion of his last few weeks groggy from some sort of blow to the head, but his experience in the matter wasn't helping him get any better at handling his concussions. The bright lights of the police station stung his eyes as he was led into yet another interrogation room. He tried to speak but the words came out disconnected and strange sounding, even for him. His jaw hurt badly from one of his many falls and he decided to try and communicate only in nods and head shakes, with the possibility of a periodic emphatic stomp if the occasion necessitated.

The deputy sat Derlin down roughly in a chair, bumping his hip against the corner of the interrogation table as he went, informing him that a detective would be in for a statement in a few minutes. Derlin nodded and laid his head as gently as he could on the table and closed his eyes.

Mavis had not yet begun to suspect Derlin missing, though she was always worried when he was away. Thinking of him as she cleaned up a small cluster of beer cans from Randy & Ollie's hay, she had no way of knowing the trouble Derlin found himself in. She looked down fondly at Randy and Ollie, smiling happily at them. She could see Derlin's face in both the boys and it made her proud. Their blank little faces and prominent jawlines always helped ease the pangs of Derlin's absence. He'd always spoken proudly about "Spurlock Men" or the "Spurlock Way" and, though she didn't understand half of what he meant, she was still happy and honored to have helped Derlin add two more Spurlock men to the family.

Being alone in the windmill did little to dissuade her fear for Derlin's well-being while he was away. He'd sworn that his kidnapping was nothing to worry about and that he'd sufficiently handled the "rake mafia," but a little part of Mavis now couldn't help but think that he wasn't ever coming back each time he left the windmill. She'd taken to spending at least an hour each day standing in the windmill doorway, staring off into the distance where Derlin's tire tracks disappeared over the rolling hills of the cornfield.

The door to the interrogation room slammed open and shut and Derlin sat up with a start. He'd managed a 15 minute nap while waiting for the detective and though the lights seemed a little less bright than before, the nap had left him in more of a fog than he'd been in beforehand.

"Alright, Spurlock," the detective began, turning his chair around at the table and sitting down backwards on it. "This should be pretty open and shut. We've got at least a dozen witnesses who saw you trying to hit those people with your rake and one of those witnesses is your arresting officer."

Derlin nodded slowly, hanging his head.

"So, let's get this over with," the detective continued, "We get you to sign a confession that says you was indeed trying to hit them. You get your mandatory six months, maybe a little less if you act right, and we all get on with our day. Save the taxpayers all the hemming and hawing of a trial. How does that sound?"

Derlin shrugged groggily, the weight of his crime being an "actual one" becoming ever-apparent.

Though his instinct told him to fight, Derlin knew when he'd been bested. Six months wasn't the longest time in the world and even he knew that it was probably best for the long term if he just cut his losses and got his jail time behind him as soon as possible. He sighed, then for the first time broke his silence.

"Alright then," Derlin sputtered quietly. "I reckon I'll sign."

"That's what I was hoping you'd say," the detective replied, tossing a pen and paper down onto the table and walking over to undo Derlin's handcuffs.

Derlin gingerly massaged his wrists for a moment before sighing again and picking up the pen.

"What do you want me to write?" Derlin asked.

"Your confession," the detective said.

Derlin stared blankly.

After a few seconds of tense silence, Derlin paused to scratch his face and scalp, soon returning to his stare.

"Just start it off saying who you are and then tell us exactly what you did down at the bank," the detective responded flatly. "That's all you have to do, son. It's not rocket science."

"I know it ain't science," Derlin snapped, shaking his head and huffing for a moment before finally putting pen to paper.

"I, Derlin Spurlock, do hear bye admit to trying to hit all them folks with a rake down at the bank. I didn't really hit nobody, but a bunch of people saw me try and y'all say that counts the same as if I really did hit them. So I guess I did it. I wasn't drunk this time though. That should count for less jail.

Muchly Sorry,
Derlin H. Spurlock"

Derlin slid the confession slowly across the table to the detective and sadly awaited his fate. The detective re-locked Derlin's handcuffs in front of him, cleared his throat and stood slowly.

"I appreciate your cooperation," the detective said, collecting the paper and getting up to leave.

"And I appreciate y'all putting me in fucking jail," Derlin responded sharply, clearing his sinuses loudly and staring angrily at the detective.

"Your old pal Deputy Higgins will be in to deal with you in a few minutes, Mr. Spurlock," the detective scoffed. "He'll get you loaded up in the van with all your criminal buddies and you'll be in your new home up at county lockup by tonight."

"They got good food up there at the county lockup?" Derlin asked hopefully.

"Yeah," the detective responded as Derlin's hopes briefly rose. "They do if you like eating bullshit."

Derlin hung his head once more, the visions of dancing burgers and shakes running through his mind slowly turning back into Mavis, Randy and Ollie. Derlin let a single tear fall onto the table, resigned to his fate and expecting the worst.

Chapter 15

March 23, 1968

Mavis knew that Derlin had disappeared time and time again since they'd been holed up in the windmill and that despite her fears, he generally turned up again no worse for wear. He always came back, weaving some fancifully-detailed tale about where he'd been. If the windmill had had a phone, she'd have likely called the Piggly Wiggly to check up on Derlin's story, but as no such line existed, she had little choice but to take him at his wildly-gesticulating word. She had no idea as to his true exploits, totally unaware of the darker side of Derlin's roving life as a "raking man of the people," treating each bizarre new "where I've been for the last couple days" anecdote as sort of her window into Derlin's day at the office.

There was no "how was your day, honey?" over the kitchen table and evening newspaper in the Spurlock household as things currently stood in their lifestyle, though Mavis still longed for that normalcy somewhere in the future once everything with the boys had finally settled down. Until then, she'd make do on Derlin's wandering, vivid descriptions of his grandest on-the-job exploits as he bloviated long-windedly on the intense territoriality of the raking industry. Cradling her sleeping children, she'd spend hours listening to Derlin rhapsodize about his chosen, however fictional life as a rugged janitorial mercenary from atop his hay-board perch by the fire.

Mavis was not particularly surprised to find that Derlin had still not returned when she woke up the morning that his incarceration began in earnest. She'd grown accustomed to his absence much the same way as the wife of a long-haul trucker would. Eventually, she had grown to expect that, like so many men in so many of the old country songs Derlin played on the car radio, his wandering absence was just part of the package. She sighed as she began to feed the boys breakfast. It was indeed less of a physical toll on her, but Mavis was displeased at Derlin's success in weaning the boys from her breast onto actual baby food while she slept. Alone in the windmill for most hours of the day, she'd cherished the bonding of her time nursing. Opening a can of baby food and setting it on the floor like she was feeding a cat didn't endear the same affection. However, as Derlin had neglected to acquire any cutlery in his gallivanting, Mavis was resigned to letting the boys paw at their jars until it was time to give them a dip in Derlin's creek water bucket. After setting up Randy and Ollie each with a jar of Salisbury steak, seemingly the only flavor Derlin had thought to stock up on in his quest to turn his boys into "meat men," Mavis found her accustomed space in the windmill doorway, staring out longingly past Derlin's tire tracks in the field. She always expected his old sedan to pop into her view over the hillside at any moment, and it made her smile just to picture Derlin skidding through the field with a trunk full of cigarettes, head out the window and a beer in his hand.

As it tended to happen, after a short time staring through the cornfields, Mavis' mind began to wander to darker places. Though Derlin had always come home thus far in their windmill residency, she couldn't help but wonder if this particular trip to town was the one that kept him away for good.

Since their early days in the windmill, Mavis often threatened Derlin with the possibility of her returning with the boys to her parents' home in town. Derlin had always dismissed it as an impossibility because of the birthmarks, but it was something Mavis had always kept on the back burner in case Derlin actually did disappear for good. With Derlin by her side, she would almost certainly stay and weather the storm of life in the windmill as long as it took for him to help them find a better situation or as long as it took for the boys to finally grow hair. But if Derlin did disappear, she knew she'd be out of her mind to stay there alone with the babies for any extended period of time and birthmarks be damned, her parents' home in town was going to be her very first stop once she'd emerged from the forest.

Derlin's van escort to his new home in Perkins County lockup arrived just as the sun was going down and the first thing the driver told them as they pulled to a stop was that they'd missed dinner.

"Goddamnit," Derlin whispered. Over the course of his whirlwind past few days, the last thing he'd eaten was a small jerky breakfast just before leaving the windmill for the bank and his stomach growled ferociously.

"Quiet back there!" the driver hollered.

"Sorry man," Derlin hollered back.

"I said be quiet!" The driver shouted angrily.

"And I said sorry," Derlin replied loudly before muttering "fuck" under his breath.

"That is enough son," the driver screamed, opening the bus door to a pair of guards and motioning in Derlin's direction.

They quickly grabbed Derlin by the backs of his arms and lifted him off the ground, carrying him off the bus as he kicked and caterwauled.

"All I want's a goddamn sandwich or somethin' man," Derlin yelled as he flailed back and forth between the guards.

Derlin continued to flail about like a large, out of water fish as the guards wrestled him out of the van and into the courtyard of the jail. His wild cartoonish kicks had already managed to catch both guards in the groin and finally, as they both struggled to catch their breath, they lowered Derlin to the ground. He calmed down a bit, content just to scowl, roll his shoulders around and periodically yell at the top of his lungs. The guards were just glad the kicking stopped.

"Jesus Christ, son," one of the guards shouted. "What in the hell's the matter with you? Would you cut all this shit out if I go and get you a damn sandwich?"

Derlin quit struggling for a moment and paused to think.

"Yeah," he said plainly.

"Alright then," the guard sighed in relief. "Just let us get you to your cell in one piece and I'll see what I can dig up."

"Two sandwiches," Derlin offered.

"No," the guard said flatly, once again tightening his grip on the back of Derlin's right arm.

"Alright, one's fine!" Derlin replied.

Derlin was quiet the rest of the walk to his cell, as he really wanted whatever type of sandwich the guard was going to locate for him. His mouth salivated at the thought of even a prison-quality meat sandwich and it was more than enough to keep him in line as he was led through the jail.

When they finally reached his cell, Derlin greeted his new home by reading the cell number aloud.

"Good ol' 658," he sighed.

"That says 65B, Spurlock," the guard snickered, pushing Derlin into his cell.

"Whatever man," Derlin countered. "It's the same damn thing. Back home, my two boys had these…" he trailed off slowly and his eyes began to water. The guard ignored him and Derlin quietly stuck his hands through the bars to be uncuffed. As they were, Derlin leaned his head against the bars and gazed blankly out into the hallway, the weight of his incarceration and his separation from Mavis and the boys finally bearing down on him.

Derlin sighed heavily and mournfully before hearing a deep voice clear its throat behind him. He turned, startled at what he saw, unsure as to how he hadn't noticed the gray-haired 400 pound black man in the orange prison jumper laying on the lower bunk of the 10x10 cell first thing during his unceremonious arrival.

"Woah!" Derlin shouted. "I ain't never seen one of y'all that big!"

"Whatchu mean "one of y'all," cracker?" the man bellowed, setting down an old issue of Parade magazine that he'd been thumbing through.

"I-I'm sorry man," Derlin stuttered. "I didn't mean nothin' by it. You just surprised me is all. I ain't ever seen a black as big as you is what I meant."

"I'm just messin' with you little man," the giant replied, laughing. "Gotta have a little fun with my new cellmate whenever I get one. I like actin' real mean and scaring the Jesus out of him. What's your name, cracker?"

"I'm Derlin," Derlin sputtered politely as he could, still unsure what to make of this seemingly-friendly mountain of a man he was expected to live with. He extended his hand toward the bed politely where the man was sprawled.

"Welcome to 65B, Derlin," the man replied, swinging a massive leg off of his bunk onto the floor and sitting up to shake Derlin's hand. "I go by the name of Oldsmobile Jenkins."

"Man, that's a pretty cool name," Derlin beamed sheepishly.

"I suppose it is," Oldsmobile replied, nodding. "Derlin ain't too bad itself." They were hitting it off fast.

"Yeah, it's alright," Derlin replied modestly. "I got it from my mama back when I was born."

"Yes, I'd imagine so," Oldsmobile replied, smiling. "That's where I got mine too!"

"Oh really?" Derlin said excitedly. "That's so cool. I can't wait till I get out of here and I'm like 'Hey Tina, I met your friend Oldsmobile when I was in lockup!' I can-"

"I meant I got my name from my mama, not yours," Oldsmobile said, laughing gently and shaking his head."

"Oh, right," Derlin said sheepishly.

"They let you read magazines and stuff in here?" he asked in an attempt to change the subject, pointing to a strewn pile of Parade, Billboard and Hollywood Confidential magazines at the foot of Olbsmobile's bunk.

"I've been here long enough the guards treat me pretty well," Olbsmobile smiled. "When my mama comes to visit, she brings me a couple magazines, and they don't say anything as long as she brings a plate of cookies with her too."

"Man, I was in weekend jail a while back and they wouldn't let me have nothin," Derlin lamented. "Although I reckon I was kind of a jackass to 'em."

"Well you catch more flies with honey than you do with vinegar," Olbsmobile said, distractedly thumbing at the issue of Parade he'd set down on his bunk.

"You one of those 'Hollywood' types I guess?" Derlin asked, pointing again at the pile of magazines.

"I guess you could say that," Oldsmobile shrugged. "I do plan on making something out of myself as an actor once my time here is up. It's always been a dream of mine to make it to Hollywood, but I haven't even made it across the Mississippi yet."

"Well you did real good at acting scary there a minute ago," Derlin offered politely. "If you're that good, I bet you could be the next... um..."

Oldsmobile waited patiently while Derlin scratched his neck sheepishly.

"What's the name of that colored fella on 'In the Heat of the Night? Sid Pointer?"

"Sidney Poitier," Oldsmobile said.

"Yeah, you could be just like him I bet!" Derlin said, nodding in affirmation. "Or that fella from the 'O-thello' movie they play sometimes when the Braves get rained out. The one what has the British accent."

"Well I sure do appreciate that, Derlin," Oldsmobile said, smiling. "I think you and I might get along just fine."

The two would talk long into the night that first evening, hitting it off so well that Derlin never noticed that the guard had failed to return with his promised sandwich. Derlin told Oldsmobile about Mavis and the boys, managing to leave out any of the drama of birthmarks, angry mobs or windmills and leaving him to assume they lived in some sort of normal home. He did manage to capture all the details of the various stops in his recent sprees of incarceration however, including the current one for attempted assault. Oldsmobile seemed to sympathize with Derlin's "but I didn't even hit nobody" defense and agreed entirely that since the officer was already charging him, he should have allowed Derlin to get back up and actually hit somebody with the rake before taking him to jail.

At first, Oldsmobile seemed reticent to spill the beans on the details of his own imprisonment, but as the evening went on, he began to open up a little more. With Derlin's prodding, Oldsmobile took a deep breath and began his tale.

As the story went, Oldsmobile had spent many years as a legitimate businessman before turning to a life of crime. He had started his career as an assistant garbage truck driver as a young man and over the years had managed to not only buy his own truck, but a dozen more alongside it. Soon, he had a growing and thriving garbage pickup business and was doing fairly well for himself. He'd even just gotten the contract to pick up all the trash in Chubb and Perkins Counties and felt like he was on top of the world the day all of his troubles began. That fateful day he was approached by a shady character in a dark suit, introducing himself as "Mr. Black." He wanted to know if Oldsmobile was interested in making a little more money on the side. "Real, walking around money," as Mr. Black put it.

Oldsmobile was skeptical, as his instincts correctly told him that this "Mr. Black" wasn't totally on the level, but when the man pulled out a stack of $5 bills two inches thick and told Oldsmobile he could make that in a week, every week, he couldn't resist the temptation.

"Man, that cat was dropping Lincoln's like he was John Wilkes Booth," he was fond of saying at this point whenever he told the story.

As he told it, Oldsmobile clearly wasn't proud of what happened next.

"I represent a group of wealthy... business associates in Hattiesburg, Mississippi," Mr. Black began. "Recently they've undertaken a new enterprise and they're looking for a man like you to help."

"What do you mean a man like me?" Oldsmobile asked.

"A man with resources," Mr. Black replied. "A man with a fleet of trucks at his disposal, and a fleet of trucks that don't even warrant a hint of suspicion by the law no matter where they're seen."

"The garbage trucks," Oldsmobile said.

"Yes, Mr. Jenkins, the garbage trucks," Mr. Black continued. "After a great deal of research we've determined that they're the ideal vehicle for this endeavor."

"You don't talk like someone from Mississippi," Oldsmobile said, narrowing his eyes slightly at Mr. Black.

"Oh, I'm not, believe me," Mr. Black continued. "Mississippi by way of Chicago, if you must know. My associates too. We're just trying to get our little business up and running down south first, to see if it's something we could bring back to the big city. You know what I mean, sort of market research on you fine southern folks."

"What am I gonna be putting in my trucks?" Oldsmobile asked sternly. "Am I gonna be carrying something illegal? I figured you were gonna have something shady up your sleeve, but I ain't gonna be no dope smuggler."

"Oh, it's nothing like that," Mr. Black assured. "No drugs. Nothing of the sort."

"Then what is it?" Oldsmobile demanded.

"Bootleg mayonnaise, my friend," Mr. Black exclaimed happily.

"Bootleg what?" Oldsmobile replied incredulously.

"Bootleg mayonnaise," Mr. Black continued. "You see, the businessmen that I represent in Hattiesburg have found a way to... circumvent a good deal of the cost involved in mayonnaise production. We've acquired ingredients that will make mayonnaise a nearly cost free item to produce and in addition, we've acquired a printing press capable of mimicking the labels of the top brands almost identically to ensure maximized sale prices and profits. We just need someone like you to help us get it over the state line into Alabama after our other point man gets it through Mississippi, without alerting the authorities."

"Uh-huh," Oldsmobile replied. He was skeptical of the entire enterprise but as far as he could tell, all of this seemed far less illegal than he originally feared.

"Is this a position that would interest you?" Mr. Black asked.

"It might be," Oldsmobile began, scratching his mighty chin. "But I don't want anything bad happening to folks either. I don't want that on my conscience. What exactly are you guys putting in this mayo that makes it so cheap to make? People aren't gonna get sick are they?"

"Oh, heavens no," said Mr. Black. "We've tested it on a range of orphanages and hospital cafeterias with minimal effects. Even if people did somehow get sick, the fallout would only affect the mayo company on the fake labels we printed. So, just as we planned, and we'd be off scot-free and still be able to keep our profits. The recipe we use took years to perfect. This is not an overnight venture, we have put our due time into this."

"That's great and all but what are you guys putting in it?" Oldsmobile asked , firmly. "I'm sure y'all got a good recipe or whatever, but If you want me in on this I need to know what I'm hauling."

"Simple, my boy," Mr. Black answered. "Instead of an olive or canola or even a vegetable oil for our blending process, we acquire used fryer oil from places all over Arkansas, Mississippi and Alabama, like The Screaming Captain for instance. And he, like most restaurant owners, is more than happy to let us have the oil for free as long as we haul it off for him."

"Is that all?" Oldsmobile asked.

"Not exactly," Mr. Black replied. "Traditional eggs are so expensive, you see. Nobody's making money on eggs but the farmer."

"Go on," Oldsmobile said, nodding slowly.

"We've found that it's far more efficient to scour the building tops for pigeon eggs," Mr. Black said plainly.

Oldsmobile laughed.

"I'm entirely serious," Mr.Black said curtly. "We have scores of men far lower on the ladder of our business organization who are more than happy to spend their time hunting out pigeon eggs atop businesses across more than 60 counties between Hattiesburg & here. All the way to Little Rock, even Tallahassee. They've gotten quite adept at finding the nests."

Oldsmobile stared at Mr. Black for a moment, his eyebrows arched.

"So, let me get this straight, one good time." Oldsmobile said.

"Sure," Mr. Black said.

"You guys take pigeon eggs off of rooftops and old dirty fryer grease from seafood and bbq restaurants and you make mayo out of it," Oldsmobile said slowly, counting points on his fingers as he went."

"That's correct," Mr. Black confirmed.

"Then you put it in jars, with fake labels you made of actual real mayo companies, and you sell it to the stores pretending to be those other companies." Oldsmobile continued.

"Right." Mr. Black nodded.

"And since you get your eggs off of buildings and get all that old oil for free, all the money you make is profit. And if it works like you plan down here, you're gonna try doing it up in the big city."

"That's the gist," Mr. Black replied. "You're really getting in on the ground floor, here. This could be nationwide by Christmas! All we need you to do is use your fleet of garbage trucks to get the stuff from our man at the warehouse in Hattiesburg and take it to our contact in Coverdale once every two weeks and you'll get one of those wads of Lincolns I showed you earlier."

"Where do I meet him once I'm back in Coverdale?" Oldsmobile asked. He wasn't thrilled about associating with gangsters, but it was hard to argue with the money offered for what seemed so mundane an operation.

"There's an old gas station on the outskirts of town," Mr. Black explained. "Lumpy's Feed & Seed. It has a big gravel lot and no one will bother you there as long as you go after dark. They close at 6pm."

At this point in the story, Derlin spoke up loudly after nearly an hour of slack-jawed, entranced silence.

"Hey I know where that is! I used to work there!" he shouted happily as though he'd seen his picture in the newspaper. "That's where my boys was conceived," he added, raising his eyebrows quickly a few times at Oldsmobile to add further validity to his claim of hanky-panky.

"It all seemed pretty good at first," Oldsmobile continued, not paying any attention to Derlin's interjection. "We went on for two or three months and I was making an extra couple grand a month, just bringin' that bootleg mayonnaise over the state line from Mississippi. I'd get to Coverdale and that cat would be waiting for me with his van behind Lumpy's and we'd unload it and load it all back up for him and I'd get that sweet, sweet stack of fives."

Derlin nodded, wide-eyed.

"But, it was all too good to be true," Oldsmobile said sadly, shaking his head. "It didn't take long for folks to start getting sick, even though them company people said nobody would. All the mayo companies started having recalls on their products, clearing out their shelves to find the problem, but we didn't know that, so we just kept on with our regular delivery and that started making the grocery folks pretty suspicious."

"Them grocery folk is a dirty bunch!" Derlin hollered.

"Yeah, some are," Oldsmobile continued. "Anyway, they got a detective to start following the van that my contact drove around and next thing you know, all 12 of my trucks got swarmed by Alabama State Troopers and the FBI one day as soon as we crossed the state line. On account of I owned all the trucks I got arrested for trafficking an illegal substance. They tried to send me up to the state pen for ten years but the judge decided since I was just driving fake mayonnaise and not heroin or cocaine or something I could do my time here in Chicken Wipe so my mamma could still come and visit me. That was seven years ago and I've been here ever since."

"Man!" Derlin shouted. "That is so cool!" Derlin briefly thought of telling Oldsmobile the harrowing tale of his false kidnapping at the hands of a different branch of organized crime but decided against it as he didn't want his new cellmate feeling as though Derlin was trying to one-up him. As cool as Oldsmobile's story was, Derlin rationalized, it didn't contain any karate, rake-scratching or dramatic escaping and it was solely to spare his new friend's supposed feelings of adequacy that Derlin kept his mouth shut. The fact that his story never actually happened didn't cross Derlin's mind as he decided against sharing, however, as he thought of the tale so often it had basically become a reality in his mind.

He leaned over his top bunk to ask Oldsmobile one more question, only to find him sound asleep. He smiled. Maybe jail was going to be alright.

Chapter 16

April 7, 1968

While the next few weeks flew along for Derlin as he eased into jail routine and life on a mattress, time dragged by slowly for Mavis and the boys. Mavis had begun to get worried after the third day, but after two weeks Derlin's absence in the windmill was becoming an oppressive force. Food wasn't an issue, as there was more than enough for Mavis and the babies to eat for several weeks more, but Mavis began to suspect more and more that Derlin was gone for good.

She felt entirely abandoned, but simply couldn't imagine Derlin just leaving. It was difficult for her to picture him doing something like hopping a train and riding the rails somewhere far away to start again. She knew that he loved her and the boys too much to ever consider doing such a thing and would never just give up and leave. The only explanation that she could provide herself was that he was hurt or in trouble somewhere. Thoughts raced through her head about the possibilities. Was he dead or alive? Was he in jail? Did he get mauled by a bear? Mavis had no one to answer these questions and, alone with just Randy and Ollie, no one to really even ask them to.

Late at night, she'd sit awake by candlelight as the boys slept, pondering their next move. She was torn constantly between leaving for her parents' house as soon as possible and waiting for Derlin till the food ran out.

Another week would pass before she finally made her decision.

It was a particularly cool and rainy night, the boys were cranky and the windmill roof had, for the first time, begun to drip. Mavis had Randy and Ollie warmly nestled in the hay, but they'd each been yell-crying for the duration of the rainstorm, at least an hour. For the first time, she dipped into Derlin's abandoned stash of Panther Cat and sipped slowly. She gazed around the windmill, a mess of hay and non-perishable groceries, making her decision then and there. With Derlin gone, the windmill was no longer the place Mavis would choose to raise her children. As soon as morning came and the rains stopped, she was taking the boys to town, birthmarks be damned. She'd call her mother from the payphone next to Lumpy's when she got there.

April 15, 1968

The first few weeks in jail were relatively uneventful for Derlin as he got used to the novelty of living inside and having three meals per day, however squalid. He'd spent the early days of his sentence bonding with Oldsmobile and doing his best to learn the lay of the land, but he was about to experience quite the rough patch as he learned that jail wasn't some parade of sunshine and daisies. His troubles began in earnest one day in the cafeteria. Sitting down to enjoy his mashed potatoes, Derlin encountered a pocket of unmixed flour during a particularly gravy-laden bite and he began to cough furiously. Frustrated, he expressed his dissatisfaction by flinging his half eaten bowl of potatoes across the room in disgust. The bowl didn't manage to hit anyone on the fly, fortunately, but it's contents splattered across the faces and into the eyes of several members of the general population as it clattered to the floor. Derlin was quickly outed as the thrower of the potatoes and, though he knew he was in trouble, he failed to grasp the magnitude of his error and didn't deny that he'd done it.

"My bad, y'all!" he hollered across the cafeteria. He waved, but his wave was only met with a series of icy glares from a half dozen gravy stained faces.

In what would become somewhat of a habit over the months of Derlin's incarceration, the guards present had seen everything as it happened and opted simply to let Derlin get what he had coming to him. The six fellow inmates whom Derlin had flung his potatoes upon locked eyes and rose to their feet in unison, each grabbing their empty trays and moving quickly toward Derlin. At first, he just assumed that they were being unusually punctual in bussing their lunches, but quickly learned that this was not the case.

The first inmate to swing his tray at Derlin connected across the shoulder blades, sending Derlin face down into the remains of his lunch. The other inmates began to work the head, arms and back while Derlin hollered for intervention from the smirking guards who stood motionless by the doorway. The group had managed to get in a good twenty-five shots with their trays before Oldsmobile was finally able to intervene. He'd seen what was happening from the beginning, but with his age and girth it took him the full length of the attack to maneuver out of his chair and make his way across the cafeteria to Derlin. Long known as a peacemaker in the jail, Oldsmobile quickly restored order, elbowing his way into the melee and convincing the group to disperse before he "brought the thunder."

"Alright y'all, get on out of here," Oldsmobile growled. "Y'all did what you came here to do, now get!"

Derlin, now covered in a mixture of blood and creamed corn, had gotten his comeuppance and they'd gotten their vengeance. By jail code, they were indeed square, but Derlin had certainly come out on the short end of the stick. He was covered in welts and bruises from the trays across his arms and back and the three good shots that he took to the back and side of his head added another to Derlin's growing collection of concussions. He was able to stand and walk under his own power but Oldsmobile had to help him back to the cell when it was time to return.

Derlin would spend most of the next week laying in his cell recovering. The amount of groaning and clanging he did would be enough to spur rumors that the wing of the jail was haunted, both by the vengeful spirit of a former inmate (responsible for the groaning and the clanging) and the spirit of a young girl (responsible for the hours of soft, high-pitched weeping each night). Oldsmobile brought Derlin his meals and helped him mash them all into a fine paste to aid his ability to chew. Despondent, Derlin was a lonely mass of lumps and bruises. He was constantly worried about Mavis and his boys and still had over five months to go on his six month sentence. If his handful of interactions since his arrival had been any indication, he'd all but assured himself to have no chance at being granted an early release for good behavior.

The hallway wall clock across from Derlin's cell had been accidentally unplugged since before he'd arrived. Though it never moved, it was this clock that Derlin stared at each night as he sadly drifted off to sleep.

Part 3: The Return

Chapter 17

April 16, 1968

As soon as dawn broke through the trees of the meadow, Mavis began loading a makeshift travel bag for her and the boys. She grabbed the remaining six jars of baby food, a pound or so of jerky and enough water to get them through the woods to Lumpy's without any issue.

Mavis slung the bag over her shoulder and gathered Randy and Ollie in her arms. She'd been dreaming of the day that she'd finally get to leave the windmill for good, but saying goodbye to it was harder than she imagined it would be. She paused in the doorway looking back as she left and felt a solitary tear trickle down her face. She gazed upon the ramshackle living quarters for a final time; the haystack next to a bacon-grease-coated fire pit, the fort that Derlin had built the boys out of his empty beer cans and the small, seemingly inconspicuous corner where Derlin thought he was secretly hiding his stash of "Plumpers" magazines. Even looking upon these tattered remnants of his person made Mavis miss Derlin all the more and though she had no idea where he was, she was certain that one day she'd find him, far beyond the treeline of the meadow.

After she and the boys left it that morning, the windmill would again be abandoned and forgotten in its little corner of the Alabama forest. Over the years, it would become increasingly dilapidated. The leak that had sprung in the roof would grow bigger and bigger until it turned from a drip into a steady pour, finally caving in upon its own remains. By the time Randy and Ollie reached their 18th birthdays, only the fireplace, one wall, a pile of rubble and a few hundred rusted cans of Panther Cat remained where it had once proudly stood.

As Mavis carefully followed Derlin's old tire tracks through the cornfield, she realized that, with each progressive step, she and the boys had gone farther from the windmill than at any point since they'd arrived, aside from periodic trips to the creek bath deeper in the forest. It was quite a freeing thought to Mavis. Even though she'd never quite felt like a prisoner at the windmill, she hadn't once strayed more than a few hundred yards from its walls during the duration of her time there. In a grand irony it was her own husband becoming an actual prisoner outside the windmill that enabled her to escape it for good herself.

The drive from Lumpy's to the windmill never took Derlin more than a few minutes after he'd gotten used to the roads, jumping logs and splashing through puddles and generally swerving about like a crazy person. On foot and carrying two babies it took Mavis the majority of the morning to arrive there, stepping carefully through the muddy ruts he'd left in his wake.

By the time Mavis had Lumpy's in her sight, the morning sun had risen high into the sky and the day was beginning to get hot. Randy and Ollie had been troopers for the majority of the trip, but were getting tired of being awkwardly carried. The blazing sun beating down on their bald little heads wasn't helping either. Thankfully, the payphone was on the shade side of the building and Mavis sat down to rest for a moment, giving the boys water and letting them crawl in the cool grass. As the boys lay fidgeting in the grass,

Mavis gazed up at the payphone and realized that she did not have the required nickel to make the call to her mother. Her heart sank, but she began to look around the base of the phone, hoping for a stroke of luck and letting out an elated "yes!" when she saw a shiny nickel sitting nestled in a tuft of grass.

She quickly dialed her parents number, hoping that at least her mother would be home. After three rings, her mother answered.

"Clapp residence, Hello?"

"Mom, 'it's Mavis!" she said excitedly. "I need your help!"

"Mavis!" Eudora cried. "Where are you? Are you and the babies okay? I've been worried sick. Is Derlin with you?"

"I'm fine and so are the babies," Mavis replied, looking over her shoulder and doing her best to keep her voice a low whisper. "I don't know where Derlin is, he disappeared a couple of weeks ago. I think he's hurt somewhere."

"Oh, I'm sure he's somewhere," Eudora said flatly. "If he's not half way to Las Vegas by now I'm sure he's probably just in jail or something."

"Mom, stop!" Mavis said, her voice rising. "Derlin may not be perfect but he'd never just leave me like that. I think he's just gotta be in some kind of trouble. I don't know where he is, but right now me and the boys need your help!"

"Where are you?" Eudora asked. "I'll come get you right now."

"We're at Lumpy's Feed & Seed out by the highway," Mavis replied. "Nobody else knows we're here, just you."

"Do the boys have hair yet?" Eudora asked quietly.

"No," Mavis said.

"Okay," Eudora sighed deeply. "Well we'll take care of that as best we can when I get you. I'll be there as soon as I can."

Mavis hung up the phone as excited as she'd been since the entire ordeal with the babies had begun. They were about to get a fresh start, whether Derlin was going to be around to see it or not.

Mavis waited anxiously for the sight of her mother's white Buick as she watched Randy and Ollie laying in the grass. She looked down at the boys and gazed across the parking lot of Lumpy's, a smile slowly coming across her face. Little did the boys know that they were mere feet from the sight of their own conception. Mavis marveled at how much life had changed in the one short year since she and Derlin had first pulled into that parking lot together on the fateful evening after Uncle Vern's fish fry. She squinted at one of the pumps, looking at what appeared to be a peanut butter stain smeared across the Pure logo.

It was no more than ten minutes later that Eudora swerved into the parking lot and came rushing out of the car. She leapt from the car emitting a low, worried hum, running up to Mavis and checking her and the babies, mostly about the head and face, to ensure that they were indeed okay. After checking that everyone seemed up to snuff, she hurried them back to the Buick. She hustled Mavis and the boys into the back seat, checking over her shoulder constantly. The back seat had been padded with pillows and blankets and Mavis got the boys comfy as Eudora began opening a large cardboard box that was sitting in the front seat. After digging through what seemed like thousands of packing peanuts, she produced two small black men's wigs from the bottom of the box.

"For the boys!" she said excitedly. "No one will know it's not really their hair. Well, except for Derlin I suppose, wherever *he* may be."

"Mama, Derlin will find me and the boys again one day," Mavis replied strongly. "As long as he's alive he's gonna come back for us, I just know it!"

"I'm sure he will," Eudora replied flatly. "I'm sure he will."

They drove in silence for the next few minutes as Mavis fashioned the new wigs upon Randy and Ollie's heads. They looked a bit strange at first and appeared to be well over a decade old, but were clearly better than the alternative of a torch and pitchfork brandishing mob chasing them back into the forest. She'd get used to them in time just as the boys would and once they'd finally grown their own hair, they'd be able to discard them like their father discarded a soiled shirt. She was perfectly content for them to look like two tiny Roy Orbisons in the meantime.

Eudora knew the gist of the trouble with the townsfolk and the reason for her daughter and grandchildren's disappearances, but this was the first time she'd seen Mavis since before the babies had been born and she'd had no idea what had happened to them after they'd fled the hospital.

Mavis explained in detail what had happened and watched her mother's face twist in horror as she learned that her daughter and two infant grandchildren had spent the past nearly two months living in a drafty, Eighteenth century windmill in the forest. She scoffed at the notion that Derlin had provided all of their groceries as trade for raking, but stopped short of connecting him to the series of rake-point grocery store robberies since their disappearance, at least aloud. She wasn't the least bit surprised by Derlin's supposed abandonment, but she was glad he'd done it at least in the sense that it allowed her daughter and grandchildren to come to a more suitable home. Despite her remarks about Derlin and Las Vegas and her general disdain for him as a person, she doubted that she was lucky enough to be done with him forever and for Mavis' sake, she didn't want to burn his bridge entirely.

Mavis' father Clebert was waiting for them on the porch when they arrived home, excited to see his only daughter and finally meet his fugitive grandchildren.

"By gar, Eudora, you got 'em!" he shouted happily at his wife as she got out of the car. He rushed to help Mavis and the boys from the back seat, hugging Mavis tightly and kissing her on the cheek before turning his attention to Randy and Ollie.

"And you two must be my grand boys!" he shouted excitedly.

Randy and Ollie each let out a happy, pleasant yell cry and gawked upward at Clebert. He scooped them both up at the same time.

"That's my boys," he exclaimed as Ollie began gumming at one of his suspenders. "What'd you name 'em, sugar?"

"That's Randy in the wig with the sideburns and that's Ollie in the Davey Jones," Mavis said happily. "They like you."

"Well, I'm a pretty likeable guy," Clebert smiled. "Now let's get you all inside and get these boys some Charleston Chews!"

At the precise moment this reunion was occurring, Derlin plodded down the hallway from his cell on his way to his hour in the yard, just like the person in front of him in line and just like the person behind him. He'd spent most of his yardtime recently just sitting on a bench next to Oldsmobile, watching people play basketball or softball or lift weights. He hadn't participated in anything even remotely sporting in the yard since his beating, but had been hit on two separate occasions by foul balls from the softball game, once on the knee and once on the crown of the head.

Each day crept by slower and slower for Derlin. Oldsmobile was the only friend he seemed to have. Since the cafeteria incident, he'd find himself getting into meaningless tussles every day with other inmates without even trying to provoke them. A little over five months remained on his sentence and each day seemed more daunting than the last. He assumed that Mavis had taken the boys from the windmill by now and only hoped that he could remember the way to the Clapp's house once his time behind bars had finally expired.

Most of the conversations he'd have with Oldsmobile revolved less and less around past glories and adventures and more about how he was going to survive his remaining incarceration. Oldsmobile tried to be helpful, suggesting everything from whittling to the Bible, but Derlin could only manage half-hearted shrugs in reply. His bleak outlook on what was left of his jail time had begun to wear on the gregarious Oldsmobile, whose weekly visits from his mother and good standing with the prison guards had begun to wear on Derlin in turn.

The two of them still got along fine, each just seemed to keep a little more distance from the other than they used to, which is difficult to do when you're sharing bunk beds in a prison cell and one of you is 400 pounds. More and more, instead of talking into the night, Derlin would just lay awake staring at the ceiling as Oldsmobile thumbed through his theater magazines, periodically calling out to ask him if the article he was reading was any good or had Clint Eastwood in it.

Chapter 18

Clebert carried Ollie into the living room, holding him aloft the way he would a golfing trophy or a prize from a cake walk. Eudora was close behind him with Randy and Mavis in tow. They hadn't seen their daughter since before she'd gone into the hospital nearly three months prior and until that afternoon had never met their grandchildren, though they'd certainly read of them in the papers.

The night of the birth, the Clapps had gotten the same frantic knock on the door that most everyone else in town had gotten: the shouting nurse with the running mascara going on and on about "devil babies" and "some little blond what took up with a Spurlock" bringing the end times to Coverdale. Putting two and two together, the Clapps had made an effort to quiet the sensationalized Satanic stories about Randy and Ollie's birthmarks amongst their friends and neighbors. Regardless, the tales had spread like wildfire through the town and by the time that Dr. Leslie had stuck his head out the hospital window attempting to persuade everyone that the marks were actually harmless it was all too late to matter.

After the riot when Mavis and Derlin escaped the hospital, the search for them and their "Demon Twins" was a hot button news item in Coverdale. Little progress was made in the police "investigation" and after the search had proved fruitless for a couple of weeks, folks mostly lost interest in the matter. By then, news of a mysterious rake-wielding masked robber had replaced the babies as the sensational story dominating the local press. This coverage, alongside the occasional photo of a proud young detective with an ax in his hand dumping a keg of bootleg mayonnaise into a local river after a bust, was enough to keep Coverdale' simple townsfolk otherwise occupied beyond the continued hunt for Derlin's townie spawn. As such, Clebert and Eudora were happy to inform their daughter that although she and Derlin had been vigorously sought after at the outset of their escape, so much had happened in Coverdale since then that it didn't seem that folks remembered it or cared about it at all.

"Long as you keep 'em Beatles wigs on my grandboys they gonna be just fine," Clebert hollered from the couch, bouncing Randy gently from a knee.

"You can stay here as long as you like, dear," Eudora began. "It's certainly a hell of a lot better than a God-forsaken windmill."

"But what about Derlin?" Mavis asked. "I don't have any way to get in touch with him to tell him everything is okay. I'm worried he's hurt, or hiding out somewhere. I-"

"Honey I'd imagine Derlin will wander up to our doorstep at some point whenever he's done gallivanting around on his beer bender," Eudora replied sweetly.

"I know he'll be back," Mavis sighed. "I just know it."

"I know you do, dear," Eudora said. "Now let's get you and the boys settled and I'll fix us all lunch."

"I already fed the boys some Charleston Chews," Clebert shouted from the living room. "They liked 'em real good."

"That's nice, dad," Mavis hollered back, "Thank you!"

April 21, 1968

Derlin had never been what he considered to be an avid bather. He'd been perfectly content to dunk himself in a creek or Vern's pond if the mood struck him and certainly wasn't above degreasing himself in a "Tennessee car wash" scenario, but the scalding hot water of the jail shower had changed his tune during his stay there. Most of his fellow inmates were in and out of the shower as quickly as possible, but Derlin began to treat the event as his own five-minute spa time. Richly lathering head to toe, twirling under the faucet like Michael Caine in "Singing in the Rain." He found these short bursts of luxury a welcome reprieve from jail life and, though he'd get his share of dirty looks while he twirled, he kept his own eyes closed and was none the wiser to anyone's business. He was already a social pariah in the jail and it seemed that his fellow inmates were content to leave him alone in his strange showering ritual until this particular day, where an exceptionally at-peace Derlin had begun letting out a steady stream of urine as he twirled. This quickly caught the attention of the other eleven men in the shower and Derlin was soon shouted out of his zen moment. He was chased, still soapy, from the shower and spent the next several minutes getting towel-whipped by his showermates as he howled in protest. The guards, going against their instinct and preparing to intervene on Derlin's behalf, stepped back out of the way once they heard Derlin hollering "I didn't mean to pee on you! I didn't mean to pee on you!" and just let the situation tucker itself out naturally.

April 27, 1968

The first few days with Mavis home passed smoothly and happily in the Clapp home. Mavis was able to introduce Randy and Ollie to household amenities like warm running water, instead of just bathing them in the bucket that Derlin would periodically fill and drag from the creek. The boys took quickly to the idea of sleeping in beds with pillows and blankets as well and soon with her parents' help, Mavis felt like she was finally able to start spoiling them like she'd always wanted to. While in the windmill, Derlin had made an effort to create toys for the boys by doing things like tying twine through the tabs of a dozen empty Panther Cat cans to make them a "rattlesnake," and Mavis appreciated his trying. It was clear after his ill-fated beer can robot that toy-making wasn't a strong suit for Derlin and Mavis was excited at the opportunity to purchase her children actual toys.

Within a few days of her arrival, Mavis had made plans to begin looking for a job in town so she could begin saving money for a place of her own. As fate would have it, her first stop in search of employment was at the Piggly Wiggly, still recovering cosmetically from Derlin's rampage several weeks prior. Most of the storefront had been replaced, but there was still a tarped-over damaged portion of the floor from where Derlin had wiped out a cash register station and if Mavis had decided to look closely as she walked by in search of a manager, she could have seen a faint tire track from the back wheel of Derlin's trusty old sedan from the moment he'd begun to floor the gas pedal and peel out in reverse to exit the store.

She was able to quickly find a manager and he was immediately ecstatic when she told him she was looking for a job. In the wake of Derlin's robbery of both local grocery stores, many of the employees quit their jobs to seek greener pastures elsewhere, away from what they suddenly considered to be such dangerous work. Both stores had been significantly understaffed in the wake of Derlin's spree as a result. Mavis confessed that she lacked any basic experience and worried at first that this would doom her chances of success, but she was hired immediately and asked if she'd like to start on the spot. A few minutes later, after the acquisition of a name tag, an apron and a very flashy "TRAINEE" visor, Mavis was at a register and on the clock.

She knew that "grocery cashier" wasn't a glamorous position, but it was her first job and she was quite proud of the efficiency with which she'd obtained it. She had no knowledge of the subtly detailed unwitting path that Derlin had sent her down which eventually led to her employment there. Still quite confident that he'd come waltzing back sooner or later, wherever he may be, she was quite happy to be able to provide for the babies in the meantime since he didn't seem to share that interest at the moment, wherever he may be.

Chapter 19

April 29, 1968

Derlin was quietly eating breakfast one day, still nursing the dozens of towel welts that covered him like chicken pox, when he overheard a pair of inmates talking about their jobs as groundskeepers around the prison. He perked up and began to eavesdrop as inconspicuously as he could manage, inching down the otherwise empty bench toward them. The pair had apparently just spent the entire morning in the sunshine, raking mulch along several of the prison walkways. For a moment, Derlin silently mocked their inefficiency of taking an entire morning to do such a task, remembering his boasts to Mavis about raking fields upon fields of mulch and hay, taking no more than "an hour a field, tops" to do so. After a few fleeting seconds of mild joy, the light bulb went on as upon further recall, Derlin remembered that he had never actually done any of his supposed exploits as a "travelling gentleman raker."

The rake had been a trusted and valuable ally of his since the fateful morning when he found it discarded behind the windmill, even if he had rarely if ever wielded it in the traditional sense. He knew how the general operation should go, as it was somewhere on the spectrum between his finely honed skills of swinging it wildly while screaming or using it as a prop to lean upon. Learning to use it properly, he thought to himself, and somehow gaining a trusted position on the grounds crew would not only get him some much needed outside time where he could stretch his legs or possibly escape, it would also provide him with the necessary displayable skills should Mavis ever question his previous alibis upon his eventual return.

"Hey, y'all!" he whispered as loudly as he could manage without drawing the attention of the guards. "Pssssst!"

They ignored him.

"Hey guys!" he continued, undeterred. "Over here. Me, Derlin!"

Finally, one of them sighed and turned to face Derlin.

"Yeah?" he replied curtly. "What do you want?"

"I don't mean to interrupt or nothin' but how do I get one of those outside raking stuff jobs y'all was talking about?"

"There's a big sign on the bulletin board that you walk by on the way to the yard every damn day," he replied. "It says 'Prisoner Work Program' in letters the size of your head with all the signups under it."

"I don't read no signs," Derlin scoffed, accidentally shooting a small bit of snot down his nose and into his shoddily-grown prison mustache.

His chortle and subsequent snot rocket was enough to attract the attention of a nearby guard, who yelled at Derlin to quiet down as the other inmate quickly turned back to his lunch.

"I'm sorry sir," Derlin hollered across two tables, "I was just trying to talk to a fella about maybe getting a job beautifying this jail up for y'all. You seen any mulch what needs raking anywhere?"

The guard stomped over to Derlin, ordering him to stand up before immediately grabbing him by his collar and standing him up.

"Are you taking me for an interview?" Derlin asked.

"When I tell you to quiet down, you will quiet down," the guard shouted.

"Is it the warden doing the interviewing?" Derlin continued. "I bet it's the warden. Seems like something as big as picking out who's gonna rake mulch at jail they'd have him doing it I bet."

By the time Derlin had finished expounding that thought, he'd garnered the attention of nearly everyone in the mess hall, including a second guard who was now helping the first drag Derlin by the arms out of the room. As Derlin had predicted, they were indeed dragging him to the warden's office but not quite for the reason he'd hoped. Derlin's series of outbursts and misunderstandings had continued to mount and much to the chagrin of the tiring guards, the beatings at the hands of his fellow inmates didn't seem to be helping Derlin's mostly well-meaning incorrigibility in the least. Since his initial beating, his act had worn thinner by the day and his seeming inability to adapt to jail life had gotten to be more than the guards were willing to bear for the amount of money they were paid to keep people in line. Had he been locked up a half century prior, they'd have probably just fire-hosed him or chucked him in the river, but the state had really been cracking down on Perkins County as far as "inmate disappearances" went over the past decade and it may have been this slight tightening up of regulations that kept Derlin and his sass-mouth from a shallow grave.

The guards were underpaid to begin with, and with the continuing number of inmate disruptions around the jail in which Derlin managed to find himself the antagonist, their workload of maintaining daily peace was growing to be too much for even the most seasoned veterans to manage. In a move that was unprecedented as far as they knew, the guards were dragging Derlin to the warden so they could beg to get rid of him in a more bureaucratic sense than simply whacking him on the head and digging a small pit near the tree line.

They knocked on the warden's office door, each man sighing nervously as he beckoned them to enter. The warden was a small, wiry man, half the size of the burly guards, but he carried his authority well and neither guard was excited about the prospect of the conversation that lay ahead of them. The warden returned their sigh from behind his bushy white mustache as soon as they opened the door. Though he'd yet to actually meet Derlin in person, he recognized him immediately from having his file so frequently come upon his desk.

"Are you who I talk to to be an outside janitor?" Derlin asked happily, throughout the entire ordeal still beaming at the prospect of landing a legitimate raking job.

"Shut up, Spurlock," one of the guards replied, whacking him with an open palm on the back of the head.

"We want rid of him, sir," the second guard blurted out.

"You what?" the warden asked incredulously.

"We want rid of him!" the first guard agreed. "He don't listen, he's loud, he picks fights with everybody over the stupidest things every damn day. He's gotten the hell beaten out of him by us and every inmate we've got 'cept Oldsmobile in the past month and we're running out of places to try and put him. We ain't got no solitary confinement on account of that lady from the state said we can't put the bad ones out in the shed anymore. He's only got five months left, I say we just cut him the hell loose and let this jail go back to normal. We didn't have hardly nobody fighting before he came along and now it's all day, every day."

The warden was indeed aware of the cavalcade of issues associated with Derlin and he didn't like having any extra stress or drama in his work day any more than the guards did, but this was going to take some finesse to pull off in a way that didn't look strange to the officials upstate.

"So I don't get the job?" Derlin began. "I didn't even get to talk none. Listen, warden. Sir. I've done a whole lot of raking in my time. I'm prideful of it, I think I could really beautify up thi---"

"Quiet!" the warden shouted angrily. "This is most certainly not an interview for employment, Mr. Spurlock. You will remain silent until we address you and tell you differently."

Derlin opened his mouth to reply, but managed to think better of it and did indeed remain silent as requested.

"Are you telling me," the warden began, addressing the guards. "That you want me to release a prisoner early because he is being too much of a pain, too much of a hassle and that you feel he is *not* someone whom we have been able to rehabilitate to enter society?"

"Well," the guard began. "It's not that he needs rehabilitation. He's kind of a crazy asshole, but he hasn't hurt anybody. He mostly just gets the hell beat out of him for being an idiot. I was reading his rap sheet and all he's in here for is attempted assault and it says he was just swinging his rake around drunk at a bank."

"I didn't even hit nobody!" Derlin hollered before being walloped in the back of the head once more by a guard while the warden glared at him incredulously.

"What I'm saying, sir," the guard continued. "Is that I think he might just be too dumb for jail. I think he's a moron. I think if we leave him here for his whole sentence somebody's gonna beat him to death and then we're gonna have all them state folks down here all over again. If we let him go, he can just go crawl back into his hole down in Coverdale and I bet we'll never see him again. We just gotta figure out a way to let him go that don't look suspicious is all."

"We could say we're letting him go on good behavior," the warden offered to the surprise of both guards. Ten minutes into his first meeting with Derlin and he was already warming to the prospect of becoming rid of him for good.

"Warden, this guy has been the biggest prick we've had since I've worked here," the second guard began, "Nobody'll buy that he's getting out early on good behavior in a million years."

"Well, on the form, we can say good behavior and they won't know the difference one way or the other up in Birmingham," the warden continued. "If any of your fellow guards who aren't in on the idea ask, just tell them he got transferred back to Coverdale. Won't be that much of a white lie anyhow."

"You mean it?" the guards asked excitedly, almost in unison.

The warden nodded. Derlin's slack jaw widened in awe as he processed what was happening before him. Quickly bypassing the initial defeat of not obtaining legitimate employment as a rake worker, Derlin let out a joyful holler.

"Y'all's letting me go?" Derlin shouted.

"Keep your voice down!" the warden shouted. "No one can ever know that this happened. I'll lose my job and I'll see to it that I find you and kill you if you ever run your mouth about this."

"But I've got a family," Derlin pleaded, "And two babies."

"Aw, how lovely! I'll kill them too," the warden said plainly. His point was clear.

"I promise I won't commit no more crimes if you let me go," Derlin whispered, leaning in toward the warden's desk in an attempt to increase his sincerity and believability. "I'll go back to that hole y'all was talking about and I won't tell nobody where I've been."

"See that you do that, Spurlock," the warden replied. He sat back in his chair and pawed a large cigar from the pocket of his sport jacket. He retrieved a brightly colored matchbook from his desk which read "Courtesy of The Screaming Captain" and featured an illustration of Poseidon stabbing an anthropomorphic starfish with his trident across the front. As he struck the match and held it to his cigar, Derlin eyed the matchbook hungrily and began to salivate. Jail food hadn't exactly been fattening him up, but a free man could eat all the fried fish he wanted.

"You men take him back to one of the processing cells while I fill out some paperwork on this. Gather his belongings if he's got any and when I'm done, one of you can take a van and drop his ass out by the city limits. I don't want any of you to ever mention this again. Not to your wives, not to each other and certainly not to me."

The guards nodded solemnly, doing their best to hold back smiles. Derlin let out a final yip of joy as they grabbed him from his chair and moved toward the door. Once again, it seemed Derlin was on his way home.

Chapter 20

Derlin paced the holding cell with anticipation as the necessary forms were processed regarding his release. He pawed at his mullet nervously, taking deep breath after deep breath. He began to count the tiles on the floor, giving up upon reaching the number seven. Under normal conditions, such a release might take days or even weeks to complete with all the accompanying bureaucratic red tape, but to Derlin's astonishment, his took a grand total of half an hour. He'd barely even broken a sweat from his pacing before he heard the jangle of the approaching guard.

"Come on Spurlock," the guard said, barely able to conceal his joy. "Let's go gather your shit."

Derlin was beaming and politely offered his hands for cuffing without so much as a gruff word. The guard locked Derlin's cuffs and led him away from his cell for what both hoped would be the final time. After a few moments of quiet hallway walking, they arrived at the desk in front of the storage area where Derlin was to collect his belongings. Sitting in an otherwise empty dilapidated cardboard box marked "D. Spurlock" were the keys to his sedan, his crumpled jeans and a small note alerting the woman at the desk that a large item that wouldn't fit in the box remained waiting for Derlin in the back.

"That'd be my rake," Derlin said proudly as the woman read the note aloud. "I've missed that old girl, I tell ya."

The woman eyed him for a minute before calling into the room behind her to ask if anyone had seen a rake lying around among the belongings. Moments later, after what seemed to Derlin to be hours of rummaging, a small old man in a sweater vest with a name tag identifying him as "Herman" emerged holding it in two hands as though he was presenting a sword. Derlin winked slyly at the woman at the desk, nodding in the rake's direction. She rolled her eyes as the guard thanked Herman for his trouble, grabbing the rake and Derlin's box in the process.

"Y'all mind if I keep this jail t-shirt?" Derlin asked hopefully, tugging at the fabric of the cheap, starchy shirt he'd been issued at his incarceration. "I didn't have no shirt when y'all picked me up and it'd sure come in handy."
"Well I don't think we'd reuse it," the woman panned. "You seem to have gotten mustard all over it."

"Aw, yeah," Derlin said sheepishly. "That's from hot dog day."

There was a moment of pause as she and Derlin looked at each other. Herman nodded in the background.

"So I can keep it then?" Derlin asked again. "I don't wanna get outside the door and then have y'all lock me right back up for stealing from jail."

"It's fine," the woman said. "It's all yours."

"Much obliged, nice lady," Derlin said, bowing slightly and offering Herman a "finger guns" salute as he grabbed his box.

"Alright, let's go Spurlock," the guard said, grabbing him by the shoulder. "I haven't got all day for you to throw yourself some little parade."

Derlin was happy to follow orders at this point. It took very little prodding to get him heading back down the hallway toward the restroom stall where he'd change back into his tiny boots and filthy civilian jeans. Tying his belt in a proper knot, Derlin emerged and joined the guard in heading toward the old county van that would drive him back to freedom awaited.

Mavis, of course, had no idea of the monumental afternoon Derlin was having as she prepared herself for work. Randy and Ollie were fatter and happier by the day and Clebert and Eudora were clearly naturals in their roles as doting grandparents. Around the house, the boys could crawl and play as they pleased in their bald splendor, and they'd quickly gotten used to having to don their wigs when leaving the house as a puppy learns a leash. Each seemed to genuinely enjoy their wigs and the two were wildly popular among the townsfolk when they'd go shopping with Eudora or to the gas station with Clebert to purchase bait. "Those thick-headed babies that just moved to town" were the talk of every grocery line or beautician's parlor they were in.

Mavis spent the majority of her days thinking about her missing husband. She no longer had the widow's walk of a windmill doorway to stand in, searching longingly over the fields of Derlin's old car tracks like they were the cold and unforgiving waters of the North Atlantic. Still, she often found herself checking out the window of her parent's home each time she heard the roaring engine or screeching tire of a passing car. Her job at the Piggly-Wiggly had provided her with more than just a chance to make it on her own, it provided her with a way to stay busy and keep her thoughts from drifting Derlin's way for hours at a time. Though her masked husband was one of the more frequently mentioned characters in the conversational daily life in the store, she hadn't the faintest idea. She imagined, just like everybody else, that the man behind these rake robberies was just some hopped-up "crazy" passing through town on a bender and, as such, she imagined that she'd never actually met him face to face.

Helping tidy up the store the evening of Derlin's release, while replacing crayons in a box mauled by a young child, Mavis glanced up and for the first time noticed a stack of yellow legal pads for sale for a dime a piece. Fishing a dime and two nickels out of her pocket, Mavis dropped them in the till on her way out the door with two pads tucked under her arm. She'd often longed for the opportunity to put pen to paper while sitting idly in the windmill and had been increasingly anxious to find a hobby to fill Derlin's void since her return to town. Between the babies and work, she had a full plate in front of her already, but if she could manage to find fifteen minutes here and there to lose herself in some distraction from her Derlin-less daily grind, she felt certain it would be good for her.

The guard slid open the van door and tossed the rake carelessly into the back. It clattered against the metal floor of the van loudly as Derlin shouted protest.

"Hey man, come on! I wouldn't do that to your rake," he hollered.

"Pipe down, Spurlock," the guard countered. "You're still a prisoner until I drop you off at the city limits."

"The city limits?" Derlin began. "My car's in the middle of town if it ain't been towed yet. Just take me down there."

"Papers say city limits, Spurlock," said the guard. "That's where I'm taking you."

"But then I'll have to walk all the way back into town to get it and then drive all the way back down the same road," Derlin continued. "That's like six miles."

"Orders are orders," the guard shrugged.

"Can I at least ride in the front?" Derlin pleaded.

The guard pushed Derlin into the back of the van, sending him careening shoulder first into the van floor. The van itself was a cargo van not typically used for the transport of prisoners, all that could be found on the short notice of Derlin's release. It had no seats in the back and thus amplified Derlin's hollering quite a bit as the guard attempted to settle in.

"Man, I'd have climbed in," said Derlin, rubbing his shoulder tenderly. "How come there ain't no chairs or nothin' back here?"

The guard shrugged again as he hit the gas and sent Derlin toppling to the floor once more. Still being handcuffed, there was little Derlin could do beyond allow himself to be tossed about with his rake each time the van took a sharp turn or stopped. It was only fitting that he earned a couple more lumps and bruises during his final stretch of imprisonment and the guard seemed to be getting some genuine enjoyment from taking the curves as fast as the van could handle based on the snickering that Derlin heard from the front each time he took a tumble.

After a brisk ten minute ride, Derlin let out a sigh of relief as he felt the van swerve off of the road and skid to a stop.

"We're here!" the guard said cheerily.

He quickly got out of the van, jogging around the side of it, sliding open the cargo door and grabbing Derlin by the arm. Derlin barely had both feet on the ground before the guard had uncuffed him and handed him his car keys, which had dropped on the floor of the van. The guard reached into the van once more, grabbing Derlin's rake and tossing it to the ground in front of him.

"I don't think I have to tell you we never want to see you in the town of Chicken Wipe again," the guard said coldly.

"But I've gotta walk back in and get my car," Derlin replied confusedly. "I promise I won't come back no more after that but I gotta go get my car."

"You know what I mean, Spurlock," the guard replied.

"You could still just drive me to my car," said Derlin hopefully.

The guard shrugged nonchalantly once again.

"Orders is orders," he said again before offering Derlin a half-hearted salute, walking back to the van and quickly driving off, spraying Derlin with gravel and leaving him in a literal cloud of dust.

Once the dust had cleared, Derlin brushed himself off and bent to pick up his trusty rake, which fell into two pieces as soon as he grabbed the handle. Derlin let out a tiny whimper as the rake head clattered to the ground and paused to stare at it in silence for several seconds, considering his options.

Derlin was wholly unaware of the existence of the legend of King Arthur and Excalibur, but he had often thought of his rake as his trusty sword since his strange dream of life as a knight riding into battle. The Alabama forest had been his own little Lady of the Lake and it was time to return his sword from whence it came.

"Well, you got me this far, old friend," he began, his voice cracking slightly. "Let's see what else you can do."

He flung the rake piece as far as he could into the woods, watching its path of flight until it was interrupted by a low hanging pine branch which snagged it and flung it to the ground. He stood for a moment staring down at the handle, his mind racing. He nodded in satisfaction as the handle was easily transformed into a makeshift walking stick. Derlin was soon on his way, bounding back in the direction of Chicken Wipe, a free man with a fresh burst of energy that he hadn't felt in ages. He began to whistle as he walked, no tune or actual note in particular. The midday sun beat down upon him, but Derlin managed to travel nearly the entire way back into downtown over the next hour and a half.

He had fully expected his car to be towed at some point during his incarceration, and it rightly should have been as it was blocking a fire hydrant. However, in what Derlin considered a massive stroke of luck, a nearby house had caught fire the very afternoon he'd parked there not an hour after he'd been arrested when a neighborhood boy named Cletus had attempted to microwave his slinky.

Responding to the call once Cletus Sr. noticed the ensuing blaze, a fire truck came swerving through the neighborhood and in the heat of the moment rear-ended Derlin's sedan, sending it flying half a dozen car spaces forward and out of the way. After tending to the fire, the firemen took one look at Derlin's precious ride and determined that it was so banged up and dilapidated that it had to have been long ago abandoned. They were in a decent neighborhood and the car clearly didn't belong to anyone who lived nearby that they'd need to contact about the accident. They thought about at least trying to shove it off the curb, as the back tire and the remains of the trunk and rear fender were blocking the sidewalk. However, they decided against the risk of cutting themselves on the rusted metal and simply went back to the station to resume the checkers tournament that little Cletus had interrupted. The trunk was badly dented, but the bumper absorbed most of the damage and the car was not really any worse off structurally than after it was used as a battering ram through the front of the Piggly Wiggly. One tire rested upon the curb where the firemen had left it and the car sat at an angle from the collision, but Derlin just assumed that was how he's parked it to begin with when he'd left it the month prior, forgetting for a moment how "not drunk" he was at the time of his arrest.

He paused for a moment as he sat down in the driver's seat, tears welling in his eyes as he leaned sobbing against the steering wheel, relishing his good fortune. He was so close to being reunited with his family he could almost see little Ollie's blank stare or Randy's slackened jaw in the reflection of his rear view mirror. He longed to wrap his arms around his beloved Mavis once more but as he knew, he had one item of business he had to take care of first. It was a promise he'd made to himself and one he fully intended to keep. Derlin was going to the fried fish buffet.

Chapter 21

Amazingly, the old sedan shuddered to life with the first crank, eliciting another celebratory yip from Derlin. Taking a quick look around for police, he pulled a quick 180 in the street, heading back away from Chicken Wipe. He'd miraculously avoided it becoming his own personal Waterloo through nothing but blind luck and a local distaste for his own abrasive personality. Still, Derlin would look back on his time in the Chicken Wipe Jail as time fraught with failure and loneliness even though it all somehow culminated in an inexplicable snatching of victory from the jaws of utter defeat. As he blazed through a stop sign at a thankfully vacant four way intersection he relished his banishment from the town, he vowed to never return and spit out the window defiantly, leaving a wad of saliva streaking across his back window and onto the rusting remains of his crumpled fender.

Derlin sped through town oblivious to the posted speed limits simply wanting to get out of dodge as soon as possible. He felt certain his requested exile from the town was permanent, but he didn't particularly want to stick around and see if anyone changed their mind about his being locked up. He glanced at the clock he kept taped to the dashboard and the time read 4:50 in the afternoon. That gave him plenty of time in his reasoning to drive back to Coverdale, head to The Screaming Captain, gorge himself on fried fish and then finally head to the windmill before dark to begin his search for Mavis and his boys.

Despite the recurring instance of running stop signs, Derlin made it out of Chicken Wipe unscathed, yelling "You goddamn right!" as he sped by the "Now Leaving Chicken Wipe" sign he'd been dropped off at earlier in the day.

Pleased at the prospects of beginning his reassimilation into the general public with an uneventful afternoon drive and a mound of seafood, Derlin spun into The Screaming Captain's parking lot 30 minutes later. After popping the car into park, Derlin clapped, rubbed his hands together and shouted a victorious "Yes!" before half jogging across the parking lot to the front door. He scowled upon reading a sign on the door saying "Buffet Closed by Health Department" but was pleased to find the remainder of the restaurant still open for business.

In stark contrast with the garish advertising it was known for, The Screaming Captain Seafood Emporium itself was a relatively unassuming building. Small, brown and unobtrusive, it was dwarfed by its own sign, a shimmering fluorescent monstrosity featuring a grinning plus-sized mermaid taking a knife and fork to her own deep-fried, dinner-plated tail. Though not as old as the restaurant itself, the sign was erected to drum up the business of nighttime long-haul truckers passing through town in the mid 1950's and it was at the ample neon bosom of the self-cannibalizing mermaid that a pre-adolescent Derlin had first noticed an attraction to women.

Inside the door, a musty mix of decades of fried fish, body odor and mildew greeted the guests and the atmosphere appeared entirely unchanged from when the mysterious Captain had opened the restaurant several decades prior. A grimy wooden pirate stood to the left of the entryway, his smiling face and pointing hook-hand offering an enticing view of worn velvet chairs, chandeliers with seeming generations of spiderwebs coiled around them and the array of strange vaguely nautical paintings dotting the walls. Lighting seemed intentionally sparse and, though Derlin was far too young to personally remember the "heyday" of the restaurant, it was clear that it was once held as a passably-nice restaurant in some long ago era. Whether it was the quality of fish or simply nostalgia that played the part, many of Derlin's fellow townsfolk shared his ravenous affinity for the old place and it remained one of the most popular restaurants in Coverdale despite its shabby appearance and the recent closing of their buffet when it was discovered to be operating at room temperature.

Derlin scampered through the door before composing himself and waiting politely by the pirate to be seated. He craned his neck, looking as far as he could into the restaurant, trying to catch a glimpse of The Captain himself; the strange, reclusive character who'd run the restaurant since its opening long before the Great Depression, still continuing daily operations though he was rumored to be approaching his 110th birthday. Derlin had only actually seen The Captain once as a boy and remembered him cutting quite the imposing figure as he strode by. Smelling of expensive cologne and whale's blood, The Captain stood well over six feet tall and probably approached 300 pounds, looking at least twice that to young Derlin at the time. His massive white beard puffed out over his thick golden sweater and seaman's coat, Derlin recalled, and he billowed massive clouds of tobacco smoke out of the hammer-sized corncob pipe he kept clinched between his teeth. He couldn't remember The Captain saying a word, only cackling through his teeth as he smoked his pipe and waved at the customers. Though he strode through the dining room like a man of full form, The Captain's gait made a dull thud as he walked because he sported a full, legitimate peg leg from the middle of his right thigh downward.

Unobtrusively, the peg-leg was fully covered by The Captain's trousers, but it was common knowledge among the townsfolk that he'd happily raise a pant leg to show it off to a curious customer. It was speculated by a few of the old timers that, if the stories they'd heard as children were true, he'd risen to the rank of Captain while fighting for the US in the Spanish American War, which he'd managed to escape unscathed despite swimming shark-filled waters from ship to ship to vanquish his Cuban adversaries. It was a few years later, while on shore leave and visiting New York City that The Captain found himself walking the banks of the East River when he noticed a passing tour steamboat, the *General Slocum*, begin billowing smoke and burst into flames. Still quite the strong swimmer, he immediately dove into the river in an attempt to aid the passengers and though he was miraculously credited with the rescue of all 321 survivors, he would have his leg ripped off by the still-rotating paddle of the steamboat while attempting to retrieve a man's hat from the deck after emptying the ship. His peg-leg, crafted days later, was made from the piece of *General Slocum's* burning timber which he clung to while paddling one-legged to shore.

Details of his life beyond that, between the *General Slocum* disaster of 1904 and his drifting into the tiny township of Coverdale, Alabama in the early twenties to open his Seafood Emporium, were not known in the slightest. That did little to curb the speculation in the little town, however.. Stories circulated claiming that he'd been everything from a Radium Watch factory owner before the poisonings started to a body double for Kaiser Wilhelm II. No one knew a detail for certain, and as such The Captain held a certain mystique in the eyes of the townsfolk. Derlin wondered how many people eating there were there as much for the chance of seeing him pass by up close as they were for the fish.

The Captain's supposed son Horatio was a waiter in the establishment and had been since he'd shown up as a teen during the early forties claiming to be a long-lost heir. The Captain was certain of the boy's illegitimacy and kept both emotional and conversational distance from him, but he did provide him room and board in exchange for employment and thus far had coaxed several thousand hours of nearly free labor out of the arrangement, costing him only the use of a haggard rear supply shed and a few pounds of old fish per week.

Horatio was now a pasty, stammering man in his mid-forties, and Derlin could see him awkwardly darting from table to table in his own definitive gait, wincing every few steps. Horatio's own peculiar step stemmed from an incident years ago during which he'd fallen from the top of a ladder while attempting to polish the chrome of the mermaid sign's massive underbelly to a point which, as his speculated father put it, "folks can comb their hair in the reflection." He suffered a hairline fracture and, against his doctor's fervent wishes, opted for amputation over treatment in a bid to forge a bond with the distant Captain. Flabbergasting his own doctor once again, Horatio quickly had a three-inch mahogany "peg foot" manufactured to attach to the bottom of his stump. The Captain's massive false appendage was much longer, more impressive and actually medically necessary, but regardless Horatio felt their now-shared peg leg life experience might facilitate some sort of emotional breakthrough. He estimated the success of this plan poorly however, as The Captain's feelings toward him remained unchanged. Aside from periodically calling him "Pegfoot" and cackling, The Captain still treated him just the same as he ever had: the nuisance of a pasty busboy-waiter with the recurring audacity to insist they were father and son.

It was Horatio himself who finally greeted Derlin by the pirate and Derlin winced a little as he heard the "clip-clop" of the peg foot approach.

"Hello, sir and welcome to The Screaming Captain" Horatio began, "And how many will be in your party this evening?"

"Well, ain't no party," Derlin started. "It's just me. I do kinda feel like partying though, now that you mention it. I did just get outta jail. Y'all got any Panther Cat?"

"I'd be happy to seat you at the bar sir, we can get you whatever beer you like there," Horatio schmoozed. "Panther Cat's actually on special tonight."

"Can I still order my fish from the bar?" Derlin asked warily.

"Oh yes sir, don't you worry!" Horatio continued, leading him to and seating him at the bar. "I'll go ahead and get a complimentary basket of hush puppies and fish tails out here for you and someone will be right here to take your drink order!"

"That's fine," Derlin said happily, leaning back on his barstool and nearly losing his balance as Horatio clop-fluttered away.

Derlin turned his attention to a strange painting of an octopus draped across a chaise-lounge in a medieval gown with a scowling knight standing behind it and was still enraptured when he noticed the wafting aroma of the aforementioned basket of hushpuppies and fishtails as they were set before him.

"And what can I get you to drink, sir?" the bartender asked.

Derlin was slightly stunned to see Horatio standing behind the bar, smiling at him and feverishly wiping a cocktail glass. He looked around the restaurant quickly, thinking he may have been mistaken, but he saw no one else working among the sea of diners and turned his befuddled attention back to Horatio.

"I'll have a Panther Cat," Derlin offered plainly. "The biggest one you got!"

"One Schooner-size coming right up!" Horatio replied.

Derlin watched intently as he heard Horatio grab something heavy from underneath the bar and drag it across to the taps. Horatio casually pulled the Panther Cat tap, following with his pale grey eyes the stream of pale grey beer into the unknown chasm still hidden below the bar taps. Derlin watched the tap pour for what seemed like several minutes before Horatio finally shut it off. Wincing again, Horatio squatted to lift something quite large. To Derlin's astonishment, the leviathan he lifted from the underside of the bar was a ship-shaped beer mug easily holding three gallons of beer which foamed over the sides like a child's science fair volcano.

"How much y'all get for one of them?" Derlin asked, a touch worried that he'd gotten in over his head from a budget standpoint.

"Two dollars," Horatio replied.

"Two bucks?" Derlin hollered incredulously as his first sips of Panther Cat in over a month cascaded down his chin. "That's pretty alright!"

"Well, to be honest," Horatio confided, "We're still on the same batch of these kegs from 1962 and we're just trying to get rid of them all as fast as we can."

"Aw hell," Derlin replied. "I had some of my first Panther Cat's in the summer of '62. That was a real good year for 'em."

Horatio laughed nervously, unsure if Derlin had processed mentally or tasted that he'd been drinking beer that had been skunked for several years. His nervousness abated however as Derlin took another guzzle, smacking his lips loudly as he set the schooner down on the bar with a mighty thud.

"Told y'all it was a good year!" he hollered, already beginning to slur just a bit. "This shit has aged nicely, I tell ya what!"

At Derlin's behest, an incredulous Horatio began to pour a second Schooner as Derlin's first was down to the final twenty ounces or so. It was upon the receipt of this second Schooner, which alongside its partner took up around 30% of the bar, that Derlin announced to Horatio that he was ready to begin ordering food.

"I'll start with the large shrimp bucket, the white fish bucket and a big old bowl of The Captain's slaw," Derlin slurred.

Horatio nodded vigorously before shuffling off to the back.

"And plenty of ketchup!" Derlin hollered after him.

In a matter of seconds, Horatio returned with a large squirt bottle of ketchup, placing it before Derlin with a flourish as though he was presenting a bottle of wine. Enjoying the pageantry, Derlin took another large swig of his Schooner. He spent a few moments squirting ketchup onto his fingertip and licking it before returning to the final ounces of his gigantic beverage.

Setting the now empty glass carefully onto the bar floor, Derlin propped his feet upon it as he leaned back and awaited the arrival of his fish bonanza. Soon, as Derlin gazed slack-jawed across the restaurant, the kitchen doors swung open with a bang. Horatio emerged, pushing a cart with the two large entree platters Derlin had selected to begin his feast. Nearly six pounds of fried fish and french fries were laid before him, alongside a good pound of slaw and another basket of hush puppies.

Derlin squealed with delight, stuffing a napkin hastily into the collar of his shirt. He began to empty the contents of the ketchup bottle across the entirety of his platters, soon hearing the fatal shart of the empty bottle. He tossed it carelessly into the empty Schooner at his feet and began to gorge. Horatio had to look away as Derlin tore into his plates like a hungry walrus. He'd seen many people go to town on a plate of fish over the years but could recall no one as violent or primal in the act. Most of the men who could compare were thrice Derlin's size at least. After a couple of minutes a few folks had even stopped their meals just to watch him cram more and more fish and slaw into his 150 pound frame as his gaping maw chomped shrimp after shrimp to bits.

Amazingly, it was over in a matter of ten minutes. Every bit of fish, fries and hushpuppies were demolished. All the shrimp, tails included, had gone down the hatch. Derlin finally felt the several sets of eyes watching him as he licked the last of the juice from the bottom of his cereal-sized slaw bowl. He slowly set the bowl down, nodded and waved at the crowd of two dozen or so diners, who burst into applause.

The applause more or less drowned out the first seven seconds of Derlin's belch, which would then continue uninterrupted for another eighteen or so. By the time it concluded, the majority of the onlookers had either burst into laughter or gasped in disgust, but all of them had quickly begun to disperse as the smell made its way around the bar area. Derlin, smacking his lips, apparently didn't notice the other diners fleeing the stench of his mighty belch and simply turned back to the last two thirds of his remaining Schooner.

Horatio, looking a little pale, nervously approached Derlin to inquire about the quality of his meal.

"And how… how was everything, sir?" Horatio asked bleakly.

"It was Grade A awesome!" Derlin replied, patting Horatio heartily on the back with a ketchupy paw. In front of him, where only ten minutes prior had been two large, nicely arranged platters of seafood and sides, it looked like a small bomb had gone off. Bits of burnt potato and smears of ketchup dotted a hellscape of balled up napkins, slaw shrapnel and hair.

"Happy to hear it," Horatio smiled thinly. "Can…" He paused briefly to put his hand over his mouth. "Can I get you anything else. Sir?"

"As a matter of fact, I'll take a couple baskets of those fried starfish if you've still got 'em. The big ones. And I'll take some extra butter mayo in there too. I like dippin' every bite and one bowl ain't gonna do the trick tonight."

"Right away, sir," Horatio said, doing his best not to recoil in horror at the stench of fish and expired beer emanating off of Derlin.

Derlin had become a bit sluggish since the first part of his meal and it took a good bit of effort to bring the Schooner to his lips as he took another mighty gulp of ancient Panther Cat. As he'd taken his time with the second Schooner more than the first, elements of the beer had begun to separate in the glass and it had begun to resemble some sort of hideous black and tan. Again, Derlin didn't seem to notice or care, simply focusing on the kitchen door between sips until Horatio burst forth once again carrying two steaming baskets toward the bar.

The parsley covered fried starfish shone with grease as they soaked the bottom of the basket and Derlin salivated. Horatio gingerly set them before him and politely inquired if he needed more ketchup.

"Naw I got plenty of the butter mayo, my good man!" Derlin began. He waved as Horatio left to make his rounds.

The Captain's famous butter mayo, a condiment which had since the 1930's seen its popularity spread through the south like Sherman's fire, was a barely-seasoned proto-ranch sauce that The Captain had discovered when he accidentally dumped a bowl of mayonnaise into a pan of melting butter and then salted it to quelch the flames. Served by the dollop on everything from seafood to ham sandwiches to ice cream sundaes, by the end of World War II, there wasn't a house in Alabama without a jug of The Captain's butter mayo in their icebox, the revenue from which only buoyed the Captain's considerable bankroll. Ideally, the jug was served with a heaping basket of The Captain's equally famous fried starfish. He'd served so many over the years that marine biologists considered him the number one predator a starfish faces in the ocean, a mantle he'd worn proudly since discovering the claim in a scientific journal in the mid-1940's.

The starfish were Derlin's favorite menu item at The Screaming Captain and he slathered each of them with butter mayo before diving in like a hungry pelican. Soon, nothing remained but two small grease puddles with a few floating flecks of parsley dotting them. Derlin spotted a loose piece of breading, using it and one index finger to scoop up the oily remains of his butter mayo. Finally, he sighed, taking a small stack of napkins and cleaning his face, neck and hands with the skills of a small child.

He turned to finish his beer, and upon guzzling the last 36 ounces or so in an uninterrupted chug, he began to look around for Horatio. Finally, seeing him emerge from a supply closet, Derlin began to snap his fingers for his attention. Horatio, hiding his irritation, quickly made his way to Derlin's side.

"I'm ready for my check, monsignor" Derlin began. "I got places to be!"

"I'm certain that you do, sir," Horatio replied. "I'll have that drawn right up for you." He made his way behind the bar and began plugging away at the ancient cash register. Derlin's eyes began to get bigger as Horatio continued pressing buttons. Reaching into his pocket, Derlin felt for the five dollar bill which Oldsmobile had slipped him during their brief goodbye.

"That'll be $22.63," Horatio stated plainly, reaching his hand out to Derlin for payment.

Derlin sheepishly pulled the five dollar bill from his pocket and slipped it into Horatio's palm.

"This is only five dollars sir," Horatio said, beginning to eye Derlin suspiciously.

"Is it?" Derlin laughed, "I'm sorry man, I thought it said fifty. He reached into his pockets again, despite knowing damn well that he had no other money on him. He pawed at his sweat-dampened T-shirt, miming the idea of patting for a wallet were he wearing a fancy dinner jacket. "Must've left the wallet in my ride." He began to make his way toward the door when he felt a firm hand grasp his shoulder.

"I don't think you've got a wallet in your car, squab," a hearty deep voice growled. "I think you're trying to run out the door on The Captain."

Derlin felt his entire body shiver as he turned around to find himself at just about eye level with The Captain's massive heaving beard.

"No! No," Derlin stammered, hiccuping. "I wasn't gonna go and do something like that. I love this place. I just came up a little short is all and I was gonna go see if I had any change hiding under my car seat."

"Oh, I know a little something about coming up a little short," The Captain menaced, before lifting his trouser leg and cackling as Derlin stared, mouth agape at his massive wooden peg leg. "You could say I know a great deal."

Horatio joined in the laughter for a brief second as The Captain's came to an abrupt stop. He eyed Horatio quietly for a second, shaking his head disdainfully before turning his attention back to Derlin.

"We've had a few fellers like you over the years," he began, staring off toward the ceiling of the restaurant. "Plenty in the Depression, sure, but they still come. Folks who come in with empty pockets and empty bellies and try to take advantage of the ol' Captain, would you believe that?"

"No… No sir," Derlin stammered.

"You wouldn't?" The Captain asked indignantly. "Why, you're doing it right now. You're covered in the grease of my own teet!" he shouted.

"I guess so," Derlin replied shamefully, gazing dejectedly at the floor.

"You guess so, son?" The Captain continued. "I can smell the butter mayo comin' off ya. And there's been rats swimming in that Panther Cat you've been chug-a-lugging on, just so ya know. You know what we do with folks who can't pay son?"

"You call the police?" Derlin asked meekly.

"No, son." The Captain began. "I'm not going to waste the policeman's valuable time because some mangy townie tried to steal my fish. I'm gonna do us both a favor. I'm gonna put you to work!"

Derlin heaved a sigh of relief, the back end of which saw him choke upon a hunk of starfish and begin gasping for air. The Captain patted him on the back with his mighty paw until the offending piece was dislodged. It caught in Derlin's mouth as it was ejected and he chewed and swallowed it slowly.

"I can do all kinds of work," Derlin offered, perking up slightly despite still fighting back the occasional cough.

"I'm sure that you can," The Captain smiled. He snatched Derlin's tab from Horatio's hand and read it to himself. "Well son, looks like I'm gonna get about $18 worth of work out of you."

He led Derlin quickly to the back, where he expected a bustling kitchen full of people hard at work. However, much to his surprise, they were the only two people in the entire place.

"I do all the cooking myself," the Captain began, answering Derlin's question before he could answer it. "I have since day one."

Many of the grease-caked appliances crammed into The Captain's kitchen looked like they'd been there since day one as well and Derlin counted no fewer than fifteen separate stove eyes and fryer baskets that the ancient Captain seemed to have well handled. A large kettle brewed atop an open fire with a strange, viscous brown liquid in it. Seeing Derlin's curiosity, The Captain identified the goo as his "Secret Slurry" before shooing Derlin away with a charred broom with which he apparently tended the fire. He lead Derlin to a massive pit of grease and ketchup stained dishes, a handful of which were his own.

"First off," he bellowed, "You're gonna clean the lot of these. After that, come grab that old broom because you're gonna be sweeping the scales up. He pointed a mighty finger to a corner of the kitchen with a massive, fishscale-filled trash can, leaking from the bottom and surrounded by haphazard piles of millions upon millions of scales, some nearly a foot taller than him. Derlin groaned.

"Usually I'll get the hose out after the mornin' scalin' but I haven't had time to in a good five days," The Captain beamed. "You're gonna have your work cut out for you at that I can tell you that. After you finish up all them dishes and getting the scales all swept up you can go." He tossed Derlin a dish rag, took a mighty puff of his billowing corn cob pipe and turned back to sauteeing what appeared to be an entire octopus in a comically small cast iron pan.

Derlin began to ask him a question, but instead turned to the mountain of dishes that were now in his charge. This was certainly a hiccup in his plan to get to the windmill and possibly all the way to Mavis's parents house before dusk, but the reunion that lay ahead of him was enough of an impetus to get the dishes done as fast as possible. He tore into the pile with as much vigor and effort as he'd ever put toward anything in his life and, after the blur of a first hour manning the dish hose, The Captain was so impressed with the chunk of dishes he'd cleaned that he offered to provide him a beer while he worked.

"You got anymore of that old '62?" Derlin asked happily. "It's got a mighty nice tang to it.

Over the next four and a half hours, Derlin plowed through the dishes and baskets with a fierce determination rival to some of the strongest efforts Spurlock men had given in generations, all the while helping The Captain purge his taps while sucking down heroic amounts of putrid, expired Panther Cat. It was nearly eleven when Derlin was finally able to turn his attention to the cascading mountains of rotting fish scales he'd been charged with sweeping up. He stared helplessly at The Captain's tiny, charred fire-broom, stomping his way through the piles and puddles to begin his cleaning. The scales themselves stuck to everything, Derlin's clothing and shoes included, as he swept through the muck one rusting dustpan load at a time. It was nearly 3:30 in the morning when he passably finished and by then The Captain had long since retired to his quarters with a bottle of brandy. Horatio had waited for him to finish, sitting uncomfortably near the pirate at the entrance. He was beginning to doze off as Derlin gingerly approached him.

"Hey." Derlin said plainly, jostling his shoulder. "Hey, man."

Horatio awoke with a start. "All done are you?" he asked briskly. "Should we have a look and see if there's anything that needs a touch up?"

"Naw," Derlin replied, brushing some scales from his shirt. "Naw, man I think I'm gonna go home now. I did $18 worth of work at least."

"I'd say so," Horatio yawned, absentmindedly handing Derlin a crisp $20 bill from his pocket.

Derlin stared at him confusedly for a moment before nodding at him in thanks and heading for the front door. Horatio, still yawning, waved goodbye and bid him a good night. By the time Derlin reached his car and revved it to life, the headlights caught sight of Horatio locking up shop and heading around back to his supply shed, where he'd nap for a while before returning to work the morning shift which began a few hours later.

Derlin, though exhausted and still stuffed beyond belief from his ample dinner, was fairly well hammered by the time he pulled away from The Screaming Captain. It took him a good twenty minutes of diligently slow and careful swerving along the road before he finally reached the familiar parking lot of Lumpy's Feed and Seed. He fully expected that Mavis and the boys had fled the windmill sometime early on during his incarceration, but knew he had to check there first just in case they'd managed to stick it out. As he followed his own crusted muddy tire tracks down the old trail and through the cornfield, it brought a flood of memories back from his brief period as an outlaw rake man, supporting his family from behind a mask and lurking on the fringes of society. He smiled and thought of how much his boys must have grown in his absence, longing for the embrace of his sweet Windmill Princess.

He plowed through the bit of recovering shrubbery separating the corn field from the windmill's meadow, skidding to a stop in his familiar fashion. He leapt from the car and began hollering for Mavis and the boys but quickly began to put two and two together when he noticed the door to the windmill ajar and the inside dark and empty. He could smell no fire and saw no fresh cans of baby food strewn about, so he quickly made his decision and headed back to the car. Suddenly, he paused at the doorway, looking back across the darkened windmill floor. Darting to the far corner of the windmill, he began scratching frantically at a pile of hay before producing his three old copies of Plumpers magazine. He clutched them to his chest with relief before running haphazardly back out the door, slamming it forcefully behind him and practically leaping back into his waiting sedan.

Recklessly careening from one side of the road to the other, Derlin drove wildly toward the Clapp residence. Surprised he was able to find it in the dark with such ease, Derlin skidded to a stop in the Clapp family yard, hitting a travelling possum in the process and sending it smashing against the side of the house.

"Mavis!" He shouted at the top of his drunken lungs. "Randy, Ollie! Where my boys at?"

Almost immediately, lights sprung on inside the house. Within a few seconds of Derlin's initial shout, Clebert was on the porch in his pajamas holding a shotgun.

"You damn fool, don't you know what time it is?" Clebert hollered. A few neighborhood dogs began to bark in the background.

"Times I gets my babies back!" Derlin hollered. "Mavis!" He continued yelling until he saw a familiar silhouette emerge in the doorway behind Clebert.

"Derlin I'm right here," Mavis shouted.

"Baby!" Derlin began. "Baby I've missed you so mu…"

"Just where the hell have you been?" Mavis cut him off. "You just left us in that windmill! We waited for you for days and you just left us." She began to cry.

"See baby, the thing is," Derlin slurred. "The thing is, I went to jail, but I got out, and now I'm back and I'm here for you and the babies and we can all be together again. I can get a real job and we can…"

"You're drunk," she cut him off again. "You're drunk and you're gonna wake up the babies." Like clockwork, Eudora emerged from the front door, holding the two crying boys, their flat hollering blending finely with the howls of the neighborhood dogs.

"My boys!" he yelled. "My two fine Spurlock boys!" He took two staggering steps across the yard toward the porch, at which point Clebert stepped forward and cocked his shotgun.

"Don't you come no closer, Derlin." he said coldly. "You stay right where you're at and there won't be trouble."

"I don't want no trouble," Derlin pleaded. "I just want my boys and my Mavis."

"I don't want you like this, Derlin" Mavis cried. "You can't just be going off and making trouble and ending up in jail. That ain't how you act if you care about your family. You can't just show up here drunk in the middle of the night after abandoning us and expect everything to be alright just cause you say it should be!"

"But I'm sorry, baby," Derlin pleaded. "You know I love you. You know I wouldn't do you like that on purpose. You know I wouldn't leave the babies and you alone in that windmill. I just got locked up is all but like I said, I'm out now. I ain't in jail no more. Lookit all the hair them babies got now. We can be a family again and everything can go back to normal."

"Honey, everything is as normal as it's ever been for me and Randy and Ollie right now," Mavis continued, tears still streaming down her cheeks. "I've got a job and the boys have beds and toys and we're living in a house. My parents love us and they don't disappear for days at a time and show up drunk with no explanation."

"I explained!" Derlin shouted, becoming agitated. "I explained I was in jail and there wasn't nothin' I could do till they let me out and they let me out yesterday."

"Well what happened between then and now?" Mavis asked, becoming a little angry herself. "Why didn't you come straight here? Why did you show up in our yard at four in the morning, reeking like beer and covered in glitter?"

"It ain't glitter, it's fish scales!" Derlin hollered as he shimmered in the moonlight.

"It doesn't matter, Spurlock," Clebert shouted. "You're acting like a horses' ass and you know it!"

"I didn't do nothin' to you old man," Derlin hollered, pointing at Clebert. He took another step forward through the yard and Clebert met him at the bottom of the porch stairs with his shotgun.

"Dad, no!" Mavis shouted, running down the stairs to get between the two of them. "Dad, please don't hurt him, I love him!"

"I love you too, baby!" Derlin shouted back, beginning to drunkenly cry himself.

Mavis wrapped her arms around Derlin and the two shared a very beery, fishy kiss as Clebert muttered profanities under his breath.

"I love you Derlin, but we can't be together like this no more," Mavis cried, pulling away from him.

"What do you mean, baby?" Derlin asked, his scale-covered brow furrowing in confusion.

"I mean I'm trying to do right by our babies," Mavis cried. "I've got a job and I'm saving up for a real place of my own to raise them in. They're gonna grow up to be good boys whether you choose to be there for it or not. And I'm not gonna let you be there for it while you're running around like a drunk idiot, getting into trouble with the law and leaving us alone in the woods."

Derlin hung his head.

"If you want to be part of this family," Mavis continued, poking him in his scaly chest. "You need to straighten up. You need to get your shit together. For me, for Randy and for Ollie. And for you, Derlin. You need to go out into the world on your own. You need to clean yourself up, get a job and make right. When you do that, you can come back stomping up in this yard. But you can do it sober. In the daytime. And you can knock on the door."

Derlin continued to stare silently at the grass before beginning to nod slowly.

"Yeah, baby," he began sullenly. "Yeah, I guess you're right about all of that. I ain't acting the way no family man should act. I'm gonna do right by you and I'm gonna do right by my boys. I want them to be prideful of their daddy when they grow up and that ain't gonna happen if their daddy is some asshole traveling rake man. I'm gonna clean up and make something outta myself."

He and Mavis hugged, tightly and silently for several seconds before she pulled back and circled up behind her father on the porch.

"My apologies, Mr. Clapp, sir," Derlin said earnestly. Mr. Clapp stared wordlessly down at him from the porch, still clenching his shotgun.

"You've got miles to go before I even think about acceptin' that apology, boy," Clebert finally replied. "Till that day I don't wanna see you around here no more. Don't come visit. Don't drive by and look at the house. Nothing."

"Yessir," Derlin replied plainly, his head still hung low. "Well, I reckon I'll be getting on my way then."

Randy and Ollie still cooed flatly from the porch as Eudora led them and Mavis back inside. After another extended stare down, Clebert followed them, slamming and locking the door behind him and leaving Derlin alone in the yard. Derlin stood there, unwavering for a moment, staring at the sky, the fish scales still sparkling resplendently in the moonlight like a sequined Hollywood gown. Finally breaking his gaunt stupor, he began to shuffle listlessly back across the yard back to his still-running sedan. Doubling over involuntarily, Derlin paused his exit to projectile vomit a frightening cascade of fish, slaw and beer into the bushes at the base of the Clapp family mailbox, rubbing his scaly arm across his dripping mouth once before groaning mightily and climbing slowly behind the wheel.

He exited the yard as quietly as he could manage, not so much as squealing the tires or revving the engine once. Doing his best to drunkenly gather himself, he decided to head downtown in search of a quiet place to park his car and sleep it off before he set forth planning his grand re-entry to functioning society.

Chapter 22

April 30, 1968

He wouldn't remember it until the next morning when he woke up on it, but in Derlin's drunken stupor he had managed to find an out-of-the-way park bench to pass out upon. He awoke, not to the pestered tapping of a concerned neighbor or local policeman, but to the pleasant sounds of birds chirping and rays of sunshine beating down upon his crusted face. He stretched, groaned and immediately vomited again upon smelling himself. After his evening's travels he'd had the unfortunate musk of an old fishing vessel, but after passing out, the mix of skunky beer and fish vomit had been allowed several hours to fester in the early morning sun and as his day began Derlin smelled like low tide at the pier.

He managed to stumble to his feet, surveying his surroundings with care as he squinted through the brightness of the morning. Spotting a small creek at the bottom of the hill about 100 yards from him Derlin lurched forward down the hill, losing his balance almost immediately. He stumbled about halfway down, managing to spin to a stop before he reached the bottom, all in all only tumbling for 15 feet. He looked at this moment as the first improvement in the turning around of his life in that he didn't fall down the entirety of the hill and this filled him with a vague sense of satisfaction that he hoped to build on throughout the afternoon.

Reaching the creek without any further issues, Derlin removed his shoes and found the deepest pool he could manage, one that was around two feet deep. It seemed a warmer, muddier version of the tub he'd dammed up in the forest. He plopped down in it like a toddler in a bathtub and began to scrub the beer, vomit and fish scales from his body. Once he felt he'd done a satisfactory job, he dunked his head under water, scrubbing his hair and face vigorously. Pulling his head from the water, he gasped loudly. He checked the surrounding area for fellow functioning citizens using the park and when he saw none, he carefully removed his jeans and shirt. Having long ago discarded his sole set of underpants, Derlin hid his biblical parts from the morning light as best he could. Naked, in the creek of a public park on a weekday morning, scrubbing fish scales from his chest and nipples, Derlin was a man clearly trying to get his life together and didn't want any pesky "Indecent Exposure" charges popping up as a roadblock to his impending successes.

Still naked, he sloshed his shirt and jeans around in the muddy water for a few minutes in an attempt to clean them. Rendering his shoddy attempt as satisfactory after a few short moments of scrubbing, Derlin put his soiled, dripping clothing back on, climbed out of the creek and began phase two of his plan, which was laying on the grass in the sun until he dried out. He spent the next 90 minutes sprawled in the grass, writhing into different positions to capture the sun until he felt that his still clearly damp clothes were passably dry. He'd done something, more or less, about the stink. He'd actually been successful in losing most of the scales. Now it was time for him to pull himself up by the bootstraps and make something of himself just as he'd promised Mavis. Hopefully in time for lunch.

Derlin climbed slowly back up the hill which he'd so recently tumbled down, wheezing slightly. Though invigorated by his creek bath, the pounding in his temples reminded him of the last vestiges of his mighty hangover and a low rumbling belch reminded him of the quantity of "fried ocean meat" he had still churning in his stomach. Reaching the top of the hill, Derlin blocked the morning sun from his eyes, looking up and down the street and surveying his options for the day.

The sedan was parked poorly across two parking spaces, with the door open, in the nearby public parking lot and as Derlin wrestled his keys from his boot, he decided he might leave the old girl parked there for a while and take in the town on foot. He waltzed across the street to the car, casually checking the crumpled and dirty fenders for any additional damage before nonchalantly slamming the door and shuffling off toward the town center. It had been several months since Derlin had been able to take a carefree daylight stroll through his hometown and he decided that he'd rather take on the challenge of self improvement as a pedestrian instead of just cruising around in the sedan, wasting gas and waiting for an idea to appear.

Not realizing he'd lost Horatio's $20 bill in the creek while washing his jeans, he didn't have a dime in his pockets, barely had the clothes on his back and, as things currently stood, he probably planned on either spending the night in his car or back on the same park bench. Despite these obstacles, he'd been legitimately stirred by the previous night's argument with Mavis. She was completely right, of course. If he wanted to be a proper father to his beloved Randy and Ollie, he really ought to straighten up and fly right. "Cool it with the rabble-rousing" as Grandpa Hoyt used to say. Functioning adults didn't tend to rob grocery stores and live in a windmill. Functioning adults didn't tend to lie to their wives about the fanciful glories of a made-up raking career instead of having a job, or go to jail for not even hitting anybody. He hadn't the slightest idea how he was going to right his personal ship, but the act of betterment was certainly the major single hurdle in his path back to Mavis and the boys and Derlin realized this clearly. So, he stuck out his proud, strong Spurlock jaw as he approached this first morning of his new beginning and held his head high. A man determined, Derlin marched toward the Coverdale town center in search of something, anything, that could help make him the respectable family havin' man that Mavis deserved.

He strode intently down the sidewalk, beginning to whistle as he approached the main street of town. Morning customers bustled around him in and out of businesses and a few even returned Derlin's "Mornin!" or "How are ya?" with a nod or a smile as they passed him. He was put at ease by the fact that he wasn't on his way to or from committing a crime and relished the pleasantry of the morning not being interrupted by a policeman throwing him to the sidewalk.

Derlin's first order of business, as he had set forth for himself on his walk, was to find employment. A respectable job would be a huge boon to Derlin's chances of reuniting with his family and though he'd thus far in life only maintained a series of real and imagined odd jobs, he was ready for the regularity and commitment of traditional 9-5 employment. Picturing himself standing in the mirror wearing a collared shirt and a name tag, slicking back his hair with a wet comb, Derlin smiled blankly. He imagined Randy and Ollie as older children, next to him getting ready for school, fighting and clamoring over which one of them got to help comb their daddy's hair.

It was this image he carried with him as he began to scan shop windows and business fronts for "Help Wanted" signs and for the first time he began to get excited about the prospect of legitimate work that lay ahead of him. Though certainly respectable places of employment, Derlin was leery of both the police station and the bank, rightfully assuming that he was woefully under qualified to be Sheriff or Bank President and that the positions were likely filled anyhow. He wandered past a small bakery and hardware store, peeking through the windows, when a gleam of red caught his eye. Whizzing by him as it neared the station down the street was the local fire engine, sparkling in the morning sun. Derlin stared, mouth agape as the engine pulled to a stop in front of the station and four firemen got out. Abandoning his original plan of entering the bakery to inquire as to their "free sample" policy, Derlin broke into a brisk jog, catching up to the firemen just as they were entering the garage of the station.

"Hey," Derlin hollered. "Hey, guys!"

The group of firemen turned in unison to see who was stomping up breathlessly behind them.

"Hey fella," one of them replied. "Everything okay?" The other firemen were much younger and in better shape, but this one was a portly man of about 50 with a large brown mustache dominating an otherwise pasty and uninteresting face. Through a combination of age and facial hair, he seemed to be in charge.

"Yeah," Derlin breathed heavily, his hands on his hips. "Yeah I just wasn't planning on running is all."

"You in some kinda trouble?" the fireman asked.

"Me? Naw, there ain't nobody chasing me or nothin'. I just seen y'all pulling up and wanted to come talk to y'all about being a fireman," Derlin answered.

"What do you mean talk to us about being a fireman?" the man asked, giving Derlin a quick and skeptical up-and-down.

"I mean are y'all hiring?" Derlin asked, still trying to catch his breath. "I'd like to apply for a job as a fireman."

The three younger men chuckled, but Derlin ignored them.
"Are you the chief?" Derlin panted. "You look like the chief."
The man nodded slowly, tapping the patch on his shirt which read "Chief."

"You want a job?" the chief asked. "You don't really… seem like the type we usually get in here. This can be a pretty physically demanding job."

"Oh I'm real strong," Derlin vouched.

The three young firemen laughed again and this time Derlin glared at them.

"No offense son, you don't really seem to have a lot of muscle definition," the chief began. "And besides that, you're still out of breath from running up in here a couple of minutes ago. I seen you on the street as we were driving by and you didn't have to run no more than a hundred feet or so. How are you gonna rescue somebody from a burning building if a jog down the street puts you down like that?"

Derlin pondered for a minute on a response, picturing an elaborate and dramatic scene of him rescuing a series of bikini models from a burning oceanside lighthouse with nothing but an ax, a bucket and his bare hands.

"I'd find a way to," he finally answered, nodding vigorously.

"Have you ever been a fireman before?" the chief asked.

"Well, not o-fficially." Derlin answered. "But I'm real good at fighting fires though. Look! Gimme some matches."

Derlin began to look around for something to light ablaze when the three younger firemen approached him and began pushing him out the door. For a moment, he resisted, still shouting for just a chance to prove his firefighting mettle in a small trash can or on an old chair, but his pleas fell on deaf ears.

"Ain't happening son," the chief hollered as Derlin was led from the station. "Thanks boys! Good work."

Derlin apologized to the men as he was deposited on the sidewalk, wishing them a good morning and thanking them for being "real firemen," but he didn't get so much as an acknowledgement as they returned to their morning duties.

A bit disappointed that his first attempt at employment had gone so poorly, Derlin dusted himself off and scoped out a nearby park bench where he could settle his mind and return to his internal drawing board. He sat down, bent over and staring at the sidewalk, wondering what his next move would be. He wanted a job with some prestige and nobility, but his borderline-entry-level skill set seemed to limit his horizons. Being a fireman seemed to be off the table and as he'd determined, being a police officer was out of the question as well. Derlin briefly considered retracing his steps to a small law practice he'd passed on his jog, but after having his confidence so shaken by the firehouse fiasco, he correctly assumed that he was vastly unprepared to be any sort of "lawyering man" either.

As he sat, running out of "prestigious professions" to list on his fingers, he noticed two young men in uniforms walking down the street. Noticing the "US Army" logo stitched onto their shirts, Derlin's face lit up as he thought of how differently Mavis and her parents would look at him as a military man.

"Y'all boys in the army?" he hollered as they walked by, pointing at their shirts.

"Yes sir!" they answered in unison.

"Y'all hiring?" he asked, smiling.

"You mean can you sign up for the army?" one asked, perplexed.

"Yeah," Derlin replied. Unlike many men his age, Derlin had avoided the draft for Vietnam entirely. His birth had occurred during a weekend woodland mud-bogging trip that his Uncle Vern had invited Clovis and a nine-months pregnant Tina to attend, where they'd gotten stranded after a washout rainstorm. By the time they made it back to town a few days later, Clovis and Tina had had enough liquor between them that they'd forgotten any notion of registering his birth with the hospital or getting him a Social Security number, though they would manage to claim him on their yearly taxes for the entirety of his upbringing.

"I was thinkin' about joining up," he continued.

"Well, the recruitment center is two blocks that way," the other young man piped up, pointing in the direction which Derlin had not yet ventured.

He thanked the men and wished them a pleasant day, saluting incorrectly and watching them walk down the street until they turned a corner. He pictured himself in the same uniform, coming home to Mavis and the boys a true American hero. He paid no attention to current affairs and would have had no idea what the Vietnam War was if you'd asked him, but the idea of having a nice haircut and marching around like John Wayne seemed like a prestigious enough set-up in his mind. Maybe they could even teach him how to actually shoot a gun.

Gathering himself from the park bench with a flourish, Derlin forgot completely about his earlier failure in the firehouse and the sting he felt from the firemen mocking him. He bounded down the street as fast as his tiny boots could carry him, his path to respectability and general admiration now clear. The firemen could keep their axes, dalmatians and fancy red trucks, Derlin was going to join the army.

Chapter 23

Derlin burst through the door to the recruitment center with a flourish, nearly as out of breath as when he first accosted the firemen. The bell above the door clanged loudly and a middle aged man in an officer's uniform looked up from his desk.

"Are y'all still hiring?" Derlin asked, panting lightly.

"Excuse me?" the officer replied.

"A couple of your boys in uniform told me I could sign up for the army here, if y'all are still hiring folks up," Derlin smiled.

"You're interested in joining the army?" the officer asked, raising his eyebrows.

"I sure am, if y'all still got any room," Derlin offered politely.

The officer smiled.

"I think we might still have a couple spots open," he replied, nonchalantly thumbing through a stack of papers in his desk pretending to look for something. "Let's get you started on some paperwork!"

Over the next twenty minutes or so, Derlin filled out the forms necessary for his admission to the army. He was curious that the form didn't indicate whether he was applying for a position as a General or a Captain, but as he stated several times, he had no problem working his way up the ladder. Soon, all that remained was his physical. While waiting for the doctor and his examination, Derlin was given a much-needed free "army" t-shirt and hat which he quickly donned, balling up the crusted, shell-shocked remains of his old t-shirt and throwing it into a nearby trash can.

Despite not necessarily being the at or near the peak of human evolution, Derlin was healthy enough for his age and in decent shape. His eyesight was strong and his bones sturdy. Though he'd suffered nearly a dozen concussions in his life, they hadn't yet affected him in any sort of debilitating way. He breezed through his physical and, aside from briefly disturbing the doctor with the discovery of a few hidden fish scales, everything went as smoothly as possible and Derlin was soon cleared for enlistment.

As it stood, Derlin would leave on a bus to Montgomery the next morning to begin his basic training with the latest batch of recruits from Southern Alabama. Officially signing his contract, the officer shook his hand and much to Derlin's surprise, gave him a $50 signing bonus for being a walk-in. It was the first $50 bill that Derlin had ever held and he gasped as he took it. Certainly, it meant he could sleep indoors and enjoy a hot lunch and dinner, though he was mildly apprehensive at the thought of breaking it so quickly. Folding it carefully and placing it in his jeans pocket, Derlin saluted the officer and headed out the door to enjoy his last day as a regular civilian.

Derlin strutted proudly down the street, puffing his chest out in his army shirt, tipping his army hat to nearly everyone who passed by. Remembering from one of his favorite episodes of The Andy Griffith Show, Derlin began whistling bars to the classic "Marine's Hymn," repeating the bars for the lyrics "From the halls of Montezuma to the shores of Tripoli," over and over as he walked happily through town truthfully unaware of the difference in separate branches of the military. Feeling a pang of hunger in his stomach, Derlin decided to treat himself with his newfound windfall and strode into a diner, taking a seat at the counter.

"I'll take the biggest hamburger sandwich you've got," Derlin said, smiling as a waitress approached him with a menu. "With fried potatoes and a cup of coffee."

"Comin' right up, hun" she replied with a wink, returning his smile. She was heavyset and probably old enough to be Derlin's grandmother, Vondene, but he blushed slightly at the attention when she winked.

"Maybe this is what life's like as an army man," he thought to himself.

She quickly returned with the coffee and Derlin struggled to make small talk as she filled his cup. He peered at her name tag.

"Mabel," he started. "That's a nice name."

"Aw, you're mighty sweet," she replied. "Do you want any cream or sugar with your coffee, hun?"

"I'll take extra sugar please," he said.

"I'll bet you will," she giggled, handing him the sugar pourer from the countertop.

Derlin poured the sugar into his cup for several seconds before he began to stir. Soon, he'd added enough that the coffee had become a viscous syrup and it was at this point that he began to drink. Over the course of his stay, he'd put down another three cups in the same manner, nearly draining the entire sugar pourer, invigorated by the caffeine and the massive cheeseburger he'd eaten in between gulps of coffee.

Mabel whistled when Derlin slapped his $50 bill on the counter to pay.

"Look at you, Hollywood!" she giggled. "Handsome and rich and an army man. There's some real lucky lady out there!"

"There sure is," Derlin smiled. "I got twin boys too. I'm sure gonna miss 'em while I'm away at army."

"Well, hun, you'll be back home to 'em before you know it," she smiled.

"I sure hope so," Derlin replied. He tipped Mabel a dollar, gave her an informal wrong-handed salute and headed for the door.

With an afternoon to kill and money to burn, Derlin felt like a kid in a candy store walking through downtown. He thought of going to a movie, but the local cinema had something called "Planet of the Apes" on the marquee and Derlin didn't particularly feel like spending his last afternoon as a civilian sitting through some cockamamie nature documentary. Wise enough to avoid the drink despite his newfound wealth, Derlin spent most of his day window shopping and eating, periodically pausing his downtown travels and coffee gulping to go and pee on the back side of the firehouse.

By dusk, Derlin had eaten burgers at four different restaurants in town and was ready to get a good night's sleep in a nice motel bed. Walking to the local Dew Drop Inn, Derlin acquired a room with a color television. He spent approximately 30 minutes moaning in a hot shower and working his way through three entire bars of complimentary soap. To his delight, he was able to find a regional wrestling show on the TV and fell asleep just a few minutes into watching a wrestler named Gary "Greased Lightning" Witherspoon battle a masked behemoth named "Cowboy" Steve Rodriguez.

He slept as soundly as he had in ages. Since the birth of Randy and Ollie, Derlin's old jail cot was the nicest bed he'd slept on and the combination of the clean motel sheets, the shower and the four burgers sent him into a deep slumber. Snoring loudly, he wouldn't so much as roll over once during the night.

Derlin would awake from his hibernation with a jolt just 15 minutes before his bus left. He quickly collected his things, a task which basically consisted of putting on his shoes and army hat, as he'd slept in his shirt and pants. He bolted from the room, tossing his key to the hotel clerk from the lobby door. Jogging down the street clean and well-rested, Derlin arrived at his bus stop with five minutes to spare. A handful of other young men, each wearing the same army shirt as Derlin, loitered around the bus stop as well.

"Y'all going to the army too?" Derlin asked, offering a wave and another wrong-handed salute. He was feeling as happy and as friendly as he had in a long time.

Part 4: The Army Man

Chapter 24

The bus had already picked up men from all over Southern Alabama before it arrived in Coverdale and there were still several more stops before Montgomery, turning an hour and a half bus-ride into a nearly four-hour excursion. Derlin attempted to make small talk with his fellow recruits a few times early on in the ride but was heatedly discouraged by the drill sergeant present from speaking out of turn. He was soon content to spend the ride in silence, staring out the bus window at the Alabama countryside. He enjoyed the little sightseeing tour that the trip had afforded him and he found it relaxing to simply zone out, jaw slackened, watching the landscape pass from his window. It was nearly noon when the bus finally arrived on the outskirts of Montgomery at Camp McQueen, the place that would be Derlin's home until his deployment.

At the behest of a small, redheaded drill sergeant named Snyder, only about shoulder height to the average cadet, Derlin jogged off of the bus with his fellow recruits, lining up among them against the side of the bus awaiting roll call. Still riding high on his whirlwind last 48 hours and seemingly oblivious to the fact that the forty-two young men whose names were called before him answered "Sir, yes sir!", when Derlin's name was called, he responded with a simple "woo."

"I said, Spurlock! Derlin!" Snyder screamed, marching up the line toward Derlin. "Sir?" Derlin replied, somewhat confused as to what he'd done to inspire such agitation so soon after arriving. This wasn't like jail, he wanted to be here and was happy to be. He wondered why the little fella with the hat was shouting at him. He could hear him just fine.

"You're Derlin Spurlock, soldier?" Snyder screamed again.

"Yes sir, that's me," he smiled, he stuck out his hand for a shake as Snyder slapped it away in disgust.

"I don't want to shake your hand, maggot!" he shouted. "Do not address me like I am your friend, understood? You drop and give me fifty, right now!"

"Fifty dollars?" Derlin hollered. "I ain't got that kind of money, I just joined up! Maybe after I get paid I can gi---"

"Pushups you retread!" Snyder yelled. "And make it 100 if you can count that high you dumb country sonofabitch."

"I can count real high," Derlin promised confidently as he slowly lowered himself to the ground.

"One fifty!" Snyder screamed, increasingly angry at Derlin's folksy, conversational inability to follow army protocol. His pale, freckled face was growing a vibrant flaming orange.

"Yeah, that too," Derlin replied nonchalantly, beginning his first and second half-hearted pushups with a sigh.

"Goddamnit Spurlock, two hundred!" the fuming drill sergeant shouted. "Do them quiet and report your ass straight to KP!"

The rest of the busload watched in silence over the next 12 minutes as Derlin struggled silently through his 200 pushups. He was doused in sweat and the shadow from Snyder's tiny frame did little to shield him from the noonday sun. Once he'd finally completed them, he lay in a puddle of his own drippings for a few seconds before feeling the gentle nudge of his drill sergeant's boot against his rib cage.

"Get your ass to the mess hall now, soldier," Snyder shouted, towering over Derlin's crumpled frame with his hands on his hips. "You're gonna be peeling potatoes till sundown. This is the Army of the United States of America, son, not a goddamn summer camp."

Managing to keep any outward reaction to himself, Derlin hoisted himself up from where he'd been wallowing in his own sweat mud and broke into a loose, lagging jog in the direction of the kitchen. He was struggling to follow the signs pointing his way, but with Snyder shouting directions at him from across the lawn, Derlin was soon able to locate the proper entrance. Ducking through a small door marked "KP," Derlin was soon face to face with the largest pile of potatoes he'd ever seen, along with five soldiers in metal folding chairs, quietly peeling away. The five of them looked up in unison, nodding to Derlin. They knew another KP duty man's face when they saw one and were happy to have another set of hands to help tackle the pile.

"Hey guys, I'm Derlin," Derlin offered, smiling and waving. "I reckon I'm supposed to help you fellas peel these taters cause I talked too much to the drill sergeant."

"So you met ol' Snyder eh?" a soldier laughed. "He's mean as a shit house rat and not much bigger than one." He laughed along with the other four men.

"Anyway, my name's Cleveland," the soldier began. "They call me that because I'm from Cleveland."

"Well I'll be!" Derlin said excitedly. "I thought they just had Alabama folks at this here army camp. I ain't never met nobody from that far up north before!"

"Oh, we've got folks from all over, sure," Cleveland replied, offering a handshake. "Over there, that's Tex, he's from Texas. That there's Other Tex, he's from Texas too. That's Memphis. Well, you guessed it, he's from Memphis. And over there, that's Brooklyn, he's from--"

The door slammed open with a bang as Sergeant Snyder stomped into the kitchen and surveyed the mountain of potatoes before him.

"I hear a lot of squawking and I don't see a lot of peeling, boys," Snyder began loudly. "Do you wanna live in here forever? Do you wanna tell your kids and grandkids you didn't get a chance to be a hero in battle because you were too stupid to do anything but peel potatoes?"

"Sorry, drill sergeant, sir," Other Tex offered.
"It won't happen again, drill sergeant, sir," Cleveland replied.

"We'll be quiet, drill sergeant, sir," Brooklyn added.

Snyder turned his eyes to Derlin, standing there quietly with his chest puffed out. He stared at him furiously for a few long seconds, giving him an up-down before sighing in disgust and stomping out of the kitchen, slamming the door behind him. The rest of the massive pile of potatoes was peeled in cautious silence as Derlin joined in. He was disappointed that their introductions had been interrupted as he had yet to learn where Brooklyn hailed from, assuming him to be an Alabama boy just like himself.

When Snyder returned to march them to their bunks later in the evening, it became quite obvious that he intended them to skip dinner and Derlin became quite glad that he'd eaten around half a dozen raw potatoes over the course of his peeling session. He was also rather happy to see that he was going to be staying in the same barracks as his five potato-peeling mates, sharing a bunk bed with Other Tex, just one down from Brooklyn and Memphis on one side, with Cleveland and Tex on the other side. Although it wasn't the most auspicious beginning to anyone's army career, Derlin was quite happy with his first day at boot camp and looked forward to what lay ahead as he worked toward his eventual goal, obtaining the position of Chief General.

"Hey Cleveland," Derlin whispered to the bunk next door. "Is this what it feels like to be an army hero?"

"I guess maybe this is a start," Cleveland replied quietly.

"I feel like I'm in a movie," Derlin smiled before drifting off to sleep, his jaw slackening. Soon, another gaping smile arrived on his sleeping face, he belched, and then began to snore.

Chapter 25

The next day began abruptly for Derlin and he got his first taste of the army morning routine that he would struggle so mightily to adapt to over the course of his time there. The morning trumpet blasts over the loudspeaker jolted him from his sleep and he sat up with a start, ramming his head on the steel bar supporting the upper bunk. By the time his days at Camp McQueen were done, he'd have a noticeable protrusion on his forehead from hitting the exact same spot every morning when he was startled awake, which would take months to fade away.

Along with his fellow soldiers, he'd shuffle out of bed, put on his uniform, boots and hat as quickly as he could and scramble to make his bed neatly before Drill Sergeant Snyder stomped through the door. Some mornings were easier than others, depending on how well he and 240 pounds of Other Tex were able to coordinate both making a bunk bed at the same time. After inspection ensuring that the bunks were made to Snyder's satisfaction, it would be time for the morning run around the perimeter of camp, which totaled just over three miles. Derlin was nearly the skinniest soldier in his barracks, but he struggled more with the cardiovascular aspects of boot camp than anyone else in his group, chalking his inadequacies up to his years of puffing away on pack after acrid pack of Old Indians.

Brooklyn too was skinny as a rail and Cleveland still had some baby fat on him, but Memphis, Tex and Other Tex were each 200+ pounds of farm muscle. It quickly became part of Derlin's morning routine to see the five of them leave him in the dust within a few hundred yards of the beginning of the run. By the time he'd finish, most of his barracks mates had been waiting for him, arms crossed, to complete the run for several minutes. Every man in the barracks had to finish the run before any man could head into the mess hall to eat and, though Derlin would indeed improve with time, he was consistently making his fellow soldiers late for breakfast, lunch and dinner each day and to say this caused resentment would be an understatement.

Aside from the support he received from his five potato peeling buddies from the KP, Derlin had not cut a very popular figure in his early days at boot camp and in a way it began to remind him of jail "but with nicer clothes." He assumed these early struggles were simply hurdles that every man had to overcome on his path to Chief General and began to remind himself that "Ain't nobody starts up as the best" each morning as his fellow recruits left him in the dust.

Derlin had grown quite used to being yelled at by authority figures for varying degrees of underperformance or loitering over the course of this life, but the verbal abuse Derlin was dealing with from Snyder and the other drill sergeants was beginning to get under his skin. Snyder barking at his heels as he shuffled through his basic training wasn't so much helping him strive to be a better soldier as it was just pissing him off, but Derlin managed to internalize it and keep his head down. He knew that his plans on returning to Mavis and the boys as an army hero would be dealt a serious blow if he decided to punch his drill sergeant in the mouth a week into basic training. Derlin would be reluctant to admit it, but Snyder's harassment was facilitating some internal growth which he'd lacked thus far in his life. Clovis had never been the type of father to yell, unless it was at something happening on the television or radio, and he had mostly dealt with Derlin's adolescent sass by returning it twofold. For the first time at the age of twenty-five, Derlin having to internalize his feelings instead of just popping off in the mouth if his feathers were rustled was very slowly building something his Grandpa Hoyt had called "character."

Regardless of his personal feelings about Snyder, he gave his 100% best at every one of his training exercises, it just happened that he was uniformly terrible at all of them. He was the slowest runner, the worst climber, far and away the worst shot. He could lift the least weight on the bench press, leg press and squat machine. Though he'd gone from squatting ten pounds to fifteen over the course of his first week, he held steady at his personal best of ⅔ of a pull-up, which was considered an army record for least impressive. Content to dangle listlessly for the remainder of his allotted pull-up time, Derlin was the subject of near-constant ridicule. During moments like this, Derlin would try to zone out from the abuse, picturing himself in an officer's uniform, dangling covertly into a Taj-Mahal-style palace to carry out a secret assassination plot or rescue the president's dog.

Doing his best, despite how poor of an effort this generally constituted, Derlin kept his head down during these early days of basic training. If jail had taught him nothing else, it was that being quiet and staring at the floor was a decent starting point to avoiding trouble. No matter what he did, Derlin couldn't seem to steer clear of Snyder's wrath entirely, but he did his best not to egg him on with attempts at kindness or friendliness, simply staring ahead blankly while he was being screamed at for polishing his boots poorly or missing large swaths of his face while shaving. He still ended up in KP more often than anyone else in his barracks, as Snyder seemed to take joy in inventing new infractions necessitating the peeling of potatoes. Sometimes various bunkmates would join him, but many times it was just him, alone with his folding chair and peeler for hours at a time.

Derlin felt he'd developed a casual friendship with Cleveland, Brooklyn, Memphis and the Tex's, but the five of them had been spending a lot more time following orders and a lot less time peeling potatoes since the evening he'd initially met them and he'd spend many of his evenings in KP staring at the empty folding chairs against the wall wishing that he had someone to talk to. Most nights, he'd arrive back to his bunk after lights out, still alone with his thoughts though he shared a room with a hundred other people.

In spirit with the general idea of basic training, Derlin's life became a routine. Unlike his fellow privates, Derlin wasn't particularly getting better, faster or stronger, but in keeping with his plan to keep his head down and get it over with he soon found himself six weeks deep into the nine week training program. He was quite proud of himself, trying to list in his head any accomplishments in his life up to this point beyond eating sandwiches and impregnating Mavis in which he'd made it more than two-thirds of the way through.

He felt like he was sweating constantly in this quest for personal betterment, whether during his daily exercises or potato peeling and the first tangible result of army life was that his right bicep and forearm began to grow markedly larger than his left from his evenings of peeling. Constantly he thought of Mavis, finding her and the boys to be all the motivation he needed to keep up his hard work instead of breaking away from his jogging group and hiding in a ditch until he could escape to the forest. Though Derlin had never written a love letter in his life, he began crafting a letter to Mavis, writing secretly after lights out. He was far from a master penman and would usually only crank out a few shaky words per night, scribbling and erasing as often as he put lead to paper. Once words turned into actual sentences, Derlin was pleased with the robust, positively-embellished letter he'd written. Hagiographically written, it glorified several aspects of his elapsed time in Camp McQueen and took pains to avoid any failures or disciplinary measures. It took him a week and a half to complete this letter, which read as follows:

Dear Baby,

I just wanted to tell you that I am verry hard at work to become a better man and husbin and daddy, all three at the same time. And a better Sittisen to Coverdale. All four of those things. I want you and your folks to be prideful of me and I want the boys to have somebody to look up to for a daddy so I decided to join up with the Army of America. It's real hard but it's good I guess. I have ben here six weeks and they say it'll be nine weeks and then I get to go be an army hero. Seems like everybody over where we're going is named Charlie, I don't know how I'm gonna tell 'em apart. I guess we're going to fight England cause Charlie sounds like a pretty brittish name to me. I hope I don't have to fight the Beatles, but if I see them little Herman's Hermits fellers lined up in the foxhole I'm gonna drop the damn hammer on them. I ain't gotten promoted up to Chief General yet but I'm sure there gonna make me one soon. Ha ha. They make us do a lot of exercise to get strong for being war heroes and I'm just about the fastest and strongest fella here. They make us do all the training every day even if it's hot and sometimes I think Army is sorta like jail but for exercising. I have been eating lots of potato's and think there real good. I have made friends from all over America! Cleveland is from Cleveland in Ohio! My friend Memphis is from up Memphis ways in Tenisee. There's Tex and Other Tex (he's my bunk mate) and they are both from Texas (the state!). Also theirs Brooklyn but I don't know where he is from yet. I will find out soon I hope. I told them they could call me Alabama but they said it would be weird since we're in Alabama. So they just call me my name. Derlin. I miss you and love you and I miss and love the babies. I'mma do rightly by you, baby. I'mma be the best Army man I can be so you and the boys can be prideful of having the Spurlock name. I hope your job is good and I hope you can buy lot's of meat and candy for the babies. Tell your mama and deddy that I said hey.

Love,
Power Sargent Derlin Spurlock, Esq.

To say the least, Derlin was putting a bit of a spit shine on his first six of weeks in the army, but he wasn't going to win back his beloved Mavis by telling her he ran slower than anyone else there, hardly talked to anybody, spent most of his time peeling potatoes and was a terrible climber. She didn't need to know that he couldn't shoot through a barn door if he was standing inside it. In his mind, by the time his grand plan of betterment was completed he'd be a fully formed army hero and she'd be none the wiser to his early days of spinning his tires in the proverbial mud. Telling her how winded he became while making the bed wasn't going to do him any favors. Still he was trying his best and in doing so was slowly becoming marginally less worse at things.

For the first time since he'd arrived, and on a 20 mile march no less, Derlin realized that he was keeping up with the rest of his fellow recruits even with the 50 pound pack on his back that he usually emptied out into some bushes once he fell behind. It was the first time in his young career that he'd managed to keep pace in an exercise and he credited the success not to his daily exercises but to the skills he gained during his days lugging stolen groceries through the forest. Drill Sergeant Snyder had noticed this progress and as he marched back and forth from the front and back of the group, shouting "Thanks for keeping up today, Spurlock!" as he jogged by.

Derlin watched as Snyder made his way to the far front of the pack and took the opportunity to make some small talk with Cleveland and the gang.

"Man it's hotter'n a jacked off bobcat out here today," he said to no one in particular. Brooklyn, Cleveland and Tex murmured agreements while Other Tex and Memphis nodded their heads in affirmation.

Derlin thought for a moment, pondering a way to engage his new friends in some interesting conversation.

"Do y'all like wrestling?" Derlin asked happily. It was taking every ounce of strength he had to keep up, but doing so had given him quite the psychological boost and he was feeling particularly engaging.

"Yeah man I love it!" Memphis whispered excitedly. The other men nodded in agreement and began to compare favorites.

"I was always a big fan of "Pistol" Pervis Money when I was a kid," Memphis began. "His elbow could take down a bear! They say it really did when he won his first title down in the Ozarks back in '38."

"No way!" Cleveland began, "I saw his son "The Eagle" Elvis Money wrestle the Steel Kaiser up at the Cleveland Coliseum before I joined up!"

"Man I hate the fuckin' Steel Kaiser," Derlin added, panting, getting a resounding agreement from the gang. "That one time he hit "The Navajo" Ricky Yamashita in the head with that big German beer stein on TV and blood went everywhere, I almost drove to Tuscaloosa to hit him with my car."

Brooklyn laughed loudly. Loud enough to get Snyder's attention from the front of the line.

"Oh man, that's great," he began, not noticing Snyder quickly heading their way. "My favorite, back when I was growing up in--"

"Private just what in the hell is so goddamned funny back here?" Snyder screamed.

"Nothing, drill sergeant. Sorry sir! Won't happen again, sir." Brooklyn replied as all six men stopped in their tracks.

Snyder peered up at the six men, sizing each of them up, pausing at Derlin to wince and sigh.

"I'm about tired of hearing y'all boys are sorry!" Snyder shouted. "Y'all boys are gettin' real good at peeling potatoes and you're gonna get plenty more practice soon as we get back from this little stroll. Y'all gonna have the strongest wrists in the army!"

"Sir, yes drill sergeant, sir," they replied in unison.

"Now let's see some hustle out of you," Snyder scowled as he jogged off.

That evening, as the six of them sat in their metal folding chairs, peeling their thousands of potatoes, they continued to swap wrestling stories. They'd been friendly enough and acquaintances by proximity so far during their army days, but it was on this evening that they truly became friends.

"Y'all remember that time at Thanksgiving Thunderdome when Kentucky Slim got his ear bitten off by Pirate Swantoon?" Other Tex asked.

"You're damn right!" Tex hollered. "He finished that match and wrestled the next night in a tag team match with The Fur Trapper against… dang, who was that big, fat tag team of colored fellas?"

"'The Great Shasta' and 'The Juice Moose' Plum Tucker?" Brooklyn asked. "The ones who came out dressed like train conductors?

"Yeah that's them!" Other Tex replied. "They were good!"

"The night before I left for army, I got to see Gary "Greased Lightning" Witherspoon fight "Cowboy" Steve Rodriguez on TV in a steel cage, watching in my motel room," Derlin offered. "That was cool, but Ricky "The Navajo" Yamashita is probably my favorite in the world."

"The Navajo is a bum!" Brooklyn shouted. "He's worse than Sheriff Jimmy Poutine. He couldn't hold a candle to "The Magic Man" Steve Jams. Back when I was growing up in--"

"Steve Jams is the worst character ever," Derlin shot back as Cleveland and Memphis began to laugh. "He comes to the ring dressed like a damn magician and he don't even do no good magic except when he hypnotizes the referee. And everybody knows that that ain't cause he's good at magic it's just cause referees are so dumb I reckon it's just way easier to hypnotize 'em. There's no way he beats Death Valley Daryl or Goose Gunderson for the title if he doesn't hypnotize the referee first."

"You're right," Cleveland began. "But it's harder than you think coming up with a good wrestling gimmick. For every Goose Gunderson, there's a Steeltoe Kid. Remember him? Just some skinny fella in steel toed boots kicking everybody in their dicks and shins."

"It ain't that hard to come up with an idea," Derlin replied confidently.

"Oh really?" Tex asked. "You got one?"

"I sure do," Derlin replied, setting down his peeler and crossing his arms.

"And?" Brooklyn asked.

"Well," Derlin began. "I'd be called The Nicotine Wolf and I'd come to the ring smoking a cigarette, maybe two at one time, and I'm dressed like a wolf and I'm all badass and I never put down my cigarette during the match but I still win cause I blow smoke in my opponent's eyes and then kick 'em in the stomach and punch 'em in the back of the head and pin them. Then when I get up I climb up on the turnbuckle and I howl, and it sounds like I'm a real wolf but really it's just a signal to all the ladies in the crowd letting them know that I like to party."

The room was quiet for a few seconds as everyone stared at Derlin. At once, the other five burst into laughter while Derlin began to nervously chuckle.

"That is awesome!" Brooklyn hollered.

Cleveland wiped tears from his eyes as the others continued to double over with laughter.

"What?" Derlin asked earnestly. "I'd probably be the Champion of the World."

Tex stopped laughing long enough to muster a reply.

"Spurlock you couldn't even beat Brooklyn in a wrestling match, let alone somebody like the Steel Kaiser or Ricky Yamashita," Tex roared.

"Oh yeah?" Derlin asked. "I may not be as fast or strong as any of y'all, but I guarantee I could beat anybody in this whole dang camp in a good old-fashioned wrestling match. I'll fly off that turnbuckle. I'll use a chair. Can't nobody stop The Nicotine Wolf once he gets going!"

"You might be onto something here," Cleveland smiled. "I bet we could get a lot of folks in on a big wrestling tournament around here. It could be like a big farewell event before we ship off to Vietnam! Might not be quite a USO show but it could still be a hell of a good time. That way we can see if Spurlock's really got the mustard for all this bullshit he's talking."

"I've got plenty of mustard," Derlin hollered.

"We'd have to keep Snyder from finding out about it though," Memphis offered. "He'd flip his lid and Vietnam or not, we'd be peeling potatoes in this room till the cows come home."

"Cows can't peel no potatoes," Derlin responded sharply. "I'll beat everybody in our barracks and then I'll beat Snyder for the title," he boasted, puffing his chest out.

"Oh sure you will," Brooklyn laughed. "You'll get your chance if we get this idea off the ground. Until then, let's keep it on the hush-hush whether you're beating the drill sergeant for the title or not there, Spurlock."

"Probably a good idea," Other Tex replied.

From there, they slowly returned to peeling their required potatoes. Gradually, as the potato pile got smaller throughout the evening, their plan began to take shape for a secret wrestling tournament with Derlin periodically howling and brashly boasting that anyone else choosing to enter was just wasting their time. It would be nearly dawn by the time they'd finish their peeling, the hours giving way to tournament ideas, raunchy jokes and more old wrestling tales from their lifetimes of enjoyment. They'd regret only getting 45 minutes of sleep when the trumpets blasted over the loudspeaker the next morning, but they were content in the fact that their plans had so quickly begun to take shape. They might just get this thing off the ground.

Chapter 26

Derlin slogged through the morning run as best he could manage, getting left behind by the group even quicker than he had in his early days of training. His back ached from spending nearly 12 hours in a metal folding chair and his already-dull brain ached for a few more hours of precious sleep. Despite his morning sluggishness, Derlin remained confident in his boasts of the evening prior. He made it a point at the beginning of the run to begin sizing up each of his possible opponents before they disappeared over the hills or curves in front of him. They were almost uniformly much larger and in comically better shape than he, but Derlin liked his chances if, as he'd put it the evening prior, "The Nicotine Wolf has a chance to spread his wings and fly."

When reminded of the fact that traditionally, wolves don't have wings, Derlin had responded with a sharp "This one does!" He peeled potatoes silently for the next twenty minutes, lopping them to bits with an aggressive motion leaving his potatoes around ⅓ the size of his comrades.

By the time lunch arrived, Derlin was famished and exhausted but also giddy to have a chance to actually discuss further tournament plans without fear of Snyder's eavesdropping. When he arrived at the mess hall, he was behind Cleveland and the gang in line by about five minutes and by the time he arrived at their table, they were already deep in discussion. Their main goal, as they'd first determined the evening prior, was to maintain secrecy while simultaneously informing as many fellow cadets as they could. While a sizable tournament would lend more credence to Derlin's prophetical claim of being a few well-landed shots from becoming "Champion of the Army, or even the Whole World Probably" it would be more difficult to keep quiet if it became particularly large. Certainly, Snyder and the other drill sergeants wouldn't cotton to a professional wrestling tournament. Derlin doubted they shared his ideas of how the cadets should be spending their time while training for a war.

While the rest of the group focused on the logistics for keeping such a tournament under wraps, Derlin set to work brainstorming on a name for the event. He was keen to create a name to rival the "Thanksgiving Thunderdomes" and "Halloween Hootenannies" which had so jubilantly filled his adolescence, furrowing his brow as he stared intently into his remaining lunch. He was silent for nearly five minutes and unblinking to boot. He cycled through rhyming but mundane titles like "Race for the Base" and "The Alabama Jammer" before his eyes lit up and he shook himself from his slack-jawed haze.

"What do y'all think about calling it 'The King of McQueen?'" he asked excitedly, absentmindedly placing his elbow into his quickly congealing mashed potatoes and gravy. Before wiping it with his napkin he briefly tried to lick it off, but when this proved impossible he gave up and returned his attention to the group.

"You know what, Spurlock?" Brooklyn began, "that's actually pretty damn good. I think we should do it."

"For serious?" Derlin asked happily.

"Yeah, I think it's great!" Texas added as Other Tex nodded in affirmation.

"Well hot dog!" Derlin brayed gleefully. "I got to name my babies that time but I ain't ever gotten to name a wrestling tournament before."

"Well then it's a big day for ya, pal," Cleveland chimed in, leaning in closely to the table. "Now all you've gotta do is win the damn thing. Hey, Brooklyn, how many people do we have signed up to wrestle so far?"

"Counting Spurlock, we've got 13. Three more folks and we've got ourselves a tournament!" Brooklyn whispered happily.

"I found the perfect place to have it, too!" Tex added. "In the basement of the old gym there's an empty swimming pool and we could take some old gym mats and rig up a ring real easy. Plus there'd be plenty of room for folks to come and watch."

"That is awesome!" Derlin said excitedly, struggling to keep his voice down. "Man this thing is really gonna come together. When are we gonna have it?"

"I heard Snyder is going on leave next weekend to take his cow of a wife to a lake upstate somewhere for their anniversary," Other Tex whispered. "With him out of the way, we won't have nobody on our asses and we should be able to pull this tournament off without a hitch!"

"You aren't worried that the other drill sergeants will wonder where all the cadets are or why they're all trying to sneak into the basement of the old gym?" Cleveland asked quietly.

"Not if we do it after lights out," Brooklyn replied. "Plus it'll be on the weekend. You know most of the sergeants have some truck shop waitress they're laying into on Saturdays anyway. You can smell it on half of 'em Monday morning."

"Ain't gonna be no drill sergeants to hear The Nicotine Wolf howl," Derlin said to no one in particular. "Best get out of the way when the Wolf Train is on the tracks."

June 22, 1968

Mavis was just returning home from a morning of shopping with the boys when she saw the familiar scrawl of the letter sitting on the kitchen counter. Seeing her name, written in poorly formed block capital letters, Mavis knew it was from Derlin as soon as she laid her eyes on it. She set Randy and Ollie gently onto the floor and ran to snatch the letter up from the counter, tearing it open hungrily. She began to cry softly as she read Derlin's glowing letter detailing his meteoric rise up the army ranks. Tears, not out of sadness but in joy that he'd seemingly taken their late night driveway conversation to heart and turned such a corner so quickly.

Randy and Ollie cooed blankly from the kitchen floor as she finished reading his florid text. She returned to them, kneeling down with the letter, holding it up to meet their unblinking gazes.

"Your daddy is gonna be an army hero," she smiled. Ollie toppled over from his sitting position and began to gum at a small piece of discarded Charleston Chew which he'd found on the floor. His poorly coordinated movements and smacking maw reminded Mavis of Derlin when he'd spill a Panther Cat on the floor of the windmill, lapping it up from the hay.

She missed him dearly, but she stood firm in her vow that he wouldn't be allowed to return until she truly felt he was a man deserving of his family, even though he did seem to be genuinely on his merry way. At the moment she finished his letter, she had never been prouder of him to that point in their young lives together. Deep down she knew that despite his growing pains, he was indeed turning into a man that could command respect. As he often said, "Someone the babies can be prideful of."

June 23, 1968

Derlin picked his nose vigorously, mining his nostril as deeply as possible, tongue stuck out in concentration before wiping the results onto the underside of the top bunk of his bed. It had been "lights out" for over an hour and his buddies were all sound asleep, but Derlin was restless with excitement about the King of McQueen tournament. He'd got the idea that it was supposed to be a surprise, but he'd overheard Cleveland and Other Tex talking about fashioning a real title belt to award the winner. Never doubting himself for a minute, he immediately began thinking of the belt as a soon-to-be-acquired family heirloom that he could one day present to the boys in some sort of ceremony. Something that would be cherished by the Spurlock clan for generations to come.

He'd spend the next nine days lost in a haze, dreaming of his soon to be wrestling glory. He barely slept at night and ate like a horse during the day, all the while continuing to be incrementally less terrible at the training exercises. The time would flash by and over it, Derlin would dedicatedly put on what appeared to be nearly ten fresh pounds of muscle. He'd periodically disappear from the bunk after lights out, only telling Other Tex that he was working on his wolf costume in a secret location "somewhere deep in the bowels of Camp McQueen."

Cleveland and the gang would pass him sometimes when they snuck out after lights out to work at building the ring. Mostly, they'd only see his silhouette perched on top of the barracks, or somewhere near the fence shrouded in shadows. Every so often, they'd hear a distant howl or catch a faint whiff of the unmistakable leaden tang of an Old Indian cigarette.

"Spurlock sure is taking this seriously," Brooklyn whispered to Cleveland one night as they passed him in the shadows, identifiable only by the lit cherries of the three cigarettes he was smoking at one time.

"Well, he did say nobody is gonna stop him from being champion," Cleveland said, shrugging. "I feel like everybody else who said 'sure, yeah, okay' and signed up for that tournament is just gonna show up the night of and try to have some fun. I don't see anybody else leaping from rooftop to rooftop of the barracks in a fucking wolf costume trying to train up for this thing."

"Well, yeah," Memphis began. "Literally like every other guy we signed up for this thing has at least a hundred pounds on him though, I don't think they've got anything to worry about."

"It's not them I'm worried about," Memphis continued. "It's Spurlock. I know he's been, um… training really hard since we came up with this idea. I saw him benching more than just the bar today! He had a ten pound weight on each side. But he's not the biggest, strongest or smartest fella out there and he's been smoking like four packs of cigarettes a day training up for his damn wolf gimmick."

"You worried he's gonna crack?" Brooklyn asked.

"I don't know, I mean there's a lot going on in that head of his," Tex added.

"Seems like he may have a screw or two loose in there, but he sure is determined about this and he really does mean well. Keeps talking about becoming an army hero to 'get his family back' and I'm not as much worried about him getting hurt as I am what'll happen if he loses."

They heard a faint howl from a rooftop a few buildings down, before seeing a shadowy figure leap from a barrack roof onto a dumpster. It paused on the dumpster lid for a moment, lighting first one cigarette and then a second from the tip before leaping from the dumpster and front-rolling back into the darkness.

Chapter 27

July 2, 1968

The Friday before the tournament, Derlin was already wide awake by the time the morning trumpets blared over the loudspeaker. He'd been up since 2:30, having snuck into his familiar KP station to practice his wrestling moves on large sacks of potatoes in the darkness of the kitchen. Though the potato sacks only weighed around 50 pounds themselves, Derlin's time power slamming and suplexing them had already begun to hone his skills noticeably. He'd returned a half hour before dawn to put the finishing touches on his wolf costume and still had a bit of work to do when the trumpets jostled him from his concentration. As the morning blasts concluded, a voice came over the speaker and began to address the cadets loudly.

"Attention all staff and cadets of Camp McQueen! We have just been informed that at 1200 hours today, Camp McQueen will be receiving a surprise visit from President Lyndon Baines Johnson as part of his tour of army bases in the south on his way home for Fourth of July vacation in Texas. All cadets are to dress and report to Field One for gun drills in preparation for the president's arrival. That is all."

"Holy shit, did you hear that guys?" Brooklyn hollered. "Lyndon Johnson is coming to Camp McQueen! I've gotta call my ma!"

"Oh, where's your mama live?" Derlin asked amicably, looking up briefly from the haphazard stitching of his costume.

The rest of the gang began to scramble to dress, digging for their "special occasion" uniforms and shining their boots as quickly as they could.

"What are all y'all fussing about?" Derlin asked, hardly bothering to look up again from his wolf costume as his friends rushed back and forth around him and their bunks.

"Lyndon B. Johnson is gonna be here in 5 hours, Spurlock," Cleveland said. "We've gotta get our asses in gear. Tex and Other Tex are about to shit themselves they're so excited."

"Johnson who?" Derlin asked, finally looking up as he cocked his head to one side and looked at them quizzically.

"The President of the United States, goddamnit! LBJ!" Tex hollered.

"Man, the only LBJ I care about is Little Baby Jesus," Derlin said. He was like the rest of the Spurlock clan, as lazily secular as they come, but remained quite pleased with the speed of his one-liner. He was not a man of quips, but would remember the line again in the future during a news program about the opening and dedication of Johnson's library and the President's death years later.

"I ain't got time for this, I gotta finish making this costume as badass as possible," he continued, shaking his head. "Y'all seen my feathers?"

"Spurlock, he's the President of the country and you're in the army. You can't not go," Brooklyn said quietly, not wanting other cadets in the bunk to hear and possibly cause a scene.

"I didn't say I wasn't going," Derlin snapped. "I just said I wasn't happy about it. Now I'mma have to finish my wolf costume later on tonight and I need to be getting as much sleep-rest as I can so I can be refresh-ified before the big day. But the president don't care about ol' Derlin."

"I'm sure he'd care if he knew about it," Tex panned, laughing.

"Oh, sure he would," Other Tex chimed in, nodding enthusiastically. "My dad says that LBJ is actually really big into wrestling. Says he saw him at an armory show down in Stonewall back when he was first running for senator."

"Is he really?" Derlin said, his mood softening. "Imagine that, President of the whole world and he likes wrestling just like you and me."

"Well, he's just President of the United States," Brooklyn started. "Not the whole entire world."

"Same thing," Derlin replied, lost in thought. He carefully placed his wolf costume in his trunk, tossing his uniform carelessly on the bed. He began to shine his boots in silence as the wheels slowly began to turn behind his blank expression. At the behest of his friends, Derlin quickened his pace and dressed himself, properly affixing his hat about three seconds before Snyder burst through the door. He let out a quick sigh of relief as the cadets awaited their instructions for preparation.

Snyder was even more agitated than usual, clearly nervous and excited about the impending visit. Naturally, he took his excitement out on his men, berating them for shabby appearances, crooked hats and scuffed boots. Clearly he had not expected so monumental a visitor to his shabby little Alabama army base, let alone on a day where he was a few hours away from vacation time. He'd imagined that surely his shaking hands with the leader of the free world was going to provide an uptick to the amorous action he saw from the missus over the weekend, but still he hoped the president's visit didn't go too long into the late afternoon. Snyder was sure that the president had better places to be than Camp McQueen and thus wouldn't doddle too long at one base or another on his tour through the south.

As Snyder shouted down private after private for minor uniform infractions, he paused at Derlin, eyeing him up and down a few times before glaring at him in silence for several seconds. Derlin stood perfectly still, staring straight ahead and finally after what seemed like an eternity Snyder moved on in disgust. After admonishing another handful of privates, Snyder marched everyone in the barracks out the door in the direction of Field One.

From several hundred feet away, Derlin could see a large wooden stage being hastily erected, with red, white and blue bunting draped over the edges. A small group of chairs were being assembled for the officers and Presidential entourage and a podium from which the President would speak. As Derlin and the gang arrived, each man was handed a wooden rifle; as greenhorns they were not being trusted with live ammunition or actual weapons around the president.

Arriving to the field at just after 7:30 am, the men would run practice rifle drills in the morning sun for four hours in preparation. It was a relatively simple routine, though many of the cadets weren't familiar enough with their rifles to make the necessary maneuvers and many a "weapon" was dropped during the rehearsal process. Derlin however took to the rifle twirling and showmanship like a fish to water. His many experiences in wielding a rake in what he felt were borderline life or death situations had readied him for deftly handling a military rifle, particularly a wooden dummy one that couldn't shoot, and he was among the most impressive soldiers at a task for the first time since his arrival at Camp McQueen when he set the record for quickest disciplinary assignment. His recent training had also stimulated a slight improvement in Derlin's hand-eye coordination and he was beginning to feel mildly impressed with his own movements.

Eager to show his prowess, Derlin was just as tired and sweaty as anyone in the group when the first signs of the presidential motorcade came rolling over the hill. A limousine surrounded by four Alabama State Trooper vehicles, eight motorcycle cops and two black vehicles carrying secret servicemen came slowly driving through the camp, each with multiple tiny American flags affixed. As the motorcade rolled to a stop, President Johnson emerged, waving to the crowd and shaking hands with a small group of army folks who Derlin didn't know, aside from the fact that they looked important. Johnson climbed the stairs to the freshly built podium slowly as a mixture of military and law enforcement folks spread behind him. The seats at the foot of the stage quickly filled with Camp McQueen higher-ups while Derlin and his fellow soldiers remained at attention with their salutes held high.

"Good afternoon, soldiers." President Johnson began. "I have to say, in the past couple of weeks, I've visited army bases up and down from Tennessee to Florida and Georgia and back and I have not seen a finer looking base than this beautiful place that you call Camp McGreen."

Derlin began to clap loudly but was the only one to do so and quickly realized the error of his ways, returning sheepishly to attention.

"Camp McGreen, with your hearty troops and valiant leadership, you will no doubt be valuable contributors in our overseas efforts in Vietnam. I salute each and every one of you and thank you for your service. Camp McGreen, you are truly one of the best army bases in all of these wonderful United States of America! God bless each and every one of you, God bless Camp McGreen and God Bless America!" the President concluded.

The seated officers and entourage rose to their feet in unison and burst into applause, with the standing rows of soldiers soon following. As the applause concluded and Johnson did 45 seconds of his best smiling and waving at the cadets, he took a seat on the stage next to some higher ups and the accompanying music began for the rehearsed rifle routine.

Derlin's plan had gradually hatched over the morning and even he considered its success to be a long shot, He knew that, while it might earn him enough potato peeling time to last through whatever war it was people kept talking about, going off-script from the routine and really showing his prowess in rifle tossing was sure to get the president's attention. As Derlin imagined, seeing his magnificent rifle twirls and finely-honed sense of pageantry, Johnson would seek him out for praise, at which point Derlin would casually invite the President of the United States of America to his secret basement wrestling tournament.

Admittedly an unlikely pursuit, Derlin was still going to try and make the most of his best opportunity to have a major dignitary watch the Nicotine Wolf in action. Derlin marched along in step with his fellow troops for the first minute or so of the routine, as "Stars & Stripes" blared over the loudspeakers. Timing the rotation of the groups to where he was nearly front and center to the podium, Derlin finally broke from the routine. He howled, spread his arms like the wings of a bird with his rifle balancing on his neck, spinning out of formation with the pageantry of an Indian rain dance. He spun forward a few feet toward the stage before he stopped, facing the President while the remaining troops continued their practiced routine. Derlin saluted, howled again and threw his rifle a good 20 feet straight up in the air, twirling like a baton. He caught it where he stood with a quick stab of the wrist and began to twirl it back and forth between his hands in a routine that could have easily been presented as the long lost footage of a strange, hillbilly-themed Akira Kurosawa film. He continued his twirling and periodic howling for the remainder of the scheduled routine, throwing the rifle in the air once more, falling to his knees, catching it underhanded and offering it gently toward the president with a solemn bow as the music concluded.

The senior officials that shared the stage paused for a moment, mouths agape, unsure of what they just saw. President Johnson immediately burst out into joyous laughter, rising to his feet and clapping heartily. They slowly began to clap along with the president, eyeing each other nervously.

"That's the most amazing thing I've ever seen," the President mused to drill sergeant Snyder, who'd gone from his usual ghost pale to beet red over the course of the routine. "Is that what you're teaching troops here sergeant? This! This, gentleman, is why we are the greatest country in the world."

"We just try to teach them to be the best, sir," Snyder replied humbly, trying to hide his shock at the president's reaction. He'd been ready to tar and feather Derlin when he'd first broken rank, but he also was quite happy with the president's accolades and more than happy to claim responsibility for Derlin's apparent skill. He was mortified when the routine started, worried that President Johnson would be upset or off-put by Derlin's high-energy and unorthodox routine, but surprisingly Snyder actually shared his opinion that the whole thing was particularly impressive. He still disliked Derlin immensely and couldn't wait until the day he left Camp McQueen forever, but now Snyder congratulated himself on being such an excellent drill sergeant that he could convert Derlin from a wet sack of feed with a cigarette to a highly-trained rifle-twirling impresser of presidents in a matter of a few weeks. He didn't understand the howling, but he could leave that part out when telling the wife about it once they got to their lake cabin. Snyder had zoned out a bit entertaining these thoughts, but was quickly brought back to Earth.

"Now that is one young man I have to meet before I go," President Johnson smiled. "I'd imagine he's probably one of your best new recruits here."

"Excuse me, sir?" Snyder replied, shaking his head in bewilderment. "I don't believe I heard you right, my apologies."

"That young fella there, the leader of your rifle routine," President Johnson continued. "He's like a white James Brown once that music gets going. I'd imagine that he's one of the top men you've got here at Camp McGreen."

"You mean *Spurlock?*" Snyder replied, trying poorly to hide his shock.

"Spurlock, eh?" President Johnson continued. "I'd like to shake that young man's hand. I am seriously impressed. Let's get him for the photo-ops, he's perfect."

"Sir, with all due respect," Snyder continued, wincing. "Spurlock ain't exactly the next John Wayne coming up through the ranks. Before that little display, pretty much the only thing he's been good at here is smoking cigarettes and peeling potatoes. I can find you all sorts of better young recruits to meet than him."

"A potato peeler, eh?" President Johnson replied. "Ah, the ol' KP. I got into a little trouble myself growing up, you know. That just shows this Spurlock fella has some spunk to him. Some character. Sounds like my kind of soldier."

"Oh he's a character, sir." Snyder replied, sighing. "I mean, pretty much any other soldier here would be a better choice but if you're sure he's the one you want for your picture taking of course I'm happy to get him for you."

"I'd be much obliged, sergeant," President Johnson smiled, patting Snyder on his shoulder. "Can't wait to meet him."

By the time Snyder was sent on his errand, most of the men had returned to their barracks from the field as the stage began a hasty deconstruction as quickly as it had been built. Nearly the entire barracks were whooping and hollering and cheering Derlin for his impromptu performance as he arrived back, but he ignored most of them except for a few quiet "Yeah, thanks brother's" and set back to work almost immediately on his wolf costume. No sooner had he made his first stitch, Snyder burst through the door.

"Spurlock!" Snyder shouted. "All you boys quiet the fuck down, right now. Where is Spurlock's stupid ass at?"

"Goddamnit," Derlin whispered to himself, sighing loudly and cramming his wolf costume quickly back into his trunk.

"I'm right here, drill sergeant!" he replied, standing at attention next to his bunk. He was certain that he was in trouble.

"Well, Mr. Fancy-Pants rifle-twirling man," Snyder began loudly. He stalked slowly toward Derlin, eyeing him up and down ominously. "Think you're pretty smooth pulling a stunt like that on my watch?"

Derlin remained silent, visions of mounds upon mounds of potatoes dancing slowly in his mind. He pictured himself as a hunchbacked 40-year-old, still sitting on the same metal chair next to a slowly dwindling pile of potatoes, his shining and muscular peeling arm massively asymmetrical in comparison to his potato-holding arm.
"Well guess what?" Snyder continued, seeming angrier with each passing word. "Each base the president stops at on this little tour, he picks out one soldier for his big photo-op for the newspapers before he hits the road. Usually, he picks the strongest, or the brightest, or somebody important. And today for some reason he's choosing you, Spurlock. Looks like your little stunt paid off. So get your shit together and come with me, because we're meeting him at the Camp McQueen sign in ten minutes."

Derlin's eyes lit up and he let out a long slow gasp. As he'd returned to the barracks, he'd begun to think his idea was a bust, but it had worked after all. The gang knew nothing of this plan, but Cleveland and the others began to cheer again, leaping to Derlin's side, hugging him and patting him on the back. He stood there silently for a few seconds before Snyder's barks got his attention.

"I said get yourself ready, Spurlock!" he shouted. "The President of the United States is not going to wait on Derlin Spurlock."

Derlin and Snyder jogged across the base to the entrance, seeing the President's limo, flags waving, waiting for them by the entrance sign. At Snyder's behest, they quickened their pace and arrived at the sign a few moments later, both a little sweatier than they'd have liked to be.

"Oh, there you are son!" President Johnson said happily, emerging from the shade of the limo. We really have to be getting on the road, but I told my driver that I just had to wait and meet you before we left. Spurlock is it?"

Derlin's eyes went wide and the color drained from his face. He gulped, his imagined confidence escaping him through the ears.

"Yes sir, Mr. President Johnson," he replied shakily. "I'm Spurlock."

"What's your first name, son?" President Johnson smiled, shaking Derlin's hand.

"Derlin, Mr. President Johnson, sir," he replied, clearing his throat cautiously both before and after. His vision of smoothly inviting the president to King of McQueen with the casual demeanor of a bar buddy was evaporating before his eyes.

"That was quite the show you put on out there today, Derlin," President Johnson continued. "May I call you Derlin?"

"Yes sir, Mr. President Johnson," Derlin replied bleakly, nodding quickly.

"Where'd you learn how to move like that Derlin?" President Johnson asked. "I have to say I was mighty impressed by it."

"Well, sir," Derlin continued. "I used to do it with a rake a bunch to protect my family and stuff but now I'm an army man so they let me do it with a wooden rifle instead on account of they want us to be war heroes."

"Are you gonna be a war hero, son?" President Johnson asked, placing his hand on Derlin's shoulder as the local newspaper cameras flashed. Snyder coughed violently.

"I'd imagine so," Derlin replied with a smile, making his first facial expression of the encounter. "I wanna be all sorts of heroes."

"Do you now?" President Johnson asked, raising his eyebrows. "Like what?"

"Well, sir," Derlin began, his confidence slowly rising once more. "I always heard from folk that you're a pretty big wrestling fan. Ain't you?"

"You know it, son," President Johnson said, patting Derlin on the shoulder firmly. "Ever since I was a boy, when my dad took me to see "Pistol" Pervis Money wrestle a bear for his first World Title, somewhere way up in the Ozarks back in '27. I still go to the shows whenever they come through DC if I don't have any other, you know, more diplomatic obligations."

"Yes sir, I bet being the President is hard," Derlin said, waiting for the proper moment to arise.

Johnson chuckled.

Derlin glanced at Snyder, who was going back and forth between checking his watch and flirting with a female newspaper reporter, paying no attention to the conversation between him and the president.

"You know, sir," Derlin continued, leaning in slightly. "Me and some of the other troops are having a big-time secret wrestling tournament here tomorrow night. Sixteen men for the base championship before we all go fight in England. None of the sergeants know about it because they'd probably get real mad and not let us do it. If you like my rifle twirlin' you should come see me wrestle in the ring! I'm going to be the champion of the whole thing I reckon. It's gonna be in the basement of the old gym if you want to sneak in but you'll have to be really quiet so we don't get caught cause ol' Snyder over there'll shit his britches if he knows we're doing this."

President Johnson stared at Derlin silently for a moment, then glanced over at Snyder, now checking his teeth in the side mirror of the presidential limousine.

"Son, are you inviting the president to your wrestling match?" President Johnson smiled, looking down at Derlin with a doting, fatherly stare.

"Yes sir," Derlin said bashfully, hanging his head.

"Well I'd love to!" President Johnson continued, slapping his leg. "You know, we're supposed to stop in some armpit in Mississippi tomorrow before I get home to Texas for my little vacation, but I think we can say something came up and the ol' president can't make it after all! I saw a motor lodge on the way in, big enough for the whole entourage to stay in. We'll saddle up there and I'll sneak back tomorrow night with a couple of secret service fellas. How's that sound?"

Derlin, never a man with the springiest lower jaw, stood silently with his mouth agape for several seconds before shaking himself from his stupor. He had never expected in a million years that the president would accept his invitation and he was beside himself with excitement.

"Of course sir, that's totally fine sir," Derlin whispered gleefully.

"I saw the old gym on my walking tour of McGreen today," President Johnson continued matter-of-factly. "We'll breach the fence behind it, then I can sneak in the side door with my secret service and I'm sure we can find our way down to the basement. What time's the bell?"

"E-Eight o'clock sir," Derlin stammered.

"Fine, just fine," President Johnson continued. "Can I bring whiskey?"

"Of course you can bring whiskey, sir," Derlin replied. "You're the president!"

"Excellent, soldier," President Johnson replied. "Now let's turn and smile for the cameras one more time."

He grabbed Derlin's hand in a firm shake and Derlin offered a toothy grin to the cameras. Just as soon as the strange encounter had began, it was over and President Johnson was marching toward his limousine. Derlin was waving awkwardly when the president turned to address him once more.

"By the way son," he began. "What's your ring name?"

"The Nicotine Wolf," Derlin responded proudly, puffing out his chest.

"The Nicotine Wolf," President Johnson replied, chuckling. "I like the sound of that. I'll see ya tomorrow night, fella. Good luck!"

With that, he got into his limousine. The motorcade moved off slowly and was soon out of sight down the road, heading at the president's behest not to Mississippi, but to the nearby Off-Ramp Suites Motor Lodge. Once there, on a steady diet of take-out chicken and Panther Cat, the only beer available at the motel-adjacent gas station, the president began his pregaming routine in earnest. By the time Saturday evening rolled around and it was time to sneak away with a pair of carefully chosen secret service agents, the president was rather drunk. Lonestar had long been his beer of choice, but he was quickly becoming a Panther Cat man.

Chapter 28

Snyder ditched Derlin as soon as the motorcade had passed out of view, frantically checking his watch as he ran to his Jeep and peeled out of the parking lot. A few moments later he'd slow down briefly and crane his neck as he passed the full parking lot of the motor lodge thinking he spotted a familiar looking limousine, but he had other, more supple things on his mind and soon returned the pedal to the floor as he drove by.

As he walked quietly back to his barracks, beaming like a schoolboy and thrice as giddy, Derlin was unsure whether or not to tell the gang about the special guest The King of McQueen was going to have. Derlin knew that everyone in the gang was incredibly nervous about the logistics of pulling off a major secret wrestling tournament without any drill sergeants or other higher-ups finding out. He also knew that telling them that the President of the United States was going to show up to watch alongside the cadets might exacerbate the gang's worry even more. On the other side of that coin, he was also quite proud of himself and his day's accomplishments thus far and didn't so much as hesitate as he strode confidently into the barracks.

"How'd it go, Spurlock?" Brooklyn asked excitedly.

"Yeah man," Cleveland added. "What was it like meeting the president?"

"He was pretty cool," Derlin replied nonchalantly, fiddling with the sheet corner on the edge of his bed.

"That's it?" Tex replied. "You just got a photo-op with the President of the United States because he specifically wanted to meet you and that's all you've got to say?"

"He was real nice," Derlin continued, smiling sheepishly.

"He was nice," Other Tex replied.

"Yeah," Derlin continued, stretching and yawning. "There was one more thing, what was it? Oh yeah. He's coming to our wrestling tournament tomorrow."

The gang gasped and Brooklyn shouted out a "Holy Moses."

"Spurlock are you insane?" Cleveland whispered. "It's gonna be hard enough having 300 people that live right here on the base at this thing and keeping it all a secret and you go and invite the President of the United States?"

"I didn't think he'd say yes," Derlin said defensively. "But he did. He's staying at the motor lodge up the road."

"How's he gonna get in without anyone at the gate noticing, you dummy?" Brooklyn scolded. "He's a pretty important guy, you know."

"He said he had it taken care of," Derlin continued. "He said he was gonna bring a couple of secret service folk and they were gonna bleach the fence by the gym and get in that way."

"You mean breach?" Memphis asked.

"Man, I don't know," Derlin replied. "I ain't the president."

"Well, what else did he say?" Cleveland asked, still far more nervous than excited about the whole development.

"Only thing he asked me was what time was the bell and if he could bring him some whiskey."

"What'd you tell him?" Other Tex asked.

"Eight and yes, on account of he's the president." Derlin replied.

"Well boys," Cleveland said, letting out a deep breath and a whistle. "Sounds like we've got a little bit of work to do tonight making sure this ring and everything is up to snuff. I know we ain't the NWA or nothin' but I don't want it to look too po-dunk if the goddamn president is gonna be there."

"He'll probably be drunk from the way he was talkin'," Derlin offered. "It don't have to be like the Birmingham Cow Dome or nothin'."

"Well, we're gonna go make sure we get it right," Tex said. "I don't want the president thinking we're a bunch of rubes and hayseeds. Derlin, you stay here and finish up that costume and get your rest, or go jump building to building and smoke a bunch of cigarettes. Whatever the hell you're gonna do. Just get yourself ready for the show and we'll have everything else locked and loaded by tomorrow."

"Oh don't you worry none about me, friends," Derlin smiled, once again retrieving his costume from his trunk. "The Nicotine Wolf is about to fly."

July 3, 1968

Derlin finally put the finishing touches on his costume, blowing dry the glue on the last of his feathers just after three in the morning, which had him in line for a little under four hours of sleep and far below the lofty threshold he'd set for his pre-match "refreshification." As he lay in bed, tired as all hell but with his heart racing in anticipation, Derlin again thought on some familial advice. Long ago, when Derlin was around nine, he complained to his half-uncle Gooch about having to get up so early the morning of a deer hunt. Gooch leaned in toward Derlin, his tobacco-soaked bottom lip protruding as much as ever. He offered Derlin a secret, one that he claimed had kept him in such "top shape" over the years.

"Trick I always use when I gotta get up early is just to sleep fast," he said plainly, spattering flecks of tobacco juice over young Derlin's face and hair. "If I sleep faster it means I don't gotta sleep as late and I get a lot more done the next day."

Derlin had never been hurried enough in his day-to-day scheduling to need to take the advice, as his youth and work history were predicated by vast swaths of taskless, empty time even once he'd grown, become a father and lived in a windmill. His full night's rest compromised for one of the few times in his life, Derlin decided this to be the night to take his half-uncle's advice. Closing his eyes as tightly as he could, he imagined himself falling asleep with thrice the efficiency. He was already exhausted and quickly fell asleep regardless, though he attributed his quickness to doze solely to his firm concentration on the matter. He awoke to the trumpets in the morning feeling refreshed, as though he'd slept a full day or more. He kept firm in his morning tradition, sitting up with a start banging his head on the support rail of the upper bunk, but he quickly shook it off and leapt from his bed ready to conquer his day.

Breezing through the Saturday morning exercises as though he was jogging on air, Derlin gobbled down nearly a dozen eggs with his breakfast, dousing them in maple syrup and chugging them with glass after glass of thick buttermilk. Following this with a pot of black coffee with a stick of butter in it, Derlin described the process as "creaming up," insisting that it was a rumored method of training shared by one of his minor wrestling heroes, the similarly-built Gary "Greased Lightning" Witherspoon. Cleveland and the gang watched in horror as Derlin gorged himself on dairy products, cringing with each bite or sip of shimmering coffee.

"Spurlock, what the hell, man?" Brooklyn began. "You're gonna make yourself sick eating like that. We won't be able to roll you into the ring."

"Naw, man," Derlin replied with confidence in between bites, not even bothering to look up. "This is gonna make me weigh like 10 more pounds tonight. I'mma be that much harder to slam."

"You're just gonna make yourself vomit and shit everywhere," Memphis offered, shaking his head in disgust.

"No way, Memphis," Derlin replied, shaking his head, still not looking up. "All this dairy just soaks into my muscles and makes me that much stronger for tonight."

"I don't think that's how science works, Spurlock," Brooklyn replied.

"Nicotine Wolf don't need no science," Derlin snapped. He stabbed his fork into a hard-boiled egg and paused, looking up with a toothy smile. "A wolf don't need no science for it to spread those wings and fly, baby."

"I don't know what that means," Brooklyn said, shrugging his shoulders emphatically.

"It means all this buttermilk and my lunch buttermilk is gonna make me strong as all hell and I'm gonna dominate these boys tonight," Derlin scoffed, snatching his fork off of his tray and downing the egg in one massive bite. He followed it with a glug of coffee and let out a slow, wet belch.

"I don't know if that's such a good idea," Cleveland began, but Derlin immediately began shaking his head vigorously.

"Wolves need milk," he interrupted. "There's your science."

The gang hadn't seen or heard from Derlin since he'd disappeared immediately following a lunch consisting of several more glasses of buttermilk and a large bowl of cottage cheese, but they hardly had the time to miss him. To the last man, they were on high alert to make sure the evening's events went off without a hitch. The first part of the plan seemed to be a success: As the sun had dipped behind the trees, Camp McQueen had basically cleared of commanding officer-types as they all headed into town for their Saturday night "slices of pie" as Brooklyn had put it. Cleveland and the gang had waited for the last sergeant to leave a little after six before they snuck down to the gym to do a final once-over of the ring before the show. Memphis and Brooklyn gave the ropes a final tightening while Tex and Other Tex remained at the doors as a security check to the soon to be arriving audience.

With nothing else to keep them on an otherwise quiet Saturday night on the base, soldiers began filtering into the gym basement two or three at a time, gradually making their way to Memphis and Cleveland's makeshift ring to admire their handywork. The ring itself had ended up more passable than they'd imagined at first. It had enough give in the mat, the ropes were springy enough to bounce off of and the turnbuckles looked totally real if you didn't get too close to them. In red, white and blue on the mat, Brooklyn and Other Tex had painted "King of McQueen" while Tex had contributed an eagle and a tank to the blank mat space. Though no one was going to mistake it for Madison Square Garden, the ring was remarkably satisfactory for the circumstances and soon the "ringside seats," being the standing room area around the inside of the emptied pool, had been filled. Soon, the tile area around the pool's edge began to fill and by seven o'clock, when the wrestlers began to arrive and report to Cleveland, well over three hundred Camp McQueen soldiers were in attendance.

The participants trickled in one by one. Most were former high school wrestlers or football players, all were in excellent shape and none aside from Derlin had entered with a gimmick of any kind, each simply using their regular names. Derlin was the last to arrive (at 7:45, via side window). The fact that he was listed on the roster only as The Nicotine Wolf created a bit of an air of mystique among his fellow participants, but the mystique was shot as soon as someone stared Derlin down long enough to determine who was behind the cape and mask.

"Spurlock is that you?" a burly combatant asked loudly, to which Derlin only howled, slowly retreating into the shadows of a nearby hallway.

A few moments later, as Cleveland was doing his best to figure out just how they were going to get everything started, he felt an excited tap on his shoulder. He turned to find a beaming Tex and Other Tex standing alongside two men in sunglasses and dark suits with a visibly inebriated President Johnson standing between them. He was holding two thirds of a bottle of Johnny Walker Blue and was nibbling on a chicken drumstick which he'd periodically return to the pocket of his jacket.

"Hey there, champ," a wobbly President Johnson said to Cleveland, offering him a greasy handshake. "Just in time for the big show, I see!"

"Y-Yes sir, Mr. President. Welcome!" Cleveland stammered. "Our buddy Brooklyn is about to step into the ring and announce the contestants for the first match. Can we get you anything sir? It's such an honor to have you here."

"Oh, no son, bless you," President Johnson began. "I've got my pocket chicken and my whiskey and my secret service, ain't that right boys?" He turned to the two men, gesturing at them with his whiskey bottle. They nodded quickly and continued to scan the area for trouble.

After a moment, the president began to wander and the two men scrambled to follow him into the crowd. By the time they'd caught up with him he was scaling the poolside next to the ladder and, to the astonishment of the young men in the ringside area, was elbowing his way toward the very front row. A murmur of disbelief followed in his wake, just ahead of the secret servicemen and he made it there just as Brooklyn entered the ring from a small makeshift ramp for the wrestlers in a far corner. The president leaned forward, putting his elbows on the edge of the ring apron and tugging lightly at one of the ropes just as Brooklyn strode to the center of the ring.

"Gentlemen! Gentleman," Brooklyn began, shouting to get everyone's attention. "Everybody quiet down for a second cause we don't have a microphone in here."

The audience gradually died down and after a few seconds, helped by President Johnson's shushing, and Brooklyn was able to continue.

"We've got quite the evening of entertainment tonight: the first ever wrestling tournament at Camp McQueen!" he shouted to a hearty round of applause. "Gentlemen, tonight, sixteen of your strongest, toughest, meanest fellow cadets will wrestle in a tournament to determine once and for all who is the King of McQueen!"

The crowd burst into raucous applause again, this round lasting nearly a full minute before Brooklyn was able to calm them again to announce the participants of the first match. Despite the build-up, the first match would end rather quickly when a soldier named McGill knocked himself out falling off of the ramshackle top rope while attempting to rally the crowd in his favor, resulting in a countout. Though the action was a far cry from what the soldiers in attendance grew up watching on their local cable station, they cheered each subsequent match with gusto as though "The Navajo" Ricky Yamashita himself was performing in front of them.

Most of the matches in the first round were quick and uneventful skirmishes, ending only when somebody was punched in the face hard enough to stay down for Memphis to make a three count. By the time Derlin's first bout arrived, the last of the first round matches, he was confident that he could run the table.

As Derlin's first round opponent, a stocky Georgia farm boy named Kenny Wilkins waited in the ring, he heard Brooklyn shout the words "The Nicotine Wolf" and heard the crowd begin to buzz. Hastily lighting four Old Indians with his rusty Zippo, Derlin billowed out his wolf cape, howled, and began to stalk toward the ring.

Kenny Wilkins had a genuinely perplexed look on his face as Derlin stomped across the ramp to the ring. Like himself, the previous 14 wrestlers had just been regular soldiers in fatigues or gym clothes and Wilkins certainly wasn't expecting a smoke-billowing hooded stranger in a costume vaguely resembling some type of wolf-badger-cat to be his opponent.

Derlin continued to smoke and howl and soon scampered into the ring under the bottom rope. The bell rang and he stood facing Wilkins for several seconds in silence. The crowd had taken to this mysterious stranger, but they soon began to get restless at Derlin's inaction.

"Do something!" a far-off voice shouted.

"You gonna take that get-up off or what, son?" Wilkins asked.

Derlin remained silent from beneath his hood, shaking his head slowly.

"Alright then, suit yourself," Wilkins replied. "At least put out your damn cigarettes and let's get this thing goin'."

Again, Derlin shook his head ominously.

"Whatever you say, freak show," an increasingly angry Wilkins replied, bounding toward Derlin and flailing wildly with an overhand punch. Derlin ducked it quickly, front rolling past Wilkins and burning him in the side of the stomach with a lit end of a cigarette. Wilkins yelped in pain and the crowd began to holler loudly.

"Got'dammit fella!" Wilkins shouted. "I said put them damn cigarettes out. Somebody's gonna get hurt and it ain't gonna be me."

Derlin stuck out his hand and wagged his index finger. With his other hand, he took a deep puff of all four cigarettes, exhaling a billowing cloud of acrid white smoke into the face of a blinded Wilkins, obscuring the vision of nearly everyone in the audience. Striking as quickly as a cobra, Derlin kicked Wilkins in the balls as hard as he could. As foretold, when Wilkins doubled over, Derlin punched him in the back of the head. As Wilkins hit the ground, Derlin quickly rolled him up for a three count pinfall and the crowd erupted. Derlin climbed to his feet, three of his cigarettes still in hand. He waved to the crowd from beneath his hood, climbing to the top turnbuckle and howling at the top of his lungs. He soaked up the attention of the crowd and revelled in it as long as he could before a smiling Brooklyn finally came to shoo him from the ring to begin the second round.

The crowd still cheered the eventual winners of the other matches, but remained mostly listless throughout the second round until it was once again time for the Nicotine Wolf to return to the ring. His first round antics had made him a clear fan-favorite and the crowd exploded as he was announced again by Brooklyn. Waiting in the ring this time as the strange pageantry of Derlin's entrance concluded was a former high school wrestling champion named Curtis Crudler who, despite being the second smallest man in the tournament behind Derlin, had breezed through his first round matchup with a textbook repertoire of classic wrestling maneuvers, winning via a wrist lock submission hold to the crowd's astonishment.

Crudler, muscle bound despite his shorter stature and wiry frame, wasted no time in trying to dissect Derlin's act after the bell rang. He immediately charged at Derlin at the bell, catching him completely off-guard. He swept Derlin's legs out from underneath him, flipping him onto his stomach and twisting his legs into a vicious reverse leg lock. Derlin yelped in pain as Crudler jerked backwards in his hold, throwing his full weight onto Derlin's knee and back. Knowing all along that his only hope lay in escaping the painful hold, Derlin took a mighty puff on the four still lit Old Indians clinched in his fist, this time sending a mushroom cloud of smoke billowing straight up into the lights of the gym ceiling. The cherried tips of the cigarettes glowed brightly in the faint, smoky light of the gym and as they shined their brightest, Derlin leaned up and jammed them into the base of Crudler's neck, right at the hairline. Derlin howled in joy as Crudler broke the hold, writhing around on the ground, clutching his neck and swearing loudly.

At ringside, President Johnson shouted his approval hoarsely taking another swig from his whiskey bottle. Derlin pointed at him enthusiastically with both hands, firing a couple of "finger guns" into the air and giving him a happy thumbs up. Not wanting to waste his opportunity, Derlin quickly leapt to the top rope, balancing himself for a moment before howling, flapping his arms like wings and leaping onto the still-incapacitated Crudler with a formidable elbow. Rolling him over and quickly hooking his leg, Derlin again secured a three count from Memphis as the crowd collectively went wild. Derlin had made his way to the semi-finals and celebrated with another spinning howl, flapping his arms as he twirled in the center of the ring.

For the first time during the tournament, Derlin lurked in view of the ring to watch an opponent's match instead of squatting quietly in the shadows of a hallway eating hard-boiled eggs from a pail he'd smuggled from KP. Derlin hadn't been concerned with the might or skill set of his early round opponents, but he definitely wanted to see who he'd be facing in the championship once he'd dispatched with his semi-final opponent.

He was too far away to hear Brooklyn's introductions, but Derlin knew who he'd be facing for the title before the bell had even hit. He recognized the larger man in the ring from his photo on the gym bulletin board, where he was listed as the weight record holder for the base in every lifting category on the charts. The man, Timmy La Fontaine, had an IQ of 76 but was 6'5 and 280 pounds of Cajun muscle. He ended his semi-final match the same way he'd won his first two. With an immediate, massive clothesline to his opponent. Derlin could see the look in his exceptionally large, dull eyes. If anyone else was taking this tournament as seriously as The Nicotine Wolf, it was Timmy La Fontaine.

Derlin did his best not to think ahead to La Fontaine as he strode confidently to the ring for his semi-final match. His opponent, a Mississippi sharecropper's son named Amos Jones, was reluctant to getting cigarette-burned by some looney wearing a wolf costume. Derlin was anxious to get in another round of practice before he squared off against La Fontaine, but as soon as he took his trademark massive puff from the four cigarettes, Jones exited the ring, shooting middle fingers at Derlin and screaming angrily at Cleveland and Brooklyn in the process.

"I didn't sign up for this shit to get cigarette burned by some nut-job fool in a wolf costume!" he shouted as he marched from the ring. "I'm trying to be an army soldier not some damned basement freak show. Y'all can have that championship, I'm out of here!"

Derlin flapped his arms and howled after Jones from the ring, raising his fists in victory as Memphis officially disqualified Jones via countout. The stage was set for the championship against Timmy La Fontaine and Derlin didn't even bother to leave the ring between matches, instead choosing to cool his heels in the corner and light a few fresh Old Indians as he prepared for La Fontaine's entrance.

As he gazed toward the makeshift ramp and tried his best to figure out how to intimidate the much larger and more muscular La Fontaine, Derlin felt a tap on his shoulder. It was President Johnson.

"Spurlock, my boy!" he slurred. "The Nicotine Wolf is flying high! Just one more match to go and you'll have done it!"

"I know, Mr. President Johnson," Derlin gushed nervously. "I can't believe it."

"You know, I thought that colored boy could have given you a run for your money, but I guess now you just have to beat the retarded fella instead," President Johnson smiled, patting Derlin heartily on the back.

"I reckon so!" Derlin hollered.

"Here," President Johnson offered. "Take a good luck swig of my Johnny Walker. It'll keep you relaxed." He extended the now quarter-full whiskey bottle to Derlin, who happily accepted.

"Aw, thanks, Mr. President Johnson!" Derlin smiled. "I reckon I could have me a little nip before the big match."

"No sir, Spurlock," President Johnson said sternly. "No little nip for the Nicotine Wolf. Kill that bottle real quick and you'll be invincible!"

"You mean he won't be able to see me?" Derlin asked excitedly.

"No! No," President Johnson shouted. "I mean he can't hurt ya. Drink that whole thing, now."

He helped Derlin tilt the bottle back as Derlin experienced the first liquor to touch his lips since being babysat by his Grandma Vondene as an infant. He experienced it in the form of six to eight shots, all at once roughly in the span of time that it took him to chug a Panther Cat. Spending the last several hours gripped in the President's sweaty hand, the whiskey was every bit as warm as the 90 degrees of the basement pool room and Derlin was not prepared for it. He coughed roughly and shook his head, slapping his cheeks against his gums.

"That stuff is mighty powerful, Chief," he said, taking several deep breaths as though he had just come up from being under water. "Man, I feel like I drank a big old pot of fire."

"Here, calm it down with a bite of this chicken," President Johnson said calmly, producing the half eaten drumstick from his jacket pocket. Derlin gnawed on it vigorously for a few seconds before Brooklyn entered the ring to preview the championship bout and introduce the competitors.

Derlin rose to his feet unsteadily and raised his fists as Brooklyn introduced him to another round of wild cheering from the crowd. Much to his surprise, however, the crowd cheered nearly as loudly when Brooklyn announced Timmy La Fontaine and he began to stomp toward the ring. Derlin quickly lit his cigarettes, coughing again from his gulps of whiskey, trying to regain his mettle as the bell rang.

Sauntering slowly to the middle of the ring, gradually feeling the warm tingle of the whiskey coursing through his veins, Derlin leered at Timmy and howled.

"I hate wolves!" Timmy shouted, screaming at Derlin and charging at him, ready to unleash his devastating lariat.

Derlin had anticipated this, rolling to Timmy's right and out of the reach of his massive arm. He log-rolled to the edge of the ring, where he jumped to his feet and bounced off the ropes behind Timmy, leaping at him with a successful flying slap to the back of the head. Timmy was unhurt, but was certainly stunned and pissed off. Having missed his clothesline, this was the first time he'd had to do any actual match wrestling and he certainly didn't like being smacked in the back of the head.

Derlin slid beneath the ropes, pulling himself to his feet and running up and down the edge of the ring apron with a fist in the air, howling happily as Timmy fumed in the center. Derlin continued his showboating parade, puffing happily on his four Old Indians and leaping to the top turnbuckle. He raised his fists in the air and blew the smoke out in a massive cloud above the crowd and was just about to turn and taunt Timmy once more when he felt his stomach turn. Throughout the day, Derlin's "creaming up" had seen him consume over a gallon of milk, a gallon of buttermilk and, just to be safe, four sticks of butter. He'd been eating from his pail of eggs since he'd arrived in the basement and had, over the course of the afternoon and evening put down nearly thirty unrefrigerated hard boiled eggs accompanied by nearly seven packs of cigarettes. He'd somehow managed triumphantly throughout the tournament, to his credit a full twelve pounds heavier, but the moment that hot whiskey made it to his stomach, he felt like he'd been punched in the gut and he broke out in an all too familiar cold sweat. He nearly fell from the turnbuckle as the crowd gasped, steadying himself with a gulp and looking up just in time to see Timmy lumbering toward his perch.

"I'm gonna kill" was all Timmy got out before it happened. He was maybe six feet from Derlin when the spew of whiskey, buttermilk and eggs began. The foamy geyser shot out of Derlin at approximately the speed of the human sneeze, a putrid white-grey firehose of filth that caught Timmy in the face and chest and continued to drench him for nearly a minute as Derlin clung to the top ropes like a gargoyle atop Notre Dame. Timmy writhed around screaming in the viscous mess for a few moments after Derlin had finally emptied himself before clutching his chest and passing out on his back.

Dazed, with vomit dripping from his mouth and nose, Derlin gazed down at the ring and at the now-hushed crowd that surrounded it. Breathing deeply from his mouth and hiccupping periodically, his nose dripping with snot, Derlin groaned and steadied himself once more on the top rope. Taking a long puff off of his only remaining lit cigarette, Derlin flapped his arms haphazardly and gurgled the best howl he could, leaping down onto the supine Timmy LaFontaine with a flying elbow. The force of the elbow sent them skidding a few feet toward the opposite corner and when Derlin hooked Timmy's leg for the pin, it took Memphis a good ten seconds to find a dry part of the ring to count the 1-2-3. The crowd remained in a stunned silence for a few seconds before bursting into their loudest cheer of the night. Memphis helped a woozy but recovering Derlin to his feet, gingerly raising his arm in victory. Derlin had done it.

Cleveland and the rest of the gang rushed into the ring, shouting and cheering, doing their best to steer clear of the stagnant pools of yellowing vomit. In Cleveland's hand was a makeshift World Title belt that Tex and Other Tex had fashioned from an old helmet, a weight-lifting belt and some metal scraps. He was about to step up and hand it to Derlin when he felt a hand on his shoulder and a deep voice say "Now, hold on just a minute son." He turned to see President Johnson standing there, a smile on his face.

"What do you say we get him a little cleaned up first?" President Johnson said. "I sent the boys to find a hose, they should be back any second. I'd like to give him that belt myself, but the president ain't getting any of old boy's egg puke on him."

"Yes sir, Mr. President!" Cleveland gushed, shaking Johnson's hand and stammering to make conversation.

As the rest of the gang shook hands and made small talk with President Johnson, the two secret service agents rushed into the ring, carrying a hose with a large spray nozzle which they'd hooked to a nearby wall at the edge of the pool.

"We found just what you were looking for, sir," one said as the other nodded.

"Well, you know what to do then, boys," President Johnson smiled. "Hose him down, get all that puke off of him."

"Yes sir," they replied in unison.

"Don't forget his hair, now," President Johnson added.

"We won't sir," they replied, again in unison.

President Johnson and the gang stepped back clear of the splatter zone to watch as the secret service agents began to spray Derlin down. He'd mostly recovered since emptying his belly and considered the cold hose bath invigorating, groaning deeply as he was washed clean of his own filth. Shaking his head and wiping his face and chest, Derlin was soon more or less free of vomit.

"Thanks for the free shower boys," Derlin smiled, waving at the secret service agents and beginning to do a little jig as he washed his back. The bouncing of the ring caused by Derlin's dancing, combined with a few fresh blasts of the hose were enough to jostle Timmy La Fontaine back to consciousness as he began to stir and moan from the ring mat. He let out a sputtering cough, followed by a small burst of vomit himself. Clearly he was in need of medical attention, but Cleveland was just relieved to see that he wasn't dead.

"Aw, man." Derlin winced. "Puking all over the damn ring, man. That's why you ain't the champion."

"Spurlock you're only champion because you puked all over the ring," Brooklyn laughed. "I still don't know why you drank all that buttermilk."

"See!" Derlin shouted. "Y'all said Gary 'Greased Lightning' Witherspoon was bullshit. Y'all said that 'Creaming Up' wasn't a real thing and that wasn't how Gary 'Greased Lightning' Witherspoon was champion. I proved all 'yall motherfuckers wrong on that one."

Derlin was riding high.

"I guess you're right about that," Cleveland said, chuckling. "It's a damn good thing there's a drain at the bottom of this pool otherwise we'd just have to burn the whole building to the ground."

Derlin nodded distractedly, reaching into his pocket to discover that his crumpled pack of Old Indians was dripping wet. Thumbing through the pack regardless, Derlin found a passably dry cigarette.

"My Uncle Gooch says Old Indians still light when they're wet 'cause they got lead in 'em or something," Derlin began to no one in particular. "I don't know nothin' about no lead but you sure can light up a damp one. Uncle Gooch said one time he took half a pack out of the papers and tried to dip it and woke up three days later in the woods out behind the Feed n' Seed covered in honey. Any of y'all fellers got a light?"

"I've got one," President Johnson said, stepping forward with a gleaming silver zippo and lighting Derlin's cigarette. The damp, leaden tobacco slowly but surely began to engulf as Derlin took a mighty drag and he was soon coughing and puffing along happily.

"Thank ya, Mr. President Johnson," Derlin said, nodding in appreciation.

"Thank you, son." President Johnson smiled. "That was a hell of a wrestling show you put on tonight and I'm awful proud of you. We could use a lot more fellas like you in the military! I tell you, Charlie wouldn't get back up from an elbow drop like that if it came flying out of a helio-copter at him! Say, your boys over here got you a little something for the occasion."

He held out the belt and Derlin's jaw dropped. Tex and Other Tex had spent a few late nights in the metal shop making the belt and they were quite proud of it. Two army helmets had been flattened and fused together in an oval, on which "World Champion, King of McQueen 1968" had been etched in cursive. It had been attached to a weight lifting belt stolen from the gym and had small steel stars affixed to the sides. Derlin gasped and his hands trembled as he reached for the belt. Taking it from President Johnson and eyeballing it closely, he ran his fingers over the metal work for a moment before flinging it proudly over his shoulder.

"Well, let's make it official," President Johnson said, producing a black marker from his pocket. Leaning over to Derlin, he began writing an inscription on the belt:

"Presented to Derlin "The Nicotine Wolf" Spurlock, the finest wrestler and finest soldier I ever saw.

Lyndon B. Johnson, President of the USA"

Damp, shirtless and still reeking to the high heavens, Derlin grabbed President Johnson in a massive bear hug, holding him tightly and moving quickly enough to briefly startle the secret service agents. President Johnson patted Derlin on the back lightly and did his best to stay uncontaminated until Derlin finally let go.

"Well fellas, I sure do appreciate y'all having me here and showing me the time y'all did," President Johnson began, shaking Derlin loose. "But it's about time for me and the boys to be saddling up and heading back to the motor lodge. Gotta get going early in the morning to head on back down to Texas. You know, folks do tend to wonder where I am every so often."

With that, a wave and a nod of the head, President Johnson strode from the basement wrestling arena in a manner no different than if he was leaving a cabinet meeting in Washington. He'd always remember the evening fondly, but once he and his secret servicemen snuck back through the hole they'd left in the fence, Johnson would never set foot on the grounds of Camp McQueen again. In a twist of fate he couldn't have imagined it at the time, Derlin wouldn't be far behind.

July 5, 1968

In hindsight, Derlin would look at it as an inevitability that they were found out. No matter what measures were taken, it was highly unlikely that the entire base could keep something the size and success of King of McQueen a secret forever, as it was wildly popular and soldier to soldier everyone in Camp McQueen was buzzing about it all of Sunday afternoon and evening. There was a small fireworks show on the base and Derlin was constantly being come up to and congratulated as champion with a handshake or pat on the back. Even the soldiers who weren't there had heard about every detail within 24 hours. Despite all of these loose lips, it wasn't any of the gossiping soldiers from the crowd who let word get to Drill Sergeant Snyder. It was Timmy La Fontaine.

After showering himself and putting on fresh clothes, a still quite ill Timmy stumbled into the sick bay at three in the morning, rambling about wrestling and President Johnson and cascades of silky white vomit. The nurses first mistook him as drunk until they began to calm him down and piece his story together. Now treating him for symptoms of a nervous breakdown, a nurse jotted down the basics of Timmy's supposed story. After dosing him with a small handful of muscle relaxers so he could manage to sleep through the night, the nurse sent Timmy to a bunk to rest. The next morning, with a clearer head, he called Snyder.

Derlin had breezed through his Sunday without a care in the world, but he feared for the worst when he heard a request for his presence in Snyder's office over the loudspeaker immediately following the trumpet blasts of Monday morning. He felt like a dead man walking as he trudged through his barracks despite the pats on the back and words of encouragement that were coming from his fellow cadets as he passed by the rows of bunks.

Timidly knocking on the door of Snyder's office, Derlin was beckoned to enter by Snyder's bark on the other side of the cheap plastic-wood door. He sheepishly walked into the room, gulping slowly when he saw Timmy La Fontaine and Curtis Crudler seated on a small couch against the wall. Timmy stared daggers at him and Curtis patted gingerly at the bandage on the back of his neck.

"Spurlock sit your ass down," Snyder snapped.

Derlin obliged without a word.

"I hear y'all had quite the time over the weekend while I was gone," Snyder said with a menacing calm.

"I," Derlin began.

"Don't say another goddamn word, Spurlock, you weird fuck," Snyder said.

"These boys filled me in on everything that happened. You running around like a wolf and burning folks with cigarettes, is that right? All sounds pretty damn crazy to me." Snyder chuckled dryly, not breaking eye contact with Derlin.

"You know, I never did think much of you, Spurlock," Snyder continued. "I knew you were trouble the second you got off that bus. I could smell it on you. That's why I believe everything these boys told me about your little wrestling show. Well, almost everything."

He leaned in slightly and whispered "the retarded boy seems to think that President Johnson was at the wrestling match, but I think he's just a little confused. President Johnson's probably sitting on his porch in Texas by now. Ol' boy is still in shock from your little puke shower I reckon."

Anyhow, I went down there to that gym basement, son," Snyder continued. "Y'all left an awful mess down there. I already know your friends who helped put it together and I know all the other boys who wrestled in this damn tournament, and I'll tell you every one of them is gonna spend the next week of their lives scrubbing every inch of that pool with toothbrushes and then they're going to peel enough potatoes to feed all of Alabama till Thanksgiving. But you ain't gonna be joining them, Spurlock."

"On account of I'm the Champion?" Derlin asked hopefully.

"Not cause you're the fuckin' Champion you idiot," Snyder said plainly. "Because we're kicking your degenerate ass out of the army. Uncle Sam don't need you anymore. You're being dishonorably discharged this afternoon."

"What?" Derlin hollered. "But, I…"

"Save it, Spurlock," Snyder barked. "You've got a couple of hours to gather your belongings and say your goodbyes. You'll meet me back here at 1pm, you'll sign your paperwork and you will be escorted from the base by security."

Curtis Crudler smirked and Timmy La Fontaine nodded in smug satisfaction.

"I'm… I'm kicked out of the army?" Derlin asked, his voice cracking.

"That's right, son," Snyder said.

"For wrestling too good?" Derlin asked, his voice raising in pitch.

"No goddamnit," Snyder shouted, exasperated. "For assaulting two of your fellow soldiers, causing bodily harm to them, destruction of army property and breaking into the damn place to begin with. You're lucky we don't send you to jail, but these boys say they won't sue the army for negligence as long as we get rid of your ass!"

"How am I gonna be a war hero, then?" Derlin asked sadly.

"That ain't my problem anymore, Spurlock," Snyder shot back. "You are dismissed. Have your shit together and be back here by one o'clock on the dot, do you hear me?"

"Yes sir," Derlin replied, hanging his head. As he began to slink from the office, he turned to face Curtis and Timmy. He paused and started to offer the pair an apology, but changed his mind and continued his dejected shuffle, closing the office door softly behind him.

He was the only one in the barracks as he gathered his belongings as all of his bunkmates were out around the base going about their daily routines or fulfilling the duties of Snyder's punishment. He paused for a moment to stare at his championship belt as he packed, a single tear falling down upon it as he crammed it into his duffel bag. Still soaked with a variety of unpleasantness, he left his once-prized wolf costume balled up in the bottom of his trunk, not wanting to soil his remaining belongings, consisting of the two uniforms he'd carefully folded at the bottom of his bag. He spent the remainder of the morning unable to track down Cleveland or anyone else from the gang, as they along with the other wrestlers from the tournament were being led on a 20-mile hill run that would take up the entirety of their late morning and early afternoon. Resigned to not saying goodbye in person, Derlin finally just scrawled a note which he left on his bunk.

"Hi everybody. I am sorry that you guys got in so much trouble for the wrestling. It is all my fault. I wish it hadn't gotten y'all up the creek. They are kicking me out of army. I tried to find y'all and say bye but couldn't. You guys are the best friends I ever had and I'mma keep my belt forever. If you're ever in Coverdale, find me and come drink a beer. Till then, the Nicotine Wolf's gotta fly. Owwwwwwww! Best of luck with army. Hit Charlie with an elbow for me if you see him and shoot me a Herman's Hermit.
-Derlin"

Finishing with a flourish in the form of a rudimentary drawing of a wolf with wings, Derlin set the page on Cleveland's pillow, wiping a single tear from his eye. With that, he trudged back to Snyder's office, arriving with five minutes to spare. He signed his paperwork quietly as Snyder peered over his shoulder. Given his papers for dishonorable discharge, Derlin was officially released from the army at 1:03pm. He was led to the gate by two armed guards, who accompanied him to the other side of the entrance and then sent him on his way.

Seeing no other option, Derlin slung his bag over his shoulder and began the long, slow walk back to Coverdale. As was so often the case, he had a plan.

Part 5: The Reunion

Chapter 29

Derlin stuck his thumb out as he walked south, hoping to catch some sympathy from a passing motorist. By three o'clock, he'd walked nearly ten miles and the only sympathy he'd encountered was a honk aimed his way when he'd stumbled on a loose piece of gravel and nearly fallen into the road. He had assumed that in his bright white t-shirt and army fatigues, he'd be both easily spottable and a have a high likelihood for hitchhiking success, but so far he had encountered no such luck. He'd go so far as to wonder if Snyder had begun phoning local radio stations, instructing them to tell drivers listening in not to pick up the wayward army hitchhiker heading down Highway 65 "on account of his dishonorable discharge," and was soon eyeballing each passing motorists for their signs of recognition.

He was another mile or two down the road before a car finally slowed, pulling to a stop on the shoulder. A wide, faded red late-1950's Cadillac gave a little toot of the horn as Derlin sauntered up to the passenger side window. Smiling at him from the driver's seat was a tall, wire-thin black man of about 60, wearing a lime green suit with a large, wide collar and a jaunty, Cuban-style fedora.

"Where you headed, young fella?" the man chirped happily.

"I'm headed back home to Coverdale, sir," Derlin began, pointing south down the highway and shielding his eyes from the sun. "You're the first person that's stopped all day, I sure would appreciate a lift."

"Hop on in my friend," the man beamed, gesturing at the front seat. "I'm headed down to Mobile myself to visit some family and I can drop you off right on the way."

"Much obliged, stranger," Derlin said, quickly opening the door and climbing inside, setting his bag at his feet.

"What's your name, friend?" the man asked as he guided the old Cadillac back onto the two-lane.

"I'm Derlin," Derlin replied, offering a handshake. "Derlin Spurlock. What about you, stranger?"

"Well, my mamma named me LeRoy," the man began, his Alabama drawl giving each word an extra millisecond of length. "But most folks just call me Satchel."

"Satchel? Like the bag?" Derlin asked, perplexed. He quietly admired Satchel's flashy green suit and shimmering golden pinky ring, making his way down slowly to the gleaming two-tone wingtips manning the gas pedal and clutch. Staring now at his own shadowy reflection in the gleam of Satchel's polished wooden dashboard, Derlin wondered to himself how he'd look in such snappy attire. As he did, his face turned into an absent-minded half-smile.

"Yeah, when I was a boy I worked as a porter down at a hotel," Satchel began. "We got paid by the bag, you see, so I wanted to carry as many as I could. I'd carry so many at one time, you could hardly see me underneath the bags and folks just started callin' me Satchel. And I've pretty much been Satchel ever since."

"Man, I bet it's hard carrying a bunch of bags at one time up a bunch of stairs like that," Derlin offered, impressed. "You ever have to drag a cart full of groceries through the woods? I'd reckon it's about the same."

"Can't say I've ever done that, my boy," Satchel replied, letting out a dry chuckle. "Though I did used to do all sorts of things."

"Like what?" Derlin asked. Having spent his entire afternoon quietly trudging along the side of the highway, he was elated to have been picked up by someone with whom he'd developed so natural a conversation. He'd been curious as to what this man did for a living since he'd first climbed into the old Cadillac and, if his army lesson of having never managed to learn where Brooklyn was from taught him nothing else, it was that Derlin was no longer going to be a man who sat on questions.

Satchel paused for a moment.

"Oh, this and that. Say, where'd you say you were headed?" he asked in a clear effort to get off the topic. "Coverdale?"

"Yes sir, that's my hometown," Derlin beamed, easily distracted as he began to gush about his family. "Heading home from army to my wife and twin boys!"

"That's mighty fine," Satchel said. "How old are your boys?"

"Well, let's see," Derlin began. He began mumbling figures to himself, counting on his fingers and periodically nodding. Satchel could hear him audibly mutter the words "devil," "jail," and "windmill" but couldn't piece together much else. He stared at Derlin warily as he calculated his children's age.

"I reckon this'd put 'em at six months, almost" Derlin calculated. "They're real good babies on account of we raised 'em rugged at first. They already probably crawling by now and I bet they're fast as all hell. They love Charleston Chews and hay and I built them a robot and,"

"Six months?" Satchel asked curiously. "You can't have been in the army that long then, eh son?"

"Well, no," Derlin began. He proceeded to recount most of the tale of his discharge from the army, leaving out any mentions of the vomit or the "dishonorable" part, spinning it as though the army was allowing him a free vacation for becoming their wrestling champion. He left out any mention of his various encounters with the president, as he doubted this "Satchel" would believe some made-up sounding story about his encounter with such a famous person anyhow.

Satisfied with Derlin's long-winded answer, though the wandering tale took up most of the hour's drive from Montgomery to Coverdale, Satchel changed the subject once more.

"Say, isn't Coverdale the place with that big old fried fish restaurant?" Satchel asked, out of the blue.

"The Screaming Captain?" Derlin replied excitedly.

"Yeah, that's the one!" Satchel answered.

"That's my favorite restaurant in the whole world," Derlin said happily.

"Yeah, I usually can't eat that way much anymore," Satchel replied, patting his stomach. "All that fried ocean meat angries up my blood. But I just can't resist when I pass down this old road. Used to stop by this place and picnic with a whole bus full of folks back in the day. We'd eat here ten, twenty times every summer."

"I went on my first bus trip when I joined army," Derlin said. "It was really nice. I'd never seen that many chairs inside of one car before!"

"Yeah, some of 'em can get mighty fancy." Satchel smiled. "Say, do you wanna join me for an early supper? My treat."

Just as he offered, they came around a bend in the road and the technicolor glory of the Captain's heavyset mermaid sign became visible a few hundred yards away. Derlin salivated.

"I'm much obliged for the offer, Mr. Satchel," Derlin said begrudgingly as the Cadillac glided into the parking lot. "But I've really gotta be getting home to my wife and kids, they're waiting on me."

Again, Derlin chose to doctor a good bit of his story here, leaving out the fact that he was currently estranged from Mavis and the boys, not to mention that he was not in particularly good standing at The Screaming Captain after his recent drunken escapade, both sort of major nuggets in the impetus for him ending up in the army and, as it was, Satchel's Cadillac in the first place.

"Well, son," Satchel said kindly. "I reckon this is where we part ways, then. It sure has been a pleasure conversatin' with you."

"You too, Mr. Satchel," Derlin replied, offering another handshake as they got out of the car.

Satchel nodded, Derlin waved and the men parted ways. Derlin watched the strange, pleasant man bob through the parking lot and up the stairs to the restaurant entrance. He jangled loosely as he walked and Derlin appreciated his gait. Derlin lingered in the parking lot a moment for a moment longer, hoping that Satchel would look back and wave once more, but he did not, sauntering on into The Captain without a glance. Slinging his bag once more over his shoulder, the afternoon sun just beginning its descent behind the tall Alabama pines, Derlin began the final steps on his trip home.

It had been what had become a normal Monday for Mavis. She was working the daytime shift at the Piggly Wiggly while her mother tended to Randy and Ollie at home. As per usual, most of her daily thoughts centered around Derlin, daydreaming of his return while she stood at the cash register. His letter was progress toward this end and though she knew he had miles to go before he became the upstanding man and father they'd discussed, she ached for his return. Having yet to receive a follow-up to Derlin's first missive, she wondered if he'd continued flying up the ranks in the army. She knew little about how the process of promotion worked, but was skeptical that someone such as Derlin would encounter such a quick, meteoric ascent to being considered for the position of General, though as he'd often told her "when a Spurlock man puts his mind good to something, he gonna do it." "Power Sargent" did sound impressive in itself and she wasn't at all skeptical of the validity of such a position.

Had she been a little less lost in thought as she stared off into the distance from her checkout counter and paid more attention to the leftover copies of the Sunday Chubb

County Register she'd been tasked with throwing away, she'd have seen Derlin's smiling face under the front page headline "President Passes Through Alabama, Meets Top Young Soldiers." Later in the shift as she walked listlessly to deposit the papers in a dumpster behind the building, she didn't so much as give them a second glance. Ironically enough, she spent her time alone on the walk to the dumpster daydreaming of a heroic and swashbuckling horse-backed Derlin, resplendent in his "Power Sargent" attire leading troops into battle in some far-off land. She kicked at an empty can of Panther Cat lying near the dumpster and sighed.

As her shift concluded at 4 o'clock, Mavis made a quick pass through the store for some necessities. Randy and Ollie had taken to exclusively eating the Salisbury steak flavor of baby food, hotly refusing all other fruit and vegetable flavors to the point where Mavis had begun to worry that it might affect their nutritional health. As she grabbed a half dozen jars of the baby food and a requested bottle of Champale for her mother, Mavis thought back to Eudora's recent warning that such an unvaried diet in the children at such a young age might stunt their growth.

"You'll have a pair of midgets running around, if that's what you want," she was fond of saying as the boys gobbled their jars of meat.

Sure, the idea of her first few months of motherhood being spent raising a pair of dwarves in a windmill in the forest had a certain "fairy tale" aspect to it, but she hoped that the boys would manage to get through their steak phase unstunted. After all, Derlin stood nearly six feet tall and seemed to exist solely on meat, tobacco and beer. Oddly enough, the boys had never been particularly picky eaters when Derlin was around, happily gobbling up every flavor he'd manage to steal during his rake-wielding raids of the very same store in which she now stood.

She sighed again, picked up another Champale for herself and headed home.

The several miles of walking Derlin had left ahead of him before he reached the Clapp house allowed him plenty of time to marinate on the formation of his latest plan. Pressing it against the outside wall of the post office, he'd already taken a marker and cleverly blacked out the "DIS" on his "Dishonorable Discharge" certificate, drawing a flag and eagle in the margins to further disguise his ruse. Thus far, that was as far as he'd gotten. The rest of the plan would, as he imagined, come to him as he walked. He pondered swinging by the park to see if his old sedan had remained there safely over the past several weeks, but decided that when compared to his earlier propensity for swerving up into the yard, the journey on foot seemed more romantic and thus more likely to stir Mavis into reunification.

By the time he had the Clapp house in his view, it was nearly dusk. He was hungry and exhausted, but he'd made it without any setbacks, which for him was a major victory in itself. Unable to utilize the several hours of uninterrupted rumination, Derlin had failed to come up with much of a plan for his attempt to win back Mavis past his masterful editing of his discharge certificate. As he wandered into the yard, he took a deep breath and decided it best to just speak from the heart.

Hiding himself behind a large tree in the yard, Derlin propped himself against the trunk, removing his boots and fatigue pants. Carefully fishing through his duffel bag, he removed his crumpled formal uniform and began to hastily put it on. Hopping on one leg for balance, Derlin was soon able to secure his boots beneath his dress pants, having ditched his formal shoes for weight considerations approximately a quarter mile into his morning journey from Camp McQueen. Freshly dressed, Derlin patted the top of his head to smooth his sweaty army stubble and made sure his shirt was properly tucked into his pants. He slung his duffel bag over his shoulder once more and headed toward the porch.

Mavis had just fed the boys their supper and was just sitting down to her own with her parents when they heard the knock at the door.

"A caller at this hour?" Clebert asked, mildly perturbed. He checked his watch and started for the door with a look of mild concern on his face.

Mavis and her mother stayed seated at the table, nibbling at a casserole and eavesdropping quietly at the goings on in the hallway. Surprise drop-in visitors were rare as their little neighborhood was fairly out of the way, and Mavis in particular was paying close attention.

"Spurlock?!" Clebert yelled as he swung open the door. "What in the damn hell are you doing here?"

"Derlin!" Mavis shouted, leaping up from the dining room table and running for the door. Eudora sighed, got up behind her and headed slowly to the door as well. As she'd often told Clebert, they'd "never be free of the Spurlock boy." Her continued correctness on the matter brought her little joy.

Mavis gasped when she saw Derlin's buzzed haircut and formal Army attire. He looked like an entirely different person until you got to the blank eyes and perpetually slackened jaw. She barged past her father and leapt into Derlin's slightly more muscular arms as they shared a long embrace.

"Why in the hell are you back so soon, boy?" Clebert snapped. "You was only gone two months and that ain't time enough to make yourself no kind of army man!"

"I did make good, sir!" Derlin began. "They let me out on account of I was doing so good, they say I earned a break."

Clebert scoffed.

"No, look!" Derlin offered, pulling his "Honorable Discharge" certificate from his duffel bag. Clebert eyed it closely. His gaze paused at Derlin's flag and eagle graphics, but he seemed to accept the legitimacy of the paper at least in the dim hallway light.

"I saved the best part for last," Derlin continued. "Mavis, baby. You know I love you. You know I love them babies. The way I was drinkin' and carrying on and getting arrested all the time wasn't gonna do no good for nobody. I knew I had to become a better man for you and the boys so they can grow up right prideful of the Spurlock name. That's why when I got to army I worked and trained as hard as I could every day and sometimes at night. For you. I got bigger and stronger and faster so I could become an army hero so I could get respectified by you. And the babies. I got so tough that I won a whole big pro-wrestling tournament they had at army, just like "The Navajo" Ricky Yamashita. They didn't let me go fight up England ways and be that kinda war hero on account of they said I was too important to defendin' Alabama, but to prove all I meant to 'em and to prove how much you mean to me, they give me this wrestlin' belt as a going away present."

"England?" Eudora asked in the background.

Derlin pulled the belt from his duffel bag, got down on a knee and presented it to Mavis as though she were some medieval princess. She took it from him in astonishment, running her hands over the etchings.

"What the hell is "The Nicotine Wolf?" Clebert asked sharply.

"Oh, that's my wrestlin' name," Derlin offered happily. "I had a costume and everything. Y'all should have heard me howl."

He took a deep breath in the beginning stages of what was going to be a bombastic unsolicited howl, but Mavis interrupted him.

"Wait a minute, Derlin," she said quietly. "Is this belt signed to you from Lyndon Johnson? You met the president at this… tournament thing?"

"He was there," Derlin said casually, shrugging his shoulders and sticking his chest out proudly. "He might have even come just to see me wrestle. I got my picture with him and he shared his chicken and his whiskey with me. He said I was one of the finest soldiers he ever saw. He even wrote it right there on the belt, so it's o-fficial."

Clebert's jaw dropped as Derlin finished his explanation. He took the belt from Mavis, eyeballing the inscription and signature closely. He glanced up at Derlin, his eyebrows raised.

"One of the finest soldiers he ever saw?" Clebert asked quietly.

"Yes sir," Derlin beamed.

"Lyndon B. Johnson said that?" Clebert asked again, clearing his throat.

"Mr. President Johnson did, yes," Derlin replied again, still puffing out his chest with pride. "He was real nice."

"You had a drink of whiskey with him?" Clebert asked, his astonishment clearly growing. "You shared the president's personal whiskey?"

"Johnny Walker! Ain't never had anything like that before. Felt like I drank a milkshake made of bees. He gave me some of his chicken leg to calm it down," Derlin added, smiling and nodding.

Clebert stayed silent for a moment, giving Derlin a long up-down as he eyed his formal attire, his haircut and now-reasonable posture, pausing for an extra second on Derlin's scuffed old size six cowboy boots.

"Maybe I was wrong about you, Spurlock," Clebert said, slowly offering a handshake. "If you're good enough to be approved by the President of the USA, I'd say you're alright by me. Heck, you just might turn out to be a good apple after all."

"It's okay," Derlin smiled. "I been wrong about stuff a bunch of times. Most of 'em was when I was a baby so I don't really remember much, but-"

"Don't push it, Spurlock," Clebert said plainly.

Mavis giggled and hugged him tightly once more.

"All I know," Derlin said happily to Mavis. "Is that we finally get to start being a normal family. I can get a good job now that I'm an army man, we can get a real house and raise those boys proper. No more hay and windmills for us."

"No more hay and windmills for us!" Mavis repeated warmly, kissing Derlin loudly on the cheek.

Clebert and Eudora still held some reservations about Derlin's very sudden transformation, but it did seem that his heart and mind were both finally in the right place at the same time, which was a first. In the event that all his fanciful stories were actually true, Clebert even found himself a little bit proud to call Derlin a son-in-law. Just a little. As things had just shaken out in his hallway, Clebert saw no way around the idea of Derlin as a relation whether or not he'd ever shared a drumstick with the president.

Surprising himself as he heard the words leave his mouth, Clebert invited him in for dinner. Happily accepting, Derlin stomped right in the house, giving Eudora a mighty bear hug.

"Them babies still up?" Derlin asked hopefully.

"Yes honey, they're in their crib in the living room," Mavis said. "But they just ate so be careful, they might be a little gassy."

"That's fine I'll just look at 'em," Derlin said. "Don't wanna get my hands all doo-dooed up before dinner."

He tip-toed slowly into the living room, wanting to catch his children by surprise. Doing his best to sneak through the room while keeping an eye on the boys, Derlin collided with a TV tray on which Clebert had been working on a jigsaw puzzle, sending it toppling to the ground and getting Randy and Ollie's immediate attention. They squealed in delight at the sight of their father, pawing at the railings of the crib. Derlin sauntered over, tussling each boy lightly on the head as they smiled up at him.

"How you doing boys?" Derlin beamed. "Y'all boys is growing like beanstalks, ain't you? Still ain't got no hair though, I see."

The boys stared up at their father, cooing happily and grunting.

"Hey," Derlin said, "Daddy's missed you, but y'all hang out in here, I'm about to go eat a plate of dinner the size of both y'all."

Eudora scrambled to set his extra place as Derlin plopped down at the table and crammed a napkin down the front of his shirt, rubbing his hands together happily. He smiled warmly as Mavis sat down across from him and Clebert began to say Grace, patting his hair down once more as Clebert's blessing began. He was just about starved to death.

Chapter 30

Derlin peered over the edge of the crib at Randy and Ollie, now sleeping soundly.

"Man, they're big as hell," Derlin offered in awe.

"That's on account of they started crawling just about right after you left and got all them Spurlock muscles built up. Doctor said he'd never seen one baby crawl at 4 ½ months, let alone two! He said most babies are almost twice their age," Mavis smiled, rubbing Derlin's back as he gazed down happily. "Mama said if they don't start eating something other than Salisbury steak that it's gonna make 'em short but I think that's just an old wives tale."

"Yeah, baby, that's made up," Derlin said. "Everybody knows steak makes you tall. That's just science."

"I figured you'd know," Mavis said.

"Yeah, in army people'd ask me all kinds of science questions on account of how smart I am," Derlin replied casually. "Math too. They said it was like I had a abacus inside my brain, but I had to tell 'em that wasn't true 'cause there ain't no way one could fit in there and still have room for brains. That's back to more science again, see."

Mavis nodded.

"I hope our boys grow up smart like you," she smiled, hugging him once more.

"They will," he said confidently. "I'mma teach 'em everything I know. I'm smarter than Elvis his self."

July 6, 1968

Derlin rose in the morning before dawn, doing his best to not wake Mavis. He slipped back into his formal army wear and spent a few moments taking a comb to his buzz cut before slinking out the door. He'd gotten up so early because he wanted to get the "early bird" jump on his big job hunt. He wanted to be waiting at the door as soon as Lumpy got to the Feed n' Seed.

He enjoyed his brisk, pre-dawn walk though the morning dew from the tall roadside grass which had soon drenched his formal pants to the knee. He did indeed arrive at Lumpy's before the old man had gotten there and was ready with a smile and a greeting before Lumpy had even ambled out of his rusty blue pick-up.

"Hey there Lumpy, good morning to ya," Derlin smiled, waving.

"Well hey there son, an army fella are ya?" Lumpy began, peering across the gravel at Derlin and not recognizing him. "What can I do for ya?"

"It's me, Derlin," Derlin offered with a second wave.

"Spurlock?" Lumpy gasped, spitting a large wad of dip into the parking lot. "I ain't seen you in a coon's age. You been in the army, huh?"

"Yes sir," Derlin said. "Just got out, made it back home with honors."

"Well, I'll be," Lumpy said. "Never had you pegged as having enough discipline to be an army feller. Bet you peeled a potato or two, yeah?"

"Oh, I mighta peeled a few of them," Derlin said sheepishly, kicking at some gravel. "But the president himself said I was one of the best soldiers in the whole army, and so they let me come home. I was lookin' to see if I might could get my old job back."

"I thought I seen your picture in the paper!" Lumpy shouted. "But it didn't have no name with it and I'd never seen you that cleaned up before."

"That sure was me," Derlin smiled, trying to seem bashful about his accomplishments.

"A real life army hero, gettin' his picture with the president and you wanna come back and work here?" Lumpy asked, wiping his forehead with a soiled handkerchief. "With all you done for the country and all, I'd say you're right near overqualified for your old job, son. Anybody can rake gravel."

"Can't nobody rake gravel like I can, sir" Derlin offered confidently.

"Now, I don't doubt that for a minute," Lumpy continued. "With all them finely tuned army muscles and all. I tell you what, I think I can do you a little better than your old job, Spurlock."

Derlin's eyes lit up.

"How's that, sir?" Derlin asked hopefully.

"Well son, this is how it is," Lumpy began, stretching his back and letting out a mighty sigh. "I been running this place for 30-something years. I remember your daddy and your Uncle Vern coming in to buy candy and firecrackers when they was just little boys. I ain't getting any younger and I'm getting mighty tired of having to drag my ass in here every morning. An old man's gotta rest sometimes."

"I hear that," Derlin agreed, thinking back to the dozens of times in that very gravel lot he'd taken a well-deserved break propped up against a rake or a gas pump. "Everybody's gotta rest sometimes. Hell, I ain't even thirty and I usually sleep a whole bunch, every night."

"You've been around this place for years, boy," Lumpy continued. "You know the ins and outs and now you're a decorated army man to boot. I think you'd be just the feller to spell me some and take over running the Feed n' Seed. Now, I'd still own it, and I'd still be in here a lot, but you'd be in charge of the daily operations. You'd be my manager, what would you think about that?"

Derlin was stunned and his bottom jaw may have reached a new personal low as he gasped at the offer he'd been presented.

"Me?" Derlin began. "Manager of the whole Feed n' Seed?" He'd come in preparing to grovel for his old part-time maintenance job back but was quickly learning the power of a man in uniform.

"That's the long and short of it," Lumpy said. "I'd have ya in here every day, 'cept Sundays. You'd deal with the customers, keep the store neat and help me out with some of the ordering as far as car parts, chicken feed, candy bars and stuff goes. You'd get a name tag and a couple of free "Lumpy's" hats and work shirts so you feel official. Does that seem like something you'd be up for?"

"Lumpy, sir, I think you might have found your huckleberry," Derlin said proudly.

"I was hoping you'd say that," Lumpy replied. "How's $120 a week sound?"

Derlin coughed. He'd never heard such a figure bandied about in his life.

"A hundred and twenty dollars?" Derlin asked, slowly articulating every syllable, feeling like a Rockafeller as they rolled across his tongue.

"Yes sir," Lumpy said.

"Each week?" Derlin asked, still a bit starstruck by the offer.

"That's right," Lumpy replied, depositing another spat of tobacco juice onto the gravel between them.

"I'd say you've got yourself a deal!" Derlin hollered.

"I was hoping you'd say that," Lumpy said, offering a meaty handshake. "If you can start tomorrow, I'll give you $100 for the first half a'week and we can go from there."

"I sure can," Derlin said.

"Great," Lumpy smiled. He scratched his mighty belly for a moment, working his way up to his chest and shoulder. "Meet me up here same time tomorrow and we'll start gettin' you all trained up."

"I'll be here ready to go," Derlin smiled. He shook Lumpy's greasy paw once more and started off through the parking lot in a gallop.

"Wait just a second, Spurlock," Lumpy shouted after him.

Derlin stopped in his tracks, worried that Lumpy had had a change of heart.

"Yes sir?" he replied cautiously.

"Knowing you as you was growing up," Lumpy began. "I never did expect you to amount to a whole bunch. I'm glad you went and made somethin' of yourself. You oughta be right prideful about that, son."

"Oh, I am," Derlin replied. "More prideful every day." He offered Lumpy a salute and sauntered off through the parking lot in the direction of town, his head held high.

Derlin realized it was a long shot, but as he'd had a remarkable string of long shots go his way lately, he set his course for the park parking lot where he'd left his trusty old sedan before leaving for the army. The beaten, nearly-unidentifiable car had taken on a vague brownish-gray hue one wouldn't necessarily find on a standard color wheel and it had thus far survived its varying abandonments at least in part because it seemed no one else wanted to touch it.

Sure enough, as Derlin crested the hill above the park, he saw the old girl glistening greasily in the morning sunlight. He let out a celebratory howl and bounded down the hill toward his prized sedan, taking a brief moment to survey the scene and think on how far he'd come in the month and a half since he'd used the park's creek to bathe himself of fish scales and excrement.

To his dismay upon reuniting with the sedan, Derlin discovered that the driver's side door was left flung wide open, but the reunion was salvaged when to his relief he discovered his keys in their familiar hiding place thrown in the floorboard. He climbed in excitedly, noticing as he sat the wetness in his seat from what appeared to be several weeks worth of rain storms. As the stale water seeped out of the cushion and into Derlin's formal pants, it let out a musty, Panther Catty smell that reminded Derlin wistfully of the windmill for a moment. Cranking the engine to life on the third try and once again howling with satisfaction, Derlin thought back on those windmill days once more, quite proud that his new found station as manager of the Feed n' Seed would soon enable him to provide a real, actual home for his wife and family.

Chapter 31

Mavis was on the porch, feeding Randy and Ollie their morning helping of Salisbury steak when Derlin careened into the driveway. He quickly clambered out of the car, slamming the door with a victorious "woo!" and jogging up onto the porch. A neighborhood dog barked at his arrival from a few yards away.

"Good morning, baby," he beamed. "Good mornin' boys. Your daddy has some extra fine news this morning!"

"Good morning, honey," Mavis smiled. "Don't you look so handsome wearing your uniform again." Her gaze slowly made it down to Derlin's formerly white, rather soiled formal pants. They were damp and green from the knee down as well as damp and brown on the back from the rainwater in his car seat. Only the thighs remained whitish and even they were beginning to discolor from where Derlin had repeatedly wiped his hands during the previous evening's dinner. From far away, they could possibly pass as camouflage, but up close Derlin looked like he'd fallen through Uncle Vern's dock. She raised her eyebrows a bit but she maintained her smile.

"What's your big news?" she asked excitedly.

"Well, I'm workin' back at the Feed n' Seed," he began, casually.

"Oh that's great honey," Mavis offered, clearly less than excited but doing her best to sound supportive. "You got your old job back, cleaning up for Lumpy I guess?"

"Even better, baby!" he smiled. "He said on account of me being an army man and meeting the president and all, I'm over-koala-fied to be just raking gravel part time, so he's gonna make me manager of the whole store!"

"Manager?" Mavis gasped. "That's wonderful, Derlin!"

"The best part is, for managing he's gonna pay me $120 a week," he continued happily. "Every week!"

"Oh my goodness," Mavis said, placing her hands over her mouth in surprise. "That means-"

"That means we can get a real house of our own soon!" Derlin smiled. "One that has lights and bathrooms and ain't got hay all over the floor."

Mavis wrapped Derlin in an enormous hug and kissed him on the cheek.

"I'm so proud of you, baby," she said, wiping a few tears out of her eyes. "My parents are going to be so proud, too."

Clebert and Eudora were indeed happy to hear of Derlin's good fortune, not only because it meant he'd be out from under their roof but because for the first time he'd be legitimately providing for their only daughter and grandchildren in a manner they saw fit. They'd had their pains with Derlin since he'd first started coming around, but with this new, honorable, more adult Derlin emerging like a phoenix from his own drunken ashes after his brief stay in the army, they were almost to the point where they'd miss having him around. Even if he did still spend a good chunk of his home time shirtless on the couch, yelling at wrestling programs and Braves games on the television.

Derlin took to his first day of training at Lumpy's like a fish to water. His original employment at the Feed n' Seed had rarely seen him allowed indoors, and as such he was quite excited that his new position of manager afforded him the ability to be "someplace where he could get out of the sun." The idea of seeing what a price tag read and then plugging that number into the cash register was also something he picked up quickly. Proudly donning a denim work shirt emblazoned with a patch reading "Derlin Spurlock, Manager" on it, Derlin schmoozed with the customers like a seasoned veteran and Lumpy soon realized that he'd made quite a hire.

Derlin's first half week at Lumpy's breezed by and between his salary and Mavis' paycheck from the Piggly Wiggly, Saturday afternoon they had enough cash on hand to pay a deposit to rent a decent house. Like Derlin, Mavis had Sunday off, and after attending church service at the behest of her parents, Mavis and Derlin carted off the boys in their be-wigged Sunday best to begin house hunting.

It didn't take long for Mavis to find a home she liked. A far cry from the squalid apartment they'd shared early in their relationship and an even further cry from the old windmill, Derlin was shocked to find such a sizable house within even his managerial budget. A two-story, three-bedroom beige number with a sizable backyard for the boys to one day play in, Mavis had found all she'd ever dreamed of in a house for her family. Though equally in love with the house, Derlin himself was more enamored with the attached two-car garage. He'd long wanted to amass a tool collection suited for such a garage where he could tinker and fix things and was also quite excited about being able to keep his old sedan covered and out of the weather, in a place where he could bang some of the old dents out of her to boot.

Later that afternoon the paperwork was signed, Derlin was handed a set of keys and the place was theirs to move in the following morning. The moving in process was remarkably quick, as having led the transient life they had over the past several months, most of their "stuff" belonged to the babies and the entirety of Derlin's worldly possessions excluding his car could fit into his pocket. The only item they owned that wouldn't fit into the old sedan was the baby crib, which Derlin simply strapped to the top for the journey across town.

Their first evening in the house, Mavis' parents surprised them with a living room couch, which they'd sleep on that first night as they had yet to acquire a bed. The next morning, using his newfound clout as a salaried manager of a respected local business, Derlin arranged for the delivery of a bedroom and kitchen set which he'd pay for on credit, once a month. The furniture store owner was a longtime friend of Lumpy's and Derlin thought fondly on how nice it was to have friends in high places. Soon, with the sound of the babies' dull chatter and their toys strewn about the house, it looked and sounded like a regular family home.

Lights, bathrooms, everything.

Chapter 32

July 14, 1968

Derlin stood in the backyard, sipping a Panther Cat and idly spraying a hose on the yard, staring off into the wooded area beyond his back fence. The sun was just setting through the trees and it set the woods aglow in a beautiful orange in between the shadows. He'd fully intended to water the yard, but had become distracted by the wooded splendor and had soon watered a large puddle a few feet in front of him and nothing else. He turned and looked into the kitchen window, watching for a moment as Mavis fed the boys their Salisbury steak dinner. He waved for a few moments trying to get her attention, but she was occupied with the boys and didn't see him so he soon returned to his spraying and staring. He was proud where he stood in this moment, in the backyard of a house in a neighborhood for the first time without it being considered loitering.

A light wind began to blow and the tree branches began to play tricks with the fading sunlight. As Derlin continued to stare off into the woods and add to his now quite sizable puddle he thought back to the windmill, to the doubt and fear that they'd experienced in the turmoil that first brought them there. Thinking as deeply as he ever really managed, Derlin realized that though he had taken a strange and roundabout course in his quest for respectability, it was in his time in the windmill that he'd begun this almost spiritual transformation from forest-dwelling grocery bandit to the bathed and combed manager of a local feed store.

Searching for the word to describe his feelings, Derlin failed. He wouldn't exactly say he missed being at the windmill. It was an incredibly tough life for him and even more grueling on Mavis and the boys during his various absences, but he looked back on the days there with a warm fuzziness he hadn't expected. Certainly he hadn't developed a nostalgia for dragging carts of stolen goods through the woods masked under the cover of darkness, more a fondness for the simplicity of it all. He was unaware of the existence of Henry David Thoreau, but his feelings at the moment weren't too far off from the basic sentiments of "Walden," and as Derlin finally broke his trance and managed to turn off the hose, he vowed to himself to not get lost in the "hustle and bustle" of his everyday work week at the Feed n' Seed. Periodically, he told himself, he'd return to nature, spending his idle time swilling a few cans of Panther Cat under a tree "somewhere real nice" where he could relax and think. He crumpled up the hose against the side of the house, took one last glance into the woods, watching the wind whip through the trees for a moment and heading inside.

Mavis had settled down on the couch with the boys and was watching an episode of Green Acres as Derlin joined them in the living room.

"Hi honey," Mavis smiled. "How was watering the yard?"

"Oh it was real nice," Derlin offered, nodding. "If I keep it up with all my maintainin' skills, we're gonna have the nicest backyard in all of Coverdale, you and me. Maybe even all of Alabama."

Derlin thought briefly of the notion that famed University of Alabama football coach Bear Bryant could have a nicer yard, but didn't want to lessen the significance of his efforts by mentioning another man's yard to his wife.

"That's great, Derlin!" Mavis said. "You're so handy around the house. You sure learned a whole lot while you were in the army."

"I did, I did," Derlin replied bashfully. "They said I learned pretty much all of it."

The next few weeks were, particularly to Derlin's standards, rather uneventful as the family adjusted to a conventional home life for the first time. At Derlin's encouragement, Mavis left the Piggly Wiggly to be able to devote more time to the boys, happy to find free time here and there to scribble story ideas onto her yellow legal pads. She had rather enjoyed her brief foray into the world of employment, but she relished the opportunity to become a stay at home mom for the first time since the "home" had been the old windmill. Indeed, becoming a homemaking mother held more esteem to Mavis than any job she could imagine ever would. Since she was old enough to first contemplate the idea of children, being a stay at home mom was all she'd ever wanted and now, with the newfound windfall of Derlin's managerial salary, she was finally getting her wish.

Ignoring the trappings of a sizable house, Derlin spent much of his spare time in the backyard staring into the forest, or in the garage banging dents out the old sedan with his burgeoning collection of tools to "keep it shaped right." He'd begun hosing down the front yard nearly as often as the back, waving at neighbors as they'd drive past and honk, or good-naturedly pretending to spray children who'd pass by on their bicycles.
In the first few weeks in the neighborhood, Derlin had struck up a friendly conversation with at least half of the folks on the block, adding the mailman and the garbage man to boot. Remembering Oldsmobile's harrowing tale about mafia goons and bootleg mayonnaise, he was at first reticent to cozy up to the garbage man, though they soon made friends when Derlin recognized him as an old fishing buddy of his Uncle Vern's and soon learned that, as such, they had a shared love of rooting for Nascar driver Bobby Allison. Mavis had made friends with a pair of fellow young mothers in the neighborhood and the trio were soon taking the babies out for strolls every afternoon while awaiting their husbands' returns from work. Though the boys still had to wear their wigs when going out in public, the Spurlocks were quickly turning into a regular neighborhood family.

Derlin had recognized a few faces around the block from the torch and pitchfork brandishing mob that had initially chased them from the town, but he had no concerns about their identities being outed as long as the boys' wigs remained in place until they grew their real hair. He hadn't been getting any friction or strange looks from the neighbors and hadn't heard a single whisper about the "devil babies" in the conspiratorial and superstitious gossip that flowed in and out of the Feed n' Seed on a daily basis, though people still often wondered to him if he ever worried about the "masked rake man" coming back to town and attempting to burgle Lumpy's. Usually he'd laugh, puff out his chest and say "not while I'm around" in his best John Wayne impersonation. The impersonation itself was terrible, especially when he took the time to add a poorly enunciated "peelgrum" to the end of it, but it endeared him to the regular customers at Lumpy's and most assumed that the rake-wielding maniac would be too smart to scuffle with a finely-tuned army man like Derlin in the first place.

Word in Coverdale about Derlin, the returning army wrestling champion, spread quickly. Not a single person in town recognized the clean-cut Derlin in his picture on the cover of the newspaper when it was printed, but since his return, Lumpy had made sure that everyone knew that his new manager had rubbed elbows and been "drinking buddies" with the president. With Derlin's ability to schmooze customers, along with his popularity and newfound stature in the community, business at Lumpy's was soon booming in a way not seen since Lumpy's father Lumpkin Senior had been selling homemade hooch out of a bathtub in the back during Prohibition.

July 29, 1968

Lumpy stared down at the papers strewn on the hood of his truck, held down by the weight of his pocket knife and two rocks from the parking lot. Squinting his eyes at the figures on the papers, Lumpy double-checked some math on his fingers before letting out a pleased "Well, I'll be," and nodding.

Lumpy would be the first to admit that one doesn't get into the "Feed n' Seed" business to get rich, but his slow trickle of profit was gradually turning into a steady stream under Derlin's watch. Satisfied with his truck hood audit, Lumpy decided that Derlin had justified a raise to $150 a week. Being a Friday afternoon, Lumpy lurked around the Feed n' Seed until the end of the afternoon under the guise of meeting his brother Greasy to go marsh dog hunting a few miles to the south. Lumpy had long been vocal about his passion for hunting the beaver-like creatures and Derlin was none the wiser to Lumpy's facade until the old man handed him his envelope at the end of the day.

Derlin yipped with joy, thanking Lumpy with the elation of a puppy, celebrating the occasion by bear-hugging him and attempting to jump up and down. Galloping through the parking lot and successfully sliding across the hood of the old sedan as Lumpy looked on fondly, Derlin waved back, shouted another "thanks" as he hopped into the car and cranked up the radio. Rolling down his window, he gave Lumpy a thumbs up as he gunned it through the parking lot and onto the dusty blacktop toward town. He was going to celebrate in style.

Minutes later, Derlin roared into the parking lot of the Piggly Wiggly and parked across the front three spaces near the entrance. He jogged into the store, forgoing a cart out of the fear of possible recognition as the masked bandit based on his posture and gait. Instinctively, he headed straight for the meat department. Grabbing the four biggest steaks he could find, he scooped up a Champale for Mavis and began to browse the beer aisle for something classy and memorable to commemorate his raise. His eyes were naturally drawn to the cases of Panther Cat on the bottom shelf, but he noticed a new, exotic looking bottle on the shelf above. Derlin gasped to himself before reaching out carefully and securing a gargantuan 66oz. Pantera Grande, tucking it carefully in the crook of his meat carrying arm. He peered open-mouthed for a moment at the Pantera Grande display sign featuring a large plastic bottle, a palm tree and the words "imported Mexican beer" in bright red letters. After a moment, he slowly broke his gaze and began wandering up to the counter. It was his first time in the Piggly Wiggly as a paying customer since his spree and he was pleased to see a few people in front of him in line so he could re-familiarize himself with the style of actually purchasing something from the store instead of taking it at rake point.

He watched the folks in front of him check out with a growing confidence and by the time it was his turn he had the routine down pat. "Just hand 'em money for your steaks and beer instead of yelling and swinging a rake around and everything will be fine" he kept reminding himself as he waited. The cashier rang up his steaks and paused as she eyed the bottle of Pantera Grande.

"The sign y'all got over there says it's important Mexican beer," Derlin beamed. "I sure am excited to try it out. I've had a lot of beer but I don't reckon none of them have ever been that important before. At least they didn't say it on the bottle."

"66 ounces for thirty nine cents," the cashier offered blandly. "I'm sure it'll be delicious, sir."

Derlin nodded enthusiastically in agreement.

"Those certainly are some pleasant looking steaks too, sir," the cashier panned.

"Oh yeah," Derlin confirmed. "I don't have much of a sweet tooth, but I sure do have a meat tooth, by golly."

The cashier winced and continued ringing Derlin up in silence.

Derlin paid, thanked her and hustled back out to the still-running sedan to hurry home. He tipped his Lumpy's hat to an elderly woman with a cane slowly making her way around his car into the store, nearly hitting her as he flung open his rear passenger door. He hastily deposited his grocery sacks on the solid side of the floorboard, slamming the door back with a dull thud. Haphazardly whipping the old sedan back out onto the street, Derlin headed for home bursting at the seams with excitement to tell Mavis his good news.

Derlin honked the horn jovially as he careened into the driveway. Mavis and the boys were in the front yard on a blanket as he arrived, with Randy and Ollie taking turns gnawing at a favorite teddy bear which had grown increasingly soggy over the course of the afternoon.

"Guess what baby?" Derlin asked excitedly, leaping unsteadily from the car with an armful of groceries. He slammed the car door closed with his hip.

"What's that, Derlin?" Mavis smiled from the blanket.

"Lumpy gave me a raise on account of how good business is with 'folks comin' to see the army wrestling hero.' He said business hasn't been this good since his deddy was selling hooch during 'probitition.' On account of all that I get $150 a week now!"

"That's great news, baby!" Mavis beamed, leaping up to hug him. "$150 a week? I feel like we're millionaires!"

"Me too, baby!" Derlin smiled. "That's why I got you this Champale and me this special new Pantera Grande for celebrating. It was on the next shelf up from the bottom, so that's how you know it's nice. I guess that makes sense since the sign was talkin' about how important it was."

"That looks delicious, Derlin," Mavis said. "And you know how I do love a good glass of Champale."

"Only the best for the Spurlocks," Derlin said proudly, almost subconsciously puffing out his chest. "That's why I got the four biggest T-bone steaks they had at the Piggly Wiggly. And I bought 'em cash, to boot."

"Honey, the babies still can't have steak," Mavis said, sighing and bracing herself for Derlin's impending disappointment. "They're still too little for stuff like that, they don't have the teeth for it."

"But they eat Salisbury steak every day," Derlin pleaded.

"I know honey, but that's baby food," Mavis began. "That's different."

"It's still steak," Derlin said.

"It's not the same, honey," Mavis continued. "They can have their Salisbury steak tonight and they'll still be celebrating with us just the same."

"Does that mean I can have three steaks again?" Derlin asked excitedly, the clouds instantly clearing around his planned celebration.

"It sure does, baby," Mavis smiled. "I'd say you've earned it."

July 31, 1968

A fine example shown in the misstep in meat purchasing, "the home life" was a daily education for Derlin on the art of parenting. He'd often done things like robbing the Piggly Wiggly or joining the army in the name of Randy and Ollie and their wellness, but he was just getting his first taste of daily, hands-on parenting and his learning curve certainly had an arch to it.

Mavis handled the dirty work of diaper changing almost exclusively, though Derlin watched in curious horror from the corner of the boys' room whenever he was home in an attempt to master the logistics in the event that he was ever thrust into action in Mavis's absence.

"Derlin, honey," Mavis smiled from the changing table. " Quit hiding behind that chair. Just come over here if you want to learn how to do this, the boys aren't going to bite you."

"'Course they ain't gonna bite me," Derlin said condescendingly. "They ain't got no teeth. That's why I got a belly full of steak meat."

"Honey all I'm saying is it's gonna be way harder for you to learn from over there behind that chair," Mavis offered sweetly.

"I ain't gettin' no pees and poops on me till I have to!" Derlin shouted from his safe perch behind the rocking chair. "I been covered in fish guts and I been sprayed by two skunks at the same time, but I ain't never smelled a smell like's coming off of Ollie right now. He smells like he's been having Bean Night at Grandpa Hoyt's every night his whole life."

"Well honey," Mavis began, gently waving Ollie's little foot in Derlin's direction. "The boys are still just eating Salisbury steak. Until we can get them eating some fruits and vegetables, their little tummies are gonna keep acting like this. Remember back in the windmill the day after you ate three pounds of bacon?"

"Yeah," Derlin said, shuddering. "Yeah I reckon I do."

Randy crawled happily along the floor as Ollie was being changed and Derlin quickly snatched him up as a distraction.

"I'mma hold the one that ain't leaking poison peanut butter," Derlin offered. He shifted Randy to his left hip and began to make a rabbit gesture with his index and middle fingers.

"Lookit! Look at the bunny, Randy," he cooed as Randy cackled with delight, pawing at his father's hand. After a few seconds of laughter, Randy closed his eyes and began to pee, soaking through his diaper and onto Derlin's arm in a matter of seconds.

"Aww, just like his daddy!" Derlin smiled, holding Randy out to Mavis as she finished up changing Ollie. "Looks like our other little race car needs a pit stop."

As Mavis reached out and gingerly took Randy from Derlin, Derlin shook the liquid from his pee arm, wiping the remainder on his jeans.

"That reminds me, I think I left the hose on in the backyard, baby," Derlin said, turning and quickly heading for the door. "I better go check it out."

Mavis hardly had a chance to call after him as he bolted from the room, galloping down the stairs two at a time. She smiled to herself as she heard the front door slam and the car start. Derlin was trying, and she was mindful of that. Watching her change a diaper from behind a rocking chair was an improvement. Derlin didn't have to be wrist deep in Salisbury steak for her to appreciate his own brand of willingness to learn the finer aspects of fatherhood. He did seem pensive about the less sanitary aspects of parenthood, but she knew that his steel trap of a Spurlock brain was soaking up every bit of the information she offered like a sponge and that it would only be a matter of time before he began taking to "the pees and poops" like a duck takes to water.

There had been a handful of times since that first pivotal night darting through the woods with Derlin and the babies where Mavis had pangs of doubt regarding Derlin's ability to raise a family and be a strong husband. She thought of the cries of the townsfolk in the distance behind them, torches blazing, and how even though she'd been completely lost in the woods Derlin had put his nose to the ground and found that windmill. In the whirlwind several months since that night, Derlin's roller coaster ride of self-betterment had helped steer their lives in the proper direction, however indirectly. Even Derlin's failed robbery and subsequent incarceration had the benefit of getting his family back to the safety and care of the Clapp's home.

Now, as Mavis gazed out the upstairs window at her husband's muddy burnout tracks cutting through the corner of the yard, those pangs of doubt were finally put to rest. There probably weren't a lot of little girls who grew up dreaming of a Prince Charming who drank too much beer or yelled at wrestling on the TV. When counting attributes of their future husbands, "eating the most fish the fastest" and "most concussions" probably wouldn't top the list, but Mavis didn't mind them in the least. She knew that, no matter what, as soon as Derlin swerved back into the driveway, half-lit, honking and smelling vaguely of wet leaves, she didn't have a worry in the world.

Chapter 33

August 5, 1969

Derlin would get his first major solo parenting test on a Sunday. Mavis had made church and social plans with her parents and a group of their friends and would be gone most of the afternoon. He hadn't actually asked the details of her plans at any point, only requesting that if she encountered a "cake walk" of some kind that he be considered. All he'd managed to piece together over the squawks of the TV was that she'd be home before dark and her parents may join them for dinner. Derlin himself, another proud member in a generations-long string of lazily-secular Spurlocks, would be staying home to watch the babies and the race.

He wasn't nearly as dedicated to NASCAR as wrestling, but it was still safe to say that Derlin had a favorite driver in Alabama native Bobby Allison, as such fanhood had run deep in the family for generations. Having grown up not far down the road from Coverdale in Hueytown, Allison and Derlin's Uncle Vern had developed quite a one-sided rivalry over the affections of a local girl during the late 1950's, with Vern traditionally coming out on the short end of the stick despite being several years Bobby's senior. Depending on who you asked, family accounts would differ slightly on the sequence of events, but the rivalry would culminate in a horribly mismatched dirt road race which ended with Uncle Vern's pickup truck flipping into a pond. Unsurprisingly, the aspiring professional racing star on the other end of the contest got the girl, not to mention the undying admiration of the rest of the Spurlock family for the kick they got out of how badly he'd embarrassed Vern. Embittered, Vern would buy the pond and the land surrounding it a few years later as a dark monument to his youthful failure. He'd never rescued the wreckage of the truck from the murky depths of the pond and despite this, Vern still fished it near daily to prepare for his weekly family fish fry. While the fact that the pond had a leaking 3,000-pound truck deteriorating in the bottom of it gave the fish in it quite the robust flavor, the Spurlocks attributed it to the "secret spice blend" that Vern so often mentioned, lauding him for his culinary efforts.

Derlin eyed the clock on the kitchen wall as he "airplaned" the boys their Salisbury steak lunch. He'd timed out all his morning fatherings remarkably in the two hours Mavis had been away and had thus far miraculously been able to get through the morning only having to change pee diapers. Gathering Randy and Ollie from their high chairs, Derlin had saddled up on the couch and managed to crack a Panther Cat with five minutes to spare before the race started. He'd fashioned a large blanket nest for them between himself and the TV, quite proud of the set-up that would enable him to watch the babies and the race at the same time without having to turn his head from one location to another.

As the race began, Derlin peered down at the boys, hoping the roar of the engines would capture their attention and they'd begin to focus more on the action on the television than gnawing on the blankets piled beneath them.

"You boys like racing?" Derlin asked hopefully. "You remember going real fast in the car with your daddy when we escaped the hospital after you was born? That was kinda like racing."

Undeterred at the lack of response, he stood up and tapped lightly on the screen, getting the boys' attention for a few fleeting moments before they returned to gumming at their blankets.

"I bet you boys could be racing brothers like them Yarborough boys," Derlin beamed. "You know, Cale and LeeRoy."

Derlin rarely rooted for him, but he'd often admired LeeRoy's pompadour.

It could very well have been a simple coincidence, but soon after the race had begun, Randy and Ollie began playing their newly-discovered favorite game, crawl-chasing each other around the blankets and across the living room floor. As they took to circling around the living room, their flat hollers reverberating just like the engines on the television, Derlin got the distinct impression that they'd somehow taken his gentle prodding and would certainly become racing prodigies once they'd learned to stand, talk and drive.

They'd tuckered themselves out quickly, the game exhausting their tiny energy reserves, and were soon back on the blanket fast asleep. Seeing this, Derlin took the opportunity to quietly sneak out during a commercial break to puff on an Old Indian from the pack that he kept hidden on top of the fridge. Standing in the doorway to the backyard, facing inward and watching Randy and Ollie sleep, being particularly careful to blow his smoke outside, Derlin chuckled to himself and shook his head at Mavis' apprehension in leaving the three of them unattended for so long.

He thought back to a recent customer at Lumpy's, a middle aged man with a mustache who'd come in drinking from a coffee mug emblazoned with the slogan "Father of the Year" and wondered what he would have to do to get on the list of folks being considered to receive one. He was snapped from his daydreaming by the sounds of the race returning to the TV, quickly stamping out his smoke and placing the butt under the "cigarette rock" he kept in the yard. Rushing in quickly to catch the returning action, Derlin accidentally left the back door ajar. As he plopped down on the couch, the crack of his fresh Panther Cat can woke Randy and Ollie from their slumber and soon, as the race began to reach its dramatic crescendo, they began their game of chase once more.

Until now, the boys had kept their chase confined to the living room or the kitchen floor where Derlin could easily keep tabs on them, but just as a major crash in the race was un-dividing Derlin's previously divided attention, Ollie had noticed the open backdoor and began to crawl for it to elude his brother, who was in hot pursuit. Once through the open backdoor, they headed quickly from the patio to the mudhole created by Derlin's recent careless watering. Soon, they were happily wallowing in the mud like a couple of baby pigs. It was nearly half an hour before the race concluded and Derlin noticed that his pair of future champions hadn't done a lap by the TV in a good while. Frantically darting through the house, half Panther Cat in hand, Derlin finally noticed the door open to the backyard and panicked.

"Shit, they escaped!" he yelled, sprinting across the kitchen. In that split second, visions of scouring the woods and finding the boys without alerting the neighborhood or Mavis flashed through his head and he broke into a cold sweat. Running out onto the patio, he was met with an instant sense of relief at the sight of Randy and Ollie safe and sound in the mud. They were covered head to toe in thick muck and from a distance one might have mistaken them for tiny baby bears.

"Aw, my boys just went to do a little dirt trackin' is all," Derlin smiled.

He'd taken two steps off the patio toward the boys when the wind shifted and the smell hit him. It seemed his lucky streak of "just pees" had evaporated majestically in one fell swoop. It became quite obvious to Derlin very quickly that, although the boys were mostly covered in mud, they'd both massively soiled themselves and were now happily rolling in a mixture of the two.

"Oh goddamn boys," Derlin pleaded, waving his hand in front of his face. "You've done got us in one shit pickle."

Randy splashed his hands about as Ollie squealed in delight.

Derlin glanced frantically at his wrist, remembering immediately that he had never once worn a wristwatch in his life. Thinking quickly back to the time the TV announcer said the race ended, Derlin figured he had maybe twenty minutes to figure things out before Mavis got home, possibly with her parents in tow.

He looked frantically around the yard for anything that could help before his eyes finally settled on the hose crumpled against the side of the house. Seeing no better option, he grabbed the hose and ran back toward the mud pit. Stepping gingerly into the pit, Derlin was able to remove Randy and Ollie's diapers and clothing, groaning and retching as he did so. Tossing them aside, he grabbed the hose and began to spray.

Spraying as gently as he could, Derlin began to hose down the babies until he could get enough brown off to grab them safely. He set them gently on the patio, leaving the hose running and sprinting around the side of the house to retrieve a small tarp from the garage. He spread the tarp on the patio, placing the boys atop it, gently hosing the toxic mixture from them while they flatly hollered and splashed about happily.

"See, y'all boys is gonna be clean as brand new babies by the time your mama gets home," Derlin beamed. "I'mma get all this shit off of you and we're never gonna tell your mama about this are we?"

Soon, the boys were clean enough to take inside. Derlin took them to the bathroom, toweled them off and had just finished putting them in fresh clothes and diapers when he heard the Clapp's car pull up in the driveway. Working quickly, he placed the boys in their playpen with a fresh Charleston Chew and darted back into the backyard. He'd left the hose running and the mudpit was now beyond repair, so he threw the tarp over it hastily. He flung the hose against the side of the house, finally managing to turn it off. He frantically gathered Randy and Ollie's soiled clothes and diapers and heaved them over the fence into the woods, wiping his hands on a clean and dry patch of grass. Leaping over the puddle, Derlin burst through the back door just as Mavis and her parents were walking through the front.

"Oh hey, I was just outside putting the hose up so the babies can't get at it," Derlin said breathlessly. "I seen on the news they call it a 'choking hazard.'"

"You're such a good father, Derlin," Mavis smiled, giving her mother a look before kissing him on the forehead, pausing briefly to sniff as though she'd caught a whiff of something unpleasant. "And to think, my folks and I were worried all day that something bad was gonna happen. You even changed them and gave them their bath!"

"Yeah, I reckon I'll be up for one of those coffee cups real soon," Derlin offered.

"You know, son that sounds great," Clebert smiled, patting Derlin on the back. "If you're making coffee, I'll take a cup too!"

Chapter 34

August 6, 1968

The next day at Lumpy's, Derlin took advantage of his managerial discount and filled the back of the sedan with several large bags of grass seed. He'd managed to keep Mavis off the trail of the destroyed backyard thus far, but as the Alabama summer peaked and the August sun continued to beat down onto the mudpit, Derlin doubted that he could keep the secret for much longer. He'd acquired enough seed to resod several acres, understanding the overkill to an extent, but operating under the theory that ten times the necessary seed would act in the same way that ten times the necessary gasoline did on a campfire, covering his trail in a much more timely fashion. He was careful to load the bags of seed when there were no customers around the store, as he didn't want word to get out around town that the manager of the Feed n' Seed was struggling with turf management on his own personal property.

Derlin arrived home that evening just before dusk. Gently shutting the car door behind him and checking the perimeter of the house, he peered into the living room window, able to see Mavis in the kitchen cooking dinner. Satisfied that she was distracted enough, he barrel-rolled away from the window, sneaking back to the car and opening the back door as quietly as he could. One by one, Derlin grabbed the bags of grass seed, a dozen in all, tossing them over the fence into the backyard as nonchalantly as anyone could throw a large heavy sack over an obstacle.

Electing to crawl over the top of the wooden picket fence instead of worrying about the noise of the rusty-hinged gate, Derlin muffled a cry of pain as he toppled over the fence, scratching his stomach badly and nearly ripping his shirt. He sat for a moment to gather himself, prodding at his quickly reddening stomach before pulling down his shirt and army crawling the ten feet or so to his pile of seed bags. He stared at the tarp for a moment, well aware of what was oozing beneath it and debating whether he should slide it off slowly or rip it like a bandaid. Choosing the latter, Derlin took and held a deep breath before ripping the tarp from the muck with all his might. The smell was overpowering at first, but was dissipating by the time he began to have to gasp for a fresh breath. Working quickly, he began to stab open the bags of seeds with a garden trowel, dumping heaping piles of them across the mudpit. Soon, he'd exhausted all twelve bags and had covered the entirety of the pit in three to six inches of pure grass seed. Grabbing his discarded seed bags, Derlin opted to slip through the gate this time around, wincing as it creaked lightly. He paused for a moment to make sure that the coast remained clear and headed back around the side of the house.

As he crumpled the bags into the trash can along the side of the garage, Derlin was startled by a crack of thunder, jumping in the air and letting out a frightened "aw, sheey-ut." He smiled as the raindrops began to fall, however. Not only would an evening thunderstorm accelerate the regrowth in the yard, but it would also keep Mavis inside and away from the smell at least until the next day. Derlin was certain that with the quantity of seeds that he put down, "enough of them would take" that he'd really only need to buy time for a day or two until the problem had fully solved itself.

"That's just science," he'd told Lumpy earlier in the day as Lumpy gazed at him in disbelief.

Making his way back to the sedan, Derlin walked over, opened his car door and slammed it as though he was just arriving home. He headed in the front door, wiping his hands on his jeans and greeting Mavis in the kitchen.

"Man that casserole smells good, baby," Derlin smiled, kissing Mavis on the cheek and pinching her butt as he tried to peer over her shoulder to check the backyard through the window. The storm had worked quickly to help mask the yard's turmoil as nightfall approached and Derlin was quite satisfied with his work.

"Thank you baby, I've been working hard on it," Mavis said happily. "It's your favorite kind, too!"

"Meat?" Derlin asked.

"Meat!" Mavis smiled. Derlin pumped his fist in excitement.

"How are my boys today?" Derlin hollered, waving across the table to Randy and Ollie perched in their high chairs for supper. He reached into the fridge and cracked a Panther Cat.

"Good I bet," he added, taking a mighty swig of his beer, taking a moment to covertly smell his hand and recoil in disgust. The boys gurgled happily in their chairs, awaiting their treasured Salisbury steak.

"Did the boys eat yet?" Derlin asked. "They're lookin' kinda lean."

"No baby, not yet, I was gonna get to it here in a minute once I check on the meat casserole," Mavis said from the sink, scrubbing caked hamburger meat and diced ham from the edge of wooden spatula.

"Aw hell," Derlin offered. "You've been workin' so hard today, making me meat casserole, I'll feed them babies."

"That would be wonderful honey," Mavis smiled, wiping her hands on her apron. "Here, I'll get the jar for you."

Mavis handed Derlin a spoon and a jar of baby food, turning her attention back to the sink. Derlin slowly opened the jar, dipping the spoon into it as one would a toe into an unfamiliar swimming pool. Looking up to make sure Mavis was still facing away, Derlin put the spoon in his mouth, stifling a cough as he did so. Far from what he'd expected for something with the word "steak" in the title, Derlin frantically looked around the kitchen for a place to spit out the baby food, determining after a few seconds that he had one option aside from actually swallowing it. Checking Mavis once more, Derlin slowly spit the bite of food back into the jar and stirred it. He paused for a moment and took a deep breath before downing the last of his Panther Cat in one giant swig.

"You boys hungry?" Derlin smiled, walking around the kitchen table. "You young fellers love meat just like your daddy!"

August 7, 1968

Derlin awoke the next morning excited to check what he hoped to be at the very least early stages of grass growing in the yard. To his astonishment, there was indeed the sprouts of fresh grass already beginning to poke up through the piles and piles of other seeds. It seemed that a combination of the already fertile Alabama soil with nearly half a gallon of potent, protein-heavy baby excrement had given the fresh seeds a rapid start on life. Quite proud of himself, especially for so early in the day, Derlin could hardly contain his smile as he headed inside for breakfast. Wolfing his eggs and bacon down quickly even by his standards, Derlin let out a painful sounding belch and popped up from the table, anxious to get a start on his business day. He kissed Mavis on the cheek, patted the boys on their heads and set to whistling a jaunty version of "The Battle of New Orleans" by Johnny Horton as he headed out the door.

Mavis huffed to herself and frowned. Derlin had eaten his breakfast so quickly that he hadn't so much as glanced at the morning newspaper set thoughtfully next to his now decimated breakfast plate. She knew he usually only looked at the sports page and the funnies, but she'd folded the paper to a page she hoped he'd at least take a glance at since it was sitting right there.

When she'd picked up the yellow legal pads in the Piggly Wiggly a few weeks prior, she'd anticipated simply jotting down little notes and stories to keep herself busy during the day when the boys were napping. Though it was slow going at first, Mavis began to hit her stride once a lightbulb went off in her head and she set aside the drab soap-opera teenie-bopper stuff she'd been tinkering with thus far. Listening to the radio one afternoon, she decided to throw her hat into the ring of fan fiction revolving around her favorite band in the world, the Everly Brothers.

Don & Phil Everly were the fourth and fifth loves in Mavis' life behind Derlin and the boys, though it was only since her and Derlin's courtship had begun that they'd been bumped down from the top spots. Still, she often joked with Derlin that she, Randy and Ollie would run off to Nashville with Don if Derlin ever started acting up again. She owned all of their records and, until she and Derlin had married, kept multiple posters up in her room. Always sure to hide it when she and Derlin first started dating, Mavis had kept a framed picture of Don Everly which she'd trimmed from a magazine on her bedside table. Until Derlin, her love for Don Everly was the deepest she'd ever felt in her life and as Mavis let that feeling start influencing her writing, she began to combine her fondness of science fiction and her childhood adoration of Nancy Drew mysteries and soon had the words flowing from her pencil. She'd intended the story just as a hobby, but upon concluding her tale she was proud enough of her handiwork to send it into the local newspaper. Mavis was shocked when the newspaper's editor, an old friend of her father, agreed to print it in installments whenever there was spare print space available over the coming few months. She hadn't felt the courage in the moment to attach her real name to the story, but the first installment of "Cathy's Clone" by a "Mrs. X" was now soaking up grease next to Derlin's spot at the table.

Cathy's Clone: A Rockin' Mystery - Mrs. X

The Everly Brothers laughed together loudly as they came strolling out of the movie theater, their shimmering, wavy pompadours sparkling in the bright mid-afternoon sunshine as they emerged. Phil slapped Don on the back as he doubled over in laughter once more.

"Say, Don, that had to be the funniest picture I ever saw!" Phil said, wiping a tear from each of his striking blue eyes as he calmed himself.

"Me too, Phil. Me too!" Don added, finishing the last of his box of popcorn and tossing it perfectly over his shoulder into the trash can.

"That poor fella got himself into so many zany situations," Phil said. "I had no idea what he was going to get into next."

Don was now half-listening to his brother, distracted by a beautiful buxom brunette walking down the other side of the street who he'd noticed while Phil was bent over laughing.

"I could go for a zany situation myself," Don smiled. He nodded toward the girl as she passed by, letting out a low whistle to Phil. They were now both watching her sashay down the street like cartoon wolves.

"Love that chewing gum walk," Phil said, smiling.

"Very wriggly," Don winked.

He took out a pack of Black Jack chewing gum, taking a piece for himself and handing his brother the pack.

"Ain't she a looker," Phil said.

"See, that's the kinda gal I need to get to go with me to the big Summer Social," Don said, staring off down the street.

"Gee, that's a swell idea," Phil said, patting his brother on the shoulder. "That'd be just the kinda gal to help you get over ol' Suzie."

"I still can't believe her folks sent her to a nunnery just because we fell asleep at the picture show and got home late," Don said wistfully. "I swore to 'em we wasn't canoodling. Except for some hand-holding and a little smooch on the cheek here and there, there was enough space for Jesus between us the whole time!"

"Parents can be so square," Phil said, waving his hand dismissively.

"Yeah," Don groused. "Real sticks in the mud."

"Say," Phil said. "Looks like she's heading down toward the soda fountain. What's say you and me go get a couple strawberry floats and see if we can't say hello?"

"Sounds great to me, Phil," Don said excitedly. "Boy howdy, let's go!"

Don started to take off running down the street in the direction of the soda fountain but soon felt Phil's hand on his shoulder.

"Slow down old top," Phil said.

"Why? What if we miss her?" Don asked. "I might not ever see her again."

"What are you gonna do, Casanova? Just run up to her out of breath and tell her you saw her a few blocks back and thought she was the bee's knees?" Phil asked, shaking his head and chuckling at his older brother's enthusiasm. Phil may have been younger, but with his blonde hair, blue eyes and outgoing personality he'd had a little more luck chasing girls than his dark-headed and moody brother.

"Should I not do that?" Don asked.

"Aw, heck no," Phil said. "You've gotta play it all casual-like. Be cool as a cucumber."

"Cool as a cucumber?" Don asked.

"Yeah, that's right," Phil continued. "You've gotta act real smooth. Not run up to her all fast like you're about to trip over your own tongue."

"Maybe you're right, Phil," Don said, nodding. He paused to fix a loose strand of his otherwise perfect hair and straightened the collar of his shirt.

"I'm always right, Don," Phil laughed. "And don't you forget it. Now let's head *on down to the soda fountain before steam starts shooting out of your ears."*

With that, they headed down the sidewalk toward the fountain, laughing and talking the way teenage boys only do when they're talking about a girl they like. Had they stood in their spot for another minute though, they'd have seen another pair of young girls walking down the same side of the street. These two had the same checkered skirt, the same blouse, same hair and same everything right down to that same chewing gum walk. It seemed Don's dream girl had a pair of doubles.

...Stay tuned next time for the exciting Part 2 to "Cathy's Clone!"

Opening up shop at Lumpy's, the morning was as slow a Tuesday as Derlin could imagine and he was glad to finally hear the bell of the front door jangle for the first time at around 9:30. Popping out from a storage room, Derlin was delighted to see that his first customer was his Uncle Vern.

"Uncle Vern!" Derlin said excitedly. "I ain't seen you in a coon's age!"

"Hey there young feller," Uncle Vern smiled, offering Derlin a wave as he waddled into the store and made his way to the counter. He limped slightly from the effects of a leg injury sustained in the infamous "Spurlock-Allison" road race as a youngster and it, coupled with his short stature and hefty physique, gave him a particularly distinct gait that Derlin probably would have recognized from a hundred yards away.

"I just come in to get some fishin' line is all," Vern began, taking a familiar path to the proper shelf and heading up to the counter with an arm full of fishing line packages.

"I been hearing about ol' Derlin Spurlock the army hero makin' good and runnin' the Feed n' Seed and I had to come see it for myself." He coughed and spat into an oily rag he produced from his back pocket, the byproduct of eating almost exclusively fish from the pond into which he'd flipped his truck so many years ago. Aside from a hamburger here and there if he was feeling "like an exotic," Vern hadn't missed a meal from the pond since he'd acquired the property in 1963 after striking it big at the local bingo hall.

"Everything they're saying about me's pretty true I reckon," Derlin began, straightening his work shirt. "I met the president and I wrestled better than anybody in the army so I could come back home and be the best daddy in the world instead of just being the best army man in the world."

"That's right!" Vern said excitedly. "You got a pretty little wife and them two boys now don't ya?"

"That's right," Derlin said proudly. "Randy and Ollie."

"Randy and Ollie, I like that," Vern offered. Suddenly, he leaned in closely and lowered his voice to a whisper. His eyes darted side to side to check for anyone else in the store before he spoke again. "And nobody's figured out it was y'all with them babies that had the "666" birthmarks that everybody was caterwaulin' about?"

The color drained from Derlin's face and he stared at Vern as though he'd just seen a ghost.

"What did you say?" he asked Vern quietly.

"Oh, you heard me old top," Vern smiled, still whispering. "I know it was y'all. I been seeing those babies out around town with their mama wearing them Don Gibson-lookin' wigs on their heads. That's a real good idea."

Derlin began to stutter a response, looking around the store and beginning to panic. He'd been so careful in his slow cultivation of the family image of the "regular old Spurlocks" since the family's return to Coverdale and Derlin honestly thought that they were past the business of the "devil babies" forever.

Seeing Derlin's angst, Vern began to laugh.

"It ain't that big a deal, son," Vern said kindly, patting Derlin on the shoulder.

"They're not..." Derlin began. "They're not... you see, they're..."

"They're not three sixes, they're just three lower case "b's," Vern said plainly, leaning against the counter and staring at Derlin with his eyebrows raised. Derlin's jaw dropped and he stared blankly at Vern.

"How did you..." he began.

"How did I know?" Vern asked. "I've got 'em too. So do you. So's your daddy Clovis and your Grandpa Hoyt." He leaned in and removed his cap. Pulling apart his thinning hair, he showed Derlin that, surely enough, he had the same birthmark as the boys. Derlin began pawing at his own hair and because of its shortness on top, Vern was soon able to help him locate his own three b's.

"But how come the whole town didn't chase after y'all when you was born?" Derlin asked incredulously.

"Oh, they did," Vern replied. "Happened when your Grandpa Hoyt was born. Happened when me and your daddy was born, even though we was only six years apart. This town just forgets quick is all, I reckon. Spurlock babies have been getting chased out of this town for having that damn birthmark at least every twenty or thirty years since before Alabama was even a state. Hoyt's daddy Chester lived in a cave by the river with his daddy Brisco till he was four years old, on account of the town mob catching up with his mama while they were running away and throwing her off the top of the church. They stayed hid out the longest, I think."

Derlin stared at Vern in disbelief.

"You got off easy, son" Vern continued, "On account of your daddy Clovis getting smart and not taking you to the hospital after we got back from that muddin' trip you was born on. He and Tina did each keep a pocket full of shoe polish on 'em after that till you grew out your hair just to be safe."

"I can't believe it," Derlin sighed, slapping his hand to his forehead. "All these years how come nobody told me to watch out for it?"

"Well, every time a Spurlock man had a child, I reckon he just kept the secret to himself and just sorta hoped it wasn't gonna happen again." Vern continued. "And it kept happenin' every time. Well, every time they had a boy anyhow. If y'all'd have had twin girls none of this ever would have come up. Grandma Vodene says we all got one of them gypsy curses, and I reckon folks in town start shouting about the devil, but we know there ain't no truth in any of that crap. No lowercase b's ain't never hurt nobody and I sure as hell ain't a spawn of the devil. I reckon being an army hero, you ain't either. It's just something the folks around here get all riled up for every time a new Spurlock boy comes slidin' into the world."

"Is that why you don't have no kids Uncle Vern?" Derlin asked.

"Partly," Vern said wistfully, staring off into the distance for a few moments.

"That and that damned sonofabitch Bobby Allison stealin' my sweet lady Jurlene away from me after that God-forsaken race."

"The race where you flipped your pickup?" Derlin asked excitedly. Nearly thirteen at the time of the race, it remained one of Derlin's most vivid childhood memories. He didn't specifically remember the truck flipping into the pond, but he had a crystal-clear image of Grandpa Hoyt doubled over, slapping his leg and laughing as Vern emerged sullen and dripping from the pond.

"Yes, the race where I flipped my damned pickup," Vern snapped. "What other racin' I been doing?"

Derlin looked hurt by Vern's outburst and, instantly realizing this, Vern was quick to lighten his tone.

"I just shouldn'ta raced a feller like that in my old pickup truck," he said wistfully.

"I should've at least taken all the logs out of it beforehand. He was driving a brand new '55 Corvette after all. Man that thing purred like a kitten."

"Yeah, well, I guess there's no shame in losing to a famous race car driver," Derlin postulated. "I was the best wrestler in the whole army but I'd probably still get knocked on my ass by somebody like 'The Navajo' Ricky Yamashita."

"Yeah, I reckon you're right," Vern sighed.

"Silver linings, the wife always says," Derlin smiled.

"Yeah. Your Grandma Vondene always talks to me about silver linings," Vern continued. "I reckon if I hadn't lost that race I wouldn't have my pond." He paused to cough heartily into his rag, cramming it back into his pocket afterwards and clearing his throat loudly.

"It's a real nice pond," Derlin offered. "Your trailer sits real pretty on that hill by it and there's worse things to do than fish all day."

"Yeah, that's true," Vern smiled. "Say, speaking of fishing, I am still cooking up a whole mess of goodness for my Friday fish fry every week. You and Mavis ain't been out to the house since you first started courtin'! Y'all should come this Friday and bring them babies to meet their Great Uncle Vern."

Derlin began to salivate at the thought of Vern's fried fish and soon began to smack his lips together slowly. Though his deep and abiding love for the Screaming Captain spawned the "ocean meat" that danced through Derlin's dreams at night, the unique flavor of everything that came out of Vern's pond was something he'd cherished since childhood and he leapt at the invite.

"Well that sounds mighty fine!" he said rather loudly, lightly startling Vern with the enthusiasm of his reply. "Mighty fine indeed. I'll get Mavis and the boys all shined up and we'll be there, sure as shit!"

"That's great news!" Vern replied, slapping his hand on the counter. He genuinely enjoyed the solitude that his life had provided him on a daily basis, and hosting his Friday fish fry was not just a personal point of pride but also his primary social outlet during the week. He loved his parents Hoyt and Vondene dearly, just as he loved Derlin's parents Clovis and Tina, but he was quite excited at the opportunity to add a fresh Spurlock to the conversational mix for the first time since Derlin's last appearance over a year prior.

"Man, I'm hungry for that good pond meat already," Derlin said, shaking his head and smiling. "You might have to wheel me out of there at the end of the night."

"That'll be fine," Vern laughed. "It's all downhill from the trailer door for a reason. Although I reckon if you're gonna be doing that much eatin' I might as well get to catchin' and cleanin'! How much is it gonna run me for all this?"

Derlin tabulated the packages in his head, every so often pausing to count on his fingers. He nearly lost track of his count when he'd run out of fingers, but he was quickly able to rebound to managerial form.

"That'll be eight dollars and sixteen cents," Derlin said, adjusting his uniform once more, hoping the light would catch his "Manager" patch in a flattering light.

"Well that ain't too bad," Vern smiled, tossing down a crumpled ten dollar bill and a fistful of pennies. "I reckon it pays to know the man in charge."

Chapter 35

It was fair to say that Mavis wasn't *as* excited as Derlin about the invitation to Uncle Vern's, but she was happy to finally get the babies some much needed exposure to the Spurlock side of the family. The Clapps were doting grandparents who'd spent immeasurable time with the boys since their arrival back to town, while the Spurlocks were more the type of family that you had to seek out and come to if you wanted any interaction. Even as they passed six months of age, Randy and Ollie had yet to meet a member of their patriarchal family.

"I can't wait for the boys to meet their daddy's family," Derlin gushed in the kitchen that evening. "Grandpa Hoyt can tell them hunting stories and Grandma Vondene can mash up some chocolate chip cookies with her whiskey and spoon it to 'em like she used to do for me when I was a little baby. These boys is fixin' to get enchanted."

"I'm sure the boys will have a good time," Mavis said, stirring a simmering pot of chili on the stove. "But I'd really prefer if your grandma doesn't give them whiskey."

"It'll be fine," Derlin smiled, offering a dismissive wave of the hand, stomping over to the stove to stick his face over the chili pot and sniff loudly.

"Honey, the babies don't need liquor," Mavis said sternly, crossing her arms. "It's bad enough that they won't eat anything but Salisbury steak and they're sure not gonna start adding in Grandma Vondene's bathtub mash whiskey to their diet. It ain't even real whiskey anyhow, she just lets it sit in the tub till it ferments and turns brown."

"Aw, baby," Derlin began, attempting to make good. "I had plenty of grandma's whiskey cookies growing up and I turned out alright." He began to paw at an itch on his lower back before satisfying it by rubbing against the kitchen table.

"I don't care honey, no booze for the babies," Mavis said firmly. "We can try and see if they like Vern's fish but as picky as they are with what they eat I don't want you to get your hopes up too much." She shook her head and returned to stirring the chili as Derlin watched eagerly over her shoulder.

"That's fine baby, but I'mma eat a whole bowl of them whiskey cookies in front of the babies and I bet they're gonna be mad as hell at you when they see me chompin' away," Derlin replied defiantly.

Randy hollered flatly from his high chair while Ollie did his best to tip himself over in pursuit of a discarded hunk of Charleston Chew on the kitchen floor, grunting periodically in frustration.

"That's a risk I think I'm willing to take," Mavis laughed. She made her way over to the boys, bending down to pick up the bit of Charleston Chew. She handed it to Ollie, who stuck it in his mouth and began gleefully smacking loudly. "You can have all the whiskey cookies you want, but we're keeping the boys sober till they're 15 at least."

"Well, that ain't the Spurlock way," Derlin began, gazing over at the boys and pausing for a few seconds, feeling his wife's glare. "But I reckon we are prone to adapt."

August 10, 1968

The next few days passed uneventfully, with the only excitement around the house being Derlin's periodic attempts to get the boys amped up for "the best goddamn fried pond meat they ever had." He did not share his wife's problem with the boys' diet of Salisbury steak as he subsisted on mostly meat products himself, but he hoped with all his fatherly being that he could teach the boys to share his deep and abiding love of fried fish.

He'd drawn a few rudimentary pictures of fish and placed them in the boys' crib in an effort to further entice them, though he was unsure of any tangible effects the hanging of his artwork may have actually had.

All of Friday morning and early afternoon at work, Derlin had been unable to take his eyes off the "Winchester" clock which hung above the front door, as it seemed to be perpetually moving slower and slower.

Even his lunch break didn't provide him the usual joy. He quietly devoured his usual lunch of beef jerky dipped in mayonnaise, but his gaze didn't break from the Winchester clock for the duration of his meal. An uneventful afternoon and a motivation to get out the door led Derlin to having his managerial side work done well before Lumpy's 6 o'clock Friday closing time and it was scarcely 6:02 by the time Derlin peeled out of the parking lot, flinging gravel as he went.

Speeding home, he began honking his horn as soon as he'd turned onto their street. Per Derlin's instructions, Mavis was ready at the door with the boys at the sound of his honking, resplendent in their black wigs. Derlin skidded to a stop in the driveway, leaving the car running. He ran to the door to assist Mavis in loading the boys and within 90 seconds of his arrival, Derlin was flooring the old sedan backward out of the driveway once more. Randy and Ollie laughed in unison as the sedan's front right tire clipped the curb and sent the car on a brief hop.

"That's my boys!" Derlin smiled from the front seat, turning and giving them each a separate heartfelt thumbs up before turning his attention back to the street, shifting into drive and accelerating back through the neighborhood. Uncle Vern had mentioned a casual arrival time of 6:30, but Derlin was hell bent on not missing any of the action. He was anxious to show off his new bride and twins to the Spurlock family for the first time, but was also keen to be right alongside Vern when the first batch of "pond meat" was pulled from the fryer as he knew how his family could put away Vern's fish.

Derlin had ignored the clock taped to his dashboard for the entirety of the drive out of superstition, but finally checked it when Vern's pond and trailer came into view. It read 6:33 and Derlin let out a victorious "Ha!" as he swung into the small dirt lot at the base of the hill reserved for Vern's guests.

"Here wifey, you relax," Derlin offered, jumping from the car. "I'll carry both them babies." He opened the backdoor, groaning as he bent over and reached inside. Seconds later he emerged with a boy in each arm, appearing quite proud of himself. He karate kicked the door closed and started up the hill with Mavis at his side.

She reached into her purse, offering a sly "pssst" at Derlin as she did so.

He paused from his walking, taking a moment to glance downward as she removed a 66oz. Pantera Grande from her purse.

"I got this for you," she smiled. "I figured it's an important occasion, so you deserved an important beer to go along with it."

"You're the smartest, best wife a man could ask for," Derlin smiled. "And she's pretty too, ain't she boys?" Derlin jostled Randy and Ollie in an attempt for affirmation but they only gurgled quietly.

Derlin grunted every few steps as he lugged the boys up the hill, salivating over what awaited him at the top.

"Man, baby," Derlin began, shaking his head at his own imagination. "That Pantera Grande is gonna set off the flavor Vern's got in that pond meat. There's gonna be two parties happening up here and the other one is gonna be in my mouth!"

"I'm glad you're excited honey, I hoped you'd be," Mavis smiled, tickling Ollie's feet as she walked next to Derlin up the hill.

When they arrived at the top of the hill, Derlin surveyed the scene in front of him. Vern, as he'd expected, was standing directly over the propane turkey fryer he used for fish. Grandpa Hoyt and Grandma Vondene were sitting on the small porch of Vern's trailer with their feet up, each sipping a glass of sweet tea mixed with Vondene's whiskey while Hoyt puffed on an Old Indian. Derlin had been particularly excited to show his parents Clovis and Tina their grandbabies for the first time when he arrived, but they were nowhere to be found as he scanned Vern's property. As he looked across the yard to the infamous pond, Uncle Vern spotted him and waved heartily.

"Derlin! Mavis!" he shouted. "Y'all come on in here and make yourselves at home. Mama, deddy, come off the porch a minute and meet your great grandbabies!" Derlin lacked the free hand to gesture and he let out a hearty "woo!" at his uncle as Mavis returned Vern's wave. He quickly swapped Mavis Ollie for his Pantera Grande and Mavis cracked it for him with her free hand as they started across the yard. Uncle Vern greeted them by the picnic table, offering a bear hug to Mavis and a big slap on the back to Derlin. He tussled Randy and Ollie's wigs and laughed.

"You know, they don't have to wear them wigs here," Vern said to Derlin quietly. "This is Spurlock land, it's a safe place."

"What do you mean?" Mavis asked, perplexed. "Those aren't wigs, that's their real hair. They're just…"

"He knows," Derlin said flatly. Mavis turned to stare at him.

"He knows what?" Mavis asked with concern.

"He knows about the boys' birthmarks," Derlin began. "Just let me explain a minute. See, um… Turns out all us Spurlock men have that same birthmark on our heads. Vern showed me his and helped me find mine."

Derlin pointed to his hairline with his beer hand and paused to take a long swig.

"It's true," Vern said comfortingly. "We've all got it, all the full-blooded male Spurlocks. All the way back to the pilgrim days. We've been getting run out of town every twenty or thirty years for having 'devil babies' since that fella on the oatmeal box was still alive."

Mavis started to speak but Vern kept right on talking.

"Ain't nothing too much to worry about though," he continued. "We been in Coverdale for damn near 200 years. America longer than that. A Spurlock'll have a baby and everybody will see that birthmark and get all riled up and their mobs together and start lightin' torches. We'll tell 'em that it ain't no devil birthmark, it's just some 'b's,' like from the alphabet, but they don't listen, so we get run out of town. After a while they forget about it all and move on, so we come back with shoe-polish or hats on the babies.

Or wigs, like y'all did. I told Derlin I thought that was a real nice idea."

Mavis stood there with her mouth agape and it took a moment for her to compose a response.

"You're kidding." she said plainly.

Vern and Derlin shook their heads.

"You guys are fucking with me," Mavis whispered, leaning in close. Derlin was taken aback as Mavis rarely swore, but Vern took it in stride and leaned forward, parting his hair to show Mavis his mark. It was a conversation he'd had in nearly the same spot twenty five years ago with Derlin's mother Tina and, though she'd also flicked her cigarette at Vern on the occasion, she'd asked the very same question word for word. Mavis gasped when she saw Vern's mark and Derlin soon followed suit.

"And you didn't know?" she asked Derlin.

"Of course I didn't baby," Derlin began. "Not till Uncle Vern showed me down at the Feed n' Seed the other day. He said they just keep hoping it'll go away each time there's a new generation, but it never does."

"So they just been keeping on and not saying anything, hoping it'll go away for over three hundred years?" Mavis asked in disbelief.

"I guess so," Derlin shrugged.

"Seems that way don't it?" Vern added, offering a sheepish smile.

"Well, I guess it's good to know we're not the first," Mavis said, doing her best to take the information in stride.

"Hell, y'all probably ain't even the first ones to hide up in that windmill," Vern began. "You had a great, great, great, great uncle named Mortimer Spurlock who used to be a whale fisherman in the way-back-when. He gave it up and moved inland up from the Gulf of Mexico to start a family with his wife. Family story says they had twin baby boys and just barely escaped town with their lives, leavin' on horseback in the dead of night. Mortimer knew about that windmill way out in the woods and headed there. It was way farther out in the country back then, it was a long time before the Feed n' Seed. The only supplies they had was what was already on the horse when they grabbed him up, a couple bags of salt and some whale oil."

Mavis gasped.

"We used some of that whale oil for light when we were first there before Derlin started bringing back regular candles!" Mavis said in amazement. "Isn't that incredible, honey? That whale oil sat there for 150 years after another Spurlock man with twins left it when him and his wife hid out. I can't believe it!"

"I hope ol' Morty got to it before it spoilt cause that whale oil sure did smell like cat piss by the time we got at it!" Derlin hollered, laughing and slapping his knee. He guzzled another long sip of his Pantera Grande.

"Funny how life is, ain't it?" Vern smiled. "That oil's probably been keepin' fugitive Spurlocks out of the dark since horse and buggy times. I'm glad to know it's still out there. I'd be loadin' some up to throw in my fryer, but I figure I ought to leave it out there for when little Randy and Ollie have babies!"

"Verny hush up about them damn birthmarks and let me meet my grandbabies," a voice from behind Vern shouted. Grandma Vondene waddled her way across the yard with a lit Old Indian in her hand and pushed past him to reach out for Ollie."

"Oh, Miss Mavis," Vondene crowed. "What fine looking boys you've got here, you and Derlin did real nice!" She took Ollie from Mavis, offering her a smoky kiss on the cheek in return.

"That's Ollie," Mavis said happily. "And this is Randy." Derlin gently grabbed Randy's hand, making him wave at his grandmother.

"They are precious," Vondene gushed. "But it is so awful hot out here, let's get those wigs off of them before they burn up. Wigs is a good idea though, dear. Your daddy had that pocket full of shoe polish that I'm sure Verny told you about, but we never did think nothin' about no baby wigs. Nice wigs too."

"Thank you so much," Mavis smiled, taking credit for her mother's idea in an effort to build some credibility among these strange Spurlock women.
Vondene pulled Ollie's wig off, brushing some dirt from it against her sleeveless floral blouse, giving him a smacking kiss on the forehead, doing the same to Randy a few seconds later. She set the wigs on the picnic table and returned to continue fawning over her great-grandchildren.

"You don't need no wig like that while you're here, sweet boy," Vondene baby-talked as Ollie cooed in delight. She tickled his forehead with her index finger as he continued to soak up the attention.

"Is that another fine generation of Spurlock men I see?" Grandpa Hoyt asked as he hobbled up to join the crowd.
He patted each boy on the head a few times, offering a handshake and an introduction:

"Hoyt Spurlock, damn glad to meet ya."

"Y'all come on in and get settled and make yourself comfortable," Vern offered, gesturing to an assortment of lawn chairs, coolers and overturned boxes that he'd set up between the picnic table, his fryer and the pond. "The fish ain't really jumping out there, but you'll see one gurgle and flap around near the bank every few minutes till he figures out how to slosh himself out of the mud."

"That sounds real nice, don't it honey?" Derlin asked, smiling at Mavis and taking another sip of his Pantera Grande.

"Miss Mavis, I've got fish to be frying but can I get you somethin' to drink before I do?" Uncle Vern asked happily.

Mavis thought for a moment, eyeing Derlin's nearly departed Pantera Grande before making up her mind.

"Do you happen to have any Champale?" she asked hopefully.

"I sure do!" Vern said. "I keep stocked up on it on account of it's all Tina drinks when she comes out here. "That old green cooler should be full of it!"

"The one with the dent and the old George Wallace sticker on it?" she asked.

"That's the one," Vern said.

"Speaking of mama, where are she and deddy at?" Derlin asked.

"Oh, they'll be here." Vern smiled. "You know how your mama can be with being on time. I bet your deddy's been sitting in the trunk honking the horn since 6:15."

Clovis stretched out on the couch and groaned. Shirtless, in underpants and yellowing white socks, he looked at the clock in the living room to see that it read 6:45.

"Ah, shit," he muttered, vigorously rubbing his hands over four days worth of beard stubble and trying to slap himself awake. Running his hands through his unkempt half-mullet as he attempted to push it back, he was the spitting image of Derlin, if you subtracted six inches and a toe, then added 22 years and a few thousand beers to the current model. He cleared his throat roughly and stood up from the couch.

"Tina!" he shouted. "We're late for Vern's goddamn fish fry. Hurry up, we gotta get in the truck." He picked a small bit of fluff from his navel and discarded it carelessly onto the couch behind him.

Tina ran in from the screened in portion of the back porch where she had been tending to a small marijuana garden. Her short, wiry frame was silhouetted in the doorway as she stomped inside.

"What the hell, Clovis," she shouted. "You were supposed to keep an eye on the time! Now I ain't got time to look nice meeting Derlin's wife and my goddamn grandbabies for the first time!"

"You ain't gonna be looking that nice anyway," Clovis shot, dragging on a pair of crumpled jeans from the living room floor.

"Coming from a man who ain't exactly Ernest Borgnine," Tina panned.

"I mean cause we're just going to Uncle Vern's is all," Clovis replied. "I just mean you don't need no ballgown to sit outside Vern's trailer and eat pond meat. You know I think you're prettier than two Ernest Borgnines."

Tina batted her eyelashes suggestively and spun in a quick circle for Clovis as though she were wearing a gown. Her eyes darted around their disheveled, poorly-lit living room at particular piles of laundry that sat throughout in varying stages between clean and dirty.

"Perfect!" she shouted. She removed the halter top she'd been gardening in, dropping it into a separate pile. Her tanned bare feet smacked across the hardwood floor as she made her way to a rumpled yellow sundress that had been sitting there since a begrudgingly-attended community potluck a month earlier. She tossed on the dress quickly over her jean shorts, removing them from underneath and flinging them into a third pile of laundry.

By this time, Clovis had at least technically put on a shirt, a faded plaid Sears number which sat unbuttoned as he stood in the kitchen drinking the remains of a warm Panther Cat from the counter.

"Well, I'm ready," Tina shouted from the living room as she slid into a pair of dirty flip-flops she'd recently found under the couch.

"I am too, let's go then!" Clovis shouted back, gurgling a belch as he finished the last sip of his Panther Cat and began to snap the buttons of his shirt.
Finally stomping out the door and climbing into Clovis's aging brown Ford pickup, they were actually on their way. The clock read 7:13.

Mavis, excited to at least be momentarily free of carrying a child, popped open the cooler to reveal an assortment of Champales and a couple of Panther Cats. Grabbing one of each, she popped the lid on her Champale and took a long, slow swig before walking over to Derlin just as he was finishing the last of his Pantera Grande. It was so large and cumbersome to manage, especially while holding Randy, that he'd begun to quietly think of the bottle as his third child. He'd downed the third child rather quickly in order to be rid of it and was already feeling the distinct early signs of a buzz when Mavis walked up offering him the Panther Cat and a kiss on the cheek.

"Watch 'iss baby," Derlin said to her, doing his best to balance Randy while gripping the empty Pantera Grande bottle like a football. "I'm Joe Namath!"

"Roll Tide!" Vern and Hoyt hollered in unison.

He cocked his arm back, using Randy's weight as a counterbalance, flinging the bottle across the pond, where it skipped to a stop about two thirds of the way across. Hoyt whistled from the picnic table.

"My grand boy's gonna play in the big leagues one day!" Vondene shouted.

"Aw, I'd have made it clean across if I wasn't holding the youngin!" Derlin said.

"Derlin if that bottle don't sink, you gotta swim out there and get it!" Vern chided from his spot behind the fryer. He'd spent so much time standing there over the years that he'd created a bare spot of oily dirt about three by five feet. Though he'd never been on a ship or in the military, he quietly referred to this grassless patch overlooking his pond as "the Captain's perch," another secret he kept from the remainder of his family for fear of ridicule.

"What happens if it does sink?" Derlin shouted back from the edge of the bank.

"Nothin'," Vern shrugged, He took a large swig of his own Panther Cat and smacked his lips in satisfaction.

Derlin nodded and grinned in approval. He'd been throwing glass bottles into the pond since long before Vern had purchased it when Derlin was a teenager, and he'd continued to do so at an increased pace over the years while attending Vern's numerous fish fries. He liked to think that, down there in the murky depths, there were hundreds upon hundreds of bottles piled around Vern's old pickup truck. He swelled with pride at the thought that someday he, or even Randy or Ollie would throw the bottle that would enable that magical pile to crest the waterline for the first time and he began to expound upon that idea as he dangled Randy out over the water's edge to familiarize him with the terrain.

"There's all sorts of fish and bottles down there, my boy," he said proudly. "There's a big old truck too. The fish is where we get all the good fried pond meat I been telling you about! I throw the bottles down there and they sink to the bottom and then the fish have to swim higher up and closer to the top of the water and that way it's easier for Vern to get at 'em to fry up his pond meat. It's science!"

Randy gurgled, staring at his own reflection in the muddy water of the pond. He squealed with delight as a large fish popped to the surface and began to roll through the mud just as Vern had described. Derlin "oohed" and "ahhed" at the fish with Randy, proud to be experiencing nature with his first born son.

"When your brother is a few minutes older, he'll appreciate this," Derlin said slowly, scratching Randy's belly like a puppy.

"Fish is ready!" Vern shouted in a piercing tone that could likely be heard for acres in every direction. "Come get ya pond meat!"

"You hear that little man?" Derlin asked happily as he galloped with Randy to Vern's side.

The Spurlock's gathered around Vern's grease slathered, paper towel covered "dumpin' platter" and began grabbing at hunks of fish as soon as Vern had dumped his fry basket. Almost immediately, they began to burn themselves on the 350 degree fish and yelps and howls began to emanate from the group as they attempted to grasp the sizzling meat without further burning their hands or faces. It was a ritual, however unintentional, that they had recreated in various numbers nearly every week for nearly a decade. Hoyt, being the oldest and most leather-skinned of the Spurlock clan managed to grab his fish without issue, only beginning to caterwaul as he shovelled it into his mouth. Mavis and Vondene picked at theirs with forks, allowing the fish to cool before taking responsible bites, but Derlin had his own method that had proven sound strategy at both Vern's and the Screaming Captain numerous times.

He still held Randy in one arm, perched upon his hip, but Derlin moved about with the grace and quickness of a dancer. Surveying his surroundings, he quickly located a bottle of tartar sauce on the picnic table. Grabbing it in his free hand, he tilted his head back and squirted the bottle with all his might into his mouth, filling it roughly halfway with sauce. Puffing his cheeks out and pursing his lips, he maintained his balance with Ollie, grabbing a paper towel to act as a makeshift glove as he clawed at the pile of fish. Picking up three pieces at once, Derlin tilted his head back once more, taking a huge bite of fish and chewing happily like some sort of dextrous pelican. Via his old pal science, Derlin had long ago deduced that keeping four to six ounces of cool tartar sauce in his mouth enabled him to gobble 350 degree "pond meat" well quicker than his other family members and thus gave him a tactical advantage. He'd downed all three pieces in his hand before Hoyt, now guzzling a Panther Cat with his eyes watering, had gotten to his second.

"I swear it's goddamn cheating keeping that city mayo in your mouth while you double fist pond meat down your gullet!" Hoyt shouted angrily, throwing his empty can of Panther Cat to the ground.

"It ain't cheatin'," Derlin countered through the fistful of coleslaw he'd just shoved into his mouth. "I seen you squirt ketchup in your mouth to get at Grammaw Vondene's fried chicken first and you never did say that was cheatin'!"

"Ain't cheatin' if it's bone meat!" Hoyt hollered. "I can sauce my mouth all I want if I'm gettin' at a turkey leg or a chicken back. You aint grabbin' no fish by the leg, you're just eatin' pond meat nuggets like they're goddamn chicklets."

"Fine," Derlin snapped, "I'm just gonna sit down and feed the babies while you catch-up on eating pond meat, Grandpa. Maybe I oughta mash it up in a bowl."

Derlin stopped speaking suddenly and his eyes lit up. Though he'd only intended to insult his grandfather, a light bulb went off in his head as the words left his mouth. Grabbing an empty plastic bowl, he threw in a few pieces of fish and some tartar sauce and began to smash them feverishly with a spoon. Soon, he'd created a fine, greasy paste. He scooped a bit with his spoon and offered it slowly to Randy. Gazing at it wide-eyed, Randy unsteadily began to lean forward, chomping down on the bit of fish paste aggressively. He swallowed and began to lick his lips, pawing at the bowl for more. Derlin happily obliged. Mavis, elated to see Randy eating something other than Salisbury steak baby food even if it was more or less fried fish and mayo paste with some bits of pickle, sat down with Ollie and he was soon joining in the feast.

"I told you these boys had a pond meat streak in them!" Derlin shouted happily as Vern began to clap.

After a few moments, Randy and Ollie had exhausted the contents of the entire bowl between them. Their round little faces were caked with the greasy paste and Derlin hurriedly began to mix a second batch, personally tasting the concoction every few stirs to "make sure he was getting it right."

"Derlin, leave some of that for the boys, there's plenty of regular fish for you," Mavis chided gently from her spot next to him at the picnic table.

"I can't help it, it's good!" Derlin replied. "Imma make extra so I can dip my fish in it. Y'all want some?"

"I'll take some," Vern hollered from the grill.

"I wanna get at it too," Vondene shouted from the picnic table.

As the first batch of fish was most of the way gone and the second batch was nearing completion, the family elected as a whole to use the remainder of the batch to fill a salad bowl for what Derlin had coined "pond mayo" to dip the subsequent batches of fish in. Vern lent Derlin the large metal pasta spoon he used to pull his fish from the fryer and, after several minutes of vigorous, grunt-filled stirring, Derlin had mixed together roughly two quarts of his greasy goodness. Just as he'd announced its completion, Vern began to pull the second batch of fish from the fryer. Not wanting to have to waste tedious time spooning his pond mayo to the babies during such a transcendent moment in Spurlock fish fry history, Derlin quickly sloshed each child a small bowl and left it sitting between their legs as he sat them down next to the picnic table. Staring down hungrily, Randy and Ollie both began to paw at their bowls, shoving their hands into their mouths and soon becoming coated in a fine, greasy sheen.

The boys developmentally lacked the motor skills necessary to coordinate eating their bowls of goo without slathering themselves in it like it was cheap suntan lotion, but the adult members of the Spurlock clan weren't much better as they jockeyed for position around Derlin's sloshing bowl of fish mayo like wild animals around a watering hole. The sauce flew in every direction as the family devoured the fish and, through the splashing and elbowing the Spurlocks soon looked as though they were wearing some strange off-white Indian war paint. They were so busy hollering and bickering amongst themselves that they didn't hear the slam of the truck doors as Clovis and Tina arrived and started following the smell up the hill.

"What in the hell are y'all doing to yourselves?" Clovis hollered as he and Tina walked into the scene of carnage.

Derlin, Vern, Mavis and Vondene stopped eating immediately, all with roughly the same frozen "deer in headlights" look on their faces and Hoyt took the opportunity of their pause to jab another piece of fish into the remaining goo, popping into his mouth before looking at his son with a "deer in headlights" of his own.

"Y'all got mayo and shit all over you," Clovis mocked. "Tina come look at mama and deddy and Vern and the boy. They look like they've been in a fight with the dumpster out back of the Screaming Captain."

"My gawd Derlin," Tina drawled.

"Hi Mama!" Derlin smiled, wiping his mouth with his hand and then wiping his hand on the seat of his jeans.

"Why in the hell are y'all making such a mess up here?" Tina hollered, carefully stepping her way through the overturned chairs and discarded beer cans that had slowly accumulated in the yard. She made her way to the dented "George Wallace" cooler and helped herself to a bottle of Champale, which she popped with her teeth mid-thought and spit toward the pond. "Trashing up Verny's nice table. It's just the same goddamn fish he's been frying up since he parked his trailer here."

As she paused to take a mighty swig of Champale, Mavis leaned toward Vern.

"What type of fish is this anyhow?" Mavis asked. "I ain't never had anything like it and it is delicious."

"I call it Elkfish," Vern smiled. "I ain't never seen it nowhere's but in this here pond. They look sorta like catfish, but they all got them little nubs on top of their heads that one day I sorta decided looked like antlers. Plus, the sound they make if you stick your head in the pond sounds a lot like elk calls I seen on hunting programs on the TV. Tastes just like catfish, just a little greasier."

"I always wanted to have one of them TV hunting shows," Derlin chimed in.

"But you can't shoot, boy!" Hoyt shouted. "Never could! You'd miss the dang sky if you shot straight up in the air."

"Hoyt don't you talk to my boy like that!" Tina interrupted.

"He ain't lying," Clovis added. "Derlin might have that Spurlock charm by the bucket full, but he couldn't shoot through a barn wall if he was standing inside it."

"Sure looks like he can do some straight shooting!" Vondene shouted from the picnic table, pointing to Randy and Ollie, who were still lost in their own little world of pond mayo and were now glistening in the early evening light.

"I reckon that's my new grandbabies, sittin' in the dirt, eating bowls of mayo?" Tina asked sternly, placing her hands on her hips and giving Derlin a dirty look.

"That's them, mama!" Derlin said. "That's Ollie with the clean leg and Randy where you can still see what color his shirt is."

"I'm sure underneath all that crap they're adorable," Tina said, smiling at the boys before returning her stern glare to Derlin. She took another large sip of Champale, sweetening her tone upon belching. "But why are they eating bowls of mayonnaise on the ground, honey?"

"Oh that's more than just mayo, mama," Derlin assured. "I stirred a whole mess of Vern's fried fish into it and been feeding it to 'em. Since we tried it, we been dipping our fish in it too, so it's like double fish. Made us all get a little wild I reckon, but it's real damn good. It's the first time the babies have ate anything but Salisbury steak flavored baby food and Charleston Chews since they was still on their mama's titty."

Derlin pointed at Mavis, who smiled and waved from the table.

"Hey Tina," she said. "Nice to see you!"

"Hey," Tina replied, smiling and waving heartily as Derlin nodded in some sort of affirmation.

Each spied the other's bottle of Champale at the same time and offered nodding "cheers" to each other as they took another swig.

"Well if it's good enough for y'all to fuss and feud over like this I reckon I'mma have to try it," Clovis said, shrugging. He flicked his cigarette into the pond, paused for a moment over the bowl and dipped his cigarette hand straight in. Slowly licking the contents from his fingers, he nodded to himself, beginning to make a pleased humming sound. Finally licking the last of it clean from his palm, he turned back to the group and offered Derlin a "Damn fine work son," in acknowledgement.

"Say Vern," Clovis asked. "You got any more of that Elkfish coming out the fryer or did Tina making us late mean we missed it all?" He dipped his cigarette and mayo hand into the cooler, digging deep to fish out a cold Panther Cat from the bottom.

"Oh I got plenty more comin'," Vern said proudly. "They was bitin' good this week on account of the bait I got from your boy down at the Feed n' Seed."

"That's right!" Clovis said. "My boy finally got done jerking off and turned himself into an army hero and a big fancy store manager, working inside and out of the sun. I ran into Lumpy at a cockfight out on a buddy's farm a couple weeks back and he sure was singing your praises, tellin' me all about how you was bringing him all sorts of business and keeping up the store for him."

"That's right, deddy!" Derlin said happily. "Doing right by the Spurlock name, I suppose. I'm glad to see y'all though! Ain't seen you since I come by about that chair when me and Mavis was still just dating. I was worried y'all had forgotten about your boy. I'm so prideful for y'all to meet Randy and Ollie."

"They look like Spurlocks," Clovis said, clearly proud of the direction Derlin's life had taken since their last encounter over a year ago. He leaned over and patted each child on his slimy head, wincing slightly as he did so.

"You oughta see them boys get after a can of Salisbury steak baby food, I tell ya." Derlin said happily as Clovis began to once again lick the pond mayo from his hand. He paused and reached into his mouth, removing and discarding a large black wig hair and staring at it wide-eyed for a moment before returning his attention to his fingers to finish the job.

"Can we hose the little fellers down so I can hug on 'em and hold 'em without getting sticky? Tina asked.

"Hose ain't workin'," Vern shouted as he ambled back to his perch behind the fryer. "I hit it with the mower the other day. Jammed my blade up pretty good, too."

"Aw hell, just get a basket and dip 'em in the pond," Vondene hollered, waving her hand dismissively at Vern's sob story about the mower. "It worked for me when y'all was babies and I'd do it for Derlin too whenever he got shit or beans all over him and y'all was down at the race track or wherever. I probably washed all y'all boys in every creek and pond in Coverdale."

Vondene stubbed out her cigarette and hoisted herself up from the picnic table, waddling over toward a discarded wicker basket that she'd brought corn in a few weeks prior. She made her way to the babies as Mavis and Tina watched in curiosity.

"Alright, oldest first," she hollered, grabbing Randy under his arms and hoisting him into the basket. She waddled down to the water's edge and out the six feet or so of Vern's ancient, rickety pier, which predated his purchase of the property by decades. Slowly getting down on her knees as the pier creaked beneath her, Vondene lowered the basket a few inches into the water and began to slowly slosh it back and forth. Randy giggled with glee looking up at his red-faced grandmother, her face shadowed against the murky reflections of the pond water. Soon, after a little help with Vondene's free hand washing his hair, Randy was free of his coating of pond mayo, though he was now somewhat silty and musky. Vondene hoisted the basket up, regained her feet and ambled up the pier to where Mavis and Tina stood, mouths agape.

"Well I'll be goddamned," Tina offered in disbelief as Vondene handed her a slightly cleaner Randy. Vondene helped herself to the pack of cigarettes that was jutting from Tina's bra and lit a fresh one before bending down to grab Ollie.

Repeating the same process, she was soon hunkered over the water's edge, dipping Ollie into the water with a steady hand. Ollie didn't seem to be as gung-ho about his pond bath as his brother, but Vondene simply attributed it to the fact that he was a few minutes younger and therefore less ready mentally for the occasion. He became noticeably calmer as she puffed her Old Indian smoke down upon him however and after a few moments, he was as relatively clean as his brother. By the time she'd made her way back up to the picnic table, Vern was throwing the next batch of fried elkfish onto his layers of grease soaked paper towels. Vondene picked Ollie up out of the basket, tossing it aside on the ground and shifting him to one hip. Bending over, she grabbed a Panther Cat and cracked it with one hand. As she watched four generations of her growing family gulp down pounds of food as quickly as they could, she beamed with pride. She took a puff from her fading Old Indian, giving Ollie a wet, smoky kiss on the cheek as she made her way to the table.

Chapter 36

"So mama, you still workin' down at Meaty's?" Derlin asked through a giant bite of coleslaw and potato chips.

Meaty's was a local dive bar "club" on the outskirts of town. Coverdale's small-town rumor mill had only recently begun to keep up with it, but for years it had been secret knowledge by those with certain social interests that Meaty's was very quietly a gay club. This was known by homosexuals throughout the region, as it was an uncommon rural occurrence in the 1960's south to say the least. Though this knowledge had spread far and wide beyond Coverdale, it would have remained news for the vast majority of the townsfolk, including the Spurlock family and surprisingly Tina, who had worked there for seven years under the blind impression that it was a gentleman's club due to it's strictly male clientele.

"Yeah, I am," Tina scoffed. "And it's just the same as ever."

"What do you mean?" Mavis asked.

"Aw, here she goes," Clovis sighed, rolling his eyes before popping another Panther Cat and taking a sizable swig.

"I just don't understand it," Tina began, taking a massive puff of her Old Indian and sending it billowing out over and around Randy's bald little head.

"Understand what?" Mavis asked again, taking a step toward Tina to better listen.

Clovis signed audibly, looking over his shoulder at Mavis and Tina as he piled nearly a dozen pieces of fish onto his plate, dousing them in a pint or so of Derlin's most recent batch of "pond mayo." He grabbed an open half-bag of potato chips, smashing it loudly in his hands and crumbling the contents over the top of his plate. Adding hearty squirts of ketchup and mustard, he finally took the sopping heap to the table where it made a dull smack against the wood as he sat down.

"I been working at this place since Derlin was in high school," Tina began. Mavis, still unaware that Derlin was seven years her senior, nodded and listened intently.

"Every day, rain or shine, this place is full of fellas," Tina continued, pausing for another swig of Champale. "Ain't seen a real lady in there the whole time I've worked there, though we do get our share of 'handsome' ones in the night time. I'm literally the only waitress in the whole place and they don't tip me for shit. I try and flirt and show a little leg, bat my eyelashes and stuff. I figure if they're sneaking out to Meaty's to get away from the wife I might as well show 'em some meat. It don't matter. If I'm lucky I'll get a dollar each from 'em for running my ass off all night fetching their martinis and Manhattans and such. I go through two jars of cherries every day making their dang 'Judy Garlins.'"

Tina took an angry puff of her cigarette and shook her head slowly, staring off at the pond. A fish flapped its way up into the mud as she looked and slowly writhed back into deeper waters, making a strange barking sound as it went. Vern threw a rock at it but missed badly.

"Well, I sure think you're pretty enough to be fetchin' drinks in a gentleman's club," Mavis said warmly.

"Hell, she ain't gonna shut up about that now, either," Clovis hollered from the picnic table. He dipped a fork into the mixture on his plate, which had begun to run over the sides at a few weaker points, shoveling some of the contents onto a piece of white bread which he then crammed into his mouth. Grabbing a second piece of bread from the loaf on the table, he began to sop up the drippings on the wood from his plate, eating the second piece before he'd finished chewing the first.

"That's mighty nice of you dear," Tina said, glaring at Clovis for a second before returning to the conversation. "Between you and Derlin, those little babies is gonna grow up to be handsomer than Elvis Presley."

"Smarter'n him too!" Derlin chimed in from the fish pile.

"You can't be smarter than the King of Rock n' Roll," Hoyt shouted.

"Can too," Derlin replied. "On account of all the science I learned in the army."

"He was in the army too, boy," Hoyt continued, brandishing a piece of fish in Derlin's direction.

"Well, he wasn't never no wrestling champ!" Derlin shouted.

"And you ain't no singing champ," Hoyt countered. "You best eat your fish and quit besmerchin' the King if you know what's good for you."

"If I could wrestle Elvis, I'd pin him to the ground," Derlin boasted, puffing his chest out and jutting out his bottom jaw.

Hoyt threw a partially full Panther Cat, hitting Derlin squarely in the chest.

"Grandpa Hoyt, that still had beer in it, that hurt!" Derlin whined.

Grandma Vondene swatted at Hoyt, as he flinched to get away.

"Ow, dammit Vondene, them claws is sharp" Hoyt spat, skittering away from her as fast as his eighty year old legs would take him.

"Don't be hurting my grandbaby!" Vondene replied. "If you mess with dynamite, you're gonna get bit."

"Ain't scared of you woman," Hoyt shouted. "I ain't never seen a wrestlin' champion get hurt by somebody throwing a beer can. I bet you couldn't even beat Elvis in an arm-wrestle if it came down to it."

Derlin opened his mouth to reply, but thought better of it. Brooding as he grabbed a fresh Panther Cat and stomped down to the pond to cool off, he wished he'd remembered to bring along his title belt.

Derlin's displeasure at his grandfather's comments faded quickly with his pond-side beer and after downing it, throwing the can and watching it sink slowly to the bottom of the pond he soon rejoined the family by the fryer. The evening sunlight had gradually been replaced with Vern's porch light and the final batch of elk fish coincided with the arrival of the evening's mosquitoes, gathering by the light by the thousands after spending the afternoon biding their time by the pond. Soon, the family's attention turned more to swatting at mosquitoes than eating fish, which was generally the signal that Vern was turning off the fryer.

"Well, looks like it's Skeeter-thirty," Vern smiled, leaning over to shut off the valve of his propane tank.

"Yeah, I reckon it's about time we start saddlin' up," Clovis groaned from the picnic table, scraping the last sloppy mess off his plate with his fork and slowly lifting it to his mouth. "Tina's got the brunch shift in the morning so we should probably get on down the road before it gets too late."

"Goddamn mimosas by the hundreds," Tina muttered. She hugged Hoyt and Vondene half-heartedly, waving at Vern before pausing to say goodbye to her new grandchildren. She called Ollie "Randy" and Randy "Ernie," but the sentiment was there. She lingered for a moment wishing Mavis and Derlin a good evening before hearing Clovis' distinctive honk from the bottom of the hill.

She bellowed an "alright dammit" and stomped off down the hill, half Champale in hand. Derlin waved, despite the fact that she was already facing down the hill and turned back to the rest of the family to begin saying his own goodbyes.

"We best be saddlin' up too, Vern." Derlin said as he stretched mightily and patted his belly. "These babies is full of fish meat and I reckon we oughta get them put to bed soon while they're still sluggish."

"Yeah, I reckon so," Vern smiled, wiping down his fryer with an oily rag, really smearing grease across it more than anything. "I'm pretty close to a pond meat nap myself."

Overhearing this conversation, Vondene hoisted herself from her seat at the picnic table to smother Randy and Ollie with one last round of smoky kisses before they left, being careful as she stood not to disturb Hoyt, who had begun to doze next to her.

Derlin took the opportunity to pat his sleeping grandfather lightly on the head while Vondene doted on the boys. As he and Mavis each received a smoky kiss of their own, Derlin offered a salute and a wave to Uncle Vern, who slapped the heel of his boot behind his back before sending "finger guns" Derlin's way. It had been his trademark goodbye since long before he'd driven that truck into the pond and though Vondene hated it so, she was glad that he'd found something beyond the trailer to make his own.

Chapter 37

"The Spurlocks," Derlin thought to himself. "It really does have a nice ring to it." He had been raised by Spurlocks, as a Spurlock, but he couldn't recall the formality of being referred to as a singular family in that matter growing up with Clovis and Tina, just "them over there who keep sneaking their toddler onto the rolly-coaster," or "those folks always in front of the gas station." He said it aloud to himself as he walked into the garage to retrieve his hammer.

While wandering around a local flea market about an hour prior, Derlin had come across a man who was selling customized wooden signs, emblazoned with family names which he burned directly onto the wood. Derlin found the designs quite fetching and stopped at the man's table, furrowing his brow and leaning close to check out the finer details of the signage.

"The Smiths," he read aloud. "The Johnsons," he followed, nodding slowly. "Hey brother, you got one of these name signs what says 'Spurlocks' on it?"

"I don't think I've got one on the table son," said the heavyset, effeminate older gentleman seated behind the table, his high-pitched accent thicker than Derlin's. "But I could make you up one real quick."

"Aw, I don't wanna be a bother," Derlin said sheepishly. "I'll just get this Smiths one here and write over it with a marker or something. Y'know, surprise the wife."

"Oh, don't do that young fella," the man smiled. "I make these for a living, I'd be happy to make one with your name. Just tell me how to spell it."

"Spur like on a cowboy boot and lock like a key goes in," Derlin smiled. It was a phrase he'd picked up from Clovis as a child, though he presented it without his father's sexual double-entendre with the key and lock.

"Excellent, I can have it ready for you in just a few minutes," the man smiled, grabbing a fresh blank sign from a box. "They're five dollars."

"That's fine, just fine. I do got one question for ya, friend," Derlin said, reaching for his wallet.

"Sure what is it?" the man asked without looking up as he began to stencil in a lovely "S" & "P".

"Where do most folks put these things?" Derlin whispered, looking around to make sure he wasn't overheard. "I seen the sharp end on the bottom but I'm not too keen on jamming it into my car hood. I feel like it'd probably fly up while I'm driving and crack my windshield or something."

The man stopped stenciling for a moment, looking up at Derlin with a slight wince.

"Well son," he began slowly. "That sharp end is on account of they're designed to be stuck in the ground."

"Like, we take it with us if we're going on a picnic or somewhere as a family and I hammer it down in the ground when we get where we're going so folks know it's us?"

Derlin asked, scratching his head.

"Not... not really," the man said, increasingly perplexed by Derlin's line of questioning and really, his visit from the start. "They're meant for your yard. Maybe in front of your porch, or by a tree... or, you know, by a mailbox if you've got one."

"I've got a mailbox," Derlin said proudly. "We get mail all the time."

"Well you could put it there if you wanted," the man replied, returning to his stenciling in a bit of a huff, shaking his head almost imperceptibly.

"Naw, I don't think I want to put it there," Derlin said, shaking his head much more perceptibly. "I don't want people thinking we live all crammed up in a mailbox. It ain't even that big of one to be honest, just normal sized. I'll put it closer to the house so folks don't get mixed up. Already lived in a danged windmill for a spell and I like folks knowing for sure that we live in a house."

"I'm sure it'll look lovely wherever you decide to put it and your wife will be just enchanted," the man said, handing Derlin the finished sign and taking his five dollars.

"Everybody will know our house is the Spurlock one just by the sign," Derlin marveled.

"Of course they will, son," the man replied, not missing a beat. "You're a Spurlock. And now you've got a sign to prove it."

"You're right fella," he nodded, raising the sign in a goodbye wave and beginning his stomp back to the car. "And a mighty nice one at that. Much obliged."

Derlin cleared the dust off of his toolbox and opened it, digging through a pile of poorly organized tools before finding his hammer. After a few moments of rummaging, he pulled the hammer out with a victorious "Aha!" and held it aloft for a moment, studying it in the light provided by the bare bulb hanging above his head. Turning quickly, he jogged through the garage slamming the door and leaving the light on. Mavis hadn't yet noticed he'd gotten home and he wanted to surprise her with the sign nicely placed somewhere in the yard before she heard him crashing about.

He hadn't warmed to the flea market man's idea of placing the sign by the mailbox, despite spending most of the drive weighing the pros and cons of its prominence from the street in such a position. As his mind had wandered on the drive home, he briefly considered affixing it to the roof above the front door, nearly turning the car around twice to confer with the man on whether or not he considered a house roof a proper place for his signage. After much deliberation, he emerged from the garage hammer in hand, firmly deciding on placing the sign in front of the bushes next to the front door.

As he leaned through his open rear window to retrieve it, he accidentally banged a new dent into the old sedan with the hammer. He looked down and winced, then shrugged. Since moving into their home and slowly building his own personal toolbox, Derlin had intended to pull his trusty old sedan into the garage to bang all of the dents out of it with the very same hammer, now he just had another reason to set aside the time. He chuckled to himself, grabbed the sign and jogged as covertly as he could across the yard. Crouching at his destination, Derlin glanced through the parlor window to make sure that he hadn't been spotted. He nodded happily when he saw Mavis on the floor and playing with the babies, oblivious to his arrival. Looking around the yard quickly once more, Derlin jammed the sign into the yard and began hammering vigorously. Naturally, the loud pounding noises coming from the other side of the front door alerted Mavis and she was soon out on the doorstep, staring down at her husband as he crouched in the shrubbery.

Derlin was startled and nearly lost his balance before propping himself up on his hammer and steadying himself.

"Baby, look what I got you!" Derlin smiled, putting his arm around the small sign as one would a new kitten or a puppy playing in the dirt. "It's got our name on it and everything. I got it from this feller what makes 'em down at the Douggie's Flea Market. He didn't have no Spurlock one done up on his table but I charmed him real good and he made us a fresh one right then and there."

"Oh Derlin, I love it," Mavis smiled. "It's adorable!"

"Also it'll help other folks know this is our house, the man said," Derlin continued. "And I figure if we go somewhere like the park or the 4th of July parade with the boys, we can take it with us and that way folks out in the town'll know it's us too."

"That's so smart, Derlin," Mavis said.

"You just stick it in the ground like this," Derlin said. "Pretty much anywhere."

"I see that baby, that's great," Mavis replied, nodding.

"You wanna bring the boys out to see it?" Derlin asked hopefully. "I reckon they'd get a kick out of seeing a sign with their name on it, right there in the yard like a congressman."

"Derlin honey, the boys still can't read," Mavis said as gently as she could.

"They're babies. It'll probably be a good long time before they learn to read and write."

"Yeah," Derlin replied, visibly disappointed. "Yeah, I guess you're right." "Especially as good as somebody smart as you," Mavis continued, patting him on the shoulder as he maintained his minutes-long crouch.

"Yeah," Derlin said proudly, slowly emerging from his crouch to stand and puff out his chest, trying to hide how painful the movements were in his now-sleeping legs. "Yeah, you're for sure right about that one honey. Although between the two of us these boys might end up smarter than the King of England."

"Maybe even the King of New England," Mavis offered, hugging Derlin tightly around the stomach.

"Yeah," Derlin replied, kissing her on top of the head. "Maybe so."

As the sign settled into its life of advertising The Spurlocks, so too did Derlin. A house with his name affixed in front of it had made him feel like quite the cock of the walk, prancing around like a grungier mayor of Coverdale as he schmoozed customers one topped-off gas tank or bag of horse manure at a time. As the weeks passed, Derlin's star continued to rise. Known townwide now as Lumpy's hard-working army hero, Derlin was getting smiles and waves from townsfolk who used to just shake their heads at him and glare as he revved his engine at a funeral procession or drank beer in the pharmacy parking lot. People were calling him "sir" without immediately asking him to leave or to stop making a scene. He reminded himself of television's Sheriff Andy Taylor and felt that Coverdale was becoming his Mayberry, though he considered himself far more of a jack-of-all-trades than Andy Griffith's character could ever be. He'd never seen the good sheriff rake.

Lumpy had begun referring to him as "the hardest working man in Coverdale," which Derlin would bashfully wave off, though he did agree with Lumpy that he'd come a long way from his rake-leaning days of yore.

"Sometimes findin' hisself a good little skirt is all it takes for a feller to straighten up and quit being a goof-off shit-for-brains at the office, whether he's pumpin' gas or doin' some big city lawyerin,'" Lumpy would often say through a mouth of chewing tobacco. Derlin, usually unsure of how to react while being simultaneously complemented and called a shit-for-brains, would nod slowly in agreement before returning to his task.

September 7, 1968

Derlin had spent the morning at Lumpy's swatting flies with a rolled up newspaper, periodically pausing to scrape a small handful of bodies off of the paper and onto the front stoop. He'd intended this as a warning to other flies, vaguely citing some kind of science in defense of Lumpy's objections, and soon he'd smashed a good twenty or thirty flies, smearing the back of the paper beyond readability. Had he managed to scrape off all of the goo, he'd have noticed the most recent piece of his wife's anonymous handiwork bringing life to the back pages between a church bulletin and the results of a nearby Labor Day car show.

Cathy's Clone: A Rockin' Mystery, Part 2 - Mrs. X

Don and Phil ambled into the soda fountain, looking around for their mystery girl. They saddled up to the counter, each taking a seat and waving at Ol' Myrtle, who'd been making them strawberry floats since before they'd started making hit records.

"Well if it isn't the Everly Brothers," Myrtle smiled warmly. "Are you boys back from your little rock n' roll tour already?"

"Yes ma'am," they said in unison.

"We finished up playing a couple big county fairs in Texas, but we went all over!" Phil said. "We had such a good time and met a lot of nice folks who sure seem to dig our records."

"That's great news boys," Myrtle said happily. "I always knew the two of you would make it big one day, ever since you were still singing with your ma and pa in front of the drug store on Saturdays."

"Thanks Miss Myrtle," Don said. "It sure is a neat way to make a livin'."

"Say, can I get you boys a couple of your usual drinks?" Myrtle asked.

"Boy can you!" Phil said. "I mean 'yes ma'am.' It sure is a scorcher out there today."

"Oh my it sure is," Myrtle said, fanning herself. "I've been about to hop in that ice cream freezer all afternoon."

"Miss Myrtle, can I get extra strawberry in mine?" Don asked hopefully.

"Oh, Donnie," she replied as she began to make the boys' floats. "You get extra strawberry every time you come in here and you have since you could barely see over this counter. In fact, with as many of these as you've drank over the years, I don't see how you haven't turned into a strawberry yet."

The three of them laughed together as she doused Don's ice cream with strawberry syrup and Don started to blush.

"Actually, Miss Myrtle, speaking of Donnie here turning into a strawberry," Phil began. "You didn't happen to see some pretty little brunette in a red and black checkered skirt walk in here a few minutes ago, did you? We saw her as we were comin' out of the picture show and I think ol' Cupid's arrow hit my brother right square in the heart."

"Aw, honey, I see all sorts of pretty girls come in and out of here," Myrtle said, handing the boys their sodas and watching them each take a long, thirsty pull on their paper straws. "I've gotta say, as bad as my eyes have gotten over the years, they just about all look the same to me nowadays."

"Oh, this wasn't one of the girls from around school," Phil said. "We'd have recognized her. Maybe she's new to town."

The bell rang as the store door opened and Myrtle nodded toward the entrance.There she was! The buxom brunette walked right through the door, removing her large black sunglasses and gazing around the room. Don and Phil quickly moved back to two seats at the counter, nearly stumbling over themselves to make it appear that they were having a normal, nonchalant conversation.

"Yeah, I think the basketball team has a chance to win all the marbles this year!" Don said, far too loudly for a normal inside conversation.

Phil whacked him on the shoulder.

"Don, you jamoke, it's summer," Phil scolded. "It ain't basketball season."

"Well she probably doesn't know that!" Don whispered back, rubbing his shoulder.

Myrtle laughed quietly to herself as the girl made her way across the room and approached the counter. Phil and Don both got so quiet you'd think they were trying to play hide and seek.

"Say boys, is this seat taken?" the girl asked, smiling as she leaned against the counter.

"The seat?" Don said, again much too loudly. "No, nobody's sitting there! Just me sitting in this one and my brother sitting in this one here!" He pointed at Phil and Phil did his best not to smirk at his brother's conversation skills.

"Yeah, slide on up on the stool next to Donnie, here," Phil offered, gesturing with his hand as Don's eyes got as big as saucers and he started to blush.

"That's mighty nice of you all. My being new to town I sure do appreciate you being so friendly," the girl replied, taking the seat and smiling flirtatiously at both of the brothers. "My name is Cathy, by the way."

"That sure is a pretty name!" Don blurted out. He startled Cathy a bit, but her smile stayed in place. Her eyes flickered seductively and a few seconds of awkward silence followed.

Phil cleared his throat.

"Well, this is my brother Don, and I'm Phil," Phil said. "It's real nice to meet *you."*

"And it's nice to meet you two as well," Cathy said. "Say, I'm sure you guys must get asked this all the time, being so handsome like you are, but you wouldn't happen to be Don and Phil, the Everly Brothers would you?"

Don started to blush, partly at Cathy calling him handsome and partly because he still got a little nervous when folks would recognize him and his brother in public. A girl as pretty as Cathy both recognizing him and calling him handsome had Don a little flustered.

"We just might be," Phil smiled. "Sorry about my brother, he can be a little shy sometimes. He always blushes like that if he thinks a girl is real pretty."

Don shushed his brother and swatted him on the leg.

"Hey, I'm doing all the heavy lifting for you!" Phil whispered. "Offer to buy her a float or somethin'."

"Oh, I just love you guys!" Cathy gushed. "I won't shriek and yell and cause a scene but I've thought you guys were the bee's knees since you first started putting out records."

"Aw, that's mighty nice of you Cathy," Don said, still as beet red in the face as his otherwise dark and golden complexion would allow. "We always like hearing that we're doing something right with our songs. It sure does mean a lot to hear that."

"I think you guys are better than Elvis," Cathy smiled.

"Well, we are a lot smarter than he is," Phil laughed.

"Say, Cathy," Don began. "Could I buy you an ice cream float?"

"That would be lovely," Cathy said, running her hand down Don's shoulder. "I'd love a strawberry float with extra strawberries. It's my favorite!"

Over the next half an hour, Don and Cathy got to know each other and Phil did his best to make small talk with ol' Myrtle when she wasn't busy with other customers, both of them sneaking glances at Don and Cathy every time she laughed or told him he was handsome.

Finally, after what seemed to Phil to be most of the afternoon, Cathy announced that she had to go meet some friends and needed to get going.

"Well, it sure was nice talkin' with you," Don said. His confidence had grown a lot over the time they'd spent talking, but he was still bashful about asking out a girl he'd just met.

"It was nice talkin' with you too, Don," Cathy said, that same smile still on her face. "I sure hope I see you around town."

"That'd be nice," Don said, shuffling his feet shyly and looking down at them. "Say, in a couple weeks they're having a big dance down at that new pavilion they built. They're callin' it the Summer Social."

"Oh, I think I've heard of it," Cathy said, batting her eyelashes. "Maybe I saw a flier for it down by the drug store."

"Maybe you did," Don said, doing his best to blurt out his question without sounding too awkward. "Well, what I was gonna ask is, seeing as how we're on tour and travelling a bunch, I don't really have a steady girl. And I figured maybe, since you're new to town, you might not have a steady fella, so maybe you might wanna go to the social with me?"

Cathy's eyes lit up and she squealed excitedly.

"I'd love to, Don," she said happily, grabbing his hands and squeezing. "I'd love it more than anything in the world."

"Well isn't that swell?" Phil said, swooping in and putting a hand on each of their shoulders. "You two birds going to the dance together? Seems like a match made in heaven to me." He winked at his brother.

"I'm so excited," Cathy smiled. "But I really do have to get going. I'm meeting my girlfriends on the corner and we're going to a ladies club meeting together."

"Well don't let us keep you," Don said. "How about tomorrow maybe I'll see you down here for another float? Maybe around two?"

"That sounds perfect!" Cathy said, waving and blowing him a kiss as she headed out the door. The bell clanged as the door shut behind her and Don fell back onto his stool with a look of wonder on his face as Phil sat down next to him.

"Would you look at that?" Phil said, shaking his head and clicking his tongue. "Ol' Donnie has got himself a date to the social."

"I can't believe it!" Don smiled, a look of shock still on his face. "We hit it off so good. We like so many of the same things. She's a real peach!"

"I just hope she's got a friend for me," Phil laughed.

They turned back around on their stools, laughing happily at Don's good fortune and deciding to have another float to celebrate. Had they decided to leave the soda fountain, they'd have seen quite a sight on the corner. There was Cathy, meeting her half dozen girlfriends, each one of whom looked and dressed identically to her, right down to the skirt, eyelashes and the chewing gum walk. As the seven Cathys disappeared around the corner together, Phil and Don continued their good-natured banter at the fountain counter.

"I bet she does, Phil," Don chided. "But I bet she won't be as pretty!"

September 8, 1968

Just as Derlin was settling down to the task of re-spooling a display of fishing wire that some unruly children had unwound during his morning smoke break, he heard a car pull up slowly in the gravel and soon heard the familiar bell of the front door. A handsome young man, probably two or three years Derlin's junior, strode through the door in a billowing white coat.

"Man, that's some jacket, stranger," Derlin offered as greeting. "Are you a colonel or something?"

"Oh heavens no," the man began, smiling. "My name's Ronald Thurbison, I'm just moving to town today." He extended his hand and Derlin shook it.

"Well, welcome to town, friend," Derlin smiled. "My name's Derlin Spurlock. Can I interest you in some discount fishing line?"

He held up the loosened spool, still wrapped around his hands and wrists.

"Not today I'm afraid, Derlin," Ronald replied. "I just stopped for gas. I'm running a little behind and need to get to town as soon as I can to meet with a few of my associates to start getting my new office set up."

"Oh that's fine," Derlin said. "We got plenty of gas, but we keep it outside."

"I'd imagine so," Ronald chuckled as Derlin motioned to the door and they began to walk outside.

"You don't sound like you're from around here," Derlin observed. "What kinda office you getting set up?"

"Oh, I'm the new pediatrician in town," Ronald said.

"Pediatrician?" Derlin asked, perplexed. He sounded out the word slowly and furrowed his brow.

"Doctor for children," Ronald explained. "I'm taking over for Dr. Leslie since he's decided to retire."

"Doctor for children?" Derlin asked, his brow maintaining its furrow. "What do kids need doctors for when they're still all young and spry? I never went to no doctor as a kid and I turned out fine." Derlin flexed his arm, pointing to his bicep.

"All sorts of ailments can get the little ones, Mr. Spurlock," Ronald replied, chuckling but a little alarmed. "They need vaccinations from diseases and check-ups on their development to make sure they're growing up right. It's very necessary."

"Huh," Derlin replied. "Vaccinations. I got some of them while I was in the army. Doctor said I can't get rabies or polio anymore even if I tried."

He began to pump the gas and leaned casually against Ronald's green Pontiac as he pumped.

"Well that's the idea," Ronald said. "Keep them as healthy and happy as we can and keep them away from the dangers of preventable diseases."

"I got two babies, they're both healthy as shit," Derlin said, trying not to sound boastful. "They're fast as hell and seem like they're gonna grow up real smart cause I seen 'em do some good figurin' in their time, but it's hard to tell since they ain't talking yet. They ain't never been to no doctor though, you reckon I should bring 'em in?"

"They've never been to a doctor?" Ronald asked, astonished. "How old are they?"

"Oh they're about seven months I guess. Twins boys, Randy and Ollie," Derlin replied, beaming with pride. "They're real nice babies too."

"I think you should bring them in as soon as you can just to be safe," Ronald said. Just call down to my office tomorrow and we'll set you guys up an appointment." He handed Derlin his card, which Derlin squinted at and crammed into his front jean pocket.

"You reckon me and the wife need to worry since the boys ain't had no formal doctoring?" Derlin asked, concerned.

"I mean, I don't doubt that they're as healthy and... fast as you say," Ronald replied. "But it never hurts to err on the side of caution and go ahead and get them checked out and caught up with everything they need to grow properly."

"Yeah, that sounds like a smart idea, Doc," Derlin agreed, finishing pumping gas and tapping the pump against the rim of the gas tank to clear the line. "I reckon me or the wife'll give you a jangle sometime tomorrow morning and see if we can't get our boys set up proper."

"Sounds good, Mr. Spurlock," Ronald smiled. "I'll take very good care of them." He paid with a five, telling Derlin to keep the change as he hopped in his Pontiac and sped off towards town. They exchanged waves and Derlin stood by the pump, hand on his hip, watching him drive away.

"Huh," Derlin chuckled, speaking aloud to himself and shaking his head slightly. "A doctor just for little babies. Who'da thunk it?

Chapter 38

Derlin presented Mavis with this new information about the "baby doctor" when he got home. They sat down at the kitchen table to have a talk about it while the boys napped in the next room.

Naturally, she agreed with the young doctor's assessment that the boys needed a check-up, as they'd had no actual medical care since fleeing the hospital. The closest thing they'd seen to a vaccination was the bucket Derlin had scavenged to wash them in and she had no doubts that they had some catching up to do medically. However, the maternal skeptic in her remained wary of Thurbison's good intentions and she expressed genuine worry to Derlin that the boys' birthmarks would be discovered and they'd be ousted from the happy life they'd built since returning to town.

"You don't want them getting all diseased up, do you?" Derlin asked. "Doc Thurbison said he needed to prod at 'em to make sure they're happy and healthy since they ain't had no formal doctorin' since the hospital."

"Of course I want to make sure they're happy and healthy," Mavis said. "But how do I know this doctor isn't going to blow our cover like that old nurse and get the town started on this whole 'devil babies' thing again?"

"Ol' Doc Thurbison wouldn't do that!" Derlin replied. "He's young and booksmart and I didn't pick up a touch of Jesus off him while we was talkin'. Plus he sure don't seem like he's from anywhere around here. I reckon he's done too much reading and studying to worry about things havin' the devil in them."

"You think he's studied and read enough to see that they ain't even sixes on the boys heads, but just lowercase B's like your mama and Uncle Vern were saying?" Mavis asked, still unsure of Derlin's proposition.

"I'd reckon so," Derlin postulated. "Plus he's new to town and being a stranger and from up north-ways and all it ain't like he's gonna be gossiping with the ladies down at the auxiliary anyhow."

"That's a good point, honey," Mavis nodded. "Maybe if we explain ourselves he'll be understanding and help us keep the boys out of trouble. It wouldn't do him no good to start that mess all up again. Being a doctor he probably doesn't want to cause no babies to have to live in the woods."

"Yeah, that wouldn't be very doctorly of him now would it?" Derlin smiled. "I'll call his office up in the mornin' and see if we can't take the boys in there and get 'em looked at. You reckon they give out trophies to parents for healthiest babies?"

"I don't think so, honey," Mavis said, shaking her head and rising from the table to check on the boys.

"What about the strongest?" Derlin hollered after her as she left the room.

September 9, 1968

Derlin called Dr. Thurbison's office first thing in the morning and was able to secure an appointment for that very afternoon. Lumpy was kind enough to let Derlin off early for the day to pick up Mavis and the boys in time to make it to their 4 o'clock appointment, though he didn't quite understand the purpose of taking such "clean and spry youngin's" to the doctor if there wasn't anything wrong with them. Derlin tried in vain to explain Dr. Thurbison's finer points on child maintenance and, while he did manage to get Lumpy to agree that the young doctor was indeed a "nice man," he refused to admit that the field of child medicine was anything more than "fancy-pants snake oil hoodoo" drummed up by slick-talking travelling hucksters like Thurbison to make a buck off of "rubes" such as Derlin.

When they arrived at the office, Derlin directed Mavis and the boys to a couch in the waiting room, parking their stroller and heading to speak with the receptionist. Their thick black wigs looked absurd sticking out of their small stroller and Mavis planned on removing them as soon as they were out of public view.

"How can I help you today, sir?" the pleasant, young receptionist asked with a smile.

"Howdy ma'am," Derlin replied, nodding politely. "My name's Spurlock and I've got an appointment set up with ol' Doc Thurbison about some babies."

Briefly off put by Derlin's phrasing, the receptionist was soon able to gather herself after staring at him blankly for a moment.

"Oh, you must be Randy and Ollie's father," she smiled. "Dr. Thurbison told us about meeting you, you're actually going to be his first appointment in town."

"Wow!" Derlin beamed. "First appointment in the whole town, you hear that boys?" he shouted across the waiting room.

The receptionist let out a nervous chuckle as Derlin craned his neck across the room at his sons, handing him a clipboard with a few forms attached.

"We just need you to fill out a little bit of paperwork and we'll get you right back to the doctor," she said, offering Derlin a pen.

"Paperwork eh?" Derlin asked, eyeing the clipboard for a moment before walking it across the room to his family. "The wife'll take care of that, she knows pretty much everything there is to know about these babies."

Mavis smiled and took the clipboard, filling in the information slowly while Derlin inspected some artwork hanging on the wall.

Upon returning the clipboard, the Spurlocks were shown to Dr. Thurbison's exam room and he soon greeted them there.

"There's old Ronnie!" Derlin hollered as he arrived, offering him a handshake and a pat on the shoulder. "This is my wife Mavis and our boys Randy and Ollie. Mavis honey this is Doc Thurbison."

"Hi there folks," Dr. Thurbison smiled, shaking Mavis' hand warmly and returning Derlin's shoulder pat gingerly. "Well, let's meet the little ones," he continued. "Let's get them out of their stroller and we can put them up on the exam table here and… what… what is that you've got on their heads there?"

There was a tense pause as Derlin thought about how to best begin.

"Well Doc, let me explain a little bit and see if I get all this to make some sense to you," Derlin began nervously. "Now, you're our doctor, and I get a real good feeling from you. I feel like we can trust you. Is that right?"

"Of course," Dr. Thurbison nodded. "Of course you can." He sensed Derlin's nerves and saw Mavis tense up as well as Derlin asked him about trust. "What seems to be the trouble? Is something the matter?"

Derlin sighed and took a deep breath.

"Well Doc, those things on their heads is their 'going in public' wigs," Derlin began, "on account of some trouble we have in my family every so often."

"I'm not sure I follow you, Mr. Spurlock," Dr. Thurbison said intently, leaning in slightly with a look of concern on his face. He prodded lightly at Randy's wig with his pencil before returning his attention to Derlin.

"Mavis, baby, let's just show him," Derlin sighed.

Mavis took a deep breath and lifted the wigs off of Randy and Ollie's heads. Sure enough, their birthmarks were as clear as day on their glistening, bald little heads.

"The family birthmark," Derlin said plainly, parting his hair to show his own. "I got it too, so did my daddy and his daddy and my Uncle Vern and every other Spurlock man going all the way back to the horse and cart days."

"It looks like three lowercase b's," Dr. Thurbison said with interest, leaning in closer for inspection, gently running his fingers across Randy and Ollie's heads as they stared blankly up at him.

"That's a keen eye, Doc," Derlin said. He felt a wave of relief wash over him.

"But why the wigs?" Dr. Thurbison asked.

"Oh, we just have 'em till the boys can grow their own hair and cover up their birthmark, like me and daddy and Vern," Derlin explained. "Grandpa Hoyt's gone mostly bald but he just always wears his old tractor hat."

"Why do you need to cover them up?" Dr. Thurbison asked. "Lots of people have birthmarks, of every shape and size, even if these are… rather distinct."

"Well, a lot of folks around here don't really look down at them marks and see three b's," Derlin explained, gaining confidence in Dr. Thurbison's trustworthiness as he went. "Lots of folks around here is real religious, see. They look at them marks and see a 666. Calling it 'the mark of the beast.' When we had the boys at the hospital a nurse run out telling everybody we give birth to twin devil babies and next thing you know we're gettin' chased out of the place by a mob of folks with torches and pitchforks and everything."

Dr. Thurbison gasped, listening to Derlin's tale in wonderment.

"We lived in an old windmill outside of town for a few months after the babies was born. Way out where nobody could find us," Derlin continued. "I reckon I don't need to tell you all the details of between then and now, but we waited till all the ruckus died down so we could come back and live in town like a normal family. We just gotta keep the wigs on the boys to hide them marks so nobody finds us out. My family said it happens every thirty years or so, whenever a male Spurlock gets born everybody sees them b's and pipes up about "devil babies" again. The folks here have been running Spurlocks out of town for them marks since we was still a territory. They just have short memories and tend to forget about the whole thing after a little while, till it all starts happening again a generation down the road."

"I don't even know what to say, Mr. Spurlock," Dr. Thurbison began. "Frankly, I'm just astonished that all of this could happen. Being chased from town by a mob in this day and age? Besides all that, I'm not sure how to even begin breaking down any of this medically."

"But, our secret's safe with you, right?" Mavis asked nervously.

"Of course," Dr. Thurbison said in a comforting whisper. "You have no need to worry about that, I've just never heard of anything like this in medicine. Of course the "devil babies" talk is nonsense, but I've never heard of every member of a family having the exact same birthmark in the exact same place! It's a phenomenon that might be unique to you Spurlocks."

"Maybe it means us Spurlock's is extra healthy," Derlin postulated, puffing his chest out slightly and winking to his sons on the table.

"Well, let's check these young fellas out and see what we can find out about them," Dr. Thurbison said warmly.

"Maybe some kind of super babies, even," Derlin nodded to Mavis.

Over the next half hour or so, Dr. Thurbison poked and prodded at Randy and Ollie, checking their temperatures, reflexes, heartbeats and the like.

"Kind of like getting a tune up on your car," Derlin observed over the doctor's shoulder.

"You mentioned at your gas station that the boys were 'fast,' Mr. Spurlock." Dr. Thurbison said. "Have they been crawling long?"

"Oh they took to crawling real quick," Derlin said. "They've been crawling since a couple weeks before I lost 'em in the yard, so I'd say getting toward a couple months."

"Lost them in the what?" Mavis whispered sharply.

"Hush baby," Derlin said, patting Mavis on the knee. "Let the doctor man speak."

"That's remarkably advanced for their age," Dr. Thurbison said in amazement. "If that's true I'm surprised they haven't started trying to stand or walk yet."

"No, they ain't been taking any tries at walking," Derlin said. "They've gotten mighty fast with the crawling though, I can barely catch onto 'em sometimes, especially if they're getting back behind the TV or something."

"They both seem to have fairly developed muscles for their age, probably from such an early affinity for crawling," Dr. Thurbison said, tapping his pen against his chin as he gazed down at the boys.

"I told you they was strong," Derlin said proudly.

"They're certainly sturdy," Dr. Thurbison smiled. "I do have a couple of tests to run in regards to their diet, their blood and organ development that will take a few weeks to complete, but honestly both of your sons seem like they are in excellent health."

"I knew they'd be in ship shape, Doc," Derlin said happily, patting Dr. Thurbison on the shoulder once again.

"You two are doing a fine job as parents," Dr. Thurbison offered. "After the ordeal you've been through and the living conditions that they had to endure as newborns, it's remarkable that they're as healthy and normal as they seem, it's a testament to both of you working very hard at it I'm sure."

Derlin nodded vigorously.

"I'll be in touch with the results from their other tests as soon as they're completed and, once again, your secret about their birthmarks is completely safe with me. Forgive my fascination."

"Much obliged to you, Doc," Derlin said sincerely. "And no forgiveness needed, I reckon us Spurlocks is pretty fascinating folks."

Chapter 39

September 22, 1968

Derlin had no idea how long "baby-doctoring" took compared to the adult variety, but he knew from his days in the army that the doctors there had found out pretty much everything they needed to know about him medically within a few hours of poking and prodding. As such, he began to get a little bit worried that he still hadn't heard back from Dr. Thurbison about the remainder of Randy and Ollie's tests after nearly two weeks. He tried to brush aside his worry, telling himself that Dr. Thurbison's office was both very new and likely very busy, but he called the office from Lumpy's as a sense of unease swelled in him. Maybe, he thought, the boys were so healthy that Dr. Thurbison hadn't even deemed it necessary to follow up with the results. Happy to hear the office sounded just as busy as he expected, Derlin wasn't particularly surprised when the receptionist told him that Dr. Thurbison would have to call him back at a later time. Satisfied at leaving his phone number, Derlin did his best not to worry as he plodded through the remainder of his afternoon at the Feed n' Seed.

He'd arrived home from work that evening, greeting Mavis with a kiss and the boys with a "finger guns" salute before rummaging through the fridge and emerging with an icy cold Panther Cat. He was just about to crack it when the phone rang. Mavis beat him to the phone and answered it on the second ring.

"Hello? Spurlock residence," she began politely as Derlin listened intently from just over her shoulder. He could hear Dr. Thurbison's voice on the other end of the line but couldn't make out what he was saying.

"Yes, hi Dr. Thurbison, this is Mavis," she continued. "So nice to hear from you. How'd the boys' tests come out? Are they healthy and hap- Oh. Oh my, yes I see."

Derlin continued unsuccessfully to mash his face into a position where he and Mavis could share the earpiece but she continued to turn away from him until she had the phone cord wrapped around her legs thrice.

"Yes, of course, Dr. Thurbison," she continued. "Yes, we can bring them in tomorrow afternoon to talk about it. I understand. I'll tell Derlin there's no reason to get too worked up. Yes. We'll see you tomorrow. Thank you. Okay. Thank you. You have a good evening too, bye."

She hung up the phone slowly as Derlin waited with bated breath.

"Well what's the matter?" Derlin asked loudly. "Is the babies the devil after all? Is that what the tests said? Dang machines! I swear, if-"

"Derlin honey, calm down," Mavis began. "Dr. Thurbison told me specifically to tell you not to get yourself so worked up, the boys are okay. They're fine. There was just an… irregularity in some of the boys blood testing and bone testing and he just wants us to bring 'em back in for a couple extra tests just to make sure everything is alright. He said lots of babies get lots of tests all the time."

"Did he say right out that my boys ain't regular?" Derlin asked. "That takes a lot of nerve after all this time of him and I being friends."

"He didn't say that because of you, baby," Mavis explained. "Remember, he was telling him how good and strong they are? He's not trying to insult them or you, just one of his doctor tests came back funny and he wants to do some more just to be on the safe side of things."

"I guess that makes sense," Derlin conceded, calming down. "We takin' 'em back tomorrow morning then?"

"Yes honey, I told him we could be there at 9 o'clock," Mavis said sweetly, rubbing Derlin's shoulder. "You should call Lumpy and see if he'll let you come in a little late and if not the boys and I can just call a taxi-cab from in town."

"I will," Derlin said quietly, the news of his irregular children clearly weighing down upon him. He glanced down at the quickly-warming Panther Cat still clenched in his fist, unopened. He stared at it unblinking for a moment before finally cracking it and taking a large, satisfying swig.

After their previous conversation on the quackery of child medicine, Derlin was caught off-guard by how understanding Lumpy was when he called to ask to come in late. Lumpy's logic was that a second trip to the doctor was infinitely more valid than the initial doctor's visit, since it was for some apparently established sort of malady.

"Well, now at least you got a reason you takin' 'em to get doctored," he said.

Derlin didn't have the energy to mention that if they didn't go to the first "unnecessary" visit there wouldn't have been a second "necessary" one, he was just glad Lumpy was so empathetic. Lumpy's kind words were framed in an almost fatherly tone before being capped with an ominous "maybe them boys ain't as spry after all." Derlin, who could only mutter a "maybe" in reply, was still gracious for the excused absence from his Feed n' Seed duties for the morning.

They arrived at Dr. Thurbison's office at the stroke of nine and were a little worried to see the doctor awaiting their arrival in the lobby.

"Good morning Spurlocks," he began. "Thank you for coming in to see me so quickly. Again, I'm sure this is startling but I don't want you to be too alarmed until we get all of this sorted out. Come on back to my office, we can go ahead and get started going over some of Randy and Ollie's charts."

"Mornin' doc," Derlin replied. "Let's whip them charts out and see what you needed to tell us about my boys, here. I've been worrying like a dog since last night."

As they entered Dr. Thurbison's office, he sat down behind his desk, motioning them to a pair of chairs across from him while Randy and Ollie stayed in the stroller.

"I'd like to start by saying that in most respects, little Randy and Ollie here are very healthy babies," Dr. Thurbison began. "In some cases, like with their crawling ability and subsequent muscle development, they're off the charts."

Derlin nodded proudly, his worry briefly ebbing.

"But in some other ways," Dr. Thurbison continued, "The boys are off the charts in the wrong direction."

"What do you mean?" Mavis asked nervously. She began to tear up.

"Well, I realize that the boys faced a difficult beginning with the months in the windmill," Dr. Thurbison began. "I'd imagine, based on the bloodwork and bone tests that we performed, they might have encountered some dietary hardships during the early parts of their lives?"

"Do what now?" Derlin asked, perplexed.

"Was it difficult to keep the boys eating a balanced diet during your time living… outside of town?" Dr. Thurbison asked.

"Oh! Oh, not at all Doc," Derlin replied. "We always had food for the babies. Fed 'em every day whether they was acting hungry or not!"

Dr. Thurbison sighed.

"That's not exactly what I'm asking," he continued. "Having enough food to be full and having a proper diet are two very different things, especially with young ones. Were you both able to make sure they were consistently getting the necessary fruits and vegetables in their meals and eating a balance of different types of food?"

Derlin laughed.

"Aw hell," he began. "We can't even get that kinda shit into 'em now. They're the pickiest eaters I ever saw."

"Derlin!" Mavis scolded.

"What, baby?" he asked. "Can't I say 'shit' to a doctor?"

"What do they eat?" Dr. Thurbison interjected.

"Well," Derlin began. "Their whole lives, since they stopped latching onto their mama, they've pretty much only eaten that Salisbury steak flavor of baby food they got down at the Piggly Wiggly. It's the only flavor they'll touch. Every now and then I'll give 'em a Charleston Chew to gnaw on but I don't know if Charleston Chews counts as a fruit or not in that little food group picture you got on the wall."

"They've only eaten steak and candy their entire lives?" Dr. Thurbison asked quietly. His face hardened.

"Well, steak baby food, not real steak," Derlin replied. "The wife says they can't have real steak on account of they don't have no teeth yet, but sometimes I forget and try to get regular-people steak for them anyhow. Twice now I've gotten to eat three steaks because of it."

"Mr. Spurlock it's very troublesome to let babies that young be picky eaters," Dr. Thurbison lectured sternly. "The amount of red meat certainly explains some of their elevated levels and possibly their impressive musculature, but regardless… It's very important that they get all of their necessary vitamins and nutrients as they grow. It's vitally important to their development as they get bigger and get older."

"They do eat some fried fish too, if I mix in the mayo just right for 'em and mash it all up," Derlin offered, shrugging and raising his eyebrows.

"I'm afraid that's not going to help much of anything, Mr. Spurlock," Dr. Thurbison continued. "In fact, this is precisely why I called you two in today."

"It is?" Derlin asked sheepishly.

"I thought you said the babies was fine, Doc," Mavis said.

"Trying to explain all of this over the phone would have been very difficult Mrs. Spurlock, and it only would have left you terribly worried," Dr. Thurbison explained. "The boys aren't in any mortal danger, so to say, but you are definitely going to have to make some significant changes to their diet to get them back on the path to proper nutrition and health."

"So no more Salisbury steak?" Mavis asked.

"Yes," Dr. Thurbison continued. "It's vital that you diversify Randy and Ollie's diet as soon as you can, though the damage may have already been done. Without the necessary nutrients to help them grow, Randy and Ollie's bones haven't matured at a normal rate through and well-past a very important time for their development. While, likely due to their affinity for crawling and a beef-heavy upbringing, their musculature around the bones is remarkable, the bones themselves aren't developed nearly to the point that they should be at their age. Think of it them like you're trying to sculpt hamburger onto a very brittle tree branch in your yard. That's the difference in their muscle and bone development right now."

Mavis began to cry and Derlin rubbed her back as the doctor continued.

"What does it mean, Doc?" Derlin asked, his face reddening as he did his best to hold his emotions in check.

"Well, Mr. Spurlock," Dr. Thurbison said. "So much of a baby's bone development occurs so early in life, in the first few months even, and at a certain point there's not really a path to catch up if development falls behind. While with a corrected diet Randy and Ollie can still lead full, happy, very normal lives, it's not likely that either of them will ever grow much beyond four or five feet in height."

Mavis wailed as Derlin processed the information with his brow as furrowed as it could possibly get.

"Four feet tall?" Derlin asked.

"I'm afraid so," Dr. Thurbison replied.

"As grown-ups?" Derlin asked.

"Yes," Dr. Thurbison said.

"Adults?" Derlin asked.

"Yes sir, Mr. Spurlock," Dr. Thurbison nodded.

"Well, that's a real kick in the dick, doc," Derlin said, sighing heavily and shaking his head, doing his best to console Mavis while Randy and Ollie lay babbling under their wigs in the stroller.

"I know it's not news you wanted to hear," Dr. Thurbison said solemnly. "But the silver lining is that if you two step up and make sure the boys start eating like they should, there's no reason they can't live a good life right up into old age like the rest of us. They just might not be playing on the varsity basketball team in school."

"Yeah, I guess you're right, doc," Derlin said quietly.

Mavis blew her nose and her wails began to subside into quiet sobs.

"Well, I guess we better be going," Derlin said, still clearly stunned by the news of his sons' stunted growth. "I reckon we should stop at the Piggly Wiggly on the way home and pick up some of them green bean and sweet potato flavors and see if we can get these boys eating right."

"Certainly the sooner starting it, the better," Dr. Thurbison said warmly. "You can get them vitamins over the counter as well, which you can mash up into their food. Every little bit helps." He offered a hug to Mavis and a handshake to Derlin and they were soon shambling out the door.

"Thank you for everything, doc," Derlin said glumly as they were leaving. "You've been mighty helpful."

"Of course," Dr. Thurbison replied. "I don't doubt at all that the boys are already on the path to better health."

"They are, doc, they are," Derlin nodded. "We'll get 'em full of apples and beans and fix 'em right up good. There ain't no way to keep a Spurlock man down, even if he's only three foot-ten."

Chapter 40

Mavis spent the next several weeks gradually weaning the boys off of Salisbury steak instead of making them go cold turkey, as she and Derlin realized that they did still have a good three dozen jars of it left in the cupboard, "already paid for and everything." At first, she started by mixing a spoon or two of carrots, peas or applesauce into their normal helpings of Salisbury steak. With Mavis gradually adding more and more fruits and vegetables while cutting down on their diminishing steak rations, Randy and Ollie were soon wolfing down sweet potatoes, corn and the rest of the garden like she'd never dreamed they would. The boys, invigorated by the rush of vitamins and nutrients, doubled down on their crawling efforts and had quickly gotten fast enough that Derlin had to jog around the house to keep them from pulling out the TV cords or getting wedged behind the couch as they whizzed around the floor.

While pleased enough with the boys' dietary progress, Derlin spent the fall mostly sulking, wallowing in the news that his boy would never be much taller than middle-schoolers because he fed them too much canned meat as infants. He put on a brave face while working, but his enthusiasm began to wane and it wasn't long before he was just going through the motions at Lumpy's. Coverdale was a small enough town and word travelled quickly that the twin boys of the local army hero were in ill health. The townsfolk never quite hit the nail on the head with attempted diagnosis, speculating everything from lead poisoning to polio to hay fever, but Derlin couldn't help but wince when a well-meaning old woman brought him a blueberry pie at Lumpy's upon "hearing that unfortunate bit about your boys catching a bout of the dwarfism."

He seemed to take it personally that Randy and Ollie had taken to eating bananas and greens, with Mavis even shunning away Derlin's famous fish paste on Fridays at Uncle Vern's.

To take his mind off of his troubles, Derlin took to spending more of his evenings in the garage with his tools, slowly and meticulously banging out the dents in the old sedan one at a time. With his salary at Lumpy's, he could have easily afforded a different car. Maybe not a new one, but a better one at the very least, especially with a family to consider. He'd grown even more attached to the old rust bucket over the past two years than he'd ever imagined, pounding out each dent slowly with the love and care of someone restoring a medieval painting.

Derlin had originally paid $200 for the car and couldn't quite remember if it was a Buick or a Studebaker. He'd acquired it at a police auction four years before he'd met Mavis and even then it had lost all recognizable symbols of brand identification. He'd always been strangely proud of it, but now that he'd courted his wife in it, conceived his children in it, saved his family from a torch and pitchfork brandishing mob in it, lived in it and used it in a string of very lightly-armed robberies, he couldn't see himself ever driving another vehicle "even if he got richer than the president." With each jarring clang of restoration, Derlin loved the sedan that much more, seeing it both like an uncle and a third son in his life.

As the autumn progressed and Derlin lurked in the garage, his two actual sons were gobbling up every flavor of baby food that the Piggly Wiggly carried and by the time their first halloween approached, they'd grown three inches a piece and were doing everything in their power to pull themselves to a standing position on the legs of furniture around the Spurlock home. Dr. Thurbison was ecstatic with the boys' improvement and though he stood by his diagnosis that they would remain quite petite, he was proud of the effort that Derlin and Mavis had made. With Randy and Ollie's growth spurt and their early signs of learning to walk, Derlin's mood brightened, though he continued to side-eye his children for other signs of normalcy.

October 24, 1968

"How can ol' Doc Thurbison tell they're gonna be little folk when they're already that small?" Derlin asked Mavis with frustration during a commercial break in The Andy Griffith Show.

"Honey, they're not "little folk,'" Mavis said sternly. "The boys are gonna grow up to be normal men like you, just shorter. They're not dwarves."

"They ain't?" Derlin asked.

"No honey," Mavis began. "You get born a dwarf, you don't turn into one if you don't eat good."

"So they ain't gonna be like them little fellas on The Wizard of Oz, they're just gonna be like me but shrunk down some?" Derlin asked, his interest rising.

"That's what the doctor said," Mavis replied.

"So they might still could race cars and not just horses?" Derlin asked.

"We'll see honey," Mavis said, patting Derlin on the thigh. "They've got a lot of time and a lot of growing to do between now and then."

"Yeah, for ol' Doc saying they're small now, I remember when they was like half that size," Derlin chuckled.

"I remember when their wigs wouldn't even stay on without falling over their eyes," Mavis smiled. "It's hard to believe they're almost nine months old."

"So do we dress up babies for Halloween and take them around getting candy or do we have to wait till they're talking and walking and not babies?" Derlin asked. He'd clearly been thinking of this topic ahead of time and the question had weighed on him more and more as October had progressed.

"Well, I don't see why we couldn't dress them up," Mavis said, smiling. "We could still walk them around the neighborhood in their little costumes and I think it would be cute! But you know, Dr. Thurbison said the boys can't have any more candy in their diet. I got daddy to throw away a whole drawer full of Charleston Chews he was keeping for them at the house."

"He threw them away?" Derlin wailed.

"Yes honey," Mavis said. "They were getting old and expired anyhow." Derlin sighed and kicked listlessly at the rug at his feet.

"So," Derlin began, pausing to make it seem as though he was trying to figure out what to say next instead of just blurting out the coldly calculated line to follow. "If we do dress 'em up and take 'em around, what do you think'll happen to the candy they would've got?"

"Well, I reckon they'll just keep it in their candy bowl and give it to other bigger kids that come by trick-or-treating," Mavis said, beginning to side-eye her husband.

The commercial break ended and soon Opie was bounding into the jail house with what appeared to be important news, but Derlin was undeterred.

"What if we got it anyway, but just didn't give it to the babies?" Derlin asked hopefully.

Mavis stared at Derlin quietly, his end game gradually revealing itself.

"We could say the babies had an older brother with polio or a game leg," Derlin continued, staring off into the distance across the living room. "They'd probably give extra candy to a polio kid."

"Honey, I think they cured polio when we were little kids," Mavis sighed. "Nobody will believe you if you tell them that."

"Well, maybe like a way older brother that was born back then," Derlin said, hastily rationalizing his imaginary crippled son. "Maybe he's been up in his little kid room with his polio since back then and now he's almost my age but he don't know no better and just wants to go trick-or-treating with his twin baby brothers?"

"So you've got a hidden third son that's almost your age that you're getting candy for instead?" Mavis laughed. "How about we just carry around one bucket for both the boys when we go, we don't make up any stories about crippled children and you can have some of the candy that we get?"

"Some of it?" Derlin asked with a snarl.

"Well, I figured I'd put it out when our folks come around," Mavis said. "And I figure we could take your Uncle Vern a little sack of it too, you told me he eats Grandma Vondene's Christmas chocolates by the fistful till he passes out every year."

"Every damn year," Derlin marvelled, shaking his head. "Quick as he can."

October 31, 1968

Mavis had given up trying to get Derlin to notice her recurring publication, but she was quite happy to see that a part of her story had been published on Halloween, just as the plot really started to thicken. She read through her handiwork, pleased with how her story arc was building and wondering if anyone else in town had taken the time to read it. She felt certain that someone somewhere must have read them, but aside from asking Derlin or the other handful of neighborhood wives that she went baby walking with, she couldn't think of anyone to ask.

Cathy's Clone: A Rockin' Mystery, Part 3 - Mrs. X

The Cathys walked quietly in unison down the sidewalk, turning through the neighborhood streets like they were walking in an army formation. Soon, they got to the end of a cul-de-sac and all walked up the stairs of the giant, gray house at the end. Locals had always said the house was haunted and it had been empty since long before Don and Phil were born. They remembered being scared of it as children and daring each other to go up and knock on the door with other neighborhood kids. Spiderwebs covered the porch railings, the windows of the house were shuttered, the yard was overgrown and the front steps had begun to crumble. It didn't look like there had been anyone inside in ages, but as the seven Cathys walked through the front door and into the parlor, they were met by 33 other Cathys just like them, milling around the living room, chatting on the stairs and lounging on the furniture. Inside, the house was immaculate. Art dotted the walls and luxury furniture filled the rooms.

"Attention everyone," shouted the Cathy who Phil and Don had met. "It's time we get started, we have a lot to talk about!"

The conversation among the other Cathys dwindled to a murmur and soon after that a hushed silence.

"I made contact today," Cathy said, spreading her arms victoriously. Thirty-nine identical squeals and hand-claps filled the room.

"I have even better news," she continued, the entire room giving her full attention. "I met them at the soda fountain just as we had planned on, but instead of just a hello they invited me to join them for an ice cream float."

The room filled with 39 identical gasps.

"I said I'd love to," Cathy began. "And then I sat down and ordered his very favorite ice cream float."

"Strawberry with extra strawberries," the other Cathy's repeated in unison.

"Strawberry with extra strawberries," the lead Cathy said, nodding in approval. "I quickly realized that Don was enamored with me and was also being encouraged by his brother. Soon, I had him in the palm of my hand. We talked for half an hour and he ended up asking me to go to the Summer Social with him!"

The room burst into cheers and loud conversations drowned out each other as Cathys processed the information their leader had just given them.

"Attention!" Cathy shouted. "There's more. Be quiet."

The room became silent. You could hear a hairpin drop.

"The Summer Social is in three weeks," Cathy continued. "Don and one of us are meeting tomorrow at the soda fountain and I imagine that we'll all be spending time with him between now and then. We've got to hypnotize Don before then, because the day after the social they leave town on their big stadium tour. If we want to achieve our objective, we have to get Don's mind under our control, so we can strap the space-activated laser-bomb to him before they go to their big concert at the Kansas City A's game. By then, it'll be too late for anyone to stop us and we can finally do what we came to this planet to do: blow up Mickey Mantle!"

All forty Cathys began cackling evilly together. One by one they each tugged at their long brown hair, removing what turned out to be human masks, revealing bubbling, green, five-eyed monster faces underneath. Their laughs turned to piercing shrieks that shook the walls of the old house. Their plan was coming together perfectly.

Over the next few weeks, Phil hardly saw Don because he and Cathy were spending so much time together. He could barely even get Don to practice guitar with him, let alone try writing new songs with him. Don was more head over heels with Cathy every day. It was almost like she knew everything about him and shared every single one of his interests. It was unreal. He felt hypnotized when he was with her, more each time they went on a date together, whether it was the soda fountain, the picture show, or just for a long walk down by the river. Little did Don know that it was a different Cathy he met each time they went out. Little did he know that they were gradually hypnotizing him with their magic space spells, a little more each day. He'd been blathering to Phil about how excited he was that the Yankees were in town the day they played at the Kansas City

A's stadium since they'd gotten the gig. He'd hoped to rub elbows with his idol Mickey Mantle before the concert and had reminded Phil of that hope every day. The Cathys shared this hope but for a very different reason. If everything went to plan, the second that Don got close enough to "The Mick" for a handshake, they'd send a laser from space to explode the alien space bomb that they'd strapped to him the night before at the Summer Social, exploding his baseball hero for good, destroying the stadium and ruining the concert.

It was only the night before the Summer Social that Phil began to suspect that something was actually wrong with his brother and decided to confront him. The fate of Mickey Mantle, the brothers and that whole stadium of people depended on whether or not it was already too late.

Stay tuned for the thrilling conclusion of "Cathy's Clone!"

Mavis had spent the past week scouring downtown for the perfect costumes for Randy and Ollie, both adorable and birthmark-covering. She was quite proud of her selections, acquiring each boy a full-body bear suit and a cowboy hat that strapped to the top of their heads just to be safe. As she expected, Derlin dug his army suit out of the closet for his costume, though she wasn't expecting that he'd be telling people he was John Wayne and doing his impersonation all night. She denied his request that she go dressed like a cheerleader, borrowing one of Derlin's flannel shirts and going as a scarecrow instead.

The young twin cowboy bears were quite the hit at every house they stopped at and, as Derlin slowly and diligently checked off every house in Coverdale with the lights on, they soon had a plastic pumpkin bucket brimming with candy. Mavis and the boys' enthusiasm had begun to wane long before Derlin's, and the last dozen houses were visited by Derlin carrying one sleeping child to the door while Mavis waited on the sidewalk with the other.

Derlin salivated at his bounty. Though he often bragged to friends, family and anyone else within earshot that he "didn't have a sweet tooth, but sure had a meat tooth," he had a significant weakness for candy. He bided his time when they returned home, helping Mavis get the exhausted babies out of their tiny bear costumes and put to bed. He went to bed with Mavis, waiting for her to fall asleep before sneaking out of the bedroom and making his way down the stairs. He walked pointedly into the kitchen and flipped on the light, beginning to paw through the contents of the boy's plastic pumpkin. Absentmindedly cramming a few chocolates into his mouth as he searched, Derlin meticulously picked out every single candy corn from the bucket. He grabbed a Mason jar from the cupboard, filling the jar two-thirds full with the candy corns and tightening the lid into place. Pausing for a moment to make sure his noise in the cupboard hadn't woken his wife or children, Derlin tucked the jar under his arm and headed out the front door toward the garage. Fumbling through a poorly lit corner of the garage, Derlin emerged with a shovel, heading toward the backyard with a look of stoic determination on his face.

Doing his best to stay quiet, Derlin creaked open the gate and snuck into the backyard. The edges of the yard were turning a crusty yellow-brown with the passing of autumn, but the center of the yard where the babies had "fertilized" was still a vibrant and luscious green. It was here that Derlin began to dig. The ground was soft and moist and Derlin had soon dug a hole two and a half feet deep without even breaking a sweat. Staring up for a moment at his darkened second story bedroom window and back into the darkness of his hole, Derlin gently placed the Mason jar of candy corn at the bottom. He stared at it for several seconds as the glass shined faintly in the moonlight. He took a deep breath and sighed as he began to shovel dirt back on top of it. Patting down the dirt gently and replacing the grass as best he could, Derlin stared down at his handiwork and back up once more at his house. He wiped the sweat from his brow and tossed the shovel on top of the hose still crumpled against the back of the house, wincing as it made a dull thud. He snuck quietly back into the house, cracking a Panther Cat in the kitchen which he drank on the stairs on his way to bed.

Chapter 41

November 20, 1968

At Lumpy's request, Derlin had spent the first few minutes of his morning taping some cardboard turkey decorations up in the front windows of the Feed n' Seed. Derlin bristled at the idea at first, as they obscured his view of the gas pumps and the parking lot. He complained to Lumpy that this increased the likelihood of gas theft, knowing deep down that he was the only person in town who'd ever been stealing any gas to begin with. "I just don't see what a couple turkeys put up in the window is gonna do for business except keep me from seeing drifters trying to rub up on your gas pumps," Derlin said from atop his small step-ladder.

"Aw hell," Lumpy said from behind the counter. "It's November, old top. Folks ain't loading up on nightcrawlers and boat gas like they was in the summertime. I can't make it through the winters just sellin' buckshot & chaw. These decorations'll get some families in the door, filling up their station wagons and buying candy bars and such. Works like a charm every year."

"How these paper turkeys gonna help business?" Derlin asked. "You wanna help business, put some real turkeys up in the window. You can't even eat these! People would stop in from all over. 'Let's go up by Lumpy's, have a bite of that nice turkey leg he's got hangin' in the window.'"

He did his best to smooth over a crumpled part of one of the turkey's legs as he taped it up, hoping his faint teeth marks were no longer visible.

November 27, 1968

Mavis felt a strange mix of simultaneous stress and relief as she'd gotten off the phone with her mother. She and Derlin hadn't concretely discussed any plans for Thanksgiving, aside from Derlin's plan to discard his belt sometime mid-afternoon, However, she had assumed that Derlin had assumed they were going to his family gathering, especially since Vern had recently shelved his fish frying until the spring. Her mother's news that she and Clebert would be attending a church potluck cleared up the mystery of which direction Derlin would be driving the old sedan, leaving Mavis with a pang of nerves at the prospect of attending her first Spurlock Thanksgiving. Summer Fridays by Vern's pond had shown her a folksy, primal side of the Spurlocks and she was unsure how that would translate into a grander, more formalized occasion.

"Derlin, honey?" Mavis called as she walked out of the kitchen looking for him.

"Back here," he hollered from the bedroom.

Mavis walked into the bedroom to find Derlin rummaging through the closet with the babies at his feet.

"What are you doing, honey?" Mavis asked.

"Looking for my good sweatpants," Derlin croaked from the back of the closet.

"What for?" Mavis asked.

"So I can eat more, baby," Derlin answered. "Denim don't stretch good, that's just science. Sweatpants stretch good."

"They sure do," Mavis said. "So, does your Uncle Vern host Thanksgiving too since he's got the turkey fryer and the picnic table at his house?"

"Aw hell no," Derlin replied, emerging from the closet empty handed. "That's Grandma Vondene's day to work her magic. She's the reason why I need those pants. Besides, anything else Vern puts in that fryer just ends up tasting like elkfish anyhow."

"I know we hadn't really made plans, but what time are they expecting us over there?" Mavis asked.

"Whenever's fine," Derlin said, waving his hand dismissively. "We don't set a time anymore, you know how mama and deddy tend to roll in."

"Well, we can head over whenever you like after I get the boys dressed," Mavis smiled. "I'm excited, I've never been to your grandparents' house."

"It's real nice," Derlin said. "I was staying on a cot on the covered porch when you and me first took up, but the regular inside is nice too."

"It sounds nice," Mavis said, picking up Randy and brushing something off of his face. "If you can't find your sweatpants, I have a pair of maternity pants you can wear in the bottom drawer of the dresser."

She was mostly kidding and was surprised when Derlin leapt at the opportunity, digging into the drawer immediately. Discarding his jeans, Derlin slid into the maternity pants and let out an impressed "Ooh, yeah!" as he pulled them up. They fit decently in the legs, but sagged badly around his scrawny midsection. He synched his belt around them as tightly as he could, crumpling the excess fabric into a ball above his groin. Pulling on an oversized flannel shirt and buttoning it, Derlin deemed himself ready to go and walked unsteadily out the bedroom door. Getting used to his new style of pant wear was going to take some practice, but Derlin was certain that the paid dividends would be worth it. Mastering the artful step of keeping the pants up in an equally ill-fitting shirt while he searched the house for his tiny boots, Derlin looked the part of a silent film-era hobo, only adding to the effect once he'd located his boots and tucked the legs of the maternity pants neatly into them.

Mavis was just about to ask Derlin how much farther they had to drive when he finally cut the sedan onto an unmarked gravel road mostly hidden by waist-high grass. Weaving slowly under an ever-thickening canopy of pine trees, Derlin laid on the horn as he pulled up to the side of Hoyt & Vondene's house. The house was a mud-brown, crusty old split level that looked from the outside as though someone had smashed two very different log cabins into one home and painted over it. Grandma Vondene's Henderson car was parked crookedly by the front door, with Hoyt and Vern's pickup trucks equally crooked on either side.

Derlin honked again as he and Mavis gathered the babies from the car. Hearing the ruckus from inside, Vern had turned to Grandpa Hoyt and remarked "I bet it's Derlin." Hoyt shook his head and sighed, eyeballing Vern as he stood and headed for the door.

"Of course it's Derlin dammit," Hoyt spat. "It ain't 5:45 so it sure ain't your brother is it? Who else would it be?"

"Just sayin'," Vern said proudly. "I'm not wrong."

"Gonna be something wrong with you if you don't cut it out," Hoyt shouted.

"Hoyt you leave Verny alone," Grandma Vondene yelled from the kitchen.

"Then tell him to shut up," Hoyt yelled back as he hobbled toward the front door. He opened it just as Derlin and Mavis were making their way up the stairs and he offered a happy wave as he saw them approach.

"Hot damn, lookit them grandbabies," Hoyt said, hooting loudly for emphasis. "They're sprouting up like bean poles ain't they?"

Grandma Vondene squealed, running to the door from the kitchen, the remnants of a pie crust still caking her hands. She kissed Derlin on the cheek, taking Ollie from him with her crusty fingers and bouncing him happily as she hugged him. Derlin dusted some flour off of his shirt and shook his grandfather's hand before leaning in for a bear hug and a few seconds of shadowboxing.

"Y'all come on in, make yourselves at home," Grandma Vondene said excitedly. "I'mma be workin' my tail off in the kitchen but y'all sit down and get comfy. Verny's in the living room watching the football game."

"The Lions is playing," Vern offered from the living room couch.

"It's always the dang Lions," Grandpa Hoyt said. "They ain't never good. I bet they ain't gonna be good for fifty years. Tina could put together a better team of folks down at Meaty's."

"If she ever did, I'd be the quarterback," Vern said. He did his best to mimic the motion of a quarterback throwing a pass from his spot on the couch.

"You'd make Greg Landry look like Joe Namath if you were out there, Vern," Grandpa Hoyt shouted. "And he can't even throw it to the right team."

"I could do that," Vern scoffed.

"Mavis, you wanna keep me company in the kitchen while the boys yell at each other in here?" Vondene asked. "I got highchairs we can set the babies in."

"That sounds great," Mavis said.

She gasped as she followed Vondene into the kitchen, seeing the countertops and stove piled high with dishes in varying degrees of completion.

"Did you do all this yourself?" Mavis asked.

"Oh, sure," Vondene said casually. "The only cooking ol' Hoyt ever does is on a meat fire if he's out hunting. Around this house it's all Grandma Vondene."

"That's amazing," Mavis said, marveling at Vondene's handiwork as she walked around the kitchen. "What all did you cook this year?"

"Well, I got the turkey and the ham in the oven," Vondene began. "I got the deer leg on the wood grill by the shed, gonna fry some chicken livers and bacon. I've got corn and beans and stuffing and sweet potatoes too, but you know how these Spurlock boys like their meats."

"Boy, do I," Mavis deadpanned, "Derlin's always talking about his meat tooth."

"That boy loves his meat," Vondene said, smiling as she looked over Mavis' shoulder into the living room.

By the time the football game ended, a variety of smells were wafting in from the kitchen and, while Vern dozed on the couch after his early-afternoon six pack, the beers Derlin and Hoyt had consumed had only made them hungrier and their stomachs were grumbling.

"I ain't waiting on Clovis to drag his ass over here to eat that much longer," Hoyt shouted at Vondene from the couch. "I'll die in this chair and come back as the ghost of Thanksgiving and wreck his plate up every damn year if I got to!"

"You hush up out there and have another beer," Vondene hollered back over Mavis' shoulder. "It's just now 6 o'clock, I'll start putting food out on the table in just a minute."

"Dang well better," Hoyt muttered, grabbing another warm beer from the floor next to the couch and passing one to his grandson. "If your deddy don't get here soon I'mma beat him with the hambone."

"Oh I bet they'll pull up any second," Derlin said, doing his best to placate his grandfather. "Mama probably just got off work late from the Thanksgiving brunch at Meaty's is all."

Grandpa Hoyt had switched the television to a repeat of an old Thanksgiving Thunderdome and Derlin had hoped that this would quell the old man's irritation long enough for Clovis and Tina to slink through the door, muttering something about traffic, the weather, or Meaty's. Once they'd stuck a turkey leg in Hoyt's massive, weathered claw of a hand, all would likely be forgiven and they could all set themselves to stuffing their faces in a fierce holiday silence like a normal family.

"I remember this one," Derlin said to Hoyt, slapping his own knee in enthusiasm. "The Fur Trapper gets blinded when Cherokee Sue accidentally throws fire water into his eyes instead of Hector Mucho's and he loses that bag of pelts right?"

Grandpa Hoyt sighed and looked at the living room clock. At 6:20, Vondene and Mavis began to carry dishes into the dining room table and at 6:40, with still no word from Clovis or Tina, Vondene called for the boys to shut off the TV and head into the dining room. Standing and stretching, Derlin licked his palm and lightly slapped Vern in the forehead, running his wet hand down Vern's face. Vern stopped snoring and rumbled to life with a start, looking around the room with bewilderment.

"Dinner time, Uncle Vern," Derlin said, reaching out with his still-damp hand and helping Vern to his feet.

"Where's your mama and deddy?" Vern asked, rubbing his eyes, arching his back and patting his belly as he shook off his mid-day nap.

"Ain't here yet," Derlin said.

"That's they own fault," Grandpa Hoyt shouted as he hobbled to the dining room. "It's dark outside already and by God I'm getting my ham and turkey meats!"

"Sit down and we'll get you your meats," Vondene said gently.

Hoyt took her advice, sitting at the head of the table and stuffing his napkin down his shirt, eyeing the spread impatiently.

"Hoyt, do you wanna cut up the turkey?" Vondene asked, holding out the necessary tools.

Hoyt stood up from his chair, leaning in and snatching the carving tools from Vondene. He quickly cut off both legs of the turkey, stabbing the carving knife and fork down firmly into the turkey's mid-section. He grabbed the legs from where they'd fallen on the platter and sat down with one in each hand, taking an aggressive bite of each and beginning to chew in silence. Uncle Vern reached out with an unusual quickness, grabbing the turkey's tail with his bare hand as a frog snatches a fly, pulling it off and shoving it into his mouth in one fluid motion.

"You boys are going to be the death of me," Grandma Vondene said crossly, leaning back across the table and ripping the carving tools from the turkey. She began to slice the turkey and dole it out among plates as everyone except Hoyt began passing the side dishes around the table.

There were soon mounds of food on everyone's plate except for Mavis (who had made a responsible pile) and Hoyt, who would be content with his turkey legs until he stood later to cut off his pie slice-sized wedge of ham. Burdened conversationally by Clovis and Tina's absence and their own exceptional hunger, the dinner table was silent aside from someone periodically congratulating Vondene on another culinary triumph or Vern's continued vigorous shaking of the salt shaker. A periodic glance would be taken at the front door during dinner and dessert, but it wasn't until Vondene began clearing pie plates that Clovis and Tina finally burst through it.

"Hey y'all," Clovis said nonchalantly. "Sorry we're running a little behind. Tina got stuck mopping up sangria at Meaty's and then the traffic was just a royal pain in the ass. Glad we made it out here at all with the weather like it's doing."

Derlin stopped picking pie crumbs from the table long enough to steal a glance out the window at the clear, cloudless night. He was about to mention it to his father when he noticed a gob of icing behind his tea glass, wiping it up with his finger.

"Ain't no dang weather out there boy," Hoyt shouted. "It was sunny all day and their ain't no traffic out here either. Your brother Vern's been here all day, runnin' his mouth, spendin' family time like a good boy and you and Tina just come waltzing up here an hour before my bedtime?"

"Oh it ain't that big a deal," Clovis said, rolling his eyes. He walked over to the dish rack next to the sink, grabbing himself a dripping wet plate and nodding at Tina to do the same. "We're here now ain't we?"

"Yeah, you are, but Thanksgiving's over," Hoyt shouted. "These is my leftovers now. You can't just come up in somebody's house and take their leftovers."

"But deddy," Clovis started.

"But nothing boy," Hoyt continued. "If you wanted to eat Thanksgiving dinner with us, you should have come to Thanksgiving dinner! Put down that plate."

"For serious, deddy?" Clovis asked, his voice rising.

"Serious as hell," Hoyt shouted.

"Fine," Clovis said. "We'll leave. It sure was great to see everybody."

"Hey deddy," Derlin said from his spot at the table, waving.

"Hello son," Clovis said politely.

There was an awkward silence for a few seconds as everyone's eyes fell on Clovis. He tossed his plate lightly onto the table where it landed with a thud, watching it slowly spin to a stop. Clovis looked around the room for a moment, seeming to size up his family, suddenly reaching down and snatching the turkey carcass off the platter, bolting toward the door with it tucked under his arm.

"Come on, Tina," Clovis shouted. "Get in the truck."

"Hey, the back!" Derlin shouted. "Don't take the back, that's my favorite. That's my second dinner!"

The rest of the family stared in disbelief as Clovis sprinted out the door. Tina followed behind him, walking slowly and waving awkwardly as she closed the front door behind her.

"Aw man," Derlin continued. "I can't believe deddy took the back."

Moments later as they passed back through town, Clovis pulled his truck quickly into the parking lot of the closed Piggly Wiggly, his greasy paw sliding across the steering wheel as he struggled to grip it. He slammed the truck into neutral and stomped down onto the parking brake. Wiping his hands uselessly on the thighs of his jeans, Clovis snatched the turkey carcass from its perch atop the dashboard wedged under the windshield. He began to pick at it hungrily and angrily.

"Grandpa Hoyt telling me I can't have no turkey on account of being late, I got news for him," he grumbled incoherently. He offered a fistful of wet dark meat to Tina, who refused, choosing to sit there silently and watch him slowly dismantle the rapidly congealing turkey carcass that now sat on his lap. The muffled tunes of Tammy Wynette's "Stand by Your Man" on the radio did little to drown out the sound of Clovis chewing and, if there was a pervading sense of irony present, it was lost on Tina as she sat blank-faced in the truck, lighting cigarette after cigarette as she watched her husband eat.

Part 6: The Salesman

Chapter 42

December 5, 1968

Derlin stared listlessly out at the gas pumps from behind the counter at Lumpy's, a small neon Christmas tree and candy cane now obscuring his view. He leaned forward with his head on his hand, his posture slouched. There was a pang Derlin felt deep in his stomach that he couldn't quite identify that he'd been unable to shake it over the course of the previous week. As good as the place had been to him, it gradually crept into Derlin's mind that he'd reached an impasse with his career at Lumpy's. Granted, he still schmoozed customers at the Feed n' Seed with his normal gusto and he was still a remarkably hard worker, but he and Lumpy's relationship had begun to strain in the time since the boys' health scare had begun a few months prior. Lumpy had always been supportive from afar and Derlin didn't doubt his sincerity, but his skittish aversion to the children since their "bout of doctoring" had begun to wear on Derlin's conscience. Lumpy was always understanding of Derlin's predicament as long as he didn't actually have to do anything, but if Mavis ever brought the boys by the store Lumpy would avoid them like the plague and Derlin was getting tired of the act.

It pained him greatly to even think it, but he even supposed that Lumpy was behind the rumor spreading of the boys' "dwarfism" and likely some of the other suspected illnesses the townsfolk had been whispering about. The Feed n' Seed had been a place where local folks would talk for generations, and Derlin couldn't imagine the firestorm of gossip if Lumpy ever happened to see the boys without their wigs on and the subsequent trouble it could bring.

He hadn't spoken to Mavis about this, as he didn't want to worry her with his inner rumblings. He had a decent-paying, steady job for the first time in their relationship and was reticent to rock the ship so soon after getting he and his family on their feet and into a life with a semblance of normalcy. Lumpy didn't often get near enough to Randy or Ollie to likely be able to see them closely, with or without their wigs, but Derlin hesitated to take such a careless chance on his family's future by staying on at the Feed n' Seed forever and simply hoping for the best.

He began to wonder what else he could do for a living in Coverdale and didn't immediately draw up a lot of prospects. Even with his newfound stature in the community stemming from his "rise through the army," Derlin still hadn't gotten over the personal embarrassment of being laughed out of the fire station. Though it had been his impetus to join the army and turn his life around, he still couldn't bring himself to show his face at the station again, so becoming a fireman was once again scratched off his list.

He considered applying for a management position at the A&P or Piggly Wiggly, as he felt the career transition would be a relatively smooth one. As he'd said to himself "groceries is just feed and seed for people." He nixed that idea too, however, as he felt a pang of guilt at the idea of managing one of the grocery stores he'd once robbed at rake-point during one of the darker points of his life. He felt as though the guilt would gnaw away at him over time and, picturing his own eventual tear-filled confession in a darkened back room of the local grocery, Derlin crossed them off his list of possibilities as well. Almost certainly, he knew that he could get brought on working under Clebert at the rubber band factory in Applebottom, but the prospects of spending his days crouched on a factory floor tying broken rubber bands back together seemed grim and he'd soon abandoned the notion as quickly as he'd thought it.

December 11, 1968

After a particularly slow day at Lumpy's, one with plenty of idle time for Derlin to spend staring slack-jawed into space pondering his future, he decided to go for a drive. As he locked up, he called Mavis to tell her he'd be staying late to catch up on some tobacco seed inventory and not to worry about waiting on him for dinner. He had no plans for a destination as he got in his trusty old sedan, turning left out onto the blacktop and heading west toward the sun.

He clicked on the radio, in the middle of the chorus of Buck Owens' new hit "Who's Gonna Mow Your Grass," and briefly considered forming a partnership with his father in the landscaping business before shuddering coldly at the idea and clicking the radio off once more. He loved his father, but the idea of spending his work days cutting grass while Clovis likely just smoked and yelled at him from the cab of his truck seemed less than enticing, in addition to being a few steps down on the employment ladder from his current position. Clovis had just barely conveyed a sense of being an authority figure as a parent and Derlin couldn't imagine the idea of taking steps to make their relationship a professional one unless it was a dead-end last resort.

Derlin hadn't travelled very far west of Coverdale since leaving the jail in Chicken Wipe several months prior and was interested to see that there appeared to be a good amount of new construction along the roadside as he drove. A new McDonalds, a small motel and an auto mechanic shop whizzed by him in rapid succession as Derlin thought, in order, of being paid in cheeseburgers, breaking Uncle Vern's family record for number of "beds" slept in in one night, and how he'd likely become one of the best "dent banger-outers" in the country from all his evenings in the garage with the old sedan, imagining how happy the shop would be to have him.

He made a mental note of each location, though he wasn't particularly keen on the idea of working at any of them, especially as he considered that even if McDonald's did have a job as "Cheeseburger Taster" it would likely be highly sought after and he was likely vastly underqualified. He'd drive another ten miles, zoned out and thinking about cheeseburgers, passing a handful of gas stations, a honky tonk and a junk shop along the way. He'd been staring off at the neon sky, missing every one of them, when finally a billboard with a familiar name drifted into his line of sight.

"Yamashita?" Derlin gasped, slamming on the brakes and skidding to a stop about twenty feet from the billboard. Luckily, no one was behind him on the road and he avoided causing any pile-ups as he gawked up at the sign.

COMING SOON: RICKY YAMASHITA DODGE SALESMEN APPLY WITHIN

Derlin gasped as he finished reading the sign. It was as if the skies had parted and the Gods had given him a sign. His wrestling hero and personal idol, "The Navajo" himself, was opening a car dealership half an hour outside his hometown. Derlin took a deep breath and checked his pulse before pinching himself on each arm to ensure that he wasn't dreaming. Slamming the old sedan back into drive, Derlin peeled off of the road and made his way hastily to the main office, where a "hiring" sign was visible in the window. It was now nearly dusk, but Derlin could make out two figures inside. Happy at his blind luck, Derlin threw the car into park and began to paw at the door handle. Leaping out of his car, he burst through the door into the office, meeting two women around his age whom he'd clearly startled.

"I'd like to talk to The Navajo Mr. Yamashita about a car sellin' position?" Derlin said, ending his inflection strangely as though he was asking a question.

"He's not in the office today, but we're actually doing the hiring," said the woman closest to him. "We're his daughters."

"The Navajo" himself had dyed his hair dark black and was well-bronzed, but his daughters were nearly identical fair-skinned blondes. Complexions notwithstanding, they shared their father's athletic build and Derlin briefly thought to himself how glad he was that he'd never tried to rob the place with a rake.

"I'm Derlin, Derlin Spurlock," Derlin said confidently.

"I'm Dixie and this is my sister Crystal Yamashita," Dixie said. They each shook Derlin's hand firmly as he did his best to maintain his composure.

"I'm manager down at the Lumpy's Feed n' Seed over in Coverdale," Derlin said.

"I been there a good while since I got out of the army, and I've done lots of good for Lumpy's business, but I'm looking to do something else for a living."

"Oh I know Lumpy's," Crystal said. "We stopped there to put some air in the tires on our way back home from The Screaming Captain a couple years ago when daddy ran over all that broken glass from the billboard."

"You folks lived around here long?" Derlin asked.

"Well, I guess by the way you come through the door, you know who our daddy is," Dixie said, chuckling. "He's on the road travelling most of the time, but we've lived on the same farm with our mamma outside of Chicken Wipe for a good twenty years."
"Is he gonna quit wrestling to sell cars?" Derlin asked, a very concerned look coming across his face.

"Oh no," Dixie said. "Not on your life."

"He's still World Champion of the whole South," Crystal added. "He's got a good ten years of wrestling left in him."

"He's done lots of other things on the side to make a living, from car washes to pool halls and bowling alleys. He always said when we grew up we were all going to go into business together," Dixie said. "And when Crystal and I graduated school at the University of the Ozarks, daddy said 'let's buy a car dealership!'"

"He owns it and it's his name on the billboard, but we're running the day to day of it all," Crystal said.

"Well, ain't that something!" Derlin said. "So, where do I sign up? Do y'all want me to fill out an application?"

"Well, Mr. Spurlock," Dixie said. "Do you have any experience selling cars?"

"I reckon I don't specifically," Derlin said sheepishly, rubbing the back of his head. "I did buy my car at a police auction though, does that---"

"This is going to be a very big lot, with 200-300 cars on sight, Mr. Spurlock," Crystal said. "Not some rinky-dink used car lot. Folks are gonna come for miles and miles to say they bought a new Dodge from Ricky "The Navajo" Yamashita. It's going to be a little more of a high-pressure environment than you may be used to at Lumpy's."

"Now, I don't reckon that selling cattle feed and birdseed is all that different than trying to talk folks into ploppin' down their cash for a fancy new mo-chine like y'all are gonna have parked out here," Derlin said. He felt something stir in his chest, a feeling he'd later identify as believing in himself. If Lumpy's had made him nothing else during his time there, it had made him quite the salesman.

"Oh yeah?" Crystal asked, legitimately curious. She leaned forward in her chair as Dixie, now standing next to her, crossed her arms. "Explain."

"Well," Derlin began, unsure entirely of where he was going to go with this. "Well, I see it like this." He cleared his throat. "Everybody that comes into the Feed n' Seed to buy something, they're already in the door because they trust what I'm sellin' there. They know that ol' Derlin ain't gonna sell them no dead nightcrawlers or bad seeds or fake manure. And they're right."

"Go on," Dixie said, a smile slowly creeping across her face.

"So I look at it as, sure I might not have ever sold a car yet," Derlin continued. He was beginning to talk with his hands and pace slowly, giving his answer a sense of presentation. "But I've sold a thousand smaller things. Maybe two thousand, I don't know. I don't count each one for sure. I figure, hey, I look up on that sign, I see Ricky 'The Navajo' Yamashita trying to sell me a Dodge, that's a man I can trust. I know he's gonna be a straight shooter, on account of he's 'The Navajo.' There ain't nobody you can trust buying a car from more than a Champion of the World. I figure your daddy's already got these folks through the door just being who he is. All I gotta do is schmooze 'em through the paperwork, make them feel real good and special about buying from 'The Navajo' and send 'em on their way in their shiny new rides, one Dodge at a time. If I can sell cow shit for Lumpy McGoon I can sure sell Dodges for Ricky Yamashita."

Dixie and Crystal looked to each other, eyebrows raised, nodding in unison.

"Mr. Spurlock, you're hired," Dixie said happily.

"If you can bring that much enthusiasm to the job we'll be damn glad to have you on board," Crystal said.

"Aw, that's great!" Derlin shouted, leaping and pumping his fist in the air. "Y'all ain't gonna be disappointed. I'mma work so hard for you and your daddy."

"We don't doubt it, Mr. Spurlock," Crystal said.

"Yall, please, call me Derlin," Derlin said.

"Alright, Derlin," Dixie said, producing a stack of papers from her desk. "Let's get you started on your paperwork and we'll make it official. What does Lumpy's pay you?"

"$180 a week," Derlin said, the thought to embellish never crossing his mind.

"How about we'll start you at $220 and you'll get a nice little commission for each sale you make? Crystal offered. "We'd usually start someone at $200 but I've got a really good feeling about you. With that enthusiasm and your community standing, I think you're going to be a very special member of our team. Plus, that's a little more incentive for you leaving Lumpy's."

"Holy shit damn that'd be fine as hell," Derlin gasped. Privately he'd been less than confident that he'd be able to find another job to pay him as handsomely as Lumpy's had and the idea of getting such a raise right off the bat almost knocked the wind out of him. He took a moment to catch his breath.

"Sorry for the swears, ladies," he squeaked, coughing. And commission too?"

"I think 5% of the profits from each of your sales is a fair start," Crystal smiled. "Daddy said he wants whoever we hire to feel like they're really part of the team and that this would be a good way to keep folks like you motivated to keep sellin' even though we pay you good money besides commission. A job you can feed a family with."

"Girls, y'all ain't gonna be able to keep 300 cars on this lot I'mma be selling them so fast," Derlin exclaimed. "When do I start?"

"We'll be open for business in two weeks time, the day after Christmas," Dixie said. "Plenty of time for you to let Lumpy know you're moving up in the world, though I don't know how he'll manage replacing somebody of your caliber."

"Sounds great!" Derlin said, giving each Yamashita sister a heartfelt and sweaty handshake. "I will put it on my calendar, that's a good idea. I'll let y'all get back to your workings, though, it's getting awful late. I gotta get home and tell the wife and the babies before they get put to bed! I'll see y'all in two weeks time."

Derlin saluted, waved and darted back out the door, the sisters waving back at him in unison. They watched in wonderment as he ran back through the parking lot, hair blowing in the breeze. Wincing as they watched him climb into his rusted, greyish mass of a car and drive away, they followed the one working tail light of the old sedan until it was out of sight over the horizon. As quickly as he'd come, he'd gone back into the night again, but it seemed the Yamashita sisters had found their salesman.

Chapter 43

December 12, 1968

Derlin spent most of the next morning tip-toeing around Lumpy, nursing the effects of the two celebratory late-night bottles of Champale that he and Mavis had shared in the yard. He didn't relish the idea of telling Lumpy that he was headed for greener pastures. Though the past few months had been a strain, Lumpy had always been very good to him, going back to when Derlin was just a lowly pump-wipe and needed an advance for his family's first squalid apartment. He'd looked up to Lumpy in some strange way since he was a boy and worried deeply about disappointing the old man. As such, Derlin spent most of the day finding ways to busy himself in different parts of the store to avoid conversation. Hed made it nearly all the way till 5 o'clock when he finally broke down.

"Lumpy, I gotta tell you something," Derlin sighed.

"What's at?" Lumpy said through a wad of tobacco.

"I gotta put in my two week notice Lumpy," Derlin continued. "I got a new job."

"Do what?" Lumpy said loudly, squinting at Derlin.

"I said I got a new job!" Derlin said louder. "I'mma be a car salesman for my hero Ricky Yamashita over out past the other side of town!"

"Oh," Lumpy said, rubbing the back of his neck. "I see… Well, I reckon I figured this day would come."

"What do you mean?" Derlin asked.

"Well, I always reckoned once you got back and settled and started helpin' this place out so much working so hard, ain't no way the "army hero" is gonna stay forever at the Feed n' Seed, pumping out gas for folks," Lumpy said.

"Oh yeah?" Derlin asked.

"Yeah," Lumpy continued. "I used to not think much of shit of you when you was a boy, but I'll be damned if you ain't got more ahead of you than workin' here, weighing out nightcrawlers and rewinding fishing line."

"Aw, Lumpy that's a real swell thing to say," Derlin replied, genuinely moved. "That might be the nicest thing anybody other than Grandma Vondene or Mavis has ever said to me."

"I mean it," Lumpy said, leaning against the counter. "I seen you wheel n' deal with these folks in here. Son, I've seen you sell chicken feed to folks who just come in for gas and don't have no chickens, and I reckon you'll do just fine selling cars for that wrestlin' man."

"Much obliged Lumpy," Derlin said. "That's mighty kind. I ain't never sold no cars before but I'mma give it my best shot."

"You did buy your car down at the police auction," Lumpy said. "Did you tell them about that?"

"They said that don't count for salesman experience," Derlin said, sounding out the last two words carefully.

"Well it should count for something," Lumpy said matter of factly. He wiped his brow with a discolored handkerchief he produced from his back pocket. "I sure will be sad to see you go."

December 15, 1968

Derlin hunkered down in the bushes, listening to the sound of a distant dog barking. He crept along the edge of the front yard, producing a small hand saw from a sack. He began to saw feverishly at the base of a decorative fir tree which he'd spotted from the roadside. Every few saw motions he'd pause and crane his neck like a prairie dog, listening to his surroundings. Content that he would remain uninterrupted, Derlin finally sawed the tree to the ground where it landed with a dull crash. A light came on in the mayor's house as Derlin muttered an inaudible swear to himself and scampered toward the road, dragging the tree behind him. He crammed it into the open trunk of the still-running sedan and did his best to close the trunk door on top of it with limited success. Just as the mayor's front door opened and he emerged, bathrobe-clad with a flashlight and a golf club, Derlin sped off into the night, tinsel spilling out of his trunk onto the road and the strains of Hank Williams' "Honky-Tonkin" blaring from his radio. He'd gotten his boys the nicest Christmas tree in town. Already decorated to boot.

December 17, 1968

As the days went on and his countdown to his exodus from Lumpy's began in earnest, Derlin began spending his evenings at home practicing his sales routine for his new job at Ricky Yamashita's.

"It's really gonna be just like selling nightcrawlers, baby." he told Mavis one evening as he began to rehearse. "Just instead of a thousand little ones at a time I'm selling one really big one."

"I guess you're right," Mavis said, fiddling with a crooked row of lights on the massive tree Derlin had acquired as a surprise and decorated in the night over the weekend.

"Like instead of selling somebody fifty packs of corn seeds," Derlin continued, talking with his hands for effect. "It's like I'll be selling them one giant corn seed. With wheels. That they ride in and drive places with their family."

"That makes sense, honey," Mavis smiled. She pictured Derlin riding atop a massive corn seed as he rolled down the road, holding onto it with stirrups as a cowboy would a horse. "You're so smart."

"Thanks, baby," Derlin smiled distractedly, combing his hair in the mirror and patting the sides down softly. He took a deep breath and turned his full attention to his reflection.

"The original owner bought it brand new," Derlin said awkwardly, pointing at himself in the mirror. He cleared his throat and patted down his shirt.

"What's it gonna take to get you behind the wheel of a Ricky Yamashita Dodge today, fella?" he asked himself. "You look like you want a fast one!"

"That's really good honey, I'm so proud!" Mavis beamed, "You're a natural."

"Aw, hell," Derlin muttered frustratedly. "That wasn't no good. I couldn't sell a jug of honey to a bear with that little routine."

"What do you mean?" Mavis asked.

"I don't like talking to myself in the mirror trying to do this," Derlin confided. "It makes me feel like an asshole."

"Well, why don't you practice with me?" Mavis smiled.

"But you're a lady," Derlin said.

"Well, what do you mean by that?" Mavis asked, raising her eyebrows.

"I mean, Grandpa Hoyt and deddy always told me there weren't no women what bought cars." Derlin said. "They said it was work for the men folk."

"That doesn't make any sense, Derlin," Mavis scolded. "There's plenty of women who buy their own cars."

"That's what I speculated when they told me," Derlin said, getting a little defensive, sensing rightly that he was about to be in trouble. "I said that same exact thing when we was on our way up to the police auction to get my car, and Grandpa Hoyt said 'Yeah maybe in New York City,' and he and deddy laughed."

"But your mama and grandma both drive cars," Mavis said.

"That's what I said too!" Derlin replied. "I said 'but mama and Grandma Vondene both drive cars!' and deddy said 'that's cause he picked out mama's and Grandpa Hoyt picked out Grandma Vondene's and that's the Spurlock way.'"

"But, I think," Mavis began.

"Besides, Grandma Vondene and mama both drive one of those women-cars that Grandpa Hoyt's friend makes himself down over in Mississippi," Derlin said casually, waving his hand dismissively.

"I'm sorry?" Mavis said.

"One of Grandpa Hoyt's friends over in Mississippi makes his own brand of car out on his property, designed just for womens," Derlin replied. "He's been doing it off and on since the depression, in between thresher accidents. Grandpa Hoyt says he's bought every one of Grandma Vondene's cars down there over the years. Mama even drives one of her old ones that deddy bought from Grandpa Hoyt."

"That doesn't make any sense, honey." Mavis said. Though certainly not something you'd see sitting in front of the boutiques in downtown Birmingham, Mavis knew that her mother's old Buick was at the very least an actual car and not made by some strange backwater farmer in between heavy equipment mishaps.

"It does too," Derlin argued. "'Henderson's Cars for Women' I think the sign on the barn says."

"How are they cars for women?" Mavis asked.

"Well, I ain't no Henderson, I don't make 'em," Derlin snorted, before softening his tone. "I mean, I have ridden with Grandma Vondene a time or two out doing stuff before. Her car seems like a regular old station wagon, but with flowers painted across the dashboard, so it smells sort of like paint. Old Mr. Henderson gets most of his parts from salvage too, so everything don't line up quite right. Her steering wheel says Chevrolet but I don't know what the dang hood ornament says. It looks like a badger. Plus I think he makes his bumper covers out of old tires too so the metal don't get all mashed up. Grandma Vondene backed into Uncle Vern's trailer one time leavin' a fish fry and just bounced off the damn thing like a tennis ball. If she'd been goin' much faster or been much drunker that Henderson might be in the pond too, right next to Uncle Vern's old pickup. Although with all the rubber it'd probably float."

"Okay," Mavis began, taking a breath and pausing to think for a moment about all the information Derlin had just given her. Certainly, there was plenty to unravel here, but Mavis needed to get her point across while the idea was fresh.

"You know honey," she continued. "There might have been a time where Henderson Cars for Women was a really good idea. But times are a little different now, honey. It's almost 1969. Women are gonna come into your dealership to buy cars, too. Probably every day. Real cars not made by some man in a barn. If we're ever rich enough to have two cars, I want to pick mine out myself."

"I guess you're right, baby," Derlin said, sighing and stretching. He leaned over and picked a few needles from the Christmas tree, placing one in his mouth and crumbling the rest between his fingers. "It is almost 1969. It is pretty much the future. I reckon that means all y'all womenfolk can buy real cars and have real jobs and wear jeans just like us mens."

"So, do you want to practice your sales pitch with me?" Mavis asked hopefully.

"Naw," Derlin shrugged. His eyes drifted over to the couch. "I think I'd rather practice on the babies."

Derlin adapted quickly to honing his skills on the babies. They weren't yet of speaking age and certainly still lacked the cognitive capacity to haggle, but Derlin spent a good hour per evening working on his technique with them as he wound out his final two weeks at Lumpy's. As Derlin would ask a question about a warranty or a clear coat, Randy and Ollie would coo and babble in delight. They hadn't yet mastered any words as they neared their first birthday, unless you counted the "Bow! Bow! Bow!" (cawed out like the side of a ship, not a ribbon) they'd shout when grasping for things they liked, or wanted. No matter their current vocabulary, this nightly back and forth with their father was certainly good for the development of their little brains, even if the advantages of good gas mileage and power steering meant nothing to them.

"Green Acres" reruns and her initial agitation at not being chosen to participate aside, this nightly routine became a favorite source of entertainment for Mavis. She'd watch Derlin from the doorway to the living room, his hair nicely combed and his shirt both tucked in and properly buttoned, waving his arms and teling Randy and Ollie that "you could barely see the scuff on the bumper" or "think of all the cooter you can run down cruising in this bad boy." She'd watch the light play on his face as he talked the boys into all the upgrades on a new Dodge Dart or Charger. He'd help them finish with the "paperwork," cheer and snatch them up, pretending to race them off into the sunset in their new sports cars. It was in these moments that Mavis realized how truly far Derlin had come in the less than two years since their little shotgun wedding on the hill and she couldn't help but wonder if Randy and Ollie would be of the first generation to have a rightful reason to be proud of being born a Spurlock.

Many times, as Derlin raced the boys through the air, whooshing and cheering after "completing a sale," he got to thinking. He was a straightforward man, as most Spurlocks were. Abstract thinking was certainly not his cup of tea but it was in these moments that he at least teetered on the cusp of it. He was sure the boys were still too young to know definitively whether cars actually flew or just drove on the "regular ground," but as Mavis had recently mentioned, it was nearly 1969. As he spun the boys one evening after a sale, gazing off into nothing in particular but the living room ceiling and imagining the future, Derlin thought to himself that by the time the boys were old enough to actually drive, cars very well could be flying.

"Why else you gonna put a big wing on the back of a Charger?" Derlin speculated to Ollie one evening. "If you ain't gonna make it drive to the moon?"

December 23, 1968

It was 4:55 and it was Derlin's last day at Lumpy's. He blew into his hand as he stepped out the door, shuddering at the cool breeze whipping through the parking lot. The day had been quiet and he was trudging outside to give the pumps one final glorious wipe down when Lumpy's truck came swerving into the parking lot behind him, skidding to a stop near a stack of old tractor tires that Lumpy kept there in case someone's brakes ever gave out.

"I was hoping I'd catch you," Lumpy hollered, climbing out of his truck with a happy wave.

"Yeah, I was just finishing up," Derlin replied, returning Lumpy's wave. "Was just gonna put a shine on these gas pumps one more time before I call it quits."

"Boy those gas pumps are so clean you can read the "Pure" sign from halfway over in that cornfield with all the tire tracks in it," Lumpy laughed. "How about you go ahead and call it a day. I got you a little going away present for all the good you've done me. I reckon you could call it a Christmas present too, if you like."

He handed Derlin a long, unwrapped rectangular box, with the words "From Lumpy" scrawled across it in what appeared to be charcoal.

"Man, thanks Lumpy," Derlin smiled. "You didn't have to go to all this trouble."

"No trouble at all, old top," Lumpy said, patting Derlin on the shoulder as he undid a piece of tape. "You've been mighty good to this old place."

Derlin finally pried open the top of the box, setting it on the hood of Lumpy's truck to paw away the bits of old newspaper Lumpy had used to wrap the contents. As he removed the last bit of paper, he gasped. He reached into the box, plucking out a large old rifle with a rusty bayonet attached to the front.

"That was my daddy's," Lumpy smiled. "He won it in a game of cards off a Spanish infantryman down in Cuba for the war back in '98. Said he killed many a gopher with it after he got back home. Beaver rats too."

"Aw, hell Lumpy that's real nice of you and all," Derlin started bashfully. "But I can't take your daddy's war gun."

"You sure as shit can," Lumpy said. "I ain't got no boy of my own to pass it to, you know. Ain't likely to be siring one anytime soon."
Derlin looked at the rifle and ran his hand down the smooth wood.

"Besides, I know what a hunter your Grandpa Hoyt is and I figure you're probably just as good as him if you ain't better," Lumpy added.

Derlin went wide-eyed for a moment before regaining his facial composure. The army had done some work on his still-shabby marksmanship, but he had never successfully hunted another living creature in his life. This problem had been exacerbated during the family's time living in the windmill and Derlin knew that he might have never had to turn to his haphazard string of grocery store robberies had he been able to trap or bludgeon any part of the ample reserves of local wildlife. On the other side of that coin was his Grandpa Hoyt, who held most Chubb County hunting records for shooting the biggest or most of something.

"Oh I could never be as good as my Grandpa Hoyt," Derlin said bashfully, playing off of Lumpy's comment as innocuously as he could.

He thought back to one of his earliest memories of Grandpa Hoyt as a child, when the two of them went fishing in some long lost river on a rickety skiff Grandpa Hoyt had dragged out from under some brush behind his shed. Derlin couldn't have been more than four at the time and was already tired from the hour-long truck ride and subsequent two mile hike to where Grandpa Hoyt planned to finally put the skiff in the water. Grandpa Hoyt quietly whistled as he fished, paying no attention to his grandson once he'd helped him cast his line. Staring blankly at the water, young Derlin soon began to nod off. Just as he was about to fall asleep, he heard a mighty splash and shrieked with terror as an alligator popped its head out of the water next to the skiff and snarled. In the commotion, Grandpa Hoyt's case of beer slid off the edge of the skiff and into the gator's mouth and soon he too was shrieking. Derlin remembered it as a much darker, angrier scream than his own, even as a small child. Steadying himself, Grandpa Hoyt pulled a pistol out of the back of his pants and calmly fired two shots, striking the gator in each eye. He retrieved his case of beer, unharmed, after spending several minutes prying it from the dead gator's mouth. Quietly he popped a beer and offered a frothy sip to Derlin, who refused. Grandpa Hoyt shrugged, watching the gator slowly float down the river for a few moments before recasting his line and returning to his whistling & fishing.

"Well I sure do hope you the best," Lumpy said, offering a tobacco filled smile. "Don't be a stranger, now."

Derlin shook himself from his memory and nodded.

"Oh I reckon you'll see plenty of me," Derlin said. "I won't be out this way for much but you're still the only place in town that sells that good spicy horse jerky."

"Aw yeah," Lumpy said. "I thought I was the only feller what liked it. That's the mayor's brother's recipe, you know."

"Well I'll be," Derlin smiled. He slapped the hood of the truck lightly. "Well old feller, I best be saddlin' up. The wife's gonna start wondering where I am if I don't get home to dinner proper. It's beef night!'

"Beef night!" Lumpy said. "Good meat! You get on home to that plate of meat and I'mma go inside and grab a fist of jerky. You take good care of that gun, now!"

"I will," Derlin said halfheartedly, staring down at the box and cramming the newspaper back around the rifle.

He slid the box quickly into the backseat and headed for home. Driving in silence for the first few minutes, Derlin glanced back at the box several times. Trying to distract himself, he clicked on the radio, tuning into approximately five seconds of Glen Campbell's "Galveston" before shutting the radio back off in frustration.

"Goddamn Glen Campbell," he muttered to himself. He stared out the side window at a passing cattle pasture for a moment before quietly adding "aw hell Derlin, you know it ain't Glen Campbell's fault."

Lumpy's gift, however well-intentioned, had stirred the memory of one of Derlin's deepest and darkest shames. Coming from a family with a master hunter like Grandpa Hoyt, Derlin's father Clovis turned into quite the crack-shot himself, though he prefered shooting cans and bottles to wildlife. Derlin however missed the ship entirely. Aside from his wrestling prowess, Derlin had ranked at or near the bottom of his entire army class in every conceivable measurable category. He was such an outlier at the bottom of the shooting chart that one could fairly assume he'd been given a small pile of rocks for target practice instead of a gun. When he was a child, Clovis used to joke to him that "he'd have better luck throwing the gun" at anything than shooting and Grandpa Hoyt would just quietly shake his head in disgust.

Shuddering as he pulled into the driveway, Derlin snatched the rifle box from the back seat, sneaking into the garage and hiding it high up in the rafters.

Chapter 44

December 24, 1968

Mavis was not particularly shocked to learn that the Spurlocks weren't much of a "Christmas" family and was quietly relieved when Derlin had informed her that they wouldn't be around for the holiday due to their attendance at a large dirt track race near the Mississippi state line.

"Oh," Mavis said, feigning disappointment. "Didn't they miss our wedding for a dirt track race too?"

"Yeah," Derlin said. "But this one's a way bigger deal. Even Uncle Vern's going to this one!"

"Well, that's too bad," Mavis said, snapping her fingers with a halfhearted "aw shucks" gesture.

"Yeah, they never was much into present giving though," Derlin said. "So we probably weren't even gonna get nothing for the babies from 'em, especially since they got a birthday in a month. Spurlocks is thrifty that way."

"Oh I don't care about presents," Mavis said. "The boys have plenty of things."

"I reckon they do," Derlin said.

"Plus, Vern already told me about the dirt track race at Thanksgiving," Mavis said. "So I went ahead and told my folks we'd have Christmas Eve dinner with them."

"Awesome!" Derlin said. "Here I was about to get a couple Swanson's out the freezer like some danged fool. What's your mama cooking?"

"She's cooking a chicken," Mavis replied. "And I think she's…"

"Chicken?" Derlin said excitedly, "That's my…"

"Third or fourth favorite kind of meat," Mavis interrupted, smiling.

"Yeah," Derlin said bashfully, giggling at his wife's prognostication. "Can we still do Santa here tomorrow morning?"

"Of course we can," Mavis smiled.

Derlin yipped and pumped his fist in the air. He nonchalantly gazed out the kitchen window at the garage, nodding imperceptibly. Though he didn't remember it, Clovis would often remind Derlin that for his first Christmas, he'd been given a jar of peanut butter to keep him occupied during a particularly heated poker game. He had long ago promised himself that he'd never go down that road of gift giving with his own children, no matter how much they'd probably love a jar of peanut butter. Their first Christmas was going to be something magical, something to remember. Derlin had an ace up his sleeve.

December 25, 1968

Derlin had racked his brain for weeks trying to think of the perfect Christmas present for the boys. He'd been pleased to learn from Mavis that her parents would be mainly getting the boys clothes for Christmas. This came as a relief because though he felt he had a keen eye for his own denim he wasn't sure how his tastes would translate to children's wear and he was grateful to be off the hook in that regard. Certainly at ten months old, Randy and Ollie weren't going to remember receiving the gift, but Derlin wanted something impressive. Something large and bombastic. At first, the idea of a puppy appealed to him before he realized that as the boys were just mastering the art of standing, it would be difficult for them to walk or play with the dog for some time. In the same vein, he also discarded the idea of acquiring them a monkey, even though he supposed that it could likely walk itself.

Derlin chuckled to himself as he walked to the garage in the wee hours just before dawn. He had kept his present hidden in the garage not from the boys, but from Mavis as well, as he'd wanted to surprise the three of them when they woke up. A few weeks prior, Derlin had gone to the local Gimbel's and purchased the largest toy train set they had, the idea coming to him near the end of the 15 minutes earlier in the day that he'd spent stuck at a railroad intersection waiting for a large freight train to pass by. He'd taken the care to purchase an extra engine, so that each of his sons could have one. After acquiring the train set, he took the engines down to Douggie's flea market to his old friend "the sign man," getting a custom painted "RANDY 69" on one and "OLLIE 69" on the other in matching red and white to help the boys remember the occasion as they got older.

"1969's gonna be a banner year for these boys," Derlin said confidently as the sign man counted out Delin's crumpled pile of one dollar bills.

Riding high on his excellent fathering, Derlin dragged the train set out of the garage and into the house as quietly as he could. He placed the engines on the mantle and slowly began assembling the tracks. By the time he heard the upstairs rumbling of Mavis and the boys waking up, Derlin had just started adding the tiny plastic trees, the rail depot and the other landscape and building pieces. Mavis slowly descended the stairs, yawning with a child in each arm.

"Merry Christmas!" Derlin shouted, startling her and the boys. He was still laying on the ground next to the tracks and it took Mavis a moment to process the scene in her living room.

"Oh honey, look at that!" Mavis said. "You got the boys a train set?"

"I sure did," Derlin said proudly. "Biggest one in the whole Gimbel's. I figure I can help 'em with the train runnin' part while they're still little and they can just crawl around on the floor and chase it or just watch it like it's a TV."

"Aww," Mavis said, her voice high pitched at the cuteness of it all.

"Plus, look!" Derlin said, clambering to his feet and grabbing the custom "RANDY 69" & "OLLIE 69" engines off of the mantle.

"That is so adorable," Mavis cooed, setting the boys down at the tracks. Ollie immediately put a tree in his mouth and Randy began gnawing on the depot.

"Aw, they love it, don't they?" Derlin asked. "Them's my good boys."

He looked over at the large pile of nicely wrapped Gimbel's boxes from Mavis' parents. Knowing Eudora's penchant for acquiring the boys matching outfits, Derlin hoped there were a couple of train conductor suits hiding in there somewhere. The kind with the little striped hats.

December 26, 1968

Derlin had been combing and re-combing his hair in the mirror for so long that his scalp underneath had begun to redden and swell, and he'd been at it for a good ten minutes before Mavis finally noticed and stopped him.

"Honey you're gonna comb all the way down to your brain," she quipped as she took the comb from him and placed it on the bathroom counter.

"That can happen?" Derlin asked, terrified. He noticed the smile Mavis had on her face and tried to play off his worry.

"Don't worry, I think your skull is probably thick enough that a plastic comb ain't gonna get through it," Mavis said.

"Us Spurlocks are a thick-headed bunch," Derlin said in agreement. "Uncle Vern headbutted me in the back one time and it sounded like a big Indian drum."

"That's nice, dear," Mavis said distractedly as she straightened Derlin's tie. "You should hurry up, you don't want to be late on your first day."

"Yeah you're right baby," Derlin said quickly, glancing at the clock on the wall. "I didn't realize I'd been combing my hair that long, I'mma have to whoop it."

He gave Mavis a kiss on the cheek, turning to dart through the hallway.

"Bye boys!" he hollered as he ran through the kitchen towards the front door. Randy and Ollie briefly stared after him blankly from their highchairs, far more interested in the morning oatmeal they'd been smearing all over themselves during their mother's brief absence.

"Bye honey, good luck!" Mavis shouted enthusiastically from the bathroom doorway. "I love you."

"I will!" Derlin shouted back as the front door slammed behind him.

Mavis listened as Derlin squealed his tires pulling out of the driveway, hearing the familiar sputtering engine of the sedan rumble down the street and fade away. As proud as she was, it was still strange for her to think of her husband as any sort of "go-getter." She smiled to herself, thinking of one day becoming the first Mrs. Spurlock since horse and buggy times to not have to drive a Henderson.

Aside from casually rolling through a few stop signs and running twice the speed limit Derlin's commute was excitement free, but he could almost feel the old sedan take a deep breath as she ground to a stop in his parking space. He'd parked behind the building as requested, jogging through the back door at the stroke of eight o'clock, waving happily to the Yamashita sisters as he entered.

"Mornin' Dixie, Mornin' Crystal," he smiled, heading straight for a box of donuts and the coffee machine. "Y'all ready to sell some cars? 'Cause I am."

"Good morning, Derlin!" they hollered from across the showroom, waving. Dixie was tying a few balloons around the showroom next to a "Grand Opening" banner and Crystal was busying herself checking through some inventory lists.

"Nice banner," Derlin said. "That's real fancy looking. All spelled good too."

"Thanks," Dixie smiled. "Daddy was planning on being here for the big day and signing some pictures for folks but he's up in Kentucky wrestling the Steel Kaiser to try and get his championship belt back."

"The "Cave Match!" Derlin said excitedly. "It was real nice of them National Parks folk to let them have a wrestling show down in the Mammoth Cave. They been talking about it on TV all week. I hope 'The Navajo' breaks off a big ol' dinosaur bone and wamps the Steel Kaiser with it right in his commie mouth."

"Yeah, daddy said it was gonna be too big of a show and he couldn't miss it even if he was opening a hundred car dealerships that day," Crystal lamented.

"Well, I sure hope he wins," Derlin smiled. "I hate the Steel Kaiser more than I hate Hitler and the Devil combined."

"We do too," Dixie shouted from her perch atop a step ladder, giving Derlin a thumbs up and briefly having to check her balance. "I'd run him over with every car in this dealership if I could."

Crystal nodded in agreement, gazing across the sea of Dodges and smiling to herself.

"Anyhow, what can I do to get started?" Derlin asked enthusiastically, taking an ambitious bite of a jelly donut.

"Well, till folks start showing up and shopping, you can just grab a shammy cloth and wipe down any bits of dust you see on cars in the showroom," Crystal said. "Just put a nice shine on any spots we might have missed."

"Sounds good to me," Derlin said happily. He was beaming internally about his rapid rise in the working world, from his humble beginnings wiping gas pumps with oily rags to wiping brand new cars with clean ones. As he plotted the course of his career arc and its logical progression upward, he wondered what millionaires must wipe off for a living and how nice the rags that they used must be.

He'd barely set to spit-shining the headlights on a new Dart when he heard the bell ring as the first customer entered the front door. Still crouched, Derlin recognized the familiar "step-clomp" of the customer as they walked slowly into the showroom. Rising to his feet, Derlin offered a greeting.

"Is that Ho-ratio I hear coming through the door?" Derlin hollered across the showroom.

"Who's asking?" Horatio asked suspiciously, startled at being recognized.

"It's me, Derlin Spurlock," Derlin said, waving happily and popping to his feet from behind a station wagon. "Remember, that one time I didn't have my fish money with me and I washed dishes and cleaned up scales for you and the nice Captain?"

Horatio walked toward Derlin with his distinctive gait, eyeing him peculiarly.

"Oh yes, I remember you," he said slowly. "You're the fella that we fed all that old beer to flushing out our taps. You wrecked up the place pretty good, I had you figured for a drifter."

"Yeah, that happens sometimes," Derlin said, chuckling softly.

"Do you work at this establishment or are you just in here trying to get out of the sun?" Horatio asked firmly.

"Oh I work here," Derlin answered confidently. "I'm a salesman."

Horatio furrowed his brow and looked around, craning his neck searching for anyone else beside Derlin that could confirm this story.

"I come a long way since you last saw me, old top," Derlin said. "I joined the army, I live inside. I got a good job now and I always pay for my fish meat."

"Well that's good for you, I certainly wouldn't have guessed it," Horatio said flatly. "How'd you recognize me so quick anyhow? You could barely stand up or see the last time that I saw you."

"You got a real specific gait to you, amigo," Derlin said, pointing downward. "Ain't a lot of folks stomping around town with a peg foot."

"Well, I could have been The Captain," Horatio said defensively. "You couldn't possibly tell the difference crouched over there."

"Yeah, well, he's got the whole peg leg, you see," Derlin said. "It makes a bit deeper a thump than just the foot does. Plus he's way bigger than you are."

"He's not that much bigger," Horatio scoffed. "Besides, since we last met I've been doing calisthenics and eating salads instead of just fried food, so I'm certainly in better shape than he is. Maybe stronger too."

"Well, he is a hundred and ten, ain't he?" Derlin shrugged. "Besides, I…"

"Anyway," Horatio said, cutting off Derlin mid-thought. "I'm not here to talk about how wonderful you think the Captain is, I'm here to purchase an automobile. Would you like to help me or not?"

"Of course, friend! That's why I'm here," Derlin said. "Everybody deserves to sit behind the wheel of a Ricky Yamashita Dodge."

Dixie smiled to herself as Derlin said this. She'd been listening intently to the conversation with her salesman's first customer and though she knew nothing of the fish scales and peg feet they spoke of, she was quite pleased to hear Derlin turn on the schmooze and quell what seemed like a potential argument about this "Captain." She certainly didn't want any scenes on the floor of the showroom on their first day of business..

"What sort of car were you wanting to look at, fella? Derlin asked. "You got any specific makes or models in mind? We've got 250 of the finest Dodge cars and trucks in the USA sitting right here on the lot."

Derlin pointed downward at the floor and then cast a wave slowly across the showroom with the pageantry of a hairier Willy Wonka.

"Well, I want something flashy," Horatio started, looking around the showroom.

"Something loud and powerful. I want something that the ladies will like, but something that men will respect."

"I get what you're saying partner," Derlin smiled, raising his eyebrows and winking. "You want something with some horsepower under the hood."

"That's right!" Horatio said excitedly.

"Something that'll make the ladies' kitties purr, but something that also lets all the fellas know that you ain't somebody to be trifled with. You're a big cat."

"Yeah!" Horatio said, clenching his fists and nodding enthusiastically. His face reddened and he felt a vague stirring of the loins.

"What do you drive now?" Derlin asked. "You trying to trade in your old car?"

"Well, that's the thing," Horatio said bashfully. "I've been working for the Captain and living out behind the restaurant since I was too young to drive, and I never really needed a car before. I took the bus here today. But I'm tired of being stuck in that fish dungeon with no transportation of my own and I'm ready to join the world of vehicle ownership. I want a car of my own, by golly. And I want a fast one."

Derlin smiled. Without exerting much in the way of effort, he had his first customer hook, line and sinker.

"Well," Derlin smiled. "Dodge makes all sorts of fast ones. They've all got pretty cool sounding names too."

"Oh yeah?" Horatio said excitedly, raising his eyebrows. "Like what?"

"You've got your Darts and Chargers," Derlin began, counting on his fingers.

"Those Chargers have a Hemi in 'em and they'll move along like a bullet."

"Like Steve McQueen in the movie?" Horatio asked.

"Well, kinda," Derlin shrugged. "He was driving Fords and these are Dodges but pretty much the same as Steve McQueen. You planning on taking your new car jumpin' and chasing, friend?"

"Not necessarily," Horatio began. "But if I need to, I want to have the horses under me to get the job done. These two fellas at the bar at the restaurant a few weeks back were telling me some story about two local guys fighting over a dame back in the day. They decided to race for her hand, but one fella just had a pick-up truck and they said he put it into a pond. I don't want that to happen to me."

"Oh that's my Uncle Vern!" Derlin said proudly, not missing a beat. "He owns that pond now and that old truck is still sitting at the bottom of it."

"So it's a true story," Horatio gasped. "I thought it was just some local fable coming out of a couple of drunks."

"Nope, everything they told you was probably true," Derlin chuckled. "Did they tell you the fella that beat him married the girl and now he's a big time race car driver?"

"They did," Horatio said, pointing at Derlin enthusiastically. "Something Allison!"

"Bobby," Derlin said.

"That's it!" Horatio said loudly.

"And you want to be Bobby in this story," Derlin nodded sagely.

"Precisely!" Horatio said. "Not a Vern. I'm tired of being a Vern!"

"I think I've got something special for you," Derlin smiled, shooting "finger guns" at Horatio and beckoning him to follow him through the showroom. Derlin waltzed through the showroom confidently. He was still unsure of Horatio's budget but his zeal to acquire a very loud, very fast car was tangible and Derlin figured it was worth a shot to see if he'd be interested in the most expensive thing on the lot. Horatio gasped as they approached it, glistening majestically in the far corner of the showroom.

"What is it?" Horatio whispered slowly, running his hand along the fender.

"That my friend is a brand new 1969 Dodge Coronet Super Bee," Derlin smiled confidently. As the words came out of his mouth he knew that all his practicing with the babies was paying off. "Not every dealership has one of these babies. We got it on account of Mr. Yamashita pulling some strings with some of the big wigs he knows. She's got all the bells and whistles. 426 Hemi with a scoop on the hood so all the ladies can hear you coming a mile away. Canary yellow paint, black racing stripe and chrome trim so they can see you coming a mile away. These babies is limited edition to boot. You ain't gonna be seeing another one of these sitting next to you at a stoplight. This is the cream of the crop."

"How much?" Horatio asked, not even looking at Derlin as he asked, staring at his reflection in the shining yellow hood.

"Well," Derlin said, taking a deep breath. "Like I said, this baby has got all the bells and whistles. Hemi and chrome and fancy tires to boot. You're looking at a sticker price today at the low, low Ricky Yamashita price of $4,250."

"I'll take it," Horatio said, opening the driver's side door and exhaling deeply as he sat down and slowly clutched the steering wheel.

"For real?" Derlin said, his voice much higher-pitched than intended.

"Absolutely," Horatio said.

"Do you wanna test drive it or something first?" Derlin asked.

"Oh I can test drive it on the way," Horatio nodded. "I'm gonna take this baby straight down to Muscle Shoals to meet up with some loose beach women, maybe Daytona after that, who knows?"

"Man, that sounds cool as hell," Derlin said. He started to ask Horatio what sort of loose beach women he hoped to encounter cruising the shoreline the day after Christmas, but couldn't bring himself to dampen the little man's spirits. "Going on a little vacation, are you?"

"I am," Horatio beamed. "My first in years. The Captain is shutting up shop for a few days to try and get our roach problem under control." He cleared his throat.

"Well that's nice of him," Derlin said. "Lord knows I've eaten a fried roach or two out of a fish basket down there in my day."

Horatio chuckled nervously.

"So, how do you plan on paying?" Derlin asked. "We can get the paperwork done and get you on the road to beach party city."

"Oh, is cash alright?" Horatio asked casually, reaching into his coat pocket.

"Ye… yeah, cash is fine," Derlin stammered.

Horatio produced a large wad of bills, thumbing through it for a few moments before counting out to Derlin forty-two hundred dollar bills and a fifty.

Derlin gasped.

"Are you in the mob or something?" he asked jokingly.

"Oh my, no," Horatio laughed, waving off the suggestion. "Like I said, I've been working for the Captain and living on the premises since I was too young to drive. My room and board is included for free and as you can imagine, my grocery bill isn't much of a worry. I've been able to stash quite the little nest-egg with this arrangement over the years. I'd been wanting a sports car for a good long time and, with a week off of work I decided it'd be a good time to clear some room under my mattress."

"Man," Derlin said. "That is so cool." He patted Horatio on the back. "Let's just get your signature on a few things and we'll get your keys and you can be on the road."

"Sounds great," Horatio said, tucking his wad of cash back into his coat pocket.

"Hey Dixie," Derlin hollered. "My good friend here wants to buy the Super Bee!"

"Did you tell him how much it costs?" she asked skeptically.

"I did, he said that's fine," Derlin said. "He's paying cash." He waved the wad of bills at her and smiled.

"Well then," she smiled. "Let's get your paperwork together, Mister…?"

"Wilson," he said, shaking Dixie's hand and smiling politely.

Derlin watched with fascination as Dixie drew up the sales slip, soaking up information and procedural knowledge like a large, slack-jawed sponge. Within a few moments, Horatio had signed on all the necessary X's and Derlin was happy to get him the key from the back room.

"Here you go brother," he said, tossing Horatio the key, which was fumbled for a moment before Horatio grabbed it against his stomach. "Congratulations!"

"Derlin," Dixie said. "In the future let's hand customers their keys instead of throwing them, okay?"

"Sure thing," Derlin said bashfully. "I just got excited is all."

"It's fine," Dixie smiled. "Mr. Wilson, I nearly forgot. Being our first customer and buying the Super Bee to boot, we've got a couple gifts to send along with you."

"Great," Horatio smiled. "This is the best day of my life!"

"First of all," Dixie said, rummaging through a nearby cabinet. "We have this stylish red 'Dodge' baseball cap."

"Aw cool!" Derlin said as Horatio took the hat and tried it on.

"As a Super Bee buyer," she continued. "You get this special, limited-edition 'Super Bee' jacket."

She produced a neon fiesta of a jacket from the cabinet, replete with checkered flags, the Dodge logo and a huge Super Bee graphic across the back. Horatio gasped. "That is bad ass!" Derlin shouted excitedly. "We got any more of them?"

Dixie looked at him sternly.

"Finally" she continued. "As the first customer here at Ricky Yamashita Dodge, you get a personally signed photo of Ricky, wishing you well and dedicating to you his quest to get his championship belt back."

The photograph, a glossy 8x10 of Ricky Yamashita holding a tomahawk and flexing, was nearly totally covered by the inscription:

"Dear Wise Brave, the strength I've gained from your purchase of this brand new Dodge car or truck will only aid my focus in gaining my treasured championship belt back. I hereby dedicate my upcoming "Cave Match" with the Steel Kaiser to you, my fellow warrior and brother or sister in battle.

All the glory,
'The Navajo' Ricky Yamashita"

It was Derlin's turn to gasp.

Horatio eyed the photo for a moment, wrinkling his face in an attempt at recognition.

"Thanks," he said plainly.

"You're quite welcome, Mr. Wilson," Dixie smiled. "You enjoy your day and that first special drive in your Ricky Yamashita Dodge."

"I will," he smiled. "You've got quite the salesman here."

"Aw, thanks Horatio," Derlin said bashfully, shaking Horatio's hand.

"Come back and get some fish sometime," Horatio said.

"I sure will," Derlin smiled. "I'd like that."

Horatio strode as confidently as a man with a peg foot could stride across the showroom floor and climbed behind the wheel of his new car. Derlin jogged over to the bay doors of the showroom and flung them open so Horatio could drive out. The engine roared to life, filling the showroom with the pungent aroma of unleaded American horsepower and Horatio was soon inching through the room, stopping and starting suddenly several times as he got a feel for his ride. Derlin and the Yamashita sisters waved as Horatio passed through the doors, watching him as he weaved slowly through the lot towards the road. Dixie and Crystal had each returned to other business as Derlin still gazed out the window. He watched as Horatio stopped and rolled the window down just before pulling into the road, gasping in shock as the signed photo of Ricky Yamashita was tossed out, fluttering slowly to the pavement.

Derlin darted quickly out the door and ran the length of the parking lot. Horatio had sped away in a flourish of squealing tires and grinding gears, but Derlin was able to rescue the picture before the breeze took it away and he clutched tightly to it as he stomped back through the parking lot.

"Is everything okay?" Crystal asked, startled, as a winded Derlin came storming back in the front door.

"He threw his goddamn picture of your daddy out the car window as he was driving off," Derlin huffed indignantly.

"Maybe he just doesn't like wrestling," Dixie offered. "It ain't for everybody."

"Still though," Derlin continued, obviously upset. "The nerve of some folk. Just throwing a picture of Ricky Yamashita on the ground like that. That's just rude."

"I guess it was kind of rude, even if Mr. Wilson isn't a fan of our daddy's work," Crystal postulated. "Maybe he roots for the Steel Kaiser."

"I bet he would," Derlin scoffed. "Squirrelly little peg-footed fella."

"I thought you liked him," Dixie said. "You kept talking about how cool you thought he was. I thought y'all were best friends."

"I was just trying to sell a car," Derlin grumbled. "He ain't exactly Mr. 'Nicest Man in Town.' I worked for him for one day a while back when I was down on my luck and it took me weeks to get all the fish scales out of my hair."

"Oh well," Crystal added, eyeing Derlin strangely for a moment. "At least he did come in and pay cash for the most expensive car on our lot."

"True," Dixie said. "I sure wasn't expecting that ten minutes into our first day of business."

"Do y'all mind if I keep it?" Derlin asked politely.

"Keep what? The picture?" Crystal asked. "Go ahead if you like."

"Cool!" Derlin yelled, his agitation fading. "I'mma nail it to the wall in my garage next to where I keep my tools!"

"That sounds nice, Derlin," Crystal said. "I'm sure daddy would appreciate that."

"And if… if y'all happen to have any extra of those Super Bee jackets laying around, I'd be happy to… model one for the town folk to help advertise us and stuff," Derlin said bashfully. "I bet all sorts of folks would come up to me asking 'Hey Derlin where'd you get that badass jacket at?' and I could be all like 'well hey, feller I got it out down at the Ricky Yamashita Dodge!'"

"We'd love to give you one, Derlin," Dixie started. "But they only give 'em out with the Super Bees, so that was the only one we've got. I've got a whole box full of those red Dodge hats though, if you want one of those you can have one."

Derlins eyes misted over with pride.

"I'd be honored to wear one," he said solemnly.

Taking a deep breath, he adjusted the size and slipped it onto his head.

"Man, what is this? Cotton?" Derlin asked, visibly impressed.

It was the nicest hat he'd ever owned and accompanying neon jacket or not, in it he felt like a king.

Chapter 45

Derlin's first few weeks as a salesman flew by in a sweaty, red-hatted blur. Just as Dixie and Crystal had envisioned, people were flocking from all over Alabama to buy or at least take a gander at a Ricky Yamashita Dodge.

Derlin had no choice but to learn on the fly, and while his practice with Randy and Ollie was certainly invaluable, getting seasoning on an actual dealership with actual customers who were both interested in purchase and old enough to talk was quite helpful.

He was quickly developing quite the salesman's acumen.

Shocked at the tangible effects of putting his mind to something, Derlin had quickly become adept at knowing the ins and outs of every car on the lot. Never the intellectual, he could spout the gas mileage stats and load capacity on the entire class of Dodge pickups, compare the zero-to-sixty speeds on the Darts and Chargers, even calculate a monthly payment in his head for any car on the lot (though he did use his fingers here). Dixie and Crystal soon began to refer to him as their "numbers man," marveling at the ground he could cover in a single afternoon at the dealership. They'd had a good feeling about him from the start based on his devout fandom of their father, but the amount of enthusiasm and energy he brought to the table was far more than they'd expected out of a single salesman.

Often, they'd see him running full speed across the lot, hair blowing behind him, whether he was tracking down a particular model for a customer or chasing a flock of birds off of the property. Keeping a shammy cloth in his back pocket, Derlin was constantly wiping down cars in between customers. They'd even caught him dragging a hose out of the trunk of his old sedan to water the grass around the lot as he had noticed a few patches that "weren't muddy seeming enough". It didn't take long for them to realize that he was doing the work of three men, both saving and making them a good deal of money as he went along.

"I'm just doing it so Mr. Yamashita is prideful of me to work here," he'd shrug nonchalantly whenever his work ethic was mentioned. "I just wanna do right by 'The Navajo' is all."

January 17, 1969

As the cars rolled off the lot daily and the sales numbers continued to mount, Dixie and Crystal had an idea. Each morning they watched as Derlin sputtered into the lot in his crusty old sedan, stashing it behind the building out of sight at their request. Each evening, they'd watch the one working tail light disappear back toward Coverdale as Derlin headed home, leaving a smoky trail of exhaust in his wake.

"Have you asked him what that car even is?" Dixie asked Crystal one evening after Derlin had said his goodbyes and they watched him chug off into the sunset.
"I don't have the slightest idea," Crystal answered. "I spent a good twenty minutes looking it up and down when he was selling that Polara to that family from Montevallo. I can't find a make or model mark on it anywhere. All I know is he got it at some police

auction and he doesn't remember if it's a Buick or a Studebaker."

"I'm surprised the damn thing still runs," Dixie said.

"Me too," Crystal answered. "It smells like burnt oil, but I swear I catch a whiff of peanut butter off of it when I walk by sometimes. Plus it looks like it's been to hell and back ten times over."

"You know," Dixie said. "He has been selling us a lot of cars. He's sold at least a couple every day since we've opened. We've already hit the goal for our first quarter of sales and it hasn't even been a month. *And* he sold that Super Bee to that weird little peg-footed man on the first day. We could give him one of these cars on the lot real cheap, or just tell him we're letting him drive it for 'advertising.'"

"That's not a bad idea," Crystal smiled. "I know he's got a family and it sounds like they've got a decent house and all that but I can't imagine driving my kids around in that thing. It looks like the bottom is about to fall out of it."

"Let's talk to him tomorrow and see if he's interested," Dixie smiled. "These new Monacos cost like fifty cents a pound and you couldn't dent one with a tank."

Mavis was beaming with pride as she saw the shine of Derlin's headlights pulling into the driveway that evening. It was 6:30, he was home just in time for dinner. She'd spent the afternoon roasting a chicken, knowing that it was "one of (Derlin's) three or four favorite kinds of meat," and the smell was beginning to waft through the entire house just as Derlin walked in the door. She gently shooed Randy and Ollie away from pawing at the oven, setting them into their high chairs as they squawked unhappily.

"Is that chicken I smell?" Derlin called happily through the hallway.

"It sure is, honey." Mavis called back. "Dressed up with all of the fixins, just now coming out of the oven."

"Oh boy!" Derlin hollered. "That's one of my three or four favorite kinds of meat!"

He took a deep sniff of a breath over the roasting pan and exhaled satisfactorily as he leaned in to kiss Mavis on the cheek.

"Nothin' like coming home from a hard day's work to a chicken meat dinner, right boys?" Derlin asked his children, tussling each of them gently on the head, where the faintest sprouts of wispy blonde hair had finally begun to grow. With his arrival, their cries had gently tapered off and their blank-faced attention soon turned entirely from the chicken to their father.

"I'm gonna mash up some of the beans and carrots with some chicken juice for the boys and I'll make your plate honey," Mavis said as Derlin walked to the fridge and popped open a Panther Cat.

"That sounds fine, baby." Derlin smiled. "You're so good to me."

Mavis rolled her eyes bashfully and blew Derlin a kiss.

"You boys got a mighty fine mama," Derlin called at Randy and Ollie, taking another mighty sip of beer.

"What piece do you want honey?" Mavis asked as she began to take a knife to the steaming bird.

"I want the back!" Derlin said enthusiastically. "The back is my favorite."

January 18, 1969

As per her usual routine, Mavis was up with Randy and Ollie about an hour before Derlin rose. The boys had their morning oatmeal and had set to crawling around the house chasing each other, periodically attempting to pull themselves up to a standing position on the sides of chairs or shelves and meeting a little more success with each try. Derlin stepped over them as he exited the bedroom, straightening the collar of his shirt and re-affixing his belt.

"There's my little race cars," he cooed as they zoomed past his feet down the hallway.

Removing a comb from his pocket, Derlin set to combing his hair in the hallway mirror. Throughout his entire life until the army robbed him of his locks, Derlin had let his hair flow wild and free "as nature intended," and though it was often bedraggled and unkempt, he seemed content to just periodically paw it back behind his ears as he saw fit. However, since his rise in the working world, he had become particularly obsessed with keeping his gradually regrown mullet neatly combed. He'd spend ten to fifteen minutes in front of the mirror, combing and recombing with no sign of satisfaction in sight until Mavis would have to jostle him from his near-hypnotic state and remind him that he was going to be late for work.

"You spend so much time combing your hair, honey," Mavis said, walking up behind him and rubbing his back as he combed away. "Then when you get to work you just put that red Dodge hat on. It doesn't make sense to me."

"Oh, I gotta look pro-fessional," Derlin answered confidently. "Nobody wants to buy a car from a fella that don't have real combed-down hair."

"I think your hair looks very professional, dear," Mavis said supportively.

"That's cause I comb it so much," Derlin answered quickly.

"I just think that maybe, if you spent a little less time doing it in the morning, you could have more time for other things," Mavis said. "You could have more time for sitting down and eating breakfast, or playing with the babies. You could even maybe sleep five minutes later if you wanted to. Maybe you could even read something good in the newspaper. You know, if anything ever catches your eye."

Derlin furrowed his brow, looking at Mavis with uncertainty.

"All I'm saying, is maybe just comb your hair a little less, that's all," Mavis said pleadingly.

"Well maybe instead of that, maybe I'll invent a hair combing robot," Derlin snapped. "Maybe I'll make it a robot chair that I can sit in and eat breakfast. Maybe it'll have arms that turn into hair combs and it'll comb my hair while I eat and talk to the babies. How about that?"

"I don't think that's what I was saying at all," Mavis started, before Derlin began talking over her.

"Maybe I'll give the robot a face," Derlin continued. He'd begun this rant as a spiteful bit of make-believe to rally against his wife's position on his excessive hair combing, but his eyes began to light up as the words fell out of his mouth. "Maybe that face will have a speaker with a bunch of songs recorded like on the radio. But maybe instead of playing real songs it just hums the songs at me like Grandma Vondene used to when she'd comb my hair when I was a boy."

It was Mavis' turn to look at Derlin with uncertainty.

"It's probably the best invention I've ever had," Derlin stated matter-of-factly.

"Honey that's not an invention, it's just an idea," Mavis said.

"Well why ain't it an invention?" Derlin asked incredulously.

"Well honey, somebody already invented robots," Mavis replied. "Plus I know you're real smart and real good at science but I don't know that you know enough science to build a robot."

"That's the meanest thing you've ever said to me," Derlin said, taken aback. "I do too know enough science."

"But honey, all the robots we see on TV and in the movies are all full of wires and computers," Mavis said. "Like that big spaceship computer "HAL" in that movie you fell asleep in when we started dating. You couldn't build a big rocket ship like that with a talking computer is all I'm saying."

"I could if I had enough lumber!" Derlin shouted. "I got a garage full of tools, I can build anything I want!"

"I don't know about that honey," Mavis said gently, stroking the side of Derlin's face with her hand. "All those computer things have all those little tiny gizmos and pieces in there. I just think it would be harder than you're expecting."

"Yeah, maybe you're right," Derlin conceded.

"Thank you," Mavis said.

"Maybe it don't matter that I don't know enough science to make space robots," Derlin said, his voice again rising in wonder. "Maybe it don't matter at all because I'm gonna make my hair-combing robot gas powered!"

"What?" Mavis asked, wincing.

"If I can't build no robot computers in the garage, I'll just make the damn thing run on gas," Derlin said excitedly. "I bet Lumpy's got an old lawnmower chassis I can have, maybe even an engine too. After that all I gotta find is a good chair or two and maybe an old mannequin head for the speaker and I'm in business."

"Honey, I just don't think that's a very good idea," Mavis said as nicely as she could muster.

"First you're standing in the way of my hair combing, now you're standing in the way of my inventin'" Derlin shouted. "I bet old Charlie Lindbergh didn't have to deal with stuff like this when he was inventin' the airplane!"

"I'm sorry baby," Mavis said. "I just think a lawnmower hair combing chair sounds like a really good way for you to get hurt."

Derlin glanced at the clock on the wall, his eyes widening once more.

"Well this conversation sounds like a really good way for me to be late for work," Derlin said, glancing back in the mirror with dissatisfaction. "And my hair ain't even combed down enough."

Putting on his red Dodge hat in a huff and quickly straightening it in the mirror, Derlin kissed Mavis on the cheek and stomped out the door to work. With that, she tossed the carefully folded morning newspaper into the hallway trash can with a disappointed sigh. Her tale now completed, it would stare at her from the top of the trash can until Derlin eventually crammed three beer cans down on top of it later that evening. She hoped someone somewhere would read the climax, even if it wasn't going to be her disinterested husband. She felt it was her best work yet.

Don had just wandered home from another night at the movies with Cathy and Phil was waiting for him on the porch when he got home. Not seeming to notice Phil sitting there in the moonlight, Don started to walk right past his brother, staring straight ahead. Phil called to him twice as he approached and passed by, finally grabbing his brother's arm as he attempted to enter the house.

"Don, I'm talking to you!" Phil said loudly.

"Oh, I'm sorry," Don said flatly, shaking his head as if awakening from a dream. "I guess I didn't hear you talking."

"Just what in the heck is the matter with you, Don?" Phil asked, waving his hand in front of his brother's face. "It's like you're in a trance. You've hardly spoken to me since you and Cathy started hanging out. I can barely get you to pick up a guitar."

"I'm sorry, Phil," Don said in a quiet monotone. "I really am. It's just Cathy and I really like each other and we're spending as much time as we can together before we go back out on tour."

"I get being sweet on a girl, Donnie, but what gives?" Phil pleaded. "We're playing in two days in front of 30,000 people at the Kansas City A's stadium and we're playing in front of your hero Mickey Mantle and the rest of the World Champion New York Yankees and you won't even rehearse for it with me!"

"Cathy's just special is all," Don shouted, his voice finally rising above a whisper. "Don't you worry about me being ready for the New York Yankees. I'm gonna play the best guitar you ever saw!"

With that, he stormed into the house, slamming the door behind him. Phil heard him climb the stairs to his room, slamming the door there too as he went. It was the last time Phil would see him before the Summer Social.

Don was already dressed and gone by the time Phil got home from the dry cleaners with his suit, and Phil was hurt but not particularly surprised that they wouldn't be going to the dance together. Phil was going stag and had counted on his brother for at least a little bit of company as he tried to navigate the dance floor before Don and Cathy slipped off somewhere. He arrived at the Summer Social about thirty minutes late and sure enough, Don and Cathy were embraced, dancing and seemingly lost in each other's eyes. To any outside observer, it just looked like a young couple in love, but Phil was beginning to have a hunch deep down that Cathy might be up to no good, he just couldn't quite put his finger on it. He tried to keep an eye on them while they danced, but they managed to give him the slip during one of his trips to the punch bowl and he lost track of them.

Having escaped the crowded pavilion, Cathy led Don down the familiar path by the riverside. They passed the lights of the social, winding around the riverbend, soon being surrounded by nothing but darkness and trees.

"What are we doing way out here?" Don asked in a hushed monotone.

"Oh we're here for a very special reason," Cathy said, maintaining her locked gaze with Don as he stood by the riverbank. "It's time we let you in on a little secret."

Cathy snapped her fingers and soon the other Cathys began to emerge from out of the shadows or behind trees and rocks. Soon, all forty had surrounded Don. He stood perfectly still and slack-shouldered, staring around at the group of them.

"Hi Cathy," he muttered quietly.

"Hi Don," they all replied in unison.

"I love you, baby" Don said drearily.

"I love you, too, sweetheart," forty identical voices replied.

"It's a shame you've got to leave for your big rock & roll tour tomorrow, Donnie, sweetie" the lead Cathy said, enhancing the sounding of hurt in her voice to an almost cartoonish thickness. "I sure am gonna miss you."

"I'm gonna miss you too," Don said blankly.

"Here," Cathy offered, producing a sleek metal box the size of a suitcase from behind her. It was the laser-space bomb! "Let me give you this parting gift. Something to remember me by when you're playing in front of all those people tomorrow."

With that, she opened the case, producing a thin metallic vest that glowed a faint orange and green. She lifted it and walked toward Don and with the help of five other Cathys removed his suit jacket, dress shirt and tie. They pulled the bomb vest over Don's head, before carefully putting his shirt, jacket and tie back on while he stood there helplessly. The next thing he knew, Don was waking up in his bed to his brother's furious pounding at the door.

"Don, wake up!" Phil shouted. "We've gotta get on the road right this second if we're making it all the way to Kansas City for this ballgame concert."

Slapping his cheeks in an effort to rouse himself, Don looked around his room uneasily, his eyes widening as he found his bedroom clock. He didn't remember any part of the last twelve hours. He didn't remember getting home, going to bed, saying goodnight to Cathy, anything. The last thing he could recall was agreeing to take a walk down by the river. How could he not remember saying goodbye to Cathy? It didn't make any sense. Don did his best to shake himself from his stupor, quickly grabbing his guitar case and quickly joining his brother in the hallway.

"Oh, wearing the same suit you did last night?" Phil said, clearly irritated. "That's gonna look great in front of 30,000 people. When's the last time you even bothered to shave? You're like a zombie. Did you guys start drinking when you left?"

"No, I swear!" Don said. Shaking his head vigorously and slapping his still-pale cheeks. "I don't know what's the matter with me."

He tugged at his collar uncomfortably, brushing down his shirt and straightening his tie.

"This dang suit sure is itchy today," he added.

"Probably because you wore it last night!" Phil said in a huff. "Let's go! We've gotta get in the car and vazoom!"

The stadium was packed as the Everly Brothers finally arrived moments before the first pitch of the game. It seems everyone in town had come out to see the A's take on the mighty Yankees. Every seat in every section was filled. Little did anyone know, however, one of those seats in each section was filled with a Cathy, there to watch the show. Each of them wore their own special vest, which would enable them to disappear instantly and transmogrify back onto their ship in space as soon as the laser to activate Don's bomb was fired.

The game passed uneventfully and quickly. The great Mick had gotten three hits and along with fellow Yankees star Roger Maris they had enough firepower to win the game. As the game ended, the stadium crew began throwing together the stage behind second base as the fans began to clamor for the Everly Brothers. Just as they were about to take the stage, the brothers heard a familiar voice shout out behind them.

"Donnie, Donnie baby!" Cathy shouted, waving at the brothers as they began climbing the stairs to the stage. "Good luck, I love you!"

Don waved back mechanically as Cathy disappeared into the crowd but didn't say a word. Phil found this strange, and his suspicions that something was amiss were proven correct as they took their positions on the stage and Phil noticed at least five different Cathys in the crowd, including one at each end of the front of the stage. Knowing that he couldn't just cancel on the show at the last second with everyone already there, Phil vowed to keep an eye on the Cathys as the show progressed to see just what they were up to. The boys went through their biggest hits like they had a thousand times before, and Phil began to worry a little less, but he got a strange and uncomfortable feeling when Don announced between songs that Mickey Mantle himself was going to join them on the microphone for a surprise rendition of Hank Thompson's "Oklahoma Hills."

The crowd went wild as The Mick ambled toward the stage, still in uniform. Phil knew something was kooky for sure now. Not only did he not know how to play "Oklahoma Hills," he and Don had never even talked about the idea of having an impromptu guest on the stage during the show, let alone Mickey Mantle. He glanced back toward the crowd, this time noticing all forty Cathys interspersed in the crowd. As the Mick walked toward Don's microphone and put his arm around him, Phil saw the lead Cathy pull a remote control from her pocket and fire it toward the stage. Out of the corner of his eye, Phil saw the giant laser being shot down from space, heading straight for Mickey Mantle and his brother. Acting as quick as a lightning bolt, he threw his guitar into the air. The guitar met the laser head on, deflecting the entire ray back to the lead Cathy and exploding her in a splash of milky green goo. Security guards rushed the stage, leading the brothers and Mickey Mantle to cover and soon the entire crowd had fled, aside from the remaining 39 Cathys who stood perfectly still, frozen in place, an unblinking gaze on each of their 39 identical blank faces.

"Holy cannoli friend," Mickey Mantle shouted, "I think you just saved my life!"

He wrapped Phil in an exuberant bear hug and this was the first thing Don saw as he woke fully from his being hypnotized.

"Well would ya look at that, my brother and The Mick are best friends," he laughed. "Thanks for snapping me out of that, Phil. I sure got us into a real pickle. We'd be toast if you hadn't acted so fast."

"He saved every last one of us, that was the best swing I saw all day!" Mickey Mantle shouted to the crowd of security personnel and fellow New York Yankees that now surrounded them. The crowd of players cheered, lifting Phil and Don each on their shoulders, carrying them around and cheering as if they'd just won the World Series themselves.

After the celebration finally died down, the other players headed to the locker room to gather their things and head to the airport. Security began to clear out other folks and soon, it was just Mick and the Everlys. It was then that they noticed the other 39 Cathys still standing in place.

"Well, what are we gonna do with them?" Phil asked.

"I don't know, but they sure are pretty," Don said. He walked up to a random Cathy, snapping his fingers in front of her face. Her eyes blinked and her face filled with *a luscious smile.*

"Well hello there, handsome stranger," she said sweetly. "My name's Cathy. We're all new to town. Aren't you going to introduce us to your friends?"

With that, Phil and Mick looked at each other grinning.

"Say," the Mick offered. "I know a club where we can all do a little dancing."

Don and Phil laughed. Maybe Cathy was gonna turn out alright after all.

Derlin arrived that morning at Ricky Yamashita Dodge and began going about his morning routine of eating three jelly donuts and drinking four cups of black coffee as quickly as he could. He'd just shoved the last two thirds of donut number two into his mouth when he was startled by a voice behind him.

"Derlin, can Crystal and I talk to you in the office for a moment?" Dixie asked. Derlin turned quickly, still wide-eyed, and nodded vigorously as he attempted to finish chewing.

"Did I eat too many donuts?" Derlin asked worriedly through his mouthful, looking frantically around the showroom. "I'm sorry, I---"

"No, no, you're not in any trouble," Dixie began. "We just wanted to speak with you about some important Dodge-related business and see what you thought about an idea we had."

"Oh that sounds fine," Derlin said, clearly relieved as he finished chewing.

"Great," Dixie said. "Crystal is already in the office, we can go ahead and talk over our idea before customers start rolling in for the day."

Derlin followed Dixie to the office, where Crystal was seated behind the desk. Crystal beckoned Derlin to sit in a chair across from her and Dixie came to stand behind her, leaning against the wall.

"So what's the idea y'all wanted to run by me? Derlin asked, shifting in the chair and attempting to get comfortable.

"Well Derlin," Crystal began. "You've been selling a lot of cars for us."

"Yeah, that's true," Derlin nodded. "Trucks too."

"Yes, trucks too," Crystal continued. "You've helped make us a very successful dealership very quickly and we appreciate that immensely."

"Aw, I'm just trying to do good for y'all and Mr. Yamashita," Derlin said bashfully. "You know he is my hero and all."

Dixie nodded.

"Well, you've already been way more than we ever could have hoped for, and we wanted to show you how valuable you are to us," Crystal continued.

"Uh-huh," Derlin nodded, leaning in to listen more closely.

"We got to thinking the other day," Dixie said. "You were talking about that 'if we had another one of those Super Bee jackets' you'd be happy to wear it around town to advertise for us."

"You guys got me a Super Bee jacket?" Derlin asked excitedly, standing up out of his chair and nearly spilling his coffee.

"Well, no," Dixie said.

Derlin slumped back into his chair.

"We know you love that old car of yours," Dixie continued. "But it is getting a little bit up there in miles and years, and we thought that maybe you'd like to start driving one of our brand new 1969 Dodge Monacos around town instead. You know, to help us advertise the dealership."

"I'd like that I reckon," Derlin said, "Those Monacos are nice but with all the boys doctorin' and the holidays and all, I can't really afford to buy a new car."

"Well Derlin," Crystal said. "The way we drew it up, if you're just driving the car to help us advertise, we're giving it to you for free."

Derlin leaned back and took a deep breath.

"Aw, that's mighty nice of y'all," he smiled. "But me and that ol' grey goose have been through so much together I don't think I could ever get rid of her."

The Yamashita sisters both looked at Derlin dumbfounded.

"I understand being sentimental, but you really wouldn't take a new car over that old thing?" Dixie asked.

"Naw, it's got too much Spurlock family history in it," Derlin said. "I've been to hell and back in it a hundred times and it's always been there when I needed it. I figure Randy and Ollie will be fighting it out to see who gets to inherit her when I die."

"Well, speaking of Randy and Ollie," Dixie chimed in. "They are babies still right now after all and they would be much safer riding around with you if they were in something new. These new Monacos are so well-built other cars would just bounce right off of them like they're made of rubber."

Derlin gasped, thinking back to the time Grandma Vondene nearly put her Henderson into Vern's pond. He thought of Mavis, whom he'd quarreled with so uncharacteristically that morning, and how she longed to one day be the first Spurlock lady to not have to get behind the wheel of a rubberized, florally-painted Henderson Car for Women. He knew that Dixie and Crystal were right about the Monaco's safety. It was a brick shit house of a vehicle and Derlin imagined that it would offer just as much of the familial protection of a Henderson without Mavis feeling demeaned at having to tote the boys around in a bedazzled Frankenstein of a station wagon coated in ground up old tires. After all it was, as Mavis had said, 1969.

"You know, y'all might be onto something." Derlin smiled. "Randy's already cut himself on the fender of the thing and Ollie's curious enough he's starting to try and put his foot through the hole in the floorboard when we're out driving. Maybe I should take you up on one of them shiny new Monacos."

"We'd be so happy if you would," Crystal smiled.

"I got one question though," Derlin said.

"What's that?" Dixie asked.

"Can I still keep the old girl though?" Derlin asked. "I always wanted to fix it up in my garage one day. Sort of a weekend project thing. That way it can still be around and be a family heirloom."

"I think that's reasonable," Crystal answered. "Just make sure you drive the Monaco to work from now on. You know, for advertising."

"Oh that's fine, I sure will," Derlin nodded.

"Well, pick out the one you like sometime today," Crystal said. "And at the end of the day we'll get our tow-truck guy to load it up and he can follow you home with it."

"Y'all are the best," Derlin smiled, standing up, leaning across the desk and hugging both of the sisters tightly with one arm. "I really don't know how to thank you. Helping my family like this, your daddy might be the champion of wrestling but y'all are champions at being nice people."

The time passed quickly as Derlin schmoozed his way through another day of sales. Two pickups, a Dart and a Polara later, Derlin had spent yet another afternoon justifying the Yamashita's faith in him. After much deliberation at the end of the day, he had finally settled on a fetching lime-green Monaco to be the new family vehicle. He looked on with pride as Larry, the dealership's go-to local towing man loaded the car up on his rig.

Derlin did his best not to speed through town as the tow truck followed, but the sedan's single functioning tail light made it relatively easy to track and soon the Monaco was being unloaded onto the street in front of the Spurlock house. Handing Larry a crumpled dollar bill and offering him a firm handshake, Derlin began to think of the best way to surprise Mavis as the tow truck rumbled down the street.

Nodding as the idea came to him, Derlin ran to the open window of his old sedan and laid on the horn as hard as he could.

Almost immediately, Mavis came running out of the house, quite startled.

"Derlin!" She shouted, a genuine look of worry on her face. "What in the world is with all the honking? Is everything okay?"

The sound of Randy and Ollie beginning to wail came softly from behind her as she stood in front of the doorway.

"Oh everything's fine baby!" Derlin shouted as he unwedged himself from the sedan window. "Everything's better than fine! Look what I got you!"

He pointed at the Monaco sitting in the street in front of the house and Mavis gasped, throwing her hands over her mouth in surprise.

"Is that…" She began, trailing off and attempting to get her bearings.

"It's a real Dodge!" Derlin shouted, waltzing over to her and putting his arm around her as they walked toward the street. "Brand new 1969 Dodge Monaco. Ain't no wife of mine gonna drive a Henderson."

Part 7: The Jet-Setters

Chapter 46

Mavis ran her fingers down the lime green fender. The smooth feel of the metal contrasted nicely to the bumpy rubber fenders of Vondene and Tina's Hendersons, and Mavis began to tear up a little when she noticed that the headlights matched. The chrome of the bumper gleamed in the evening light and Mavis leaned in closely, fogging it with her breath and wiping it away.

Derlin sauntered proudly into the house to grab his children, whose wails from being startled by their father's horn blasting were finally starting to subside.

"Hey fellas," Derlin cooed. "Come check out this badass chariot I just got your mama. Y'all gonna feel like Elvis riding in the back of this thing."

He scooped the boys up with a grunt and carried them back out to the yard. Mavis was sitting in the car with the front windows down, listening to the radio blaring a commercial about an upcoming local rodeo.

"There's no flowers on the dashboard!" Mavis shouted happily over the radio. "It doesn't smell like paint in here!"

"I knew you'd like it, baby." Derlin smiled. "Ain't it nice?"
He set the boys down in the grass and strode toward Mavis, leaning in the opening passenger window.

"It's wonderful, Derlin, I love it!" Mavis said. "The radio even gets FM!"

"Both kinds of radio for my wife," Derlin said proudly. "Maybe we can save up a little and even get you an eight-track player put in there soon. You can play whatever song you want on it!"

"I'll be like the Queen of England," Mavis said.

"Or New England," Derlin laughed.

"Speaking of saving up though, honey," Mavis said, turning down the radio. "I know you're making good money now, but how did you afford this thing?"

"Oh don't worry about that," Derlin said, offering a dismissive wave of the hand.

"The Yamashitas give it to me for to help advertise in town. Plus, on account of me selling so many damn cars already, they said they were making so much money we could just have one. I figured this would be a good one for driving the babies around. Dixie said it's real safe on account of it's like 8,000 pounds of American steel."
Mavis started to reply, but was interrupted by a startled gasp from Derlin as he felt an unexpected tug on his jeans. He looked down to see Randy standing next to him, staring up at him with his moon face from roughly knee height. Derlin looked up as Ollie slowly but confidently tottered up behind him.

"Baby!" Derlin shouted, turning back into the window. "The boys is walking! They's taking their first steps!"

Mavis leapt from the car, running around the massive front end and catching the last few steps of Ollie's trek toward his father. Seeing their elated mother, the boys turned their attention to walking awkwardly toward her. This time, it was Ollie's turn to shine as Randy lost his footing, falling butt first into the grass. Ollie arrived cackling into his mother's arms just as Derlin scooped Randy up from the grass, brushing him off and offering words of encouragement.

"Careful little buddy," Derlin smiled. "You're walking like your daddy after he had that spoiled beer down at the fish restaurant."

"I can't believe they're walking!" Mavis beamed, a joyful tear sliding down her cheek. "It seems like just the other day we were making them a hay bed in the windmill and now they're growing up and turning into little people!"

"But Doc Thurbison already told us they were gonna grow up to be little people," Derlin said, furrowing his brow.

"That's not what I meant honey," Mavis sighed. "I just meant now that they're walking, soon they'll be talking. Next thing you know they'll be going to school and kissing girls and getting in trouble."

"Just like their daddy," Derlin winked. "Except for the school, I reckon."

"I think we should celebrate," Mavis said.

"Well the boys do have a birthday coming up really soon," Derlin said, looking at his wrist again as though he were wearing a watch. "Just a couple of weeks away. Plus there ain't no dirt track racing happening again till March, so mama and deddy and Vern can come too!"

"I reckon that means we've got a party to start planning!" Mavis smiled. "I can't believe it. Almost a year old."

"They're getting old so quick, pretty soon they'll have caught up to us," Derlin smiled, tussling Ollie's hair and winking. He caught his own reflection in the chrome of the Monaco' bumper. As he had recently said, they were "pretty much living in the future" and if the first few weeks of 1969 were any indication, the future was going to be just fine.

February 2, 1969

Derlin swerved into the parking lot of the Piggly Wiggly, nearly sideswiping the repaired wall of the entrance way and briefly thinking back fondly on the time he'd driven right through it. He parked crookedly and hurried into the store. Quickly, he set to acquiring his list of items: a birthday cake, a candle shaped like the number one, a few party hats, balloons and four cases of Panther Cat.

"Somebody's having a party today," the cashier smiled as Derlin unloaded his gathered sundries onto the counter.

"Oh yeah, who?" Derlin asked happily.

The cashier pointed at the child's cake and 96 beers, raising her eyebrows and gesturing to the cluster of balloons still in Derlin's left hand.

"Oh, right," Derlin said sheepishly, chuckling.

He paid and left, returning to his car and quickly loading the beer into the trunk. Carefully setting the cake and balloons in the back, Derlin backed over a patch of grass and sidewalk straight into the road and slammed the car in drive. Though he was nearly past due to be home, he'd promised to pick up Uncle Vern for the boys' party so that Vern could drink more and not have to worry about driving.

Vern was waiting outside his trailer when Derlin arrived, leaning against the back of his pickup truck and sipping a beer. A small, poorly-wrapped present sat next to two empty cans on the hood of his truck. He waved at Derlin and finished his beer, tossing the can in the back of the truck. Derlin had been honking continuously since he pulled into the driveway and Vern did his hefty best to go quickly. Grabbing the boys' gift, Vern hopped into the passenger seat, slamming the door and producing a fresh beer from his shirt pocket, which he then cracked.

"I sure do appreciate the ride, old top," Vern smiled. "I hate drinkin' and drivin' anymore."

"Sure thing, Uncle Vern," Derlin smiled. "Just like daddy always says we don't want you flippin' another truck into the pond."

"Goddamnit, you and Clovis never are gonna leave that alone are you?" Vern asked angrily. "I flip one truck into one pond one time and it's all any of y'all ever talk about. If I'da won that race I'd be a goddamn senator by now."

"No you wouldn't, Uncle Vern," Derlin laughed.

"I would too," Vern snapped.

"There ain't never been no senator that smells like fish and beer, Uncle Vern," Derlin said sarcastically.

"But you told me yourself that Lyndon Johnson smelled like chicken and whiskey, why can't I smell like fish and beer and be a senator goddamnit?" Vern shouted.

He offered Derlin his can of beer.

"Can't get bit by a gift horse if you don't look him in the mouth!" Derlin said, taking a mighty swig.

"Tell me I would so be a senator," Vern demanded.

"Fine, fine," Derlin said, conceding the argument and taking another swig of Vern's beer and belching lightly. "You'd have been a dang senator. But listen, you got to dial it down a notch. This is a little kid birthday party, we got all day to drink."

Clovis sat in the truck, smoking a cigarette while Tina went birthday shopping in the gas station. He watched her try and lose at the claw machine three times before wandering down the aisles and it was a good five minutes before she finally came jogging out of the gas station carrying a paper sack.

"What'd you find?" Clovis asked, throwing his still-lit cigarette onto the ground and turning to Tina as she climbed into the truck.

"I got 'em each a little toy wind-up car and a yo-yo, I think we did pretty good!" Tina said excitedly. "I still can't believe you said you had their presents 'taken care of' and you thought that was a good idea."

"Pocket knives is a perfectly good gift for little boys," Clovis argued.

"They're babies, they play with toys," Tina shouted.

"They're nice knives!" Clovis shouted back.

Mavis looked at the clock worriedly. The party started at two o'clock and, though Derlin had promised to be home by noon, the time was creeping toward 12:30. She had done her best to get as much work done as possible before Derlin arrived and had dressed the boys in matching sailor suits which she'd recently acquired from her mother. The accompanying blue and white hats covered the boys' birthmarks perfectly should any neighbors drop by and they looked quite dapper to boot.

Hearing a familiar squeal of brakes in the driveway, she peered out the living room curtain happy to see Derlin finally home, though she was less than thrilled when she saw Uncle Vern clamber out of the passenger seat, beer in hand. Derlin waved enthusiastically and grabbed the cake and balloons from the back seat, instructing Vern to pop the trunk and grab the beer. Mavis winced upon seeing Vern slowly stack the four cases of Panther Cat on top of eachother as he tried and failed to slam the trunk with his foot. Leaving the trunk open, he marched through the yard behind Derlin and Mavis soon heard them come stomping in the front door.

"Hey baby, I'm back!" Derlin smiled, setting the cake down on the dining room table and letting the balloons go in the hallway with the low ceiling.

"Hey honey," Mavis said. "The cake looks perfect and so do the balloons! I didn't know that you were picking up your uncle, though."

"Hey Mavis!" Vern shouted, setting the beers down with a thud on the kitchen counter and beginning immediately to load them into the fridge. "I sure am excited about the party."

"Hello Vern," Mavis said. "Derlin did tell you that this is Randy and Ollie's birthday party right? So I don't know if everybody is gonna be just… you know, getting hammered."

"I sure am!" Derlin hollered, cracking a beer. "Where them boys at? I wanna see them in them little sailor suits your mama got 'em."

"They're in their crib, but they can come on out if you like," Mavis said, rubbing Derlin's back. "Do try and maybe go a little easy on the beers at least while it's daytime? Today is about the boys, you know, and I think Uncle Vern already has a buzz."

"Oh of course I'll go easy, baby," Derlin said. "Eight beers, maybe nine tops, I'll be good to go."

"Okay honey, thank you," Mavis smiled. "And no wrestling Vern till my parents leave please."

"Alright then," Derlin sighed.

"Hey Mavis," Vern hollered.

"Yes Vern?" Mavis answered.

"I do too know that it's Randy and Ollie's birthday party," Vern said. "I got 'em a present and everything."

He produced the small package from his hip pocket and tossed it underhanded to Mavis, who caught it and smiled at Vern, quite surprised at his actually bringing a gift.

At that moment, Derlin emerged from the hallway carrying both the boys, resplendent in their sailor suits.

"Honey, bring them over here and let's let them open their present from Uncle Vern," Mavis said excitedly. "This will be the first birthday present they've opened in their lives. Look boys! It's your first birthday present. This is for you!"

She took Ollie while Derlin held Randy and began to tear the paper away as the boys gazed at the package in blank-faced wonderment.

"It's… a deck of cards," Mavis said flatly. "Thanks Uncle Vern."

Vern smiled and nodded enthusiastically as the boys began to claw at the bits of wrapping paper.

"I knew they'd love it," he said, grinning and taking another sip of beer. "They got boats and stuff on the back so they can learn about boats… and stuff."

"Great job Uncle Vern!" Derlin said happily, patting Vern on the back with his free hand and mouthing the word "boats" to Randy.

Just then, the door opened and Clovis and Tina came storming in, well over an hour early and still shouting at each other.

"Well now at least I've already got their birthday present for next year," Clovis yelled, immediately going to the fridge for a beer without bothering to greet anyone else in the house.

"That's still too young," Tina shouted, producing a bottle of Champale from the boy's birthday bag and tossing the bag on the table next to the cake.

"Hey mama!" Derlin hollered over them. Tina stopped getting after Clovis and came running over to greet Derlin and Randy.

"Look how cute they are in their little outfits!" Tina said happily, tickling Randy on the belly and kissing Derlin on the cheek.

Clovis sat down on the couch, offering Derlin a "Hey" and a cheers with his beer can. "You think we could put on the race?"

"I reckon we can if we keep the sound off," Derlin said. "It is the boy's birthday party after all."

"Aw, hell," Clovis started. "It ain't no good without the sound on. Don't my grand boys like racing?"

"You guys are a little bit early, I'm surprised," Mavis grinned thinly as she came in with Ollie. "We didn't expect anybody till two o'clock."

Vern smiled and nodded.

"Well, shit, I thought it started at noon," Clovis shouted from the couch. "I could have slept another hour and a half, goddamnit."

"We're so glad you could make it," Mavis said, gritting her teeth. "We were just about to start putting decorations up before everybody else starts getting here."

"Well I won't be in your way," Clovis said, sipping his beer and scratching his stomach as he propped his feet up on the coffee table.

Randy and Ollie were both set down to roam as Mavis and Derlin began retrieving the balloons from the low-ceiling hallway and tying them around the house. Mavis stacked the presents she and Derlin had gotten the boys next to the cake, careful to place Clovis and Tina's paper bag on the top. She'd gotten a few other decorations and a happy birthday banner during a recent sale at the drug store and was soon directing Derlin and Vern to hang it high upon the dining room wall.

"Baby, I thought you said the babies couldn't read," Derlin said as he stretched his arm higher and pressed himself against the wall.

"They can't, Derlin, honey," Mavis reminded him. "The boys still cannot read."

"Then who is this sign for?" Derlin asked.

"It's for all of us," Mavis replied. "To celebrate."

"But it ain't our birthdays," Derlin said, growing agitated as he and Vern were finally able to thumb-tack the banner into proper position.

"Mine was last week," Vern offered.

"Shut up, Vern!" Clovis shouted from the couch. "I'm trying to watch the dang race with no sound on and it's hard enough without you jabbering in there about God knows what."

"If the sound ain't on, how's my jabbering hurting it?" Vern shouted.

"Cause I'm trying to concentrate," Clovis shouted. "Don't you wanna come see your best friend Bobby Allison be a race car star?"

"Dammit, Clovis," Vern yelled. "I swear to God,"

"Boys!" Tina interrupted, smacking Clovis on the shoulder. "Clovis it's your dang grandson's birthday party, get off the couch and come mingle."

Clovis looked down to see Ollie crawl by and begin trying to raise himself up on the coffee table. He snatched Ollie up under his arms and plopped him down on his lap, bouncing him up and down and tickling him.

"I am mingling," he replied, turning his attention back to the race.

Derlin and Vern soon joined him on the couch while Mavis and Tina watched Randy and began making a batch of kool aid in the kitchen.

Much to Derlin's surprise, when he and Vern sat down, Clovis seemed to be genuinely enjoying his time with his grandson.

"That's my good boy Ollie," Clovis smiled. "Look at that race car! Look at that fast race car! Vroom, vroooooom!"

Ollie cackled happily as Clovis peered around him at the television.

"Lookit that big, fast, gold number 29 car, Ollie," Clovis continued. "Look how good he is! That's Bobby Allison, Ollie."

"Goddamnit Clovis, quit it," Vern shouted.

"He's the best race car driver in the whole state of Alabama and he's your Uncle Vern's best friend," Clovis laughed.

"Clovis, I mean it," Vern shouted, beginning to swat at him across Derlin. He caught him in the ear with a grazing blow causing Clovis to yelp and start using Ollie as a shield. Derlin snatched Ollie out of harm's way and turned his attention back to the race as his father and uncle continued to bicker on the couch.

Mavis and Tina made small talk in the kitchen as the menfolk shouted over the muted race and "bonded" with Ollie in the long-standing family tradition of disparaging Uncle Vern. The party was still an hour from actually starting and Mavis was already beginning to tire of the energy required to host a Spurlock gathering. She loved Derlin's family, even Clovis and Vern, despite their constant drunken bickering. The Spurlocks were indeed higher maintenance than she was accustomed to with her own family, but she knew that they had good intentions. Her mother would often take this declaration and mention something about paving the road to Hell but since reuniting with Derlin, Mavis had quickly come to view the Spurlocks in all their grimy majesty as her own family. She loved Derlin endlessly and was certain that both Tina and Vondene could be mined for helpful information should he ever prove to be excessively difficult or enigmatic. After all, Tina had been dealing with Spurlock men for nearly thirty years, Vondene more than twice that, and Mavis was certain that some wisdom lay beneath their leathery hides.

"I was gonna bring the boys some leftover brunch cupcakes from down at Meaty's," Tina said, lighting a fresh cigarette and offering Mavis a sip of her Champale, which she accepted, chasing it with a sip of coffee.

"Oh yeah?" Mavis asked, eying the clock and doing her best to fan cigarette smoke away from the rim of her kool aid pitcher.

"Yeah, the handsome woman who plays show tunes on Sundays left almost a dozen of 'em, sitting right up on top of the piano. I think she must've forgotten 'em up underneath all them fake flowers," Tina sighed. "I was like 'hey if nobody wants these, I'mma take 'em to my grandbabies,' and this fella Ricardo who's always in there was like 'aw honey, there's rum in those you can't take 'em to your grandbabies!'"

Tina laughed and it soon turned into a cough.

"Aww, well that's too bad," Mavis smiled. Tina continued to cough but soon solved the problem with a swig of Champale and was back to the conversation.

"Yeah, no kidding," Tina said. "I told him 'thanks for the tip, I don't want no messed up grandbabies, mine are gonna be big and strong!'"

Tina laughed and this time it stayed one. Mavis looked at the floor.

"The thing is," Tina continued. "After everybody left, and I was sweeping up all the glitter and mopping up sangria and whatnot, I ate five or six of 'em real fast off the tray and I didn't even catch a buzz!"

"She still talking about those cupcakes?" Clovis asked Mavis as he wandered in for a beer. "That happened Sunday before last! I keep telling her they'd have been thirteen days old and crusty by the time the party came around but she wasn't having none of it from me."

"The rum would have kept 'em fresh!" Tina yelled.

"Well you and Vern just would'a ate 'em all anyhow because babies ain't supposed to have rum!" Clovis shouted, "Look at Derlin!"

"At least I didn't try to give the babies knives for their birthday," Tina said snidely.

"They're nice knives!" Clovis said sternly through clenched teeth. "The boy could have kept 'em in a drawer till they was old enough not to get all cut up. Me and Vern was playing 'Pirates' with knives bigger than that by the time we was four."

"And you got all cut up!" Tina replied, pointing at a long, winding scar on Clovis' right forearm.

"Aw, I got him better than he got me," Clovis muttered.

"You sure did brother," Vern agreed happily as he waddled into the kitchen, lifting his shirt to reveal a large haphazard attempt at a "Z" carved into his stomach. "Is that what's taking you so long to get the beer? Is we telling stories?"

"Not really, we--" Mavis began.

"Derlin come in here," Vern shouted. "We're telling stories!"
Derlin quickly hopped to his feet with a straining "hyut!" under Ollie's weight, wooshing him around like a spaceship and heading for the kitchen.

"Come on daddy, Vern's telling stories," Derlin said. "The race is on commercial anyhow, you ain't gonna miss nothing. Plus you already got to make fun of Uncle Vern a bunch about Bobby Allison."

"Aw, hell," Clovis said. "Ain't barely catching none of the action anyhow with all this caterwauling and commotion. I've heard every one of Vern's dang stories 500 times but I reckon today is a family day after all like your wife was saying."

"Yeah," Derlin replied. "Science-wise, I reckon the boys is still too young to be able to pay too close of attention to any of Vern's story-tellin' but I bet they can still pick up on the mood he's settin' when he talks."

"Or they could be like Tina at a party and just laugh when everybody else does," Clovis said snidely. "I swear, Vern's truck at the bottom of that danged pond has a better sense of humor than that woman does."

Clovis hoisted himself from the couch, making a nearly identical sound effect as his son had moments prior. He lightly shook the empty Panther Cat can on the coffee table, assuring himself that it was drained of its contents before setting it back down. The pair headed for the kitchen just as Vern was getting wound up telling one of his many anecdotes.

"So Mavis, you'll never believe it," Vern began. "There I was just minding my own business out by the Gimbel's one day."

Tina sighed and took a seat at the kitchen table, leaning back in her chair and staring at the ceiling as Derlin and Clovis wandered in.

"Dammit, not this one again, Vern," Clovis hollered. "We heard it last Thanksgiving and it ain't even that good."

"Mavis ain't heard it and it is too good!" Vern replied. "You don't have to listen."

"Well I can't listen to the dang race and I gotta listen to something so quit running your mouth and get back to talkin'," Clovis said shortly, grabbing a beer from the fridge for himself, tossing one to Derlin and a second to Vern, unaware that he'd just grabbed his own fresh one.

"No, Clovis," Vern whined. "I can't hold two beers during this one cause I need my hands for my story telling!"

"Then set it on the counter, I don't care," Clovis said, shrugging. Vern nodded and set the extra beer down on the counter, which Derlin began to eyeball.

"Anyway," Vern snapped. "Sorry Mavis. So there I was, just minding my own business out by the Gimbel's one day."

Tina sighed again and lit a cigarette.

"I seen this tour bus pull up at the stop across the street, there were all these folks getting out to go eat at that little hamburger restaurant they used to have down there before the grease fire," Vern continued.

"Hamburger Dan's?" Mavis asked.

"That's the one!" Vern smiled. He'd told these stories to listless family members so often that he wasn't used to having a fresh participant like Mavis to engage with. Derlin first realized this on that fateful night where they'd attended Vern's fish fry and Derlin had peanut-buttered his gas tank, when Vern sequestered Mavis for a solid twenty minutes telling her about the time he'd lost his boots in the pond and caught them with his fishing pole a few months later. One could postulate that if it wasn't for that particular story that Derlin never would have had time to sneak away to sabotage his car. He wouldn't have had the opportunity to woo Mavis in the Lumpy's parking lot that evening and thus, without going into everything else in between, none of them would be sitting around the kitchen table celebrating Randy and Ollie's first birthday if Uncle Vern had never lost his boots in the pond stomping after a lizard. Silently, Derlin felt a lot of gratitude toward Vern and his stories for that very reason, so while Clovis and Tina griped and bitched, Derlin was happy to let the lonely old man talk.

"So I figure, they look like nice people, I could use a hamburger sandwich," Vern continued. "So I walked right over there and I joined 'em. Turns out they were taking a big church trip from Tallahassee to Branson, Missouri. After they did all their churchin's up there, they were going to this place called Silver Dollar City."

"What's Silver Dollar City?" Mavis asked, enraptured by Uncle Vern's glowing oratory majesty.

"Silver Dollar City?" Vern replied, positively beaming. "It might be the finest theme park in the country outside of Disney World! Everybody's dressed like the old west and you feel like you step off a bus right back smack dab into the 1880's!"

"Neat!" Mavis said. "Honey, we should take the boys there when they're a little older and can enjoy it."

Derlin rolled his eyes and took a sip of beer.

"Uh-huh, you should!" Vern continued. "So here's what I did." He paused here, spending a good ten seconds stifling a giant laugh before regaining his composure. "After I finished my hamburger sandwich and they was all leaving, I took up with 'em and got on the bus right there with 'em and found me a seat toward the back. I rode up to Branson with 'em, stowing away like a boy on an old ship."

"Dammit Vern," Clovis interjected. "It ain't stowing away if you're sitting out in the open talkin' to 'em the whole time. I told you, stowaways hide."

Clovis slammed his empty beer can into the kitchen trash can as Tina began to rub her face with her hands.

"Tell Mavis why they let you on the bus, Vern," Tina said flatly. "Can't be leaving that part out now, can you?"

Vern looked embarrassed for a moment and hung his head.

"They thought I was simple," Vern said quietly.

"I don't know if she heard that last part or not Vern, you were kinda mumbling," said Tina, a smile creeping across her face.

"They thought he was a retarded," Clovis laughed. "They felt bad about kicking him off a church bus and all, so they just let him ride along to Cowboy Town like he was part of the gang."

"It ain't Cowboy Town it's Silver Dollar City!" Vern snapped. "Anyway, that part don't matter. Thing is we get up there and as soon as we get off the bus, there's folks doing old time chores and blowing glass and doing cowboy tricks. There's a fella handing out sarsaparilla for a nickel and I must'a give him two dollars while I was there. There's women in bonnets making old time clothes and blankets, there's mustached fellas in matching shirts singin' "Home on the Range" all fancy, there's a fella smoking up turkey legs. They smelled so good that I forgot about the hamburger sandwich I'd just ate and I went through four or five of them, easy."

"That sounds like a wonderful day for you, Vern" Mavis smiled. She too began to think about Vern's story about his boots and the pond and how thirty seconds worth of information had been crafted into a finely-honed, gently-nuanced twenty-minute anecdote that the rest of the family had instinctively avoided like the plague. She was unsure of where this story of hamburgers and false retardation was going to go, but she realized that she was clearly strapped in for the ride and, as a new member to the Spurlock clan, she was probably going to have to live through each of Vern's many stories at least once before she joined the rest of the family in their distaste.

"I ain't even got to the best part!" Vern said excitedly. "I paid a dollar to go up in this big Ferris Wheel. They let me take my turkey leg on, which was nice, but I did spill my sarsaparilla when I was at the top and they wasn't happy about that. But while I was up there, I seen this booth with a big totem pole sticking up next to it and right in front of it with his teepee was a real, live Indian chief! A real one!"

"Vern, you know that feller wasn't no chief to no Indian tribe," Clovis said. "I bet he was just a Mexican feller they hired up in a big fancy costume and you fell for it, hook, line and sinker!"

"He was too real, otherwise how'd he get a totem pole?" Vern barked. "They don't just hand out totem poles."

Vern took an angry sip of his beer before continuing onward unabated.

"I got down off that Ferris Wheel and finished my turkey leg and washed my hands real good in the bathroom," Vern said. "I wiped 'em off real good on my jeans and I walked over there and talked to him a spell. He told me about this one time he tomahawked a deer and how if he wanted to, he could dance a certain way and it'd start thunderstorming on top of just me. On top of my head!"

"Wow!" Mavis said. Derlin nodded in approval, proud of his wife's pandering. As far as Vern's stories went, "Meeting the Indian in Branson" was near the bottom and Mavis was handling it like a champ.

"He let me get a polaroid picture with him and I still got it on the wall of my trailer," Vern beamed.

The room was silent for five seconds or so as Vern let that sink in.

"Then what happened?" Mavis asked.

"Well, all the nice church folk had reservations at this motel nearby, and it was pretty full up, but they let me sleep on the bus," Vern continued. "I got to stretch out wherever I wanted and I musta slept sprawled out over at least half them seats over the course of the night."

"Why are you so proud of that part?" Tina pleaded.

Vern ignored her.

"The next morning, they woke me up as they was getting on the bus to head home," Vern said. "This one nice lady brought me a danish from the breakfast bar and told me she was proud of me for taking a big trip like this. We rode back and they dropped me off right in front of the hamburger place that night and we all waved goodbye and I walked the rest of the way back home and stuck my picture of me and the Indian up on the wall."

"That's great Vern," Mavis smiled thinly. "I'm so glad that you shared that with me, today of all days."

"Those were probably the best two days of my whole li--" Vern was interrupted as the doorbell rang loudly through the hallway.

"Thank fuckin' God," Clovis shouted, stomping out of the kitchen and beating Mavis to the door.

Clovis swung the door open widely and stared a second.

"Who the hell are y'all?" Clovis asked.

"We're Mavis's parents," Clebert said, offering a handshake. I'm Clebert and this is my wife Eudora. Who the hell are you?" He smiled.

"I'm Clovis," Clovis replied. "I'm Derlin's deddy."

"Well that makes sense," Eudora mused, handing Clovis a large shopping bag full of nicely wrapped gifts for the boys. "How exciting to finally meet our fellow grandparents!"

"Hey," Tina waved from the hallway. "I'm Tina, Derlin's mama."

Tina and Eudora exchanged looks and pleasantries while Clovis, groaning under the weight of the sack of presents, led Clebert to the kitchen and offered him a beer.

"I reckon one couldn't hurt," Clebert smiled, cracking open his Panther Cat and wincing as he took a sip.

"So where are the birthday boys?" Eudora called out to Mavis as she fluttered into the kitchen. "I can't wait to see their little sailor outfits."

Just then, as if on cue, the boys crawled out from under the kitchen table where they'd instinctively hunkered down during Vern's anecdote. Smiling and cooing at the sight of their grandparents, Randy and Ollie were both soon scooped from the floor. Eudora smothered them both with kisses while Clebert went to his "go-to" baby move of tickling them on the belly like a puppy and calling them "good."

"Honey you sure picked out some good baby outfits," Clebert smiled. "These boys look like they could positively up and join the navy."

"They wouldn't let me in the navy," Vern offered from his spot leaning against the countertop. "They said no matter how many times I tried to sign up it didn't matter because something in my brainpan got shook loose when I flipped my truck into the pond and if my ship ever got hit by a torpedo I'd probably forget where I was and fall into the ocean. They just kept on deferrin' me."

"That's Uncle Vern," Mavis said, introducing her parents as Vern nodded and waved from across the kitchen table.

"Yeah, that's him," Clovis said, huffing and puffing from the effort it took him attempting to hoist Eudora's large sack of birthday gifts on top of the dining room table without smashing the boys' birthday cake. He'd given up putting it on top of the table almost immediately but had taken a few moments care to wedge the contents safely into a dining room chair, even pushing it back in when he finished. He felt a little bit of shame in his personal physique that the bag was being effortlessly carried by a small fifty-year-old woman moments earlier, but he shrugged it off and headed to the fridge for another couple of beers.

"So what do you do, Clebe?" Clovis asked, propping an arm up on the door frame and leaning against it as he took a loud sip of Panther Cat.

"I'm the head foreman at the rubber band plant they got over in Applebottom," Clebert replied. "Got a job there sweepin' up and re-tying the broken ones right out of high school and I've worked my way all the way up to the top."

"Well hot dang, that sounds like a mighty fine job," Clovis replied. "No wonder you got such a pretty wife." He winked at Eudora, who raised her eyebrows but otherwise ignored him.

"Um, thank you Clovis," Clebert replied. "But to be fair she was my pretty wife back when I was still just the simple young fella trying to unjam the rubber band machine with a broom handle before it started smokin' and made everybody pass out. Ain't nothing too glamorous about it."

"Not a lot of glamour in my line of work either," Clovis sniffed.

"And what is it that you do?" Clebert asked, taking another careful sip of his quickly-warming Panther Cat.

"Mow grass, mostly," Clovis said. "A little other yard work and maintenance. That boy Derlin, he's got my raking bone in him. Got that skill straight from his daddy."

"I don't rake no more, deddy," Derlin said happily. "I got me a job sellin' cars for Ricky Yamashita."

"Don't interrupt us when we're talkin' boy," Clovis snapped. "This is grandpa-to-grandpa time." He smiled at Clebert, offering him a "cheers" with his beer.

"Anyhow, Clebe," he continued. "What's the wife do?"

"Oh she's a homemaker," Clebert replied, as though there was no other possible answer. "Why? Does your wife work?"

"Yeah, she works down over at the Meaty's," Clovis replied, nodding his head in a general direction. "She's been waitressin' down there a good long time."

"I see," Clebert said. "That must be... an experience for her."

"Cause you know, sometimes my back gets all messed up," Clovis said, feeling the sudden need to justify his wife's employment. "And I can't do no lawn mowin', no raking, no..."

"Definitely not any raking," Derlin chimed in. "Fine way to mess up a back."

"Dammit, son, what did I just tell you about interrupting?" Clovis hollered.

"Sorry deddy," Derlin said sheepishly, turning his attention back to his children, in the midst of splitting a Charleston Chew that Clebert had slipped them when they first arrived in the kitchen.

"So what I was saying," Clovis continued, side-eyeing Derlin, "is that when I'm all laid up cause my spine got janky, the wife can hop around slingin' cocktails and we can still keep the lights on and the water runnin'. I'm just glad, with all the fellas that come in there, that she hasn't took up and run off with one of 'em yet."

Clebert began to laugh heartily, slowly tapering off as he realized that Clovis seemed to be unaware that he'd told a joke. He'd been hearing stories about Meaty's ever since a few of his factory men had dropped in one night for a beer over a decade ago. Surely, he thought, the husband of probably the only female employee in the whole operation would have an idea what went on there.

"You laughing cause you don't think none of them fellas would want to take up with Tina?" Clovis asked angrily. "Look, I know she ain't no prize pig, but---"

"You ain't no prize pig either, y'asshole," Tina shouted from across the kitchen.

"No, no," Clebert started, doing his best to backtrack as much as possible and diffuse the situation. "All I was saying, I mean, I think Tina's a fine example of a woman." He winced as Eudora shot him a dirty look. "I just think that... the men there might tend to have other interests, right?"

He looked to Tina and Clovis for support and they both stared at him blankly for a moment.

"You mean like, they all got wives at home and they wouldn't never step out on 'em with a waitress from the men's bar?" Clovis asked.

"Sort of," Clebert shrugged.

"Since they're just in there with their guy friends, they're too busy chatting each other up about sports and hunting and men's stuff to worry about chasing any tail?"

Clovis asked.

"More or less," Clebert said. He was fine with the picture of spousal nobility Clovis was painting at Meaty's as it seemed to get him off the hook for his perceived besmirching of Tina. He really couldn't care less that somehow Clovis and Tina were oblivious to the lifestyle exclusively held by Tina's clientele and he was becoming concerned that the current line of conversation might soon derail his grandsons' birthday party. He sighed in relief as Clovis accepted the scenario which he'd slowly drawn up for himself.

"That's mighty noble, Clebe," Clovis said calmly. "I hadn't thought about that. Thanks for the kind words about m'wife."

"Who's the prize pig now?" Tina asked sarcastically from across the table.

"Still me," Clovis replied, smiling. He opened his mouth to say something else, but once again, the doorbell rang.

"Ooh, I bet that's mama & deddy," Vern said, and for the second time in an hour a Spurlock man dashed past Mavis in her own hallway to beat her to her own front door."

Vern's prognostication did indeed turn out to be correct, as there were no other invited guests who hadn't yet arrived. Still, Vern boasted of his deduction.

"I'm real good at guessing who's at doors," he told Clebert. "I got so good at guessing, they started calling me the 'Sherlock Holmes of Spurlock Homes.'"

"Nobody calls you that, Vern," Clovis shouted.

"Never did," Grandpa Hoyt said, shaking his head as he walked in.

"Not one time," Grandma Vondene added behind him.

"The only reason you ever used to guess right is cause you'd cheat by looking out the window to see what car pulled up," Clovis said.

"And you can't really call me on the phone to come over and then yell 'I bet it's Derlin' fifteen minutes later when I knock on the door," Derlin said. "Plus you can't really guess it's Grandpa Hoyt and Grandma Vondene if you know they're the only folks that ain't showed up yet."

Vern scoffed, looking around for support and finding little.

Derlin had actually invited one more person, Lumpy, but he'd refused on the grounds that the boys were likely still rabidly contagious with whatever ailments they'd been suffering through. Meaning well as always, he'd patted Derlin on the back when he'd dropped by the Feed n' Seed, smiling and telling him that if the boys make it, he'd be happy to come to their fifth or sixth birthday when he could feel a little safer about his personal health.

"Hey everyone!" Mavis shouted, surprised at her own volume trying to be heard over the Spurlock rabble. "I figure since everybody is here, we can quit bickering and pickin' on Vern and start celebrating Randy and Ollie's special day!"

She began to herd the group toward the dining room, grabbing Randy off the floor while Vondene covered Ollie's face in kiss marks of her smokey lipstick.

The boys were too young to truly conceptualize what was happening around them, but Mavis and Eudora began to stack presents in front of them as they both sat in Grandma Vondene's lap staring at the balloons. Derlin tried in vain to draw their attention to the banner he and Vern had hung, but had soon given up and was helping the boys tear the wrapping from their pile of gifts. Instinctively knowing that the brown grocery sack with the race cars and the receipt from the gas station a few blocks away came from his parents, Derlin enthusiastically thanked Clovis and Tina as Vondene made Randy and Ollie's hands wave in excitement.

Mavis, Eudora and Vondene had all enthusiastically over-shopped for the boys and they were soon practically buried in an avalanche of stuffed animals, toys, matching outfits and candy. Randy and Ollie's eyes widened with the joy of overstimulation as they pawed at their new collection of toddler sundries. Derlin and Mavis had just begun thanking people when Hoyt piped up from the edge of the dining room.

"I got one more present for 'em, Miss Mavis," he smiled, producing a plain, neatly wrapped package from behind his back.

He tossed it to Derlin, still crouched next to his boys and grandmother. Derlin pawed away at the wrapping paper before letting out a surprised gasp and a long "cool!"

Mounted nicely in a wooden box was a matching pair of incredibly ornate hunting knives, each with the head of a deer carved into their bone handles.

"Goddamn it, it's knives," Clovis shouted, throwing his hands in the air in exasperation. "Tina, I fuckin' told you."

"Deddy, hush!" Derlin said sternly. Clovis, surprised, complied immediately. "These are really nice, Grandpa Hoyt!" he said, looking them over carefully.

"Both them handles is made out of antler bones from the Kaiser's deer that I killed with my bayonet back in W-W one," Grandpa Hoyt said proudly. "Had to kill him for his hide to stay warm in the winter of '17. I wore him like a coat for four months while we trudged through the Alps, eatin' bits of frozen meat off from the inside whenever I got hungry. Right about the time I was fixin' to gnaw through the old bastard's ribcage, Woodrow and Pershing got their Armistice and I got to go home. They wouldn't let me take the coat back on the ship with me so I sawed his antlers off right there at the slipway ramp and tossed the rest of him in the ocean. Made a smackin' sound when it hit the water that's always stuck with me over the years."

"Wasn't that the war your brother Lester got killed in?" Vern asked.

"Yeah, that's the one," Grandpa Hoyt nodded. "But we don't need to be talking about that on such a happy day." Lester had been a sore spot with Hoyt ever since Hoyt had returned from the Great War and Lester hadn't. Both of them lived through combat unscathed and both were set to return home the same week, but Lester, mis-hearing the terms of the Armistice, attempted to defect to the Kaiser two days after the Treaty of Versailles was signed and was summarily shot in the back by a fellow soldier as he attempted to flee the allies and clamber up the barbed fence into German territory. Though some witnesses on the allied side claimed that he wasn't fleeing and was simply chasing a bunny, he was officially listed as a deserter as several soldiers and countless other witnesses stated in a court martial proceeding that there had been no rabbit and that Lester had wet himself before beginning his run.

"I figure the boys ain't old enough to have 'em yet, but you could find some place to stick 'em safe till they are," Grandpa Hoyt smiled.

"That's a great idea, Grandpa Hoyt," Mavis said, patting him warmly on the back.

"You've gotta be kidding me," Clovis muttered under his breath.

The rest of the party flowed gleefully, if uneventfully. The boys managed to cover themselves in icing while getting their first taste of birthday cake. Vern helped himself to second, third and fourth pieces and as Derlin looked across the table at their three icing covered faces, he gazed over to his wife and realized that whether the boys grew up to be four feet tall or forty, he could still be truly happy.

February 8, 1969

Mavis was in the yard with Randy and Ollie when Derlin arrived home from work. She sat Indian-style as the boys toddled around her in a circle, periodically tumbling to the grass. Derlin honked the robust, fresh horn of the Monaco as he pulled into the driveway, ambling over to join his family in the yard.

"I've got a surprise for you," Mavis smiled as Derlin plopped down next to her in the grass.

"Oh yeah, what's that?" Derlin asked.

"You've got the weekend off!" Mavis replied. "I called Dixie and Crystal right after you left work to see if they would give you a couple extra days so we could go on a road trip! We can load up the boys and do some sight-seeing. They agreed that you've been working so hard you could use a little weekend getaway."

"That sounds great, baby," Derlin said. "I ain't never been on a vacation before unless you count jail or the army."

"I don't know if that counts, honey," Mavis said.

"Well, besides, it'd still be cool to go on one," Derlin shrugged, nodding. "We can drive anywhere we want to. Look at us! A couple of jet setters."

"Just like Frank and Nancy Sinatra," Mavis smiled dreamily.
And I could teach you how to drive the Monaco good while we're out on the real country parts of the road too!" Derlin said.

"That sounds nice," Mavis said. "I'll be outracing Uncle Vern by the summertime."

Derlin doubled over with laughter, cackling for a solid ten seconds before Mavis interrupted.

"Where should we go?" she asked. "I've only been out of Alabama once, when I went with daddy to the rubber band convention in San Antonio when I was a girl."

"We could go to Daytona Beach!" Derlin offered loudly, thinking back to Horatio's plan to cruise for loose women.

"Oh honey," Mavis began. "I'd love to, but the boys are still too young for the beach. They don't have enough hair to cover their heads yet and wearing their wigs on the beach would be too hot for them, even this time of year. Let's save the beach trip for when they're older."

"That's fine," Derlin said. "That does make sense."

"We could go to Atlanta," Mavis offered. "I've always wanted to go. We could go see Braves game and the boys would love going to the zoo."

"Nah, it ain't baseball season, baby. Plus Grandpa Hoyt and Clovis both told me it ain't safe to travel with families north of the Mason-Dixon line." Derlin said, shaking his head. "I wouldn't go no farther north than Birmingham just to be safe."

"Well what ain't safe about it?" Mavis asked.

"Oh, mobsters, bandits, stuff like that I think," Derlin said. "I don't really know for sure. Grandma Vondene always said it gets dark real early up in them big cities, so I reckon folks have a lot more night time where they can do their robbin' and swindlin'."

"Oh that makes sense too, since it is north," Mavis said. "I remember learning in school that there's some places so far up north that in the winter it's dark all the time."

"I bet those poor folks get robbed blind," Derlin said, sighing and shaking his head in empathy.

"Well, where should we go?" Mavis asked.

"Well, we knocked off going north and south," Derlin began, counting on his fingers. "There ain't nothing east but a bunch of damn pig farmers. So I guess that just leaves…"

"West!" Mavis shouted.

Derlin thought for a moment, still counting slowly on his fingers.

"Yep, you're right!" Derlin said happily. "West it is."

"Well, what's west?" Mavis asked.

"My mama's got cousins in New Mexico," Derlin offered. "But every time we'd talk about visiting them growing up, deddy would just snort and say 'more like Jew Mexico' and we never went."

"Hmm," Mavis said. "As much as I'd love to hang out with your mama's cousins, I think New Mexico might be a little far for the boys' first road trip."

"Yeah, it is way the hell out there," Derlin said.

"What about New Orleans?" Mavis asked. "We could eat good cajun food, there'd be parades and stuff that the boys would love. It's south, but not the beach. You could even get as drunk as you like as long as I don't have to carry you anywhere."

"I can't think of anything wrong with that," Derlin smiled slyly.

"Your daddy didn't used to say Jew Orleans too did he?" Mavis said jokingly.

"Not as much!" Derlin laughed.

February 9, 1969

The morning sun shone brightly in through the bedroom window as Mavis giddily packed the family's bags. Randy and Ollie played at her feet and Derlin lurked in her periphery.

"Baby do you wanna make a bet how many crawdads I can fit in my mouth?" Derlin asked as Mavis set up the boys' outfits for the weekend on the bedspread.

"Oh I don't know honey," Mavis said distractedly. "I bet you can fit a bunch."

"The family record is fourteen," Derlin said proudly. "Uncle Vern's done it three times. He keeps trying to beat it but he can't. Grandpa Hoyt said that fifteenth crawdad is gonna put Vern in his grave."

"Well baby, let's try and stay out of your grave on this trip, okay?" Mavis asked dotingly.

"Yeah that ain't a bad idea," Derlin said, stretching. "I do like being alive."

"We like you being alive, too," Mavis said, smiling down at her children and stuffing their sailor outfits into a suitcase.

"Yeah, I'll probably just try and see how many hushpuppies or something I can fit in my mouth," Derlin said casually. "Something way easier to chew."

"How many hushpuppies can Uncle Vern fit in his mouth?" Mavis asked sarcastically.

"Eleven," Derlin said. "He said he probably could have made it to twelve or thirteen if he'd let 'em cool proper when they came out of the fryer. Burned his mouth up pretty good. I think he even had to live on buttermilk for a few days."

"That's awful," Mavis gasped.

"Well don't worry about me, baby," Derlin said, puffing out his chest. "I'm smart enough to let mine cool first."

As Derlin pulled the Monaco out of the driveway, Mavis began to calculate their route from Coverdale. A four-hour journey lay ahead of them, which would put them at their destination around two o'clock in the afternoon, just in time for Randy and Ollie's nap and Derlin's first vacation beverage.

The boys were nearly as fascinated with the new family car as Mavis was, expressing their interest by gnawing on the seatbelts which held them in place while Mavis fiddled with the radio.

Scrolling slowly through the static on the dial, Mavis squealed with excitement when she tuned in Loretta Lynn's "Squaw is on the Warpath."

"I bet it'd be fun being an old-time Indian like she's singing about," Mavis postulated, looking out the car window as they drove past a field with a handful of goats grazing in the grass.

"I imagine it wouldn't be too different from living in the windmill," Derlin answered. "No electricity, finding whatever food you can to survive. Sleeping in hay."

"But, Indians hunted for their food," Mavis said. "We pretty much ate out of cans you brought home, or steaks that people gave you for raking."

"Yeah, I guess," Derlin said dismissively. "It was still kind of like hunting, but instead of having a bow and arrow or a tomahawk, I had my rake."

"Yeah, I guess so." Mavis said. It was her turn to sound dismissive.

Derlin nodded.

"You know, I always thought going hunting would be pretty fun," Mavis said.

"Do you think your Grandpa Hoyt would take us out with him one day?"

Derlin's eyes got wide and he could feel himself blush.

"No, no I don't think he'd do that," Derlin stammered. "He's pretty famous for hunting around the county and I think he probably just hunts with the mayor and maybe the mayor's brother."

"Oh," Mavis said, surprised. "Well, Clovis and Uncle Vern go all the time too, don't they? I'm surprised you don't go too."

"I used to," Derlin said. "I just, I just don't like it is all."

He clenched the steering wheel and stared straight ahead at the road. His father, grandfather and uncle had been shaming him about his inability to hunt since he was in grade school and despite his prowess in other areas he had hoped that his wife would never find out that he was, by army metrics, the worst shot with a rifle in their documented history.

He thought back to the sound of laughter the last time he'd gone hunting with his family as a surly seventeen year old, when he'd missed an oblivious deer standing in an open meadow from no more than twelve feet away. Grandpa Hoyt's words echoed through his mind every time he'd held a gun since then, generating the shame he'd felt at Lumpy's in the parking lot on his last day there and the shame he felt in front of Mavis now. Clear as day, he could still hear Grandpa Hoyt yelling "Jesus W. Christ, son, you couldn't shoot him from point blank range!" as Clovis and Vern doubled over with laughter.

Aside from this deep shame, his age and the fact that he'd described his string of drunken armed robberies and subsequent jail time as hired yard work and being kidnapped, he'd never kept anything from Mavis during their relationship and he decided to relieve himself of the burden of the former.

"Baby, I can't go hunting with them because I can't shoot no good and they make fun of me a bunch and they're mean," Derlin blurted.

"Oh," Mavis said nonchalantly. "Well, I can't shoot either, so we'd be the same if we ever went."

She put her hand on Derlin's thigh, patting it supportively.

"I guess you're right," he said quietly, a wave of relief washing over him.

He smiled, looking back in the rear-view mirror at his sons, each staring blankly out the window. The boys were each sporting a new vacation hat in lieu of their usual "going in public" wigs, as the late winter weather was already unusually mild and Mavis had assumed that New Orleans would only be warmer. In place of the wigs she'd found a pair of baby-sized Atlanta Braves hats on the shelf at the local Gimbel's, which fit just well enough to hide the boys' birthmarks as they traveled. Their wisps of blonde hair continued to grow by the day, but their dark birthmarks remained quite the attention-grabber beneath them.

"Y'all boys look good in them hats," Derlin said happily. "You look like Hank and Tommie Aaron, just with a lot more cream in their coffee."

"Ooh, speaking of coffee," Mavis said. "I could sure use a pick-me-up, do you mind if we stop at a filling station so we can get some? I bet you could use some, too. According to the map, we're almost to the state line of Mississippi."

"Can we look for one of them fancy new rest stops they got with the vending machines of drinks and snacks and stuff?" Derlin asked hopefully. "We stopped at one of them when I was on the army bus up to Montgomery and I'd never seen anything like it! They had bathrooms too, with sinks *and* mirrors. They've got good snacks to boot! It ain't just some shack with a feller and bunch of road apples."

"I'd love to," Mavis said excitedly. "Uncle Vern was telling me about one he stopped at on his Branson trip. He made it sound like a palace."

Derlin rolled his eyes. He began to scoff before seeing a sign along the roadside advertising a "Public Rest Stop" just over the Mississippi state line. He'd always taken back roads on his way into Chicken Wipe and was pleased with the bounty that interstate highway travel had provided him.

"Baby!" he shouted, startling the children from their sightseeing stupors. "Baby there's one of 'em three miles up the road."

"I see that honey," Mavis smiled. "That'll be perfect. We can let the babies out of their seat belts and all stretch our legs a little bit."

"If nobody else is in there, I'm gonna see how many urinals I can pee in!" Derlin said excitedly.

"How many did Uncle Vern get?" Mavis asked, humoring Derlin's strange family record keeping.

"Oh, Uncle Vern don't have the record for that," Derlin explained. "He's not spry enough. My deddy's got the record for that, but it wasn't real fair."

"How was it not fair?" Mavis asked, no longer humoring and actually interested in the direction of this particular Spurlock tale.

"Well, he made me and Vern sit in the parking lot of a Stuckey's while he drank three six packs of Panther Cat, one after the other, not even sharing," Derlin started. "And this was one of them big truck-stop Stuckey's and the bathroom in there had ten urinals in a row, right there on the wall. Well, deddy walked in there, he was already stumbling pretty good, he walked up to the first urinal and let her rip. He started moving to his right and hit that second urinal for a few seconds, you gotta be there long enough to hear the splash echo or it don't count. Next thing he's on to the third and fourth and fifth and he's going faster and faster, but he got kinda sloppy and clipped his knee on the ninth one and fell down and pissed himself and hit his head."

"Oh no!" Mavis gasped.

"Aw, it wouldn't have been that bad if it wasn't my birthday," Derlin started. "I was turning ten years old and he was trying to do it for my birthday present. I was pretty sad until Vern explained that it didn't mean that I had to stay nine for another year."

"Honey, you get older every year," Mavis said.

"I know," Derlin answered flatly, turning his attention fully to looking for his exit.

Chapter 46

Derlin guided the Monaco gently into the middle of two parking spaces as Mavis "ooh'd" and "ahh'd" at a picnic bench perched next to a few pine trees and an already-blooming bush. He craned his neck trying to spot how many vending machines there were lined under the awning of the building, grabbing a softball-sized bag of change out of the glove box. He'd been stashing the change since his return from the army and during his employment at Lumpy's under the off-chance that he'd return to another similar rest area one day. Acquired a nickel at a time, mostly from the Lumpy's parking lot, Derlin marvelled at the weight of the sack, immensely proud of his resourcefulness as he tucked it under his arm like a football and grinned.

"I'm going to let the boys play in the grass," Mavis said. "Would you please grab me a coffee while you're getting your snacks?"

"I sure will baby," Derlin said, opening the door and hopping from the car. "I'm gonna hit the pisser, then it's vending machine city!"

"Good luck with both of those things," Mavis smiled.

Derlin shot her a thumbs up with his free hand as he turned to jog to the men's room. He was disappointed when he arrived there however, as there were only four urinals lining the wall, with someone using one to boot. He briefly thought about waiting till the bathroom was entirely unoccupied and attempting some sort of back and forth relay with the four provided urinals as he made his run at the family record, but with no witnesses he decided to just use one of them like a normal person, privately dedicating it to his sons as a belated first birthday present in the fine gift giving tradition of his father Clovis.

Derlin felt a bounce in his step as he had freed himself from the burden of what he estimated to be fifteen to eighteen urinals worth of pee, had he been attempting to break his father's record. He yipped happily as he headed to the row of vending machines, looking off fondly at the nearby patch of grass where Mavis sat as Randy and Ollie toddled confidently about.

With precision and form reminiscent of a championship golfer churning through a back nine, Derlin began inserting coins and collecting snacks, slowly walking back and forth between machines and eyeballing his choices carefully. As his armload began to grow and his change satchel began to dwindle, Derlin's grasp on his several dollars worth of ten and fifteen cent snacks was beginning to slip. Loading a final pack of Razzles onto his heap with his final nickel and forgetting his wife's coffee, Derlin turned to head back toward the car.

He'd made it around two-thirds of the way back, slowly weaving from one side of the sidewalk to the other. As he wobbled back and forth, his load prevented him from seeing the edge of the concrete and he took a tumble. In a surprised attempt to pinwheel his arms for support, Derlin flung his candy in a huge radius around as he crashed to the ground, howling. Mavis had seen all of this unfold slowly from where she sat watching the boys some twenty feet away and immediately rushed to her husband's aid. At first worried he'd broken an ankle, her fears of injury were soon dissipated as Derlin was on his hands and knees frantically attempting to gather his treats by the time Mavis had arrived to help, muttering "Oh God, oh God, oh God," under his breath as he crawled along the ground.

They spent the next few moments carefully rounding up Derlin's bounty and when it was fully recovered they turned to gather the boys and load it all into the car. It was then that they noticed that Randy and Ollie were nowhere to be found.

Mavis gasped and ran frantically back to the now-empty patch of grass where they'd been playing happily moments prior.

"Damn are they that fast already?" Derlin asked. He glanced over to the row of vending machines, half expecting to see the boys pawing up at some desired snack stuck behind the glass, but there was no trace of them there either.

"They can't have gone that far," Mavis shouted, tears beginning to well in her eyes and fall down her face.

Randy and Ollie had toddled away from their designated patch in the grass as soon as Mavis had rushed to Derlin's aid. Though their first few steps were following behind their mother, the boys were soon distracted by the vibrant green of a patch of bushes, their wobbly path taking a detour to and through the patch. Pawing at their branches, each boy soon found that the leaves weren't as tasty as their appearance would indicate. They turned to locate Mavis, their sight hindered both by the bushes and their own diminutive builds. Thus unable to see both their mother and father crawling around gathering up armloads of dusty snacks, the boys continued their journey down the sidewalk, heading slowly into the men's room which Derlin had so recently vacated. What the boys lacked in walking speed, they made up for in blank-faced determination. They hadn't yet passed their particularly impressive brand of crawling in terms of total velocity yet, but were quite literally taking strides every day in regard to getting better at putting one foot in front of the other. Between the two of them, their bare feet were making quite a patter as they stomped flat-footed into the men's room, stopping in their tracks as they saw a dark, hulking figure examining his ghoulish face in the mirror.

—

Oldsmobile Jenkins' life had gotten pretty quiet after Derlin had been released from jail. He could read a theater magazine article without being interrupted about whether or not the article concerned "Batman." He hadn't had to break up a fight in over a year and his mother still came to visit him twice a week. Whether it was his actual disposition or just a quality of being generally inert for most of the day, Oldsmobile was looked at as a model prisoner by the guards. He'd never actually expected it to happen, but he wasn't all that surprised when the warden called him into his office that he was being let out of jail almost eighteen months early on account of good behavior.

"Plus you never killed that Spurlock boy in the night," the warden added. "So I figure you must be rehabilitated."

Oldsmobile had spent a few weeks staying with his mother as he reacclimated to life on the outside. He'd spend his mornings and evenings browsing the help-wanted section in the newspaper for what he called a "straight job," being certain to avoid any listings that seemed to have the trappings of mob affiliation. He certainly wasn't going to be a garbage man again. Anything with a union seemed too risky.

Nothing had stuck out at him employment-wise after several days of searching, and as he flipped through another set of ads waiting for his mother to cook dinner one evening, he began to think that there weren't a lot of possibilities on the job market for a 400-pound, freshly-released ex-con. He was about to give up and apply for the vacant dishwashing position available at The Screaming Captain when an ad in the back of one of his theater magazines caught his eye.

"NEW ORLEANS VOODOO THEATER SEEKING ACTORS"
Daily Shows in front of Hundreds of Tourists
Wanted: Large Black-Negro Men to Play Head Voodoo Priest
Well-Paid Gig, Guaranteed Summer Hours
Apply in Person, in Costume
M. Alexander Voodoo Theater, 133 N. Water St.

Oldsmobile gasped. Though he'd spent most of his days as a simple garbage man before his time in jail, he'd kept no secret his desire to be an actor. He'd long dreamed of playing Othello, but had resigned himself to the idea of simply being, as he put it "the Laurence Olivier of throwin' yo shit away." Now, embittered by and spurned from his earlier life of a theatrical garbage man, he saw a light at the end of his tunnel. After combing through days of help wanted ads for ditch-diggers and dishwashers, he took the placement of this ad as a sign from above. After years of dreaming, he felt he finally had a chance to get his foot in the door.

That night over dinner, Oldsmobile explained the plan to his mother, who immediately agreed to loan him her old Edsel for the weekend so that he could travel to New Orleans and apply in person as the ad suggested. For the first time since he'd been released from jail, he felt that his dreams were within reach. Once they'd finished eating, the pair headed down to the basement to find Oldsmobile a costume. Conveniently enough, Oldsmobile found a box of his grandfather's church clothes, producing a dusty black chimney hat that was somehow not too small atop his massive head. Though his grandfather's coat began to groan and tear before Oldsmobile had managed to get an entire arm into it, the accompanying cloak fit quite nicely draped across his massive shoulders. Only minutes into their search, Oldsmobile and his mother agreed that he had a fine basis for a Voodoo priest costume and that his appearance coupled with his size would certainly impress whoever was taking his interview at the M. Alexander Theater.

The next morning, Oldsmobile headed off toward New Orleans to make his appearance and hopefully start down the path of his newfound life in the theater. He beamed with excitement as he headed down the road, but with each passing mile his brain began to plant small seeds of doubt about his ability and he was soon letting his nerves get the better of him. He wondered how many people had seen this magazine ad and how many might be showing up to apply for the job. There wasn't a phone number listed, as far as he knew the job could have already been filled. Sure, he was exactly as the ad specified, "large and black." Just as surely, he figured there was someone else out there who was large, black and had acting experience beyond just thumbing through two decades worth of "Playbill."

Oldsmobile did his best to tuck these thoughts away and remain confident. As he drove and thought, he began to wonder if it would put his mind at ease if he actually tried on his costume before his interview. All he'd done was make sure the items fit him in his mother's dimly-lit basement the evening prior before cramming them into his suitcase. He hadn't taken the time to look at the entire ensemble in a mirror, but he imagined that he must look fairly daunting.

Not five minutes after having this thought, Oldsmobile saw the sign for an upcoming rest area just over the Alabama-Mississippi line. Having heard tales of the luxury of these modernized highway stops from a few fellow inmates over the years, Oldsmobile decided that they likely had facilities large enough to accommodate his girth as he tried on his costume. Oldsmobile slowly pulled his mother's old Edsel into a spot next to a green Monaco and headed for the restrooms.

Smiling and nodding politely as he passed a lady and her two young children on his way, Oldsmobile chuckled at a man pounding on the side of a vending machine and tucked quietly into the men's room. He was relieved to have the whole place to himself as he put himself into his costume. Donning his hat and cloak, his speculation was correct as he certainly cut quite the striking figure in the mirror. However, he felt something was missing were he to appear as an actual hulking Voodoo priest and not just any old heavy-set black man in a cape and top hat. Looking around, a small, half-used bar of soap sitting atop the sink caught his eye. Grabbing it and wetting it to a fine lather, he had just finished applying his white, bubbly "face paint" when Randy and Ollie came toddling into the room and stopped in their tracks.

Oldsmobile turned, gasping, just as startled to see them as they were at him. He loved children dearly but he'd always been genuinely off-put by twins, unable to put his finger on exactly why. Encountering them here in the bathroom seemed like a strange omen to him but he was determined to not tempt fate and be kind to them.

"Well, hi there little fellas!" he smiled, waving warmly and forgetting his ghastly appearance as the soapy "makeup" dripped down his face.
Randy and Ollie shrieked in unison, with Oldsmobile shrieking in turn, and the boys turned to flee the bathroom with the most speed they'd shown yet. Getting his bearings and shaking his head at the odd disturbance, Oldsmobile went back to touching up his soap "makeup" in the mirror, humming lightly.

"The type of people you see at these places," he muttered to himself, shaking his head and chuckling.

The boys ran back out into the outdoors, Ollie's hat flying off in the breeze and landing on the ground next to a trucker's discarded can of baked beans. Scared out of their wits and in an unfamiliar place, the boys were disoriented and soon became separated, with Randy taking a left toward the vending machines and Ollie taking off toward a parked convoy of 18-wheelers.

Randy was quickly spotted by Derlin, who was scouting from the top of a small charcoal grill mounted on the property. He rushed over to scoop up his son as a wave of relief washed over him.

"Good God'amighty, there you are fella," Derlin said. "You had us worried sick. Y'all can't go running off like that, you're too little! Now where's your brother?"

Derlin looked around, gradually turning a full circle in search of Ollie, seeing nothing. The wave of relief had disappeared.

"Mavis!" he shouted. "I got Randy!"

"Oh thank God," Mavis yelled, running over from the parking lot, where she'd been looking under parked cars and inside open doors and windows.

"I still don't know where Ollie got to," Derlin said, peering off into the distance. "But he can't be too far from here."

Derlin handed off Randy to Mavis, watching stone-faced as an exiting 18-wheeler with the words "MISSISSIPPI HAM" emblazoned on the trailer nearly sideswiped the Monaco pulling out of the parking lot.

"Baby, you take Randy over there to that group of long-haul truckers," Derlin said. "And show 'em Randy and ask them if anybody's seen a baby what looks just like him. Just explain that there's two of him and we need to find the other one."

"That's a good idea honey," Mavis said, doing her best to hold back another wave of tears.

"Now everything's gonna be alright," Derlin said, rubbing his wife's back in consolation and squeezing her tightly. "We'll find Ollie. He's around here somewhere. I'm gonna do another lap around the building and see what I can see."

"Okay, good luck," Mavis said, sniffling.

She took a deep breath and began to walk across the parking lot to the truck parking area. Scouting the parking lot and the surrounding wooded area as she walked, Mavis had made it about thirty feet when she heard Derlin scream.

Turning in fright, Derlin was already sprinting toward her by the time she'd been able to react. Panting as he arrived, his face white with fear, he held out Ollie's Braves hat and the can of beans.

"Baby," he gasped. "We need to call the police."

Mavis did her best to hold it together as she called the police from a nearby pay phone to report her missing son. The woman on the other end of the line promised multiple units arriving as quickly as possible and, though Derlin continued to speculate wildly about what had happened, Mavis hesitated to use the word "kidnapped" over the phone as her husband repeatedly requested.

"Damn gypsies come through here with their caravans," Derlin muttered, half under his breath as he paced back and forth. "Think they can ride in here on their dope-wagons and trade my boy for a can of beans? They got another thing coming, that's for goddamn sure."

"Honey, I don't think it was gypsies," Mavis said, wiping away tears. "He's probably just hiding in the woods somewhere. He's probably just lost and scared. The police will find him as soon as they start looking."

Just as Mavis said that, three Mississippi State Troopers pulled into the parking lot, sirens blaring, quickly followed by two more. Derlin waved to get their attention and jogged up to the lead car.

"Hey y'all, we're the ones what called in that disappeared baby," Derlin said loudly, pointing over his shoulder at the rest area.

"Hi there, Mr. Spurlock is it?" the trooper said. "I'm Sergeant Johnston, I'm going to take a statement from you and your wife while the other troopers start combing the grounds for little Ollie."

"Okay," Derlin said, instinctively fidgeting with his own comb in his back pocket.

As Derlin and Mavis laid out the chain of events for Sergeant Johnston, the other dozen officers began to fan out around the rest area. Derlin was just getting to the part about dropping his candy when one of the other state troopers began shouting from the men's room.

"Hands in the air! Freeze! Get down on the ground! Don't move!" the trooper shouted in rapid succession. Three other troopers rushed into the restroom behind him, guns and batons drawn, and they soon emerged with a bewildered and handcuffed Oldsmobile Jenkins, sporting a large lump atop his forehead. One of the troopers carried Oldsmobile's now-dented top hat as he walked behind, and it was clear by the look on their faces that they believed they had found their man.

"Hey Sarge," one of the other troopers shouted, "I think we found our perpetrator, here. Looks like he's one of them Voo-Doo priests you hear about on the TV, bringing his godless ceremonies up from New Orleans."

"More like Jew Orleans," one of the other troopers whispered from behind him, eliciting a few snickers from his fellow troopers.

"Look at him, he's got his face painted like some kinda crazy warlock," another trooper shouted. "He's wearing a damn cloak. You don't wear a cloak if you ain't some kind of witch or wizard."

Sergeant Johnston glared at Oldsmobile for a moment as he was being led toward him before looking down at Ollie's hat and the can of beans. The three troopers holding Oldsmobile stopped about ten feet away and Sergeant Johnston gave Oldsmobile a quick up-down look as he struggled to regain his senses after the baton blow he'd taken in the men's room.

"Mr. Spurlock, your wife said on the phone that you found your boy Randy when he came running up to you by the vending machines?" Sergeant Johnston asked.

"Yes sir, running as fast as I've ever seen him," Derlin said.

"Like something might have startled him." Sergeant Johnston said.

"Yessir, I guess you could say that," Derlin answered. He sure was wide-eyed."

"Well, here's what I think happened," said Sergeant Johnston, taking a look around as the other troopers listened intently. His eyes fell on Oldsmobile once again and he glared at him fiercely.

"I think when these boys, Randy and Ollie, ran off from their mama," Sergeant Johnston continued. "They ran past all the candy machines their daddy had just emptied out and they run into the men's room, maybe looking to see if he was still making use of the facilities."

Derlin nodded, listening closely and putting his arm around Mavis and Randy.

"They didn't find their daddy, though!" Sergeant Johnston said dramatically. "They found this man, in the middle of some type of evil black magic ceremony in the mirror, doing God knows what in his own reflection. They interrupted his demonic ritual and they scared him and pissed him off. They tried to run, but they're just little baby boys still learning to walk for Christ's sake. Randy made it around the corner just in time to be spared, but this big fella Voodoo-zapped little Ollie and turned him into this can of baked beans as punishment for breaking up his demon summonings. It's the only theory that makes a lick of sense."

At this point, Sergeant Johnston took Ollie's Braves hat and placed it atop the can of baked beans, eliciting gasps and shouts from the officers. Derlin began to wail at the top of his lungs, snatching the can and hat from Sergeant Johnston and falling to the ground clutching his "son" as Mavis crouched down to join him.

Oldsmobile was hastily led to the back of a waiting squad car. Still woozy and possibly concussed, Oldsmobile never recognized Derlin as the distraught father of the boy he'd been accused of 'Voodoo zapping." Likewise, despite his distinctive size and girth, Oldsmobile's cloak and shabby face paint kept Derlin from recognizing him in turn. Mavis was giving it her best to console a still-wailing Derlin as he clutched the can of beans and the hat sitting on the ground, but she wasn't anywhere near convinced that the State Trooper's prevailing theory was true. Though acutely aware that she certainly didn't know everything in life, Mavis wasn't dumb, and she found it incredibly unlikely that her son had been magically turned into a can of baked beans by a Voodoo priest in the bathroom of a Mississippi rest area. Sergeant Johnston seemed quite pleased with his theory considering how quickly he'd been able to "crack" the case, but hid his smile long enough to offer his sincere condolences to Mavis and Derlin before saluting solemnly from the passenger seat of the squad car containing Oldsmobile as it sped away.
Mavis and Derlin sat with Randy at the rest area long after the troopers had finished their business and left. Derlin was fully convinced that he now had a can of baked beans for a son, but Mavis kept her eye out for Ollie as they sat. She waited expectantly for him to come tottering over the horizon at any second, though he never did. After a couple of hours, Derlin began to dig absentmindedly into his pile of snacks, eating a Mounds bar in one bite in the way one feeds a log into a wood chipper. Handing Randy a Charleston Chew, he offered Mavis a bag of peanuts, but she refused, not even breaking her stare looking off into the distance.

Cars came and went as the hours passed, and the moon was high in the Alabama sky when Mavis finally woke Derlin up from the ground and the three of them climbed back into the Monaco for the long and somber drive back to Coverdale.

Chapter 47

Ollie, as it happened, hadn't been turned into a can of beans. He'd simply zigged when his brother had zagged as they'd left the restroom. Wandering over to the bank of 18-wheelers, he soon continued a long-standing Spurlock tradition of becoming disoriented on gas fumes. Following a smell of stale Panther Cat and meat grease, likely because it carried the familiarity of his father, Ollie soon found the source of the smell in a large, brownish duffel bag sitting unattended next to a "Mississippi Ham" truck. Clambering inside it and discovering it to be full of denim and flannel reeking of the same magic odors, Ollie soon fell asleep, not even waking as the bag was hoisted into the cab of the truck.

Exhausted from the stressful journey of his day, Ollie didn't wake up until the truck was nearly a hundred miles down the road. Strange, exotic-sounding fiddle music blared from the radio and the smoke of Old Indians filled the air as Ollie clawed his way out of the bag, emerging on the passenger-side floorboard of the cab of the truck.

"Well shit damn, a bag baby!" the trucker shouted. "I heard about y'all from the fellers down at the truck stop diner."

Ollie stared up at the man and smiled. Tall, gaunt and bespectacled, the man had a well-sculpted dirty blonde mustache which in another fifteen years would be known as a "Hulk Hogan." Long, wiry brown hair lay shaggily across his shoulders and his face had a certain hawkish quality to it accentuated by his Spurlock-like lack of chin. The man pushed up his glasses, cleared his nostrils and leaned over to take a closer look at Ollie, periodically looking away to glance back at the road.

"Yep, I've heard stories about babies like you, little fella," the man continued in his strange, Cajun-by-way-of-Baltimore accent. "You musta got dropped off in my bag when I was at that nice rest area, trying to pee in all four urinals at one time."
He paused and took a guzzle of a giant thermos of black coffee.

"Lot Lizards like your mama have babies sometimes," he continued, talking loudly and enrapturing Ollie as he held onto the seat. "You know, doing what they do for a livin,' they're gonna have little babies like you sometimes and they can't take care of 'em, so they look for unlocked doors of truck cabs and luggage that ain't being kept after and they put their babies in there, hopin' whoever finds it'll take better care of it than she can. Waitress at the diner called it 'Truck Stop Storkin' among a whole bunch of other things. You leave a bag out and some poor Sally or Mary's gonna come leave a baby in it so she can get back to polishin' gear shafts, if you know what I mean."

He winked at Ollie and Ollie cooed back happily, climbing up slowly on his belly into the seat.

"You know, they say that if you get visited by one of them truck stop storks, you're supposed to take the baby to the church or the fire house or some such wheres, so they can get a proper upbringin'," the man said, talking to Ollie as though he was any other adult passenger.

"But you know," he continued. "I always said that if one of 'em ever visited me, I might have to keep the youngin'. See, I ain't got no wife, and I'm getting a little old for my goose juice to be workin' proper anyhow. I'd always wanted a boy of my own to raise right here on the open road."

He stared out over the steering wheel for a few minutes, thinking.
So here's what I'm gonna do, Slim." He continued. I'm gonna take this as a sign from ol' baby Jesus his'self that you and me was supposed to cross paths like this. I think he put you in this 'Mississippi Ham' truck for a reason. Strap yourself in, little fella. Ain't gonna be no churches or orphanages for you today, because I'm keepin' ya."

He tooted the horn of his rig in celebration and Ollie let out a delighted laugh.

The man began to fiddle with the radio dial, landing on an evening AM radio magic show, where an announcer mimicked excitement about a studio magician making things disappear or guessing a proper playing card. Some of the luster was lost on the reveal without the benefit of sight, but the announcer's excitement was palpable and he did more than enough to makeup for the show's improper medium.

"I bet you'll like this program," the man offered, tussling Ollie's wispy hair and glancing over at him, doing a quick double-take. "Well look at that birthmark! Looks just like three lowercase b's."

They arrived home in silence, and after shuffling inside dejectedly from the car Mavis and Derlin put Randy to bed, doing their best not to look at Ollie's vacant pillow. Derlin began to sniffle once more, shuffling to the living room where he placed the can of beans, still wearing the hat, next to a picture of Ollie on the mantle. He lit a candle and began to blubber.

Mavis tried her best to console her husband, but he remained convinced that Sergeant Johnston was correct about the "voodooing" and couldn't accept the possibility that Ollie had just wandered off into the forest or gotten into a strange car. She wept alongside Derlin that evening but stayed steadfast in her belief that Ollie would pop up alive and well, tucked accidentally into the back of someone's station wagon or laundry cart and no worse for wear.

She fully expected a phone call from someone, from somewhere the next morning, hoping to one day file the story away as an anecdote they'd all laugh about together on holidays. Mavis pictured that moment then: she and Derlin a little older, Derlin's mustache and mullet accented with gray. The boys were grown, not quite normal adults, but tall enough to at least stand over the Thanksgiving turkey they were laughing around as they shared their imaginary family moment. As the future-Derlin called dibs on the turkey's back, Mavis shook herself from her daydream and took in her surroundings. It was the middle of the night, nearly four, and the real Derlin lay next to her curled up in a ball beneath the hearth snoring away. She peeked in on Randy, who remained sound asleep as well. She walked slowly through the darkness of her strangely empty-feeling home and eventually wandered into the dining room, flicking the light switch on the wall. Not knowing what else to do with the time until the morning, she sat down with her yellow legal pad and once again began to write.

Made in the USA
Middletown, DE
03 October 2024

61999016R00152